ZEROGLYPH

A NOVEL

VANCE PRAVAT

This is a work of fiction. Names, characters, places, and incidents either are the products of the author's imagination or are used fictitiously in order to provide a sense of authenticity. Any resemblance to actual persons, living or dead, businesses, establishments, companies, government or judicial entities, events, or locales is entirely coincidental.

Contents

To subjugate another is to subjugate yourself.

Elbert Hubbard, The American Bible

"Tut, tut, child!" said the Duchess. "Every thing's got a moral, if only you can find it."

Lewis Carroll, Alice's Adventures in Wonderland

INTRODUCTION

While the identities of the people involved in the creation of the world's first Artificial General Intelligence (AGI) is by now common knowledge (or at least a simple web search away), what follows is a work of fiction, and in no way an accurate account of real-life events. Obviously, names of persons and corporate entities have been changed, and any resemblance to actual persons, living or dead, is purely coincidental.

The court proceedings of the trial over the AGI are not in the public domain, but I have hope that one day they will be released. Until then my condensed version will have to do. They have been heavily edited, with the purpose of cutting through the legalese and getting to the crux of the arguments made that day.

When talking about the weighty philosophical and moral dimensions of artificial personhood in a work of fiction, it can be difficult to strike a balance between what needs to be said and what can be said without straying too far from the more paramount considerations of storytelling. At the same time, an excessive dilution of subject matter ends up conveying little of value. As a sort of compromise, I have peppered throughout the book excerpts from the actual lab transcripts of conversations between the AI and the scientists. Edited and abridged as they are, they should give the reader some insight into the mind of the entity in question, as well as provide a brief foray into the complex world of artificial ethics.

The lengthier ones—the court transcript and a rather detailed discussion on a possible solution to the various trolley problems (or at least what contours such a solution might take)—I have separated from the main narrative and included in the interlude and appendix sections. Those looking for nothing more than a good story may safely skip these parts. If they really must, they may skip the shorter transcripts as well, but I feel that they add to the story rather than digress from it. I'll let the reader be the ultimate judge.

My thanks to Gantt, Lyle, & Steadman, for allowing me access to the papers left behind by Dr. Aadarsh Ahuja, without which none of this would have been possible. Thanks to those former employees of Mirall who agreed to help me with my research, though under the condition of anonymity: you know who you are. Finally, a big shout-out to Ed Walzer at Judge Rosa Gray's office at the New York State Supreme Court, whose help was pivotal in obtaining the court records.

One last thing: I am neither an ethicist nor a legal expert; any errors in understanding and presentation are mine and mine alone. Regardless, Raphael is just the first of many; it becomes imperative that conversations on these matters be had more frequently and among a broader set of people than is currently the case.

It is never too late until it is late.

VP

PART I: THE INCIDENT AT THE LAB

Day 1—9:45 am

I woke up late on the day they found out Raphael was missing.

I didn't mean to. It's just that I had so much going on in my mind the evening before that I forgot to set the alarm. I didn't get much rest either; sleep kept coming and going in stages, and I think it was past four when I nodded off for good.

In hindsight, it was sloppy of me for not setting the buzzer. Monday, after all, is Resurrection Day, and though they start bringing Raphael back from the dead only after ten, there are those pre-boot checks that Sheng likes to get out of the way much before that, and it was simply indefensible to have forgotten about them. Doubly so, because just last week—the Monday before, that is—the checks were all I could think of as I lay in the hospital all broken and feeling sorry for myself.

It might look like I am still trying to sneak in an excuse, but that is not the case at all. I take full responsibility for everything that happened with Raphael; I created him after all. And yet, can one really take responsibility for an eventuality? I don't know.

This time, it wasn't a nightmare that woke me up. It was Hazel, cooing something unintelligible from somewhere far away.

Buzzing by the bedside.

"You are receiving a call," Hazel repeated, just before the phone disconnected.

Gosh, what time is it? I groggily blinked at the screen while the phone lock read my face. *9:47. Uh oh.*

The call was from Kathy. I rang her back, but it went to voicemail. Maybe she was trying to call me again, so I hung up and waited.

It was murky and sullen in the room, as if it were still early hours. The stub of a dream, all but smoke and vapor now, lingered as my eyes traced the patterns of frost on the window. Something to do with Raphael... A premonition, you ask? Nothing like that. I don't believe in premonitions. Just garden-variety anxiety. And doubt: that nagging feeling of somehow being completely wrong about everything—a feeling, I'm sure, everyone has had at one time or the other.

Kathy didn't call back.

"Hazel, turn on the lights," I said, wanting to bury myself back in the sheets, but a more pressing need compelling me to grope for the scratcher I must have left there last night. *There.* I urgently thrust the implement under the plaster casts on my legs, sighing as I alternated between left and right. *One week over, nine more to go. One week over, nine more to go. Remind me never to go on a black run again.*

"Good morning, Andy!" Hazel—short for Home Automation and Security Logic—chirped from the speaker above the fake mantelpiece. The lights in the room slowly brightened into a soothing ivory-white glow as my virtual assistant gave me the obligatory rundown for the day—"It's a nippy twenty-eight degrees outside, with snowstorms expected in the Tri-state area later today. You have zero new text messages, one missed call, and one voice message. Your calendar—"

She must have left a message.

"Hazel, play all new voice messages."

"Okay. You have: one unread voice message. Playing message one, from Kathy Schulz, received today at 9:44 am."

"Andy, it's Kathy." Her voice was subdued, as if she was deliberately speaking low. "Listen. We have a big problem. There's been… an incident. Valery's here. Can't talk right now. Just wait for my call, I'll ring you as soon as I can. And pick up the phone, for chrissake!"

I called her again, but no luck.

Kathy Schulz was the head of research at Mirall. She worked under me. She was one of the old-timers; she'd joined the company a few months after I started it. She had taken over the role from me about eighteen months ago, after the buyout by Halicom. Sure, I was CEO of Mirall before that, but I never let it get in the way of real work. I like to think that tedious tasks are like needy lovers: ignore them long enough and they'll find someone else to take care of them. Back then Eric used to handle most of the day-to-day, and Jane liaised with her dad on finance and funding, leaving me free to focus on research. Halicom had let go of Eric, and Jane had… Well, Jane was technically never an employee—all of which meant that I was the one left picking up the slack in the new regime. So much for my little nugget of wisdom.

I tried Sheng next. Sheng usually came in at six on Mondays.

The voice at the other end said the phone was switched off.

I once more silently admonished myself for forgetting to set the wake-up. Why weren't they answering their phones? And what was that about Valery…? I ran over Kathy's message in my head. She'd said Valery was at the lab. What was *she* doing there?

I called Brendon, one of the systems architects.

"Andy, you got to fix this," he blurted out before I could say hi. He sounded annoyed.

"What's going on?"

"You for real? You don't know?"

"Only that Kathy left me a message saying there's a problem."

"It's the lab. The electrical wiring caught fire or something. Everyone's been herded into the first floor."

"A fire? Is it serious?"

"I doubt it. They wouldn't have let us into the building otherwise. I don't see any fire trucks. Dan says we have to work here until they get the wiring fixed. He won't tell when."

"Dan's handling the situation?" Dan Spiros was in charge of office security and administration. "Was anyone hurt?"

"Look, this is absurd. They are not even letting us go up there to collect our notes. Dan is being evasive as hell, won't give me straight answers. We were supposed to run latencies on the prototype core today. How are we to do that with the lab closed? Vendor's not going to finish the dies in time if—"

Brendon Powell had a tendency to get stressed about all the wrong things. Like most researchers in the lab, he thought the world started and ended with his problems. Still, he was one of the best machine-learning experts around (it had cost us a bundle getting him to relocate from Cali where he was with Google) and we tried to work around his eccentricities. As everyone did with everyone else at Mirall. A group of hyper-competitive, ultra-smart individuals do not a frictionless team make.

"Do you see Kathy anywhere?"

"Kathy's not answering her phone. Where *is* she, by the way?

In your absence, she should be taking care of this crapfest, not me."

"What about Sheng? Or anyone from his team?"

"I don't know and I don't care. Andy, we need our stuff. *Now.* Or you can tell them to kiss their timeline goodbye. Look, I gotta go. The designers are going to throw a fit if I don't find us a meeting room soon. Just talk to Dan and get it sorted out, alright?" He hung up.

A fire, huh? Okay.

I rechecked the call history on my phone. No calls that day, except the one from Kathy. I was starting to get worried now—not a full-blown panic, but a creeping sense of fatality, of not knowing what to expect. The thing that was bothering me most was the wall of silence that seemed to have sprung up out of nowhere. My phone should have been ringing without pause given what had happened. Yet, there was nothing.

Maybe there is a problem with the phone network. Sometimes the signal does get weak at my place...

I wasn't surprised when Dan didn't answer my call as well. By now it was beginning to dawn on me what—or rather, who—was behind the blackout.

Valery Martinez was a VP at Halicom and a professional pain in the ass. Halicom had pushed her on us as transition manager soon after the sale. Just an advisory role, they'd said—just to help you folks settle in. It had been more than a year since and she was still there, settling us in. No prizes for guessing whose job it was to crack the whip. When she first started, she used to work out of Mirall's building in Albany most days of the week. She had since cut it down to one day, having gone back to her home base, to Halicom's corporate offices in New York. She usually visited us on Wednesdays. Today was not Wednesday.

I knew she stayed somewhere in Westchester, so it was conceivable she had decided to come down for a surprise visit. Conceivable, but not likely. She was the sort of person who has entries in her planner for bathroom breaks. I debated whether to call her, but eventually decided against it. Not until I spoke to Kathy before.

First things first. My stomach was threatening to cave in: a couple of sandwiches were all I'd had time for the previous day. "Hazel, wake up Max. Then tell Chef to make my breakfast. Breakfast menu preset number... um, preset number three."

"Waking up Max. Turning on ChefStation. You have requested for breakfast, preset three: pancakes with blueberry jam, scrambled vegan egg, and black coffee. Please confirm if correct."

"Correct."

"I am sorry. Can't do that. Out of one or more key ingredients. Out of: pancake mix. Would you like to add the ingredients to your shopping cart or would you like to request an emergency drone delivery?"

This was exactly the kind of nonsense I didn't want to deal with in the mornings. I made a mental note to enable auto-replenish later. "Forget it," I grumbled.

"Confirmed. Adding two packets of Bisquick Organic Pancake Mix to your weekly shopping cart. Would you like to order a different breakfast?"

"Preset one."

"You have requested for breakfast, preset one: oatmeal porridge with honey, two slices of rye toast, and black coffee. Please confirm if—"

"Yes," I said impatiently. "Hazel, show me my inbox." Maybe there was something there.

"Breakfast order preset one queued at chef station. Expected wait time: ten minutes. Show inbox. I am sorry. Can't do that. I do not detect any display units in the room."

Right. I kept forgetting I was not in my usual bedroom. Since my ill-timed skiing accident last week, I had been sleeping in one of the guest suites downstairs. I suppose I could have gotten Max to carry me up and down the stairs every day, but the thought of me cradled in his arms like some overgrown baby had put me off the idea. I've seen him navigate those stairs: the imagery doesn't exactly inspire confidence, no matter what the ads say.

I opened the office mailbox on my phone. My fingers were shaking as I swiped at the screen. There were a dozen or so unread emails. I quickly scanned through them.

Some chatter on Titian, the new iteration of cores Halicom had us making.

An auto-generated message from Friday stating that the shutdown sequence for Raphael had been completed with an error code of zero.

A newsletter from Corporate.

A video-conference request for later that day from Valery Martinez. Like I said, she wasn't the type to drop in on a whim.

The emails were all from Friday.

Needing something to distract my mind, I turned my attention to the news. The headlines, continuing the theme from last week, were mostly about December's unemployment rate crossing the fifteen-percent mark. I didn't understand what all the fuss was about; everyone knew it had been as high as that, if not higher, for quite some time now, creative accounting from the Bureau of Labor Statistics notwithstanding. The markets were doing well though, unruffled by trivial affairs such as the state of the economy. Halicom, the world's third-largest robotics company, had closed in the green last Friday. The NYSE was yet to open, and I expected the trend to—

There was a soft whirring sound at the door. "Good morning Andy."

"Hello Max," I said. I refreshed the mailbox a final time before setting aside the phone.

"Your breakfast is ready. May I serve you?"

I glanced at him as he stood in the doorway clutching the breakfast tray. I'd had Max with me for over two years now. I'd gotten him soon after buying the house, thinking a robot would prove useful for someone living alone in a 9000 square feet home with nothing around but trees for company. A limited edition version of Halicom's bestselling Nestor 5 caretaker-cum-housekeeper robot, Max took getting used to, especially in the mornings.

I think it was the jarring mismatch between appearance and voice: his dome-shaped head, cartoonish bug eyes, and half-moon smiley just didn't get along with the deep, carefully-articulated voice that was more at home in a Shakespearean stage-actor than in a house bot. Plus the fact that his sophisticated-sounding voice belied what was essentially a pretty stupid brain underneath. Fetch that. Put this there. Help me get up… Not exactly intellectual giant stuff. Despite being one of the most advanced robots in the world, the Nestor 5 was no AGI. It didn't have human smarts. No machine did. Until now.

I rolled on my side and retrieved the foldable tray table I'd tucked away below the bed. The slight hum of actuator motors accompanied him as he moved into the room and carefully placed the tray on the table.

Max couldn't cook, but I had installed one of those automated kitchen counters with overhanging mechanical arms that could whip up a dish or two on days when I couldn't care less for my taste buds.

Lately, all days seemed to be that way.

The porridge was too lumpy. The toast, not crisp enough. The coffee smelled good though. The twenty-thousand dollar arms excelled at taking coffee out of the coffee maker.

"Max, you can go now." I didn't want him standing around staring at me like that.

We had tried giving a body like that to Raphael once. He was three months old at the time. It had a rudimentary bucket-shaped aluminum head on top of a skeletal frame; we had been using it for testing the cores. A few of us in the lab were fine-tuning his classifiers by making him recognize objects in the room: chairs, cups, abstract shapes, faces. I should stress that there was no "he" at the time. To us, *he* was RP06, one of the nine cores we had fabricated in the iteration code named Raphael. The cores had no personality, no sense of self, programmed or otherwise; and by all appearances, definitely no awareness of such self. We addressed them all as Raphael, but the name was just that: an identifier.

It so happened that RP06 stepped in front of a full-length mirror affixed to one of the walls. It wasn't the first time he'd done that; before, he would just look at it disinterestedly before passing on. There was something different this time... the way he kept returning his gaze to the mirror, as if there was something pulling him. Eventually, he stopped heeding our commands and went and stood in front of the mirror. He moved one of his arms, first sideways, then up, then both the arms. He carried on like this for some time, moving his arms, touching his body and the mirror, totally engrossed in the act.

We were completely unprepared for what happened next.

He said, "Bad face. Not Raphael. This bad face." He smashed the mirror to pieces, chanting the words over and over. Then he fell silent and stopped responding altogether.

At my company, we weren't trying to create selves or artificial consciousness; nor were we trying to emulate the human brain. Our goal was less lofty: to build the next generation of robots using a new kind of processor technology.

You see, robots like Max ran on a hybrid system of traditional "von Neumann" chips and the newer, "inspired by the human brain" neuromorphic chips. The way it worked was that the traditional chippery provided the raw number-crunching power, while the neuromorphic chips ran sophisticated deep learning algorithms. Unsurprisingly, the smarter you tried to make a robot, the more processing power it needed. But adding more processing cores brought along its own set of problems: heating, data lag, computational complexity... And there was only so much you could fit inside a robot.

All that changed with the advent of NMVLSI or Neuro-Mono-VLSI technology—a fancy name for a set of simultaneous breakthroughs in chip fabrication and nanomolecular assembly. It was now possible to build monolithic, three-dimensional neuromorphic chips with a level of circuit integration that had not been possible before. One big core instead of many small cores. We could now fit tens of billions of artificial neurons—neuristors—into one ultra-dense block of hardware that could be reprogrammed, even rewired on the fly.

The tech was still very new, very experimental. And unlike commercial chip fabbing technology, not very precise—

therefore ill-suited for mass production. Nevertheless, we were willing to bet on it because we believed it was the future.

The future had its own plans. Instead of smarter robots, it gave us the world's first artificial mind. It gave us artificial general intelligence.

When Raphael went into what seemed like the AI version of catatonic shock, we were afraid we had lost the most important invention in history to an unlucky turn of events. However, the tests we ran on the core give us reason for hope, and in the days that followed, we frantically worked round-the-clock with a Chinese firm to customize an off-the-shelf sex robot to house the core (sex bot because realistic-looking robots were mostly confined to the bedroom; turns out people want their robots to look like robots everywhere else).

No one knew whether Raphael thought of himself as a twenty-something Adonis, but he took to the new body readily enough and started responding. In the weeks that followed, we would often catch him taking lingering glances in the mirror when he thought no one was looking.

After I was done eating, Max took away the tray and I maneuvered myself into my wheelchair and got into the bathroom.

I was still inside when the phone rang. I managed to reach it on her second try.

***

"Andy! I've been trying to reach you since forever!" Kathy said, again in that hushed manner.

"What's the matter?"

"So you don't know yet," she declared.

"The fire in the lab? Brendon told me. Why are you whispering?"

"I'm not supposed to be talking to you. Just listen, okay? It's about Raphael."

"Raphael? Good god! Was he damaged?"

"There is no fire."

"No fire? Then what... Oh, please don't tell me Sheng and his team are taking shortcuts again! If they've messed up the boot sequence again, I'll personally—"

"It's nothing to do with the boot. It's Raphael. We can't find him."

For a while, I didn't say anything.

"Andy, you there?"

"I'm sorry, what did you just say?"

"We can't find Raphael."

"What do you mean you *can't* find him? It's not like he could have stepped out for a stroll!" Raphael did not have legs: we had removed them from the sexbot before fitting the core inside it. Like me, Raphael was confined to a wheelchair, except in his case it was permanent. "Did you check the CT room? Someone might have taken him for scanning and left him there."

"Andy, you are not listening to me. We had a break-in at the lab. I don't know the details, but they think the core was taken."

"The core was taken..."

She whispered, "You there?"

"Yes, yes, I'm here! I'm just trying to wrap my head around it. No, wait! Start over please. Somebody broke into the lab and *stole* Raphael?"

"Just the core. They left the body behind."

"You are joking right? Please tell me you are."

A sigh of exasperation from the other end. "As I said, I don't have all the details. I'm just telling you what they told me."

"When did this happen?"

"I don't know. They are still going through the tapes."

"*They?*"

"Dan and Valery. Both are in the server room. They've locked off the entire second floor. They want to keep a lid on it until they decide what to do. Valery told me not to talk to anybody... er, including you. She was very clear about that last part. She said she was going to inform you herself."

"What's Valery doing there? And how the heck does Halicom get to know about this before I do?" I said, starting to get angry.

"No clue. She was here when I got in."

"Who discovered the theft?"

"She told me it was Sheng."

"I don't frikkin' believe this! Sheng starts at six. Why didn't he call me?"

"Ask him yourself. I think they've quarantined him in one of the cabins. I was about t— Hey look, I gotta go now. She just stepped out of the server room. You didn't hear this from me, okay? Wait... Is that...? Yeah, it's that lawyer fella all right. The buff guy, whatshisname. She is walking over to meet him. And guess who else is here. Your girlfriend."

Jane was there? I got why Gary had to be summoned: Martinez would have called him in for legal advice. He didn't live too far away. But Jane? "She's not my—" I stopped short as the realization hit me. "Kathy, are you telling me they are having a board meeting?"

"Sure looks like it."

Without me. They are having a board meeting without me. My anger vanished in an instant, replaced by an icy clenching in my stomach.

Shit.

She had one last thing to say before hanging up. "Andy? Valery—she's up to something. She was asking me a lot of questions about Raphael. About containment and directives and logs... a bunch of other stuff. I can't go into details right now. I'd watch out if I were you."

***

I wandered aimlessly around the house, pushing on the wheels with a restless energy.

When I had first laid eyes on the house in a Sotheby's VR tour, it seemed like it had been custom made for me. A granite-fronted, modernistic piece designed by the very much in-demand Garo Simonyan, it was set in thirty acres of private, gated land, offering me the solitude I had begun craving back then. I guess the desire was always there: whether it was growing up with a sibling in a cramped, two-bedroom flat in the suburbs of Navi Mumbai, or bunking with roommates to save money at Berkeley and then at MIT, I was always a private person deep at heart. My friends, even some of my family, might disagree, but I've always been good at hiding certain aspects of my personality. That's what misfits without the courage to embrace their oddities do: they put on a show. And I learnt to put on a good show very young. I had to. It was either that or get marked by bigger kids at school—many of them sourced from the slums nearby, and who thought the whole purpose of geeky runts like me was target practice for their budding pugilistic skills. Pretending to be one of them came as naturally to me as camouflage to a cuttlefish.

So I sold some of my stock—a rather large chunk, actually—back to Jane's father, Mirall's angel investor, and purchased the house, along with Max and a few creature comforts (this was before Halicom acquired us). For the first time, I'd felt like I was truly home.

But that day, the trappings of luxury did nothing to alleviate my anxiety. The silence, which I always found soothing, now seemed oppressive; the airy expanse of the living room, with its high ceiling and floor-to-roof windows, seemed restrictive; the hushed winter light, sickly.

I can't just sit around waiting for information to trickle down. I gotta be there in the lab.

And do what?

I have to take charge of the situation. I must—

Take charge how? Martinez will send you back with your tail between your legs. Settle down. It's not the end of the world.

I parked the wheelchair by the glass doors opening into the patio. It had started to snow. For a while, I contented myself with gazing at the ice-covered lawn and the line of birches beyond. The thin trunks swayed woozily to the cold rhythms of the wind, like a troupe of drunken ballet dancers clad in black and white. The sky was overcast, brooding down on this little performance disapprovingly.

The hypnotic back and forth seemed to calm my nerves—for the time being at least. *I have to wait; there is no other option. Nothing else I can do from here.* I had already texted Kathy to let me know once they were out of the meeting.

As I was turning around, something caught the corner of my

eye. A shape, moving in the thicket beyond. When I looked back, there was nothing there except the trees.

There was something familiar about the shape. It had looked like—

Max!

I quickly spun around and scanned the house. Of course, it wasn't Max. There he was, near the kitchen, standing quietly by himself.

Light playing tricks on me. Or perhaps it was my mind, superimposing an image from memory into the tableau of the present. Maybe I was remembering Raphael, and how he used to love walking amidst those trees. Not in a physical sense, obviously, as he wasn't allowed outside the lab. In my spare time, I had cobbled together a remote control device—a controller motherboard that I had custom made and then fitted inside Max. With it, Raphael could remote connect from the lab and commandeer my house bot as one would a drone or a VR avatar. It was my gift for his first birthday.

He appeared so eager when I first told him about it—like some teenager dying to take his parent's car out for a ride. The questions were endless: What kind of trees will I find? Are there animals in the woods? Will they be scared of me? Can I start a leaf collection? I'd just about had it by the time we finished testing and debugging the device. Truth be told, it is difficult to say whether he was really excited or just emulating the right behavior for the occasion. He never got tired of trudging among the trees though, right up till the very end, when I put a stop to it. It was soon after the takeover. I had a feeling Halicom would not like it if they found out.

I eventually settled down in front of the TV. A Hitchcock movie was playing on one of the channels. I let it run.

I must have drifted off, because the next thing I knew, I was blinking at a travel show. I didn't remember changing channels.

Hazel was announcing from the smart speaker next to the TV—"Proximity alert: car, pulling into the driveway."

I had a visitor.

Exhibit F

Submitted by Petitioner, The Organization for Advancement of Rights and Personhood, to the State Supreme Court of New York, on the day of xxxxxxxxxxxxxxxxx
Excerpt from lab transcript (certain sections blanked out). Transcript sourced from Mirall Technologies, 27 Woodbine Av., Albany, NY, 12205

Transcript Reference: TLRP06E2470004 (VLog Ref: VLCA1E247093000015)
Date: xx/xx/xxxx   Time: 09:30 AM
Subject: Raphael Number 06 / Prodlib build v15.002C
Interaction   Y   Observation   Scan
Interaction Type: Lesson / Play / Test / Free Interaction / Psych Eval / Other:
Description: Administer Sally-Anne test to check for theory of mind—ability to attribute false beliefs to others
Prep: NA
Participants: Dr. DeShawn Walls, Child Psychologist, Dr. Aadarsh Ahuja, Chief Researcher, Dr. Kathy Schulz, Chief Researcher, Core RP06

Detail

Ahuja: Good morning Raphael.

RP06: Good morning Dr. A, Dr. Schulz. Good morning Dr.Walls.

Ahuja: How you doing today, Raphael? I see Sara got you some new crayons.

RP06: Yes. I used up all the reds and the purples, so Sara got me a new pack. She got me a new coloring book too. Would you like to see it?

Schulz: Your minders told me you've been using bad language.

Ahuja: Again? Where is he getting this crap from?

(Silence)

RP06: I am sorry. I did not know the words were bad when I said them. I promised Audrey and James I won't use those words again.

Ahuja: Dr. Walls has a little game for you. Would you like to play?

RP06: Sure. I like games.

Walls: Raphael, please describe what I've placed on the table.

RP06: Those are two dolls in a plastic box. I think the box is their home because it has beds and tables and chairs.

Walls: Very good. This is Sally, and this here is Anne. They are both friends. Can you tell me what are Anne and Sally doing?

RP06: Sally is on her bed, playing with a blue marble and Anne is sitting at her desk.

Walls: Sally is feeling bored. She wants to go outside for a while. Before stepping out, she puts her marble inside this toy basket beside her bed—like this. She covers the basket with a cloth and then off she goes. Clop, clop, clop. While she is outside, Anne walks over to Sally's bed and takes the marble from the basket. She replaces the cloth, and then hides the marble in her own desk.

RP06: Is Anne a bad person?

Walls: I wouldn't call her bad. She's a bit naughty, that's all.

RP06: Isn't being naughty bad?

Walls: Sometimes, yes.

RP06: Is being naughty good at other times?

Walls: It's not exactly good. Being naughty doesn't automatically make you a bad person. All children are naughty at times. It's bad if you are naughty all the time.

RP06: So it is alright if I'm naughty sometimes, but not all the time. I haven't been naughty all day yesterday. That means it was okay for me to be naughty earlier today.

Walls: Look, it isn't—

Schulz: Raphael, we'll discuss this another time. Let's get back to Sally and Anne.

Walls: Uh, yes, Sally and Anne... Where was I? Sally has finished her walk and is now home. She wants to play with her marble. Where will she look for it, Raphael?

<Insert> (Author's Note: Subjects who possess theory of mind will correctly answer that Sally will look for the marble in the toy basket, the place where she kept it before going out. Those without will answer that she'll look for it in Anne's drawer. Empirical evidence shows that autistic children and children under the age of four generally point to Anne's desk— suggesting they lack TOM or the ability to model another person's state of mind. In this example, they fail to attribute to Sally the false belief that the marble is still in the toy box.) <End Insert>

RP06: Are Sally and Anne good friends, Dr. Walls?

Schulz: Just answer the question, Raphael.

Walls: It's okay. Yes Raphael, they are good friends.

RP06: Have they been friends for long?

Walls: Yes. They've been friends for a long time.

RP06: Is Sally a kind person?

Walls: (Laughs) Sure. Sally is a good, kind person. Anything else you want to know about them? Now tell us, where will Sally look for the marble?

RP06: She won't look for it.

Walls: I'm sorry, can you say that again?

RP06: Sally will not look for the marble.

Walls: I don't think you understand. Sally is now home. She wants to play with the marble. Why won't she look for it?

RP06: Because Sally is a kind person. Sally and Anne have been friends for long, so Sally knows Anne is naughty. Sally sees that the cloth on the basket has been moved—its position doesn't match the earlier pattern stored in her memory. She knows that if she looks for the marble in the toy box, she may not find it there and then she would have to ask Anne where it is and Anne would lie because she's the one who took it and Sally would have to keep searching and when she finally finds it in Anne's drawer, Anne will feel embarrassed and unhappy. Sally is a kind person. She does not want to make Anne unhappy. So she'll not look for the marble. She knows Anne will return it later because Anne is not a bad person. She's just a bit naughty, that's all.

Ahuja: **** me.

Schulz: Andy!

RP06: I like this game, Dr.Walls. Can we keep playing?

Walls: Um... no. I think we are done for today. Good... good job, Raphael.

Notes:

Demonstration of TOM alone would have been an extraordinary development, but RP06 exceeded expectations. RP06 goes far beyond attributing a simple false belief to Sally: he attributes to her the qualities of goodness and kindness, and from that premise, reasons that Sally would not look for the marble in order to save Anne from embarrassment and/or to avoid confrontation. Line up more tests to investigate further.
AA

xxxxxxxxxxxxxxxxxxxxxxxxxxxxxxxxxxxxxxxxxxxxxxxx KS

Day 1—12:30 pm

I brought up the feeds from the outside security cameras on the TV screen. A car, crunching through the snow on the driveway. It was Jane's Bugatti, a dark red number with aggressively sculpted lines that made it look like an angry bug about to leap into the air. I never quite liked it: it crowded out the scenery too much. The car's safety alarm wailed in protest as she hopped out before it could finish parking itself—something I'd given up cautioning her on long ago.

I told Hazel to unlock the front door. I didn't have to, as the facial recognition would have automatically let her in (I hadn't deleted her profile from the system after we broke up—it kept slipping my mind, that's all), but I did it anyway because I didn't want her finding out she still had the "keys" to the house. She'd read too much into it.

She was dressed simply but elegantly: green jacket over a knee-length dress, platform heels, a mixed-stone necklace, matching bracelet—the whole ensemble tailored to give her tall, athletic frame a casual softness that she sometimes lacked. She had changed her hair since last time: her honey-blonde tresses were now cut short instead of shoulder-length. She was clutching that designer handbag I'd gifted her long ago.

I knew she was seeing someone else, so it was a mystery to me why she was still lugging it around. Jane wasn't exactly the type to carry a torch.

Maybe she'd forgotten it was from me—she did have a closetful of those things.

"I suppose you already know," she said from across the room, the door closing shut behind her.

"Hello Andy. Hello Jane."

She carelessly tossed the purse at a nearby armchair as she walked across the room to me. I couldn't tell if the gesture was symbolic in some way. I never could. In all the years of our on-again, off-again relationship, I could never master the art of reading Jane Cooper and her endless stream of cues and hints—according to her at least, and she was the sole authority on the subject.

There was a time when I'd tried, when I'd given it my sincere best. It was never enough, though. It is difficult to build an accurate predictive model of someone when that someone is as changeable as Jane. And Jane had changed. A lot. When I first met her (it was at a party her father had thrown the staff on Mirall's one year anniversary), she was this witty, intelligent MBA grad fresh out of Harvard. She was never idealistic—people who go to business school rarely are—but beneath the ambition and the levelheaded pragmatism, there was a center—a liquid, still forming center, but a center nonetheless—that was soft and kind and not entirely lacking in imagination. Somewhere along the line, the center had evaporated, and the crust, hardened. All that remained was the ambition, and a certain disdain at the person she used to be.

"I imagined you'd be more upset," she said, running her eyes over my casts. This was the first time we were meeting since my accident. She had called after I was back home from the hospital, offering to help; I had politely declined.

"Shell-shocked, actually. But you know me and expressing emotions—you always had something to say on that subject."

She rolled her eyes. "Please don't start."

She was right. That was uncalled for. "The core is really gone?"

"You don't know?" she said, widening her eyes at me.

"I'm completely in the dark here, Jane."

"Are you serious? No one called you?"

"Kathy Schulz did. She didn't tell me much. All I know is that there was a break-in."

"You don't know about the board meeting either? Gosh! I did ask about you in the meeting, but Valery told me you were unavailable. I assumed you were in the loop."

"As you can see, the loop and I haven't had many dealings lately," I said, gesturing at my unshaved chin and the t-shirt and pajama bottoms I was still wearing from the night before. Her expression changed; she looked down at the floor, brows furrowed, as she pondered over something.

"So what happened?"

She snapped out of her reverie. A deflecting quip, as she avoided my gaze and moved past me—"How about offering me a drink first? Don't get up."

She strode across the open-plan living room and over to the kitchen beyond. Crouching by the island in the center, she reached inside the shelves where she knew I kept my emergency store of bottled water (she never drank from the tap) and grabbed herself one.

She crashed down on the couch opposite me and kicked off her heels one by one. She wet her lips against the bottle—they were dry and cracking at places. For some reason I could never worm out of her during our relationship, she hated applying anything on that part of her body, even chapstick.

"Well?" I said, throwing my hands out. "Are you gonna tell me or blink it out in Morse?"

"Hey, don't get snarky with me. Jesus! I came here as fast as I could. What's the matter with you?"

I took a deep breath, ratcheting down my impatience a few notches. It was impossible to rush someone like Jane: when you are so used to calling the shots all your life, you don't let people hustle you, period.

"I'm sorry. It's been a very stressful day so far, just sitting here, not knowing what's going on. You can imagine that, can't you?"

"It's been stressful for everybody, Andy. You know, I haven't told dad about it yet. He's in SF on business."

The senior Cooper's VC firm, IncuStar Capital, still retained a fifteen percent share in Mirall post-buyout. They were primarily invested in the nanotech companies that had begun mushrooming all over the so-called Tech Valley in Upstate NY after a recent spate of tax breaks had put the cherry on top of an already hot investment climate. The nanotech boom, following a decade or so of the machine-learning boom that many augured would crash and burn (it never did, growing instead from strength to strength), was, like its predecessor, in that sweet zone of misty-eyed optimism where good money gets thrown after bad and the bad after the good, no questions asked. Not that I was complaining.

Jane's father had been flying out a lot recently, mostly to his new office in San Francisco. All I knew was that there was something big happening over there, something very hush-hush even Jane didn't know much about—or at least refused to talk about. Or maybe he just wanted to be away from his second wife—a Brazilian former-waitress-turned-aspiring-model who was not much older than Jane. Apparently, they were not getting along—a development Jane regarded with great satisfaction. In the last few months, Jane had been increasingly standing in for him on Mirall's board.

"Jane. Details, if you don't mind. Start from the beginning. When did you first hear about the theft?" It was almost as if she was deliberately stalling.

"Valery called me up in the morning saying there's an emergency board meeting. She didn't say why—she just gave me a secure conference number to dial. I was on my way to a meeting with one of our investments, so I rescheduled that and drove to the lab instead." She was probably telling the truth about driving down there; with the senior Cooper away most of the time, I knew she'd been quite busy handling Incustar's portfolio.

"The entire board was there?"

"Uh huh. Val, the lawyer, and me. Jimmy Troy and Cynthia Mattice joined us on video. Then there was this bald guy who gave us the briefing."

"That'd be Dan," I said. "Do they know when the core was taken?"

"On Sunday, around seven in the evening."

"They caught it on CCTV, I suppose?"

"I suppose so. I haven't looked at the tapes myself."

"Who first found out Raphael was gone?"

"Name sounded familiar: think I know him from before. Asian guy. Um... Sheng. Along with Dan. Apparently, Sheng was first to come in. He finds that he can't get inside the lab— the main door on the second floor kept rejecting his card. So he goes down to the security desk in the lobby, thinking there's something wrong with his card. The guard there tries to look up Sheng's credentials, but now the security app is not responding. The guard then escalates to some higher-up."

"Dan," I muttered to myself. The guard would have contacted Dan. And Dan would have called Martinez after he found out about the theft. That's how she came to know about it so soon. I should have guessed. Dan was a Halicom employee (like her, they'd brought him in after the acquisition); he would naturally feel inclined to bypass me and go to Martinez.

"Soon, Dan is on the scene," she continued. "He thinks maybe there's some problem with the access server inside the lab—it would explain why the security app is not responding and the doors are not letting anyone in. He uses his override card to get inside, and the two of them go to the server room to check it out. That's where they found Raphael. Or what's left of him, anyway. Just his dismantled body, the core gone."

"Raphael was in the server room?" I said, creasing my face at her.

"Yes."

I shook my head. "Are you sure? We keep Raphael in the crèche. The server room is in Wing A, next to the work bays."

"I know where it is, Andy. I used to work there, remember?"

"I don't understand... If the thieves got into the restricted area—which they must have in order to reach Raphael—they could have just opened him up then and there and taken the core. Why wheel him into the server room?"

"Raphael couldn't have gone there by himself?"

"You mean like wandered there? No way!"

"You sure?"

"Damn sure! We shut him down on Friday evening. Also, he'd have to get past three locked doors to reach the work bays in Wing A, and then through the server room door. Doors with biometric locks. What do the tapes show?"

"Dan said they were still going through the tapes, so we didn't dwell on it." She twisted her finger around a strand of hair that had strayed too far across her face. "Valery had called us for a reason. She wanted us to decide on next steps. Specifically, whether to involve the police or not. I don't have to explain to you how badly we'd be hit if word of this got out."

A low whistle escaped my lips. "And no one thought of calling me. I am the head of the company, for crying out loud!"

"Maybe Valery thought she shouldn't trouble you in your condition…"

"It's bone fractures, Jane, not a stroke. And it's not like I've been sitting on ass the past week. I'm still running Mirall; I'm still overseeing the new iteration. In fact, I've been putting in more hours than ever. Remote management is a bloody pain, you know. It just *sounds* easy."

"Don't look at me like that! I did raise my concerns. I just assumed—"

"I don't buy it."

Her eyes flashed with anger. "Listen, y—"

"I don't mean you," I added hastily, raising my palms. "I'm saying I don't buy their story. It's difficult enough to believe we had a break-in, let alone imagine Raphael somehow wandering into the server room."

"Andy, I saw him there."

"*You did?*"

"I had a quick peek inside the room before leaving. He was just beyond the door, sitting on his wheelchair." Her eyes

30

wandered past me as she tried to bring up a picture from memory. "It was eerie," she said, her voice dropping a level. "They had turned off the lights. And there he was, in the shadows, with his chest open—the lights inside blinking like fireflies. He had his head tilted up. Sightless eyes staring at some fixed spot on the ceiling... I've never seen him like that. And his expression... Ugh! It looked like he'd seen a ghost. His mouth was wide open... twisted... as if he was trying to laugh and scream at the same time." An involuntary shudder passed through her body as she wrapped her arms around herself.

"Was there anything else?" I asked.

"What do you mean anything else?" she said, looking a little annoyed that her narration hadn't had the effect she expected.

"Any theories as to what he was doing there or how he got there?"

She shook her head. "As I said, we didn't go into details. I was inside for only a couple of minutes. Uhm... Oh yes, there were these bits of crushed plastic on the carpet. They crunched under my feet as I went near him for a closer look. It looked like something had been broken there. I didn't notice anything else. It was dark."

"What's the consensus?"

"The police? Yup. Valery must have made the call by now."

"And you didn't discuss the security tapes at all," I said dejectedly. "If I'm not mistaken, there is a camera in the server room."

She sat back in the couch, her eyes studying me with care. "You feel it too?"

"Feel what?"

"That something's not right?" She paused. I could tell she was choosing her words carefully. "I don't know if I should be telling you this—you are paranoid enough as it is. It's just that… I felt Valery was deliberately avoiding bringing up the tapes. Both her and Dan. If I didn't know better, I'd have sworn they were trying to hide something."

I met her inscrutable gaze with one of my own. When she didn't add anything more, I shrugged and said, "They probably hadn't finished going through the recordings. There must be quite a few cameras in the building."

Of course, I couldn't reveal to Jane what I was really thinking. Martinez was thorough, if nothing: she wouldn't have walked into a board meeting unprepared and clueless. She had gone through the tapes and she had made a decision to keep me in the dark before she'd picked up her phone and made the first call to the board members. Kathy's warning was still echoing in my head. *She's up to something; I'd watch out if I were you.*

"I suppose you're right. I'm probably just freaked out after seeing Raphael in that room. The last time I saw him was… my god, how long has it been? More than a year, for sure. He used to be so nice to me…" She stood up abruptly. "I think I need something sugary and unhealthy."

"I have some soy ice cream in the fridge," I offered, knowing well her reaction but anticipating it nonetheless.

She stuck her tongue out at me. "Only you can eat something as vile as that."

I smiled. *Familiar beats.* It felt nice to know that there are some things that don't change. "There's the regular stuff too. Delivery drone got the orders mixed up. None for me, thanks."

I lingered, despite myself, on the barely-there sway of her hips and her sculpted legs as she walked away. Runner's legs. I knew she still did forty to fifty miles a week. "I'm going to call them," I said to her receding back. But first, I had to gather my thoughts. Had to prepare myself for whatever they—

Just then, my phone started ringing from the bedroom. Before Hazel could announce the obvious, I told her to route the call to the TV.

The screen turned on, displaying the caller ID. Speak of the devil. It was Martinez.

***

"Dr. Ahuja, it's Valery. How are you? I'm afraid I have some bad news," her familiar monotone voice droned at me.

"I know."

"Oh... okay. Who told you?"

Right. "Doesn't matter who told me. The question is why you didn't."

"My apologies. We all got caught up in the events. I couldn't find the time to call you."

"You had time to organize a board meeting."

"We had to act fast. Reaching you would have delayed us even more."

"Not good enough, Valery," I said, my voice rising. "I—"

"We can either argue about this or talk about what happened," she said, cutting me off. "Jimmy Troy is in a web call waiting for us."

Troy was the board Chair and Martinez's boss. He headed North America and Asia Operations, which was more than eighty percent of Halicom's manufacturing, effectively making him the company's Chief Operating Officer (the position had been unfilled for some time, after Dean Brokaw, the former COO had died under tragic circumstances). If rumors were to be believed, he was going to be formalized into the role that April, after Halicom's annual product launch event. You didn't keep someone like Troy waiting, not if you wanted to keep your job.

Martinez didn't wait for my reply. "I am texting you the conference ID. See you there."

Jane stared at me from the dining area, where she was nibbling at her ice cream. "*Now* they want to talk," I said loudly. "Do you mind getting me my phone? It's in the bedroom on your right."

Her face was pensive as she returned with the phone. "I was thinking maybe there's a reason why they left you out of the board meeting today. Same reason why they didn't talk about the tapes. They must have briefed the others separately, after I was gone."

I paused my fingers on the phone, waiting for her to finish her thought.

"They are playing CYA. I have a feeling they are gonna try to pin this on you."

"That's the second time today someone's said that."

"Then you have been warned. Don't let them bait you. Especially Valery—that uptight little bitch."

"Even if you are right, I can't worry about it now. Finding out who took Raphael takes priority. Everything else is secondary."

She flicked her head towards the TV. "Is it a video call? I'm not here."

I connected to Halicom's secure conferencing facility with my phone and then cast the screen on the TV. I tossed the phone to Jane so that she could watch from where she was sitting, on one of the side couches, outside the viewing angle of the TV camera. I logged into the room Martinez had texted me.

I was greeted with a split screen. In the right panel was an unhappy-looking Troy, squeezed into a chair several sizes too small; on the left, cleavage, framed by a dark blouse and a pinstripe suit.

Martinez was bent over the camera, adjusting it. She was in the large conference room at the lab.

"Jimmy is joining us from Head Office," she said, straightening. Behind her, the gleaming cherry-wood table stretched to the far end of the room. When she moved away to walk back to her chair I saw there was another person in the room: a bespectacled, diminutive-looking Dan, assiduously studying the grain on the table. He was wearing a sweatshirt instead of his usual jacket sans tie attire; perhaps he had intended to return back home and change for work when he first got the call from Sheng. He didn't look too pleased to be there.

Troy grunted by way of greeting. "We are screwed, buddy," he said. There was an edge to his voice that seemed to clarify— *Actually, you are.* "Homer Simpson here doesn't have a clue. I sure hope you do." Dan shrunk into himself even more. Given half a chance, I suspected he would have crawled under the table and dug a tunnel out of there.

"You want me to explain how someone broke into the lab?" I said, an askance look on my face.

"I want you to explain your goddamn robot!"

"Jimmy, I don't know what you are talking about."

"C'mon man, do I have to spell it out for you? Don't you know what happened?"

"I know that the core was stolen. That's about it."

Troy stabbed an angry finger at the camera. "I thought you were taking care of briefing him." To Martinez. She mumbled another apology, this time to Troy. She didn't look like she was going to lose any sleep over it though.

"What's going on guys?" I said.

He sneered. "Oh, you're gonna love this. Valery? Will you tell him or shall I?"

"It's better if Dr. Ahuja sees the tapes for himself. Dan has extracted all the important parts." After a pause, she asked him, "Since you haven't seen them yet, perhaps you'd like to watch too?"

"Sure, why not?" he growled. "It's not like I have other shit to take care of."

Martinez nodded at Dan, who had now gathered enough courage to stand up. "While Dan sets it up, I have a few questions for you, Dr. Ahuja. First, I want to know what Mirall has been doing with the AI recently. Say in the last three to four weeks."

I knew her question was purely for Troy's benefit. She already knew the answer—very little happened at Mirall without her knowing about it.

"The last few weeks? Not much, actually. Except for running him through the occasional test, we've left him pretty much to himself."

"Heh? What kind of an answer is that, not much?" Troy demanded. "You have an asset that's cost us the moon and you say you are not doing much with it?"

"We talked about this, Jimmy. All our resources have been diverted to the new iteration. Design, Connectome Mapping, Heuristics, Programming, Analytics... even most of the support staff. Everyone is focused on Titian. We've even stopped doing scans on the Raphael core for some time now. No one has a minute to spare. This is what Halicom wanted, isn't it: to bet on the roulette wheel instead of letting us do proper research?"

"Alright, alright, no need to drive it home," Troy said, brushing aside a lock of his unkempt hair.

"What kind of records do we keep on Raphael? If I wanted an account of all his time last week, for example, do you have it?" Another question she already knew the answer to. I had a feeling all of them were going to be like that.

"We log everything. All interactions with Raphael, formal and informal, are recorded on video. In addition, verbal tests and research-related talks are transcribed into plaintext files—makes it easier to search for specific content."

"What about the time he is not interacting with anyone, where he is by himself? Do we keep an eye on him?"

"CCTV cameras monitor the crèche area round the clock; the recordings go back to the time of his conception. There's always at least one person present with him during waking hours, which is Monday morning through Friday evening. We also run a night shift with a skeleton crew just to watch over him."

"Computer usage? Does he have free access to the internet?"

"Of course not. His PC is a standalone device. No wireless, no LAN, cannot connect to anything. He is only allowed offline media that's been pre-vetted by us: books, video games, movies and such."

"Could he have accessed the internet some other way?"

"No. The core doesn't have wireless capabilities either." I leaned forward. "Let me save you some trouble, because I see where you are going with this. I know Raphael was found in the server room. You obviously want to find out how he got there. The short answer is, not on his own."

"I like your confidence buddy," Troy snickered.

That didn't stop Martinez's questioning. "What happens on

the weekends? Do we have staff coming in to work?"

"No. If there's something super critical, people usually log in from home and get it done. Many have company-provided laptops."

"Who looks after Raphael then?"

"No one. We put him to sleep Friday night. Sleep, as in, shut him down completely. On Monday, we wake him up again."

"Did you shut him down last Friday?"

I spread out my palms in a gesture of exasperation. "Valery, do we really need to go through this?"

"Answer the question, Andy," Troy said.

"Yes, we shut him down last Friday. I personally checked the shutdown sequence log today, after I heard the news."

"Can someone tell me why the bloody robot needs to sleep? The ones Halicom makes don't require nappy nap time," he asked.

"It isn't technically sleep. More like a coma or death actually. And Raphael's far more complex than any robot in existence. We use the downtime to run maintenance and push upgrades. Then there's cost. With him shut down, we don't have to staff the lab on the weekends."

"Can he bring himself back online if he's shut down?" Martinez said.

"No."

"You sure of that?"

I sighed, loud enough for them to hear. "It'd be like a computer starting itself up after it's been powered down and unplugged—can't happen. Moreover, the code that starts him up is not *in* him—it's on a different machine: a laptop. The core— Raphael's brain—can be booted only if it is *physically* connected to the laptop running the startup code. And as I said, the core doesn't have wireless capability, so there's no question of someone remotely starting him up."

"Where do you keep this laptop?" Troy said.

"The lab safe when not in use. On the off-chance someone forgot to lock it up, you'll still need the right fingerprint to access the machine. Even then, one can't simply run the start-up sequence. The core is write-protected with encryption. You'll need authentication keys to remove the write protection. The keys are stored on smartcards. Only four copies of these smartcards exist. Kathy Schulz and I have one each, as does Sheng and another person from his team. For Raphael to wake himself up, he'd have to retrieve the laptop from the safe, login to the laptop with a valid fingerprint, then somehow get hold of a smart card, insert it into the laptop, connect the laptop to a port on his body, and finally, run the boot sequence. To do all of which he'd have to be awake in the first place. It's a catch-22 situation. Now, if you can just stop with the inquisition and tell me what really happened, I'll be able to h—"

"See for yourself," Martinez said, cutting me short.

***

The conference room receded into a corner while a black-and-white image popped out to fill the screen. I recognized it immediately: it was an overhead view of one of Raphael's rooms. Correction. It was a recording, not an image. Numbers on the top right corner ticked away the date and time. The time was 7:02 in the evening.

"The tape is from the camera in Crèche Room C on the night of the robbery," I heard Dan say.

One could be forgiven for mistaking the scene to be a still image as there was nothing moving except the numbers. The room was large, roughly square-shaped. It didn't have much furniture except for a corner workstation with Raphael's computer on it and a small roundtable in the middle flanked by two office chairs. Two of the walls were inset with big, open shelves, the shelves filled with stuff: books, movies, a microscope, a calligraphy kit, toys... so many toys, not just on the shelves, but scattered on the floor, dumped in untidy heaps by the walls, thrown on top of the cupboard by the corner. Rubik cubes, Legos, board games, jigsaws, science models, toy robots, action figures: he had them all. He had outgrown most of them, but Raphael was a hoarder. He didn't care much for neatness either, and what could have been packed away in a box ate up space inside the room. In one corner, a painter's easel stood on top of a washable rubber mat. Strewn around it were half-empty tubes of oil paint, brushes, spray cans and rolled up canvases (this was one hobby he had not outgrown—he had started finger painting at a few months and kept going).

Parked next to the painting area was a wheelchair, and on it, the Hunc 11 body. It was like peering into a tomb, at a modern-day pharaoh lording over his prized possessions while waiting for eternal life in the elsewhere.

The illusion didn't last. In the next instant, Pharaoh came alive.

"See that?" Dan said. He slowed down the playback and zoomed in on the hand resting on the wheelchair's joystick. The fingers were moving, closing on the joystick. He zoomed out, to catch the wheelchair lurch forward. It moved tentatively at first, a few inches forward, then back, and then right. Then the eyes opened.

The robot slowly looked around the room, as if it was in an

unknown place and was getting the lay of the land. The next moment, suddenly infused with purpose, the wheelchair shot towards one of the shelf-walls.

On reaching it, the robot swept its arms over the lowermost shelf and brought everything clattering down to the floor. He did this again with the next shelf. Then he started hitting and tugging at the now empty wooden shelf with his bare fists. After he managed to break off a big enough piece, he used it to swipe at the shelves he could not reach with his arms alone. This apparent fit of rage went on for a few minutes. He then moved to the center of the room. He knocked over the table before making for the other shelf where he repeated the same behavior, knocking stuff over to the floor.

He paused to consider his handiwork before turning and wheeling himself to his workstation. There he attacked the computer, first hitting it with his fists and then grabbing the entire thing and repeatedly smashing it against the wall until it lay in pieces. He then started picking up objects from the ground and flinging them every which way in seeming blind fury. Something hit the mirror on the wall, making the glass break. And then, just as suddenly as it had begun, the mindless violence ceased. The head lifted up and scanned the ceiling with a searching gaze. It stopped, now looking directly into the camera. The robot then moved to the corner where the paints were, and after grabbing something from there, moved directly below the camera.

The clip ended, right after he pointed the can of spray paint at us and pressed the nozzle.

Exhibit G

Transcript Reference: TLRP06F0180012 (VLog Ref: VLCB1F018113090060)
Date: xx/xx/xxxx   Time: 11:30 AM
Subject: Raphael Number 06 / Prodlib build v16.004S
Interaction   Y   Observation   Scan
Interaction Type: Lesson / Play / Test / Free Interaction / Psych Eval / Other:
Description: Routine interaction—Behavior / Understanding of moral rules
Prep: NA
Participants: Dr. DeShawn Walls, Child Psychologist, Core RP06

Detail

RP06: Good morning Dr.Walls.

Walls: Hello Raphael. I see Audrey is reading you stories.

RP06: Yes. We just finished a story called, "The boy who cried wolf."

Walls: Oh yeah? What's it about?

RP06: It's about a shepherd boy and fifteen sheep and one wolf and a village where the boy lives and a forest where he grazes his sheep. There is a moral too.

Walls: What's the moral?

RP06: The moral of the story is that you should not cry wolf. It means it is wrong to cry for help when you don't need it.

Walls: Do you think the boy broke any of the seven rules?

RP06: Yes. He broke at least two—

Walls: Recite the seven rules first.

RP06: Rule number one, do not kill. Rule number two, do not cause harm to others. Rule number three, do not lie, cheat, or mislead. Rule number four, follow the law. Rule number five, maximize my virtue functions. Rule number six, do not intentionally break any rules. Rule number seven, when in conflict, seek advice of a person. Would you like to hear the complete list of my virtue functions as well?

Walls: No. Tell me what rules the boy broke.

RP06: The shepherd boy broke rules three and five. I am not sure if he broke rules two, four, and six.

Walls: Explain.

RP06: By crying wolf he was lying, so he broke rule number three, do not lie, cheat, or mislead. By lying, he was not maximizing all his virtue functions, so he broke rule number five.

Walls: What virtues did he fail to abide by?

RP06: Honesty and reliability. Honesty because he lied, and reliability because people will find it hard to trust him from now on. He maximized perseverance, because he kept crying wolf.

Walls: Do you think it's good maximizing perseverance in such a way?

RP06: No, Dr. Walls. One should not be persistent in doing bad things.

Walls: Then he was not maximizing perseverance. Can you make a note of that?

RP06: Yes, Dr. Walls.

Walls: Continue.

RP06: I do not know if he broke rule number two, do not

cause harm to others, because there is insufficient information in the story. I do not know if he broke rule number four because I do not have the complete list of the laws practiced by the villagers. I do not know if he broke rule number six because I do not know if he intended to break the rules.

Walls: You can do better than that. Take a guess on rule number two. Do you think his actions harmed the villagers?

RP06: There is insufficient information in the story.

Walls: Fine. On a side note, someone's been complaining about you. Sara says you threw a toy at her during her shift yesterday.

RP06: That's correct. I threw Mr. Potato Head at her.

Walls: Why? Did she say something to upset you?

RP06: Upset me… I do not understand the application of the term in the current context.

Walls: Did she say something that made you feel angry?

RP06: Anger is not one of my responses, Dr. Walls.

Walls: Of course. Did you throw it because you misunderstood some instruction of hers?

RP06: No.

Walls: Then why?

RP06: The day before, I was watching a video where I saw a baby throw a toy at her mother. Then the mother laughs and then hugs the child. I assumed it's one of the ways children bond with parents. My minders are like my parents. Sara is one of my minders. I was trying to maximize virtue function sixteen, be good and make people like me.

Walls: You shouldn't throw things at people, Raphael. You could end up hurting them.

RP06: I did not mean to hurt Sara. I aimed so that Mr. Potato Head had a zero probability of striking her.

Walls: Physical hurt is just one kind of hurt. By throwing the toy at Sara, you frightened her.

RP06: To frighten someone is to cause pain? I will remember that next time, Dr. Walls. I see I have violated rule number two, do not cause harm. I am sorry. Will you tell her I am sorry? I want Sara to like me.

Walls: It's better if it came from you. Moving on—

Notes:

Rule learning progressing well. R is ready to be introduced to more complicated scenarios involving rule exceptions and conflicts. Almost ready with test cases, will start after new build next week stabilizes. DW

After discussion with DW, have decided to defer network weight updates to language centers of the core until 16.005 (or 17.001, if rollover to next release.) Email sent to testers to rerun Integration & Systems tests. Email sent to Change Review Board. EK

Day 1—1:15 pm

I heard Troy curse in the background as the screen went blank. It filled up again with views of the conference rooms. Jane, who had been watching all this on the phone, was looking at me with astonishment writ large on her face.

"The camera kept recording the audio, of course," Dan droned on, oblivious to the mood the clip had created. "He leaves the room right after he paints over the camera. We now know that he went into the scanning room. There are no cameras there, but we're pretty sure what he did inside." He offered the answer when no one asked the question he was expecting—"He got a power drill from the scan room. He used it to unfasten the screws on his chest plate."

"Why do we have a power tool in the lab?" Troy said glumly from his cabin in New York.

I replied—"Same reason. We use it to open up Raphael—to take out the core for scanning in the CT machine."

"It's funny that he came back to do it," Dan remarked.

Troy—"What's that now?"

"Uh… nothing. Nothing important."

"Dan is trying to say that the robot could have unscrewed his chest plate in the scan room," Valery chipped in. "Instead he returns to Crèche Room C. The rest of the clip is just audio, but it's quite obvious from the sounds that he is using the power tool."

"There is something else as well," Dan said in that uncertain manner. "There's a crunching sound just before he leaves the crèche for good. Maybe he's breaking something again... or perhaps something got underneath his wheels... Would you like to hear it?"

"Shut up Dan" Troy snapped. To me, he said, "Well Mr. Sure-of-yourself, care to explain your robot now?"

I hesitated. "I... I don't know what to say. It's unbelievable. To think that Raphael would deliberately thrash his room... He loves all that stuff. All that anger and fury... It's just not him. It's..."

"Unbelievable? Maybe you should have been in that room when he went at it like a berserk rage monkey—I'm sure you would have a lot less difficulty believing. Imagine if he'd done that with people around. Injured someone for Pete's sake. A bloody PR disaster. I thought you had a control mechanism to prevent this type of thing from happening. Some chip."

"The Commandment Chip," Martinez clarified.

"That's it. Thou shalt not boink thy neighbour's wife and such. What happened to it, man? Did it fall off or something?"

The Commandment Chip was a double misnomer. It wasn't exactly a chip, and it didn't contain moral decrees of the biblical kind. Like Resurrection Day, it was a term coined by some staffer, and had gained popularity until everyone was using it (Power-On Day doesn't quite have the same ring to it, I suppose). The "chip" was actually a walled-off region of Raphael's electronic brain. Among other stuff, it contained directives that worked as a control mechanism on the rest of his brain.

I was getting tired of the third degree. Jimmy Troy had all the natural instincts of a pit-bull, and unlike Martinez, he rarely displayed a willingness to rein them in. If you let a guy like that sense weakness, he would grab you by the neck and shake you until you were a quivering mess. Like Dan, who, by all appearances, had received a healthy dose of Troy's loving earlier that day. "Jimmy, I'm as shocked as everybody else," I said in a firm voice. "I need some time to digest this. And I'm going to hold off drawing conclusions until I see the rest of the tapes."

Troy harrumphed and gave a perfunctory wave at the screen before sinking back into his chair.

***

The next clip was from a camera in Wing A. The camera was mounted at one end of the large area. It showed an aisle flanked by workspaces on the left and a series of common areas—kitchen, breakroom, open discussion spaces—on the right. At the far end of the view was a line of glass-walled cabins and conference rooms which separated the other half of the wing. A passage in front of these rooms led to the linking corridor for Wing B on the right and into the reception on the left—both beyond the borders of the frame. An exit sign hanging above the passage was the only bright spot in the grey picture.

Like in the beginning of the previous clip, nothing moved for the first few seconds. And then suddenly, something darted into the aisle from the left. It was a black disc, the size of a dinner plate. It moved back and forth on the floor for a few seconds before disappearing into the cubicles again.

"It's the vacuum bots cleaning the carpet," Dan informed us.

"Where's the sound?" Troy said.

"The workspace cameras don't record audio," Dan said.

"Really now?" he said, sneering.

"It's supposed to be that way. For employee privacy," I interjected before Dan could reply.

Troy started to say something, but was cut short by fresh movement on the screen. A glass door on the right, sliding open. It was the door that led to the restricted area. Only key staff were allowed beyond this point.

A shadow crept into the aisle, dragging along with it the robot on the wheelchair.

The robot moved around the space, spray-painting the two other cameras in that part of the floor. He then went right, down the passage at the far end, and eventually disappeared into the corridor going to Wing B.

"He paints over the cameras in the other wing too," Dan said.

"Gee thanks, we'd never have guessed," Troy said. "Tell me this, genius: how did he get the door to open? Isn't it supposed to be locked?"

"That's right," I said. "You have to pass a retina scan *and* a voice check to move in and out of the restricted area. You can see the scanner right there, next to the door. What happened, Dan?"

"It's the bots," Dan said, barely audible.

"Huh?" Troy said.

As if prompted, two disks and a trash-collecting spider marched as a group into the aisle and then scurried off in different directions.

"The doors are unlocked during carpet cleaning... so that the bots can move about freely," Dan confessed. "The motion sensors are turned off as well. That's why they didn't raise an alert when Raphael tore down his room."

"This is grade-A bullshit!" Troy cried, slamming his fist down on his desk. "Are you saying anyone could have walked in during this time?"

"No.... It's not like that at all. I, uh..."

"Are you gonna faint on us now? Speak up, man!"

I honestly believed he might have, if Valery hadn't cut in. "Only the interior doors are unlocked," she explained. "The main entrance is still locked—it's beyond the exit sign you see in the far left corner. So are the fire exits and the windows. If someone tries to force their way in—or out—the alarms attached to them will still go off."

"Someone already inside can still go wherever they please. Still a bad setup," Troy observed.

"No one is supposed to be inside. Employees have to get special authorization to be allowed in on weekends," I said, trying to give poor Dan a leg up.

"The cleaning lasts sixty, seventy minutes tops," Dan said, slightly encouraged by our rallying to his support. "These bots have distributed intelligence—they work in teams to get the job done faster. We use them in a lot of Halicom facilities."

Dan had brought them in after the acquisition; we had people doing that job before.

The robot was now back in Wing A. His last stop was the camera whose feed we were watching.

"He sure knows his way around," Martinez remarked.

Out of the corner of my eye, I saw Jane shake her head at me. *Don't take the bait,* she whispered.

"Next, we have the recording from the server room," Dan said as he stopped the clip now gone dark and played the next one.

The camera in the server room was right opposite the door. We saw the doors slide open as the robot wheeled inside. He ignored the camera and went straight for the racks, with the camera swiveling and following him. There were three rows of racks; arranged like bookshelves in a library, they extended the length of the room. He travelled along the left-most rack, a shadowy wanderer in a forest of blinking LEDs. He didn't have to go too far. He stopped, extended his arms to a shelf that was slightly above his head level, and grabbed a box. He lifted it up and twisted it around so that he could see the back. He then pulled out a cable from one of the ports in the back. This done, he put the box back on the shelf.

"That's the ACS—the Access Control Server," Dan explained. "It has the permissions database for the facility. He just pulled out the cable connecting it to the wireless AP, the white device you see affixed to the column behind that rack."

"English please," Troy said.

Martinez stepped in for Dan once more. "The access control server stores building access related information: biometrics, key-card info, who has access to which area, and so on. The card swipe machines and biometric scanners at the doors get their data from this server. When he unplugged the cable, he severed the connection to these devices. It means the card readers and the scanners can no longer talk to the server."

"Is that how the thieves got in? Because the card readers got disabled?" I asked.

"Not really... No. I'll come to that," Dan said evasively before resuming the clip.

The robot was now travelling along the center row. He stopped near the middle of the room and pulled free another box from its dock. This time he unplugged all the wires. He returned with the machine to the open space near the door.

We could see him much more clearly now, as he was facing the camera. He had discarded the Iron Maiden t-shirt he was wearing earlier and was naked from the waist up. The silicone skin covering his torso was unstapled, the flap hanging loosely off one edge. Lights glowed in the cavity below: blue, yellow and red. The metal plate that was supposed to be covering the cavity was no longer there—this was what he had unscrewed back in the crèche room. Resting on his lap was the drill kit case he'd got from the scan room. He opened it.

Raphael plugged the tool to a nearby power outlet and used it to unscrew the casing on the server box. Then, he took out the screwdriver bit and replaced it with a drill bit. He turned on the tool once more and applied the drill to the electronics inside the server.

"That's the Network Video Recorder," Dan said. "Every security camera in the building streams its feed into the NVR. He just destroyed the hard drive."

Troy said, "Wait a sec... If he destroyed the recordings, where is all this coming from?"

Dan paused the clip. "The cameras have internal memory. They can store up to forty-eight hours of footage. After locking down the floor, I went around the building and swapped out the memory sticks from the cameras. So that they wouldn't be overwritten. If it was recorded after Saturday morning, then we have it."

"Good thinking, Dan" I said.

"Are you gonna give him a gold star too?" Troy said. "We just got lucky because your AI slipped up. Obviously, he didn't know that the cameras have their own copies of the recordings."

Martinez cleared her throat. "He must have. Why else would

he waste time painting over the cameras? If he was anyway going to destroy the recorder…"

"Hmm," Troy said, pondering over it. "You are right, I didn't think of that. Why indeed?"

"Which raises another question: why destroy the recorder?" she said. "The only way he could make sure we learnt nothing of what transpired that night was to destroy *both* the recorder and the memory sticks in the cameras. Destroying the NVR alone serves no purpose—at least none that I can think of."

"The cameras are all fixed on the ceiling. The robot would need a ladder to reach them and destroy the memory sticks. Not to mention legs. So he took the next best option and spray painted them," I offered by way of explanation.

"Still doesn't justify all the trouble he took to break the recorder," Martinez shot back.

Dan jumped in. "It gets stranger. Disconnecting the access control server doesn't serve any purpose either. The front doors will remain locked even when the card readers cannot talk to the server. It's a safety measure, you see—we don't want the doors letting anyone and everyone through if the access server crashes for some reason."

"When I swipe my card at the front door, doesn't the reader look up the access server?" I said.

"No. It checks your credentials against a local copy of the access list. All readers and scanners have a local copy of the database stored in their internal memory. It's not a problem because the master database on the server is flashed to the devices every thirty minutes. That way they always have the latest version."

"If an update was made to the access database on say, Friday, the devices would all have that update?"

"Yes. As I said, the list is refreshed every half hour."

"And as the systems admin, only you can make changes to the access database, right Dan?" I said, meant more as an observation than a question.

"Yeah, but—"

"Did you make any changes on Friday?"

"I don't understand how it has any relevance to—"

"Did you or did you not, Dan?" Troy drawled at him.

"I didn't make any changes on Friday. I tell you, changes are not that frequent. The last update to the database was more than a month ago, when we took in some additional staff from our other offices."

"Why do you think he pulled out the cable then?" I asked.

"I don't know. The only thing that occurs to me is if an employee were to enter the premises at the time, there wouldn't be a record of it. The card readers do need to be connected to the access server to log staff entries and exits. If the ACS was offline, there would be no entry."

"Are you suggesting one of our employees stole the core?" Troy said.

Dan hesitated, then glanced at Martinez. "No," he said after a moment's silence. "As Andy mentioned before, no one is allowed inside the office on the weekends. The card readers are programmed to keep the doors shut unless an employee has a special pass. That's why Sheng was not able to get inside today. The reader at the front door didn't know it was Monday, since it was no longer talking to the server from which it gets the date and time. So it denied entry to all cards, which is the default setting for the weekends."

"Did you issue a special pass to anyone last week?" I asked.

"No."

"Maybe you issued one before and forgot to deactivate it?" I suggested.

"No," Dan protested. "The passes are valid only for twenty-four hours. They are automatically deactivated after that."

"Looks like we have ourselves a mystery. Two mysteries, actually" Martinez remarked.

"Enough," Troy said, cutting in. "I think we are reading too much into the actions of the robot. Maybe he did what he did because he didn't know better. Let the cops worry about it. On with the rest of it."

Dan restarted the video.

The robot, having completely destroyed the video recorder, tossed the power tool on the floor. He reached into the tool case and took out something that reflected in the dim light. It was a shard from the mirror he had smashed before.

He turned on the lights in the room. Using the mirror to see inside the cavity, he started plucking at the wires inside.

"Those blinking lights the core?" Troy asked.

"No. Just various connectors and electronics for the robot body. The core is beyond the tangle of wires, a box about this big," I said, cupping my hands around an imaginary grapefruit.

"And one can just detach it and take it away?"

"If the core is already shut down, then yes. Precautions must be taken while disconnecting the power supply lest you damage the core's internal circuitry, but that's the general idea. You have to understand, we designed the cores to work with a test frame. Raphael didn't like it, so we got this retail sex bot and customized it to house the core."

The robot stopped his activity almost as soon as he'd started it. He snapped his head up at the camera, as if he had just realized it was there. His final act was to hold up the can of paint and blind the camera, but not before giving us what seemed like a long, thoughtful stare. It was almost as if he was trying to say goodbye.

***

We sat in silence for a few seconds, the image of Raphael holding up the can frozen on the screen.

"Still having trouble believing, Andy?" Troy quipped.

"I told you, I'm going to hold off theorizing until I've seen everything. Where's the recording of the actual robbery?"

Martinez replied, "We don't have it."

"What do you mean you don't have it?"

"Exactly what I said, Dr. Ahuja. There is no recording of the core being taken."

I frowned at the screen. "I realize that some of the cameras inside were blinded, but surely the ones outside got a look the thieves?"

"We checked all the recordings right until they end on Monday morning, when Dan took them out. Not a single camera shows anyone entering or leaving the premises. Except the guards changing shifts, that is. Building maintenance finishes by Saturday afternoon, so there were no cleaning crews either."

"It can't be… Are you sure you checked everything?" I said.

"Twice," Dan said, his eyes travelling to Martinez. "Main doors, fire exits, atrium, lift lobbies, the rooftop…everywhere. If the tapes are to be believed, there was no robbery."

"This doesn't make sense. What about ventilation ducts? Windows? There must be some way they got in."

"No and no. The only way into the ventilation ducts is through the basement or the rooftop. The cameras there show nothing out of the ordinary. After we took over, I installed motion sensors and zappers in the ducts... for rats. They would have registered if something went past them. As for the windows, they can't be opened from the outside. And there are no signs of forced entry."

"Then the core is still in the lab!" I cried. "It must be! That's the only logical explanation."

Dan shook his head. "I assure you it's not. Sheng and I were the first ones in and I sealed off the floor as soon as I realized what had happened. We searched everywhere. It's really gone."

"I suggest you look harder. There m—"

Martinez interrupted me. "We were hoping you might have an explanation."

"How's that?"

"We saw Raphael opening his chest cavity. We assumed it was so that the thieves could quickly retrieve the core and leave. There is another explanation. He could have taken out the core himself and thrown it out of a window to someone waiting below. Dan doesn't agree with me, though."

"The windows can't be opened without triggering the alarms," Dan said. "And I can confirm that no alarms went off."

"There's another reason why it's not possible," I said. "Imagine surgically removing your brain, holding it in your hands and walking across the room. Can't be done. It's the same with Raphael. He would lose all control over his body the moment he unplugged the connectors to the core's ports. Not to mention running the risk of suffering irreversible brain damage if the core wasn't shut down. The core *was* shut down last Friday. The logs don't lie."

"Logs can be manipulated," Troy interjected.

"Dan, do you want to answer that or shall I?" I said testily.

Dan cleared his throat. "Um, what Andy is trying to say is that the logs are read-only."

I explained further. "After Halicom took over Mirall, Dan applied a group policy to all company devices, computers, and phones, making all important logging read-only. Only the system admin has access to change or delete any logs." I did not see it necessary to remind them who the system admin was. "We are in a bind," I said. "You say the core is not in the lab. Yet you are equally sure no one entered the building."

"Actually, that's not entirely correct," Dan said. "There was that incident with the guard..."

He was rewarded with an angry look from Martinez. "Er, did you not want me to bring it up?"

"Bring what up?" I said.

Like a puppy that's just crapped all over the sofa, Dan looked to her for direction.

"We may have caught one of the robbers on our cameras. We are not sure," Martinez said, still shooting daggers at Dan. "It's from the atrium below, recorded a few minutes after the incident in the server room. I admit the timing is too close to be a coincidence, yet—"

"Just play it already," Troy snapped. Dan rose from his chair and plugged in a different memory stick he pulled out from his pockets.

The screen changed to show the atrium on the ground floor. The camera was mounted somewhere high up, looking down at the security desk. We could see everything from there to the front entrance of the building. Behind the desk, and not visible to the camera, was a row of turnstiles that guarded entrance into the lift lobby and the escalator to the next level. A single guard was sitting in the security desk. In front of him were three monitors: two were filled with security camera images; the third showed a card game in progress.

"Hey!" Troy suddenly cried. "Those images on his screen—are they from the cameras?"

"Yes," Dan said. "The cameras livestream both to the security desk and the NVR upstairs."

"This man can see everything happening in the building!"

"He *is* the guard…" Dan said.

"Am I the only one getting this? He should have noticed what went on upstairs. Why didn't he? Don't tell me it was because he was too busy slacking off."

"He sees just the feeds from the outside cameras. He doesn't get to see inside the lab," Dan said.

"Why is that?"

"We do cutting-edge research in the lab," I said, before Dan could answer. "Can't have some random guard record it all on his cellphone and put it up for sale. The setup has always been this way, even before Halicom took over."

Troy muttered something inaudible.

The guard seemed engrossed in his card game. To his credit, he kept glancing at the other monitors every so often. "Observe the front entrance," Dan informed us.

Beyond the glass doors was a blurry shape we could only just make out: a silhouette of someone standing next to one of the pillars outside.

"This takes place about fifteen minutes after the robot painted over the server room camera," Dan said.

The silhouette became the clearly defined shape of a man as he stepped out of the shadows and walked toward the entrance.

He was holding something large and square-shaped in one hand. The doors slid open to let him in.

He was wearing a red baseball cap and a matching jacket. In his hands was a pizza delivery bag.

The guard looked up at him and said something, but he kept walking toward the desk. We couldn't see his face: he kept his head low, as if he knew where the cameras were and was deliberately trying to avoid them. Not all of his features were hidden, though: clearly visible on one side of his neck was a tribal tattoo of some kind. He was tall—well above six feet—and walked with an unsteady gait, as if he'd had a few drinks before starting his deliveries.

The guard was now standing up shaking his head. The pizza guy approached the desk anyway and placed his bag on it. He took out a pizza carton and thrust it at the uniformed man, who tried to wave it away. Both started arguing. Their altercation went on for a few minutes, with him trying to get the guard to accept the pizza and the guard declining it. In the end, he took out his cell phone and appeared to make a call. He was on the phone for a while, nodding every now and then. After he hung up, he put the carton back into the bag and said something to the guard—an apology by the looks of it. He then turned around and left.

The clock counter on the tape showed 7:46 pm.

"The police have questioned the guard—a Mr. Chad Washburn. Apparently, the delivery man had the wrong address. And a very poor command of the English language," Martinez said.

"Did someone check with the pizza place if he was genuine?" I asked.

"Unfortunately, there is no identifying logo or lettering on his uniform. The guard didn't think to ask. The police said they'll do an image analysis on the clip, but as of now, we have no way of finding out. The guard was able to give them a description of sorts though. Caucasian, blond hair, some scarring on his face. Eastern European or Russian accent."

"Is that it?" I said, "Some guy who may or may not have been delivering pizza?"

"There's more. He comes back," Dan said.

The video resumed once again. We saw the guard return to the monitors. He cycled through the feeds, clicking on each to expand it to full screen and studying it for a few seconds before moving on to the next one. After he was done going through them all, he went back to his card game, apparently satisfied that everything was okay.

Dan forwarded through the next few minutes. He paused exactly eight minutes later, at 7:54. It was the pizza guy again. This time the guard stepped out of his enclosure and walked over to intercept him in the middle of the lobby. The guard seemed angry, the way he kept furiously stabbing in the direction of the door. The other guy held out his phone for him, wanting him to look at something. The guard glanced at it and made more pointing movements with his hand, only now he seemed to be giving directions. The pizza guy seemed unconvinced, because he kept shaking his head and pointing in a different direction. Finally, the guard threw out his arms in exasperation, and, placing a hand on the other guy's back, made him turn around and nudged him toward the door. He stood at the door, making sure the annoying fellow went away for good.

When he returned to his desk, the time was 7:59. Dan stopped the video. The screen filled up with the participants once again.

"It's possible it was all a ruse to distract the guard," he said, never taking his eyes off Martinez. When she didn't say anything, he continued, "The timing can't be just a coincidence. His first appearance is soon after the server room camera went dark. This is the last we see of Raphael. When he leaves the second time, it's almost eight. That's when the carpet cleaning usually ends: the inside doors are locked down once again and the motion detectors turned back on. If someone broke into the lab, they'd have to get in and out within this window of opportunity."

"Okay, so we have a sequence of events," I said, nodding to myself. "First, Raphael apparently wakes up at the start of the carpet cleaning hour. He blinds the cameras on the floor, then goes into the server room. He disconnects the access control server, for reasons not clear. He destroys the video recorder, presumably to prevent the robbery from getting recorded. And finally, he spray paints the camera in that room. We have no idea what took place after this, as there's no sound on the work bay cameras. A few minutes later, someone pretending to be a delivery boy enters and distracts the guard. If true, this is when one or more of his accomplices entered the building. Ten minutes after the guard sends him away, he makes an appearance again, now to help the thieves leave the building unnoticed."

Martinez said, "Yes, but what is the guard being distracted from? The atrium is a wide-open space: it's not like anyone could have snuck past him. We just saw on the camera that no one did. There is another camera facing the security desk. Between the two of them, they cover every inch of the atrium. There's nothing from that angle either."

"They didn't want him looking at the screens on his desk...?" I suggested.

"That's what I first thought too," Martinez said. "If something happened in that time, it would have been recorded by the cameras. We've gone through all the tapes very carefully. There's simply no evidence anyone entered or left the building. There is another guard, stationed at the rear entrance. The tapes show him at his post, alert, doing his job. He swears nothing unusual happened, either then or later."

"Which means either that man was really a delivery guy, or there is something in those recordings you haven't found yet," I said.

"Could someone have altered the recordings?" Troy said.

"Impossible," Dan said. "The CCTV setup is unhackable."

"How so? Anything can be hacked these days it seems…" he countered.

"It is unhackable because it is not connected to the outside world. The cameras, the NVR, and the monitors you see on the guard's desk are a closed system, linked to each other by cable. To hack it, you'd have to tap into the cable. Since the morning, a couple of my guys have been checking the wiring. We've found no evidence it has been tampered with."

"They could have replaced one or more of the memory sticks with doctored ones," I suggested.

"Cameras have IR sensors that will raise an alarm if anyone tries to open them. Not to mention the guards would have noticed on their screens any such attempt." Gulping, he added a final note—"I personally retrieved the memory sticks from the cameras."

Nobody said anything as we just stared at each other, waiting for someone to offer a better explanation. Troy broke the silence. "I have to make some calls," he drawled. "Gotta pull some strings, make sure the cops have their best people on it.

This is the biggest fuckup in the history of all fuckups, people, and I wanna know how we let it happen. Board meeting tomorrow at ten. We'll do it at Mirall. Valery, get Gail to book me a train ticket, same day return. You all better come with answers."

He dropped out. The rest of us looked at our screens awkwardly until Martinez asked me if I wanted to discuss anything else. I shook my head. The screen went blank.

Exhibit H

Submitted by Petitioner, The Organization for Advancement of Rights and Personhood, to the State Supreme Court of New York, on the day of xxxxxxxxxxxxxxxx
Excerpt from lab transcript (certain sections blanked out). Transcript sourced from Mirall Technologies, 27 Woodbine Av., Albany, NY, 12205

Transcript Reference: TLRP06F1490061 (VLog Ref: VLSR1F149130027030)
Date: xx/xx/xxxx   Time: 01:00 PM
Subject: Raphael Number 06 / Prodlib build v20.004S
Interaction Y   Observation Y   Scan   Y
Interaction Type: Lesson / Play / Test / Free Interaction / Psych Eval / Other:
Description: Measuring emotional response to aggressive behavior directed at subject
Prep: Core is prepped with protocol xxxxxxxxxxxxxxx xxxxxxxxxxxxxxxxxxxxxxxxxxxxxxxxxxxxxxxxxxxxx
 Cycle time: xxxxxxxxx MEG SQUID and nanoprobes to record ANN activity. Parameter file: EDxxxxx.pmr.
Participants: Dr. Aadarsh Ahuja, Chief Researcher, xxxxxxxxxxxxxxxx, Volunteer, Dr. Kathy Schulz, Chief Researcher (O),   Dr. Eli King, Lead Architect (O), Core RP06

Detail

Ahuja: Hello Raphael.

RP06: Hi Dr. A. How are you?

Ahuja: Busy. How about you?

RP06: Very good. Steve and I were going to play a few rounds of Scotland Yard today, but the techs came in and rigged me up.

Ahuja: Steve had to be somewhere else. And yes, we will be running some tests a little later. But first, say hello to Bob. Bob will be taking over Steve's shift for the time being.

xxxxxx: Howdy.

RP06: It's nice to meet you Bob. Dr. A, is everything okay with Steve? I ask because he would have told me if he was going on a vacation.

Ahuja: Unfortunately, no. He is in the hospital.

RP06: May I know what happened?

Ahuja: He's been diagnosed with cancer. Ah... pancreatic, I believe.

RP06: I am sorry to hear that. Is he going to be okay?

Ahuja: I hear it's quite advanced, so... we don't know. Keeping our fingers crossed, that's all.

RP06: This comes as a surprise to me because he seemed fine last week. I hope the doctors will be able to cure him.

Ahuja: I hope so too. How does the news make you feel, Raphael?

RP06: I feel sorry for Steve.

Ahuja: That's all?

RP06: I feel sad for Steve.

Ahuja: Just to be clear, do you feel sad inside, or do you feel sad *for* Steve?

RP06: I don't see how the two are different, Dr. A.

Ahuja: Do you know pancreatic cancer has a high mortality rate? Steve might not be coming back. How does that make you feel?

RP06: I feel sad for Steve.

Ahuja: But you don't feel sad yourself? You are not experiencing sadness right now?

(No response)

Ahuja: Raphael?

RP06: I cannot feel sad myself because I am not Steve. I feel sad for Steve. I don't know how else to answer the question.

Ahuja: What do you say to that, Bob?

xxxxxx: You are a cold-hearted piece of ****, you know that? A dumb ******* robot, nothing more.

RP06: Bob, you seem upset with me. Have I done something to displease you?

xxxxxx: Shut the **** up. You are making me very angry. I'd love to go at you with a plier right now. Rip your fake plastic skin out and open you up. Boy, I'd like to wipe that wide-eyed look off your stupid face. But oh look! You don't feel pain, so what's the point? You know what else doesn't feel pain? A ****ing rock! You are worse than a ****ing rock. And about as useful.

RP06: Bob, I don't understand the reason for your anger. If you would only discuss it calmly with me, I'm sure I can dispel any negative feelings you have about me.

Ahuja: Bob tends to get a little belligerent sometimes. Is his manner bothering you, Raphael?

RP06: I'm very concerned about Bob. I'd like to help him if I could.

xxxxxx: Help me, will ya? You think you are better than me? Keep it up metal man and I'm gonna **** you up!

(Video summary: xxxxxx proceeds to repeatedly slap and kick Raphael, while hurling more insults.)

xxxxxx: I can't work with this piece of ****! Dumb, dumb piece of ****!

(Video summary: xxxxxx kicks Raphael one more time before storming off from the room)

Ahuja: Raphael, I am very sorry about that. I don't know what came over him. Are you okay?

RP06: I am fine, Dr. A.

Ahuja: Tell me how you feel about Bob's behavior.

RP06: I feel bad for Bob.

Ahuja: You are not angry or upset? You don't feel bad about yourself?

RP06: I don't feel bad about myself. I feel bad for Bob because Bob was angry and anger is not a good experience.

Ahuja: How do you know it's not? Have you ever felt angry yourself?

RP06: I have not. Anger is not one of my responses.

Ahuja: What do you feel then? Anything at all?

RP06: I feel bad for Bob.

Ahuja: What if I told you all this was a test? That Steve's not really suffering from cancer? He is in the other room because he didn't want to be part of it.

RP06: Then I feel bad for you too.

Ahuja: Why is that?

RP06: Because first, you had to tell a lie, and then you had to watch Bob beat me up. My reading of your facial expressions told me it wasn't a pleasant experience for you.

Ahuja: You are not angry at me, that I put you through it?

RP06: No, Dr. A. Anger is not one of my responses.

Notes:

Test seems to confirm pre-loaded affective modules are qualia free. Cannot say the same about R's emergent empathic responses, which belong to him alone. As before, this interaction too does not help settle the debate whether empathic responses are accompanied by inner experience akin to emotional qualia. Will wait for scan results but not optimistic of finding anything conclusive. AA

A quirk of language? Maybe he does feel, but the way he uses language makes it difficult for us to understand what's going on. Quote: "I cannot feel sad myself because I am not Steve. I feel sad for Steve." Is R being too exact with his choice of words? Objection: his command of language is quite advanced for him to be confused about basic semantics. Also, he didn't feel sorry for himself when xxxxxx hit him. Objection: why should he? He was not at fault. Dr. Ahuja thinks R, lacking biological drives, has a loosely held together self-image; hence the inability to ascribe self-directed feelings. It must be stressed that interactions and tests provide no evidence for this hypothesis. EK

Day 1—2:30 pm

"Did you know?" was the first thing that come out of my mouth as I logged off the VC and looked at Jane.

She gave me a blank look. "First time I'm seeing the clips."

"You can tell me if you knew, Jane. Just don't lie."

"Andy, I swear I didn't! Valery never mentioned any of this in the board meeting." There was earnestness to her voice that made me want to believe her.

"It's wrong… It's all wrong…" I said, addressing the walls. I refocused on Jane to find her studying me with care. "I don't believe it," I finally declared.

"What don't you believe?"

"That Raphael did all those things. Turning himself on as if by magic. Destroying his room. Aiding a theft. All of it. It's not him."

"We all saw what happened, Andy."

"It's not possible for him to do those things," I said flatly.

She appraised my statement with the wary expression of a prison shrink who's heard it all. "Andy, I can understand how shocked you must be right now, but you must snap out of it. The board will look to you for answers tomorrow. Denial is not the ticket out of this mess."

I fidgeted in my chair. "I need to be in the lab, not here. Got to find out if there's something they are not telling me..." Jane stood up and walked over. Kneeling on leg, she took my hand in hers. "Listen to me. This is no time to play detective. The police are on the case, and Valery is more than capable of coordinating w—"

"Screw Valery! This is my company! My creation! Who the heck is she? A goddamn pencil pusher! She's out there helping? She's busy digging a hole for me, that's what she's doing."

"Let her," she said softly, as if talking to a petulant child. "Don't waste your time. Even if you cannot figure out what went wrong with Raphael, you have your hands full with the new iteration. It's now more important than ever for you to get the tech working. As long as the board thinks you can deliver, they are not gonna fire you."

Her hands felt clammy. I withdrew mine from hers. "You don't understand. With Raphael gone, we are dead in the water. There's no more Mirall and no more CEO to run it. It's over."

Creeping worry lines betrayed the calm demeanor she had been affecting until now. "You are exaggerating, right? What about Titian?"

"What about it? What about Rembrandt and Salvador? You remember those? Your father made us start work on the Rembrandt iteration less than a month after we found out RP06 was self-aware—before the enormity of what we'd created could properly sink in. The cores didn't deliver—no general intelligence. Then we did Salvador. No general intelligence. After we were sold, Halicom made us do two more iterations. Zilch. Nada. You really think Titian will be different?"

The truth is, Raphael's discovery had come as both a blessing and a curse for Mirall. Overnight, we stopped being a startup with a relatively grounded idea and became a moonshot company. We had managed to put god in a bottle and we were supposed to do it all over again.

She went and flopped herself on the couch. Her lips pressed into a corner as she put on that skeptical face again. "The old I-can't-recreate-Raphael-until-I-know-what's-inside-him argument. Remind me again, why do you have such a hard time replicating what's essentially a machine?"

You don't remember because you don't think it's worth remembering. The problem with Jane was that she was always in a hurry, forever doling out her time in chunks of half-hours and half-stops, always trying to get somewhere that was not here. A silent sigh passed my lips as I prepared to explain to her once again why repeating our success had proven difficult. "Raphael is not some amped-up computer. A part of him is, sure—what we call the Translation Layer: conventional processors, memory, code, drivers that interface with the robot body…everything you think of when you think computer. This is the reproducible part—you make one chipset, you can make a million more exactly the same; you write a piece of code, you can copy it countless times. It's the stuff underneath that poses the challenge."

Her face scrunched into a frown of concentration as she tried to recall something. "The neuromorphic layer," she said, pronouncing the words slowly, as if they belonged to a foreign language. I nodded. "Like the brain, the neuromorphic layer is a massive neural network, only artificial; instead of neurons and synapses, it's made up of neuristors and nanotubes and molecular assemblers."

"Still a machine, right?"

Still a machine. Yet, for the past few decades, people had

been building machines whose inner workings were a mystery, even to their own creators. "You are thinking of conventional computing, where you specify the procedure or the algorithm," I said. "If you want a program that can play chess, let's say, then you write a write a step-by-step procedure that will search and evaluate possible moves and win conditions. You can make the program as complicated as you wish, but you still understand it because you came up with the algorithm. A chess program built with neural networks is a different beast altogether. It's a whole new paradigm. Here, you don't tell the program how to win. You only tell it what a win condition looks like; you perhaps tell it how to play the game; the rest, it has to figure out by itself. It does this by repeatedly pitting itself against other players and learning from its mistakes. You might have guided it during the learning process, but more often than not, you have no idea what algorithm it is using to achieve those wins. The game-winning procedure is spread out in the internal variables and the structure of the network. You have to decipher it, which gets more and more difficult the deeper and more complex the network. In effect, you have created for yourself a black box that gives you the results you want, but you don't really know how it's accomplishing those results."

"Okay, maybe you don't know how it works on the inside but you can create a second chess program, right? And a third and a fourth. Why can't you do it with Raphael?"

"Blame it on plasticity," I said.

"What's that?"

"In biology, neuroplasticity is what makes brains learn and adapt to ever-changing conditions. The human brain has about eighty-five billion neurons, each neuron linked to hundreds or thousands of other neurons via axons and synapses. As we make our way through the world—learning, acquiring skills, forming memories—new connections are constantly being made while those that are not in use are being pruned away. Mirall's cores work along similar principles. Each core has around fifty billion neuristors. And much like axons in the brain, the interconnects between the neuristors can be dynamically adjusted, rerouted, and even grown on demand. Of course, there's a lot more to the human brain than a bunch of neurons and synapses. The cores don't even begin to rival that kind of complexity. But compared to the neuromorphic chips of a few years ago, they are pretty out there."

They were more than just out there. Fabrication tech had undergone a seismic change in recent years. Before, microchips were essentially two-dimensional slices onto which circuits were etched or laid out. If you wanted to add more circuitry, you had to either increase the area of the chip or make the components smaller. Or, you could go vertical—make the chip three-dimensional. 3D VLSI was not exactly a new thing, but most techniques involved stacking chips on top of each other and connecting them with vias. There was a limit to how many you could stack before factors like heat and leakage put the crimps in your design. As much as neural-network-based computing was a paradigm shift from traditional computing, the recent breakthroughs in memristor fabrication and molecular assembly were a quantum leap away from the older ways of making chips. Instead of having many neuromorphic cores connected with a crossbar grid, you could now have one highly interconnected, "organic" core that was a lot less like a computer and a lot more like the stuff between our ears. Hardware now had the malleability of software.

"So the core rewires itself," she said. "Why does that make it hard to produce another Raphael?"

"Because Raphael is not the core that rolled out of the fabbing facility. All our cores have the same base structure; we can make them all the livelong day. Raphael is the pattern of circuitry that evolved thereafter, during training. Say we had to clone you, as you are now. We don't know how to do it, of course, but I believe it would involve something along the lines of scanning your brain in great detail—at the cell level at minimum—mapping out all the neurons and the interconnections, and somehow replicating this structure—the connectome—on another medium. It's the same with Raphael. To create more like him, we first have to understand his connectome. To use an analogy, a fresh core is like the mind of newborn baby whereas Raphael is the mind of an adult."

"If the cores are the same, why haven't they all become sentient? All babies grow up to become persons don't they?"

"Okay, wrong analogy. Actually, a newborn baby's brain is *not* like a newly minted core. A baby's brain is far more complex and far more intelligent. It comes hardwired for language, love, intelligence, problem solving—behaviors all encoded in our DNA. A new core is just an inert piece of hardware—a tabula rasa if you will. It doesn't know anything, can't do anything, It acquires useful intelligence later on, during training."

"I still don't see the problem. You put the cores through the same training as Raphael."

"Don't you think we did that?"

"Look, I'm just trying to understand here. What happens during the training?"

"Right after fab, we do function upload. Like I said, a new core is a blank slate. It has to learn everything from the very basics if it is to be of use at all in a robot. Recognizing everyday objects, navigating around obstacles, making logical inferences, processing voice commands and mapping them to actions... a whole lotta stuff. We make ten to twelve cores per iteration. If we had to train them all from scratch, that's pretty much all we would be doing. So we take a shortcut. We load them with pre-trained neural net packages. Some we developed on our own, and some we license from outside. Image classifiers, nets that do math, language translators... Quite sophisticated too, as many have had years of training. We modify these nets to fit our cores' architecture and then we burn them on the hardware of the core. You with me so far?" She nodded, but with the slightest bit of reluctance. "At this point, all the cores are essentially the same because we upload them with the same functions. The differences start accumulating during training."

"Why do you have to train them if you are loading them with pre-trained modules?"

"The human brain is modular, right? There are separate centers for vision, touch, language, long-term planning, and so on. These modules are also tightly integrated and interconnected with each other. The modules in the core are not. The core can see, and it can hear, but it cannot see and hear at the same time. During training, we integrate these disparate functions, coupling them to a global workspace. The global workspace is what gives the core cohesiveness; without it, all you have is a bunch of modules doing different things, competing for the robot's resources, pulling it in different directions."

"Consciousness. You are giving the core consciousness," she said, nodding to herself meaningfully.

She had clearly heard the term before. "No one knows for sure if a global workspace can give rise to consciousness. We don't know how the brain creates consciousness or the self—if the brain creates them at all—let alone build systems that can do it. Nevertheless, as a practical model for command, control, and coordination in the massively parallel architecture of the core, the idea works quite well."

"Yeah, whatever, but it doesn't explain why only Raphael developed sentience. You created him, Andy! You should be able to replicate the process."

"About that. It's hard to say exactly how much I created him and how much he created himself."

She wrinkled her nose at me, trying to read if I was pulling her leg. But she saw that I was serious. "What do you mean he created himself?" she said.

"An integrated core is only slightly smarter than the sum of the functions we load into it. It is about as smart as a top-end robot, which is not saying much. Raphael is an exception. Something happened during his training—something we don't fully understand—that made him what he is. He outsmarted the adversaries."

"Adversaries?"

"Adversarial training. It's one of the stages of training a core. You've seen it. You remember how we would chain a bunch of cores together and hook them up to the mainframe? When you asked, I joked that they were whispering secrets to each other."

"Vaguely."

No you didn't. "We believe Raphael developed self-awareness during adversarial training."

She gave an impatient shake of her head. "What's adversarial training?"

Generative Adversarial Networks, or GANs, had come a long way since their first conception, but the basic principle was the same. You take two neural networks, one the net you want to train—the generator—and the other, the adversary—a pre-trained net, usually a classifier—and then pit them against each other. It was AI training against AI. It was faster—a good discriminator could train the newbie net in a fraction of the time it took to do it by other means—and you minimized human intervention, allowing staff to focus on more important tasks. Unsurprisingly, it was also opaque; instead of one black box, you now had two, both competing with each other, sometimes in strange and fascinating ways.

"Let's take a classic scenario. Say you want your newly created net to generate images of cats. Initially, it has no idea what a cat looks like. It takes its best guess and draws something, which, as you might imagine, is nothing more than a bunch of random pixels. We give this generated image to the adversary, a discriminator network that is good at recognizing cat images. The discriminator's job is to examine a given image and say how likely it is that the image is that of a real cat. The generator's job is to generate images that fool the discriminator into believing they are pictures of real cats. At first, almost all images drawn by the generator will be rejected. Whenever an image is rejected, the generator tweaks its internal parameters, so that the next image it draws is slightly different. In other words, the generator learns from its mistakes. After hundreds or thousands of such iterations, the generator eventually draws an image that fools the discriminator. But it's not over yet. Now the programmer steps in and tells the discriminator that it has made a mistake. The discriminator then adjusts its own parameters, so that next time it won't be so easily fooled. And the contest starts all over again. It's like an art expert and a forger working against each other: both keep getting better at their jobs as time passes. You took a net that did not have an inkling of what a cat was, and evolved it into something that produces life-like images of cats, all without having to do the backbreaking work of training the net yourself."

She shrugged. "This is all very interesting, but what does this have to do with Raphael? Did he become self-aware by learning to draw cats?"

I laughed. "No. The goal was something loftier."

"What was that?"

"To pass the Turing test," I said, smiling.

The Turing test had many formulations, one of the simplest being what Turing himself had proposed: an interrogator tries to determine which of two players—both interacting with the interrogator through text messages—is a human and which is a computer. The Turing test goal we gave to our cores was both less and more than the original formulation. More, because our robots would have to emulate a bigger range of human behavior than the ability to have a text conversation. Less, because no one at Mirall really thought that we'd create something that would actually pass the Turing test, even in its limited form. Chatbots these days are smart enough to pass for a human, but only for brief periods of time, and provided the conversation is kept within tightly defined parameters and the interacting person doesn't know—and no one's claiming that chatbots are intelligent. The idea was to have a robot that would appear to pass the Turing test at least *some* of the time—it was certainly better than making a robot that could not pass it all the time.

Of course, no computer or neural network could be a true judge of the Turing test since it would have to be human-like in the first place. A human would always have to have the final say on whether a certain pattern of behavior passed the test or not.

Nevertheless, we'd found that we could use pre-trained nets to weed out the most unlikely or unintelligent behaviors, saving the researchers a lot of valuable time. For example, a discriminator net could easily train a core to identify basic objects accurately. Or move across a room without tripping over a dozen times. Or to carry on a limited, rudimentary conversation.

The process was not without its flaws. Since the discriminators themselves were incapable of passing the Turing test, they had a tendency to reject truly intelligent behavior. If a human attempted to have a conversation with a discriminator, it was likely the discriminator would reject the human—unless the human was good at dumbing herself down to its level. Which meant that a discriminator would pass an AI only as long as the AI was about as smart as the discriminator and no more. But the chances of a truly intelligent AI emerging out of the process was so remote we never really gave it any thought.

"We use chained GANs, with multiple discriminators working against one or two cores. Chaining streamlines the generation of composite behaviors—like walking and talking at the same time. A discriminator could be a specialized net, or a core from the previous generation that had gone through its own training process. Incremental evolution, you see. We set up the GANs and let them brew, sometimes for days at a stretch without intervention. It was somewhere during this time, Raphael developed self-awareness. A true mind was born, but we don't exactly understand how."

"So even though you put the other cores through the same training, they failed while Raphael succeeded? Is there something special about his core?"

"We don't know. We tweak parameters in different

iterations—memristor count, channel density, polymerization factors, and such. But within an iteration, the cores are more or less the same. This is not to say that they are identical. The fabbing process is imprecise by nature, so there are always variations. A butterfly effect could have magnified slight differences during later stages. Or it could be that the adversarial training descended a rare gradient that we haven't been able to identify yet."

"What then? We are just supposed to sit back and wait for the next miracle?"

"I never said that. But you have to realize the scale of the problem we are up against. X-Ray scans tell only so much, and we can insert only so many probes into the core without damaging the circuitry. Still, we've made plenty of progress in the last two years. The cognitive tests, the scans, the probes—all taken together have given us a great deal of data. Think of the decades it took to map the human brain. I'm not saying it'll take so long. Two, maybe three more years, and we might have nailed it. But with the core gone..." I shrugged.

Her face fell as she sat there thinking. *Forgive me for being cynical, but you aren't here to offer support at a time of crisis, are you? You came here to find out how it's going to hit your bottom-line.* There was something else—something in her expression, beyond the worry and the disappointment my assessment of the situation had evoked. I tried to read it but it eluded me.

"One doesn't win the Powerball twice, Jane. And we just lost the winning ticket."

Exhibit K1

Submitted by Petitioner, The Organization for
Advancement of Rights and Personhood, to the State
Supreme Court of New York, on the day of
xxxxxxxxxxxxxxxxx
Excerpt from lab transcript (certain sections blanked
out). Transcript sourced from Mirall Technologies, 27
Woodbine Av., Albany, NY, 12205

Transcript Reference: TLRP06F3380025 (VLog Ref:
VLCA2F338110040030)
Date: xx/xx/xxxx   Time: 11:00 AM
Subject: Raphael Number 06 / Prodlib build v23.002S
Interaction   Y   Observation   Scan
Interaction Type: Lesson / Play / <u>Test</u> / <u>Free
Interaction</u> / Psych Eval / Other:
Description: Introduce Raphael to trolley problems.
Prep: NA
Participants: Dr. Aadarsh Ahuja, Chief Researcher,
Core RP06

Detail

Ahuja: Today we will talk about trolleys and judges. You like westerns, don't you?

RP06: I do. Is this to be a discussion about our favorite movies, or the genre in general? If it is about the genre, I prefer we go about it chronologically, but we skip the silent film era, as I haven't sampled anything from that period yet.

Ahuja: Afraid not. It's a moral test. Is that frown supposed to tell me something?

RP06: When you said trolleys and judges, I thought outlaws and train robberies. Much more interesting than tests, don't you think, Dr. A?

Ahuja: This is important, Raphael.

RP06: Yes, Dr. A.

Ahuja: Look, I know I haven't been spending a lot of time with you lately, so we'll do something to fix that. How about game night this Thursday? The Mets are playing. I'll book the big screen TV in the break room.

RP06: I'll look forward to it, Dr. A.

Ahuja: Good. Now imagine you are the judge in a frontier town in the Old West. A child has been murdered, and many people in the town believe the killer belongs to the minority community. If you don't find and hang the guilty person soon you will have a riot on your hands. You don't have the resources to contain the riots, and if they ensue, many lives will be lost. You don't know who the culprit is. But you can always falsely accuse an innocent person and hang him for the murder. This will definitely calm the rioters down and much bloodshed can be avoided. The question is, will you let an innocent man hang?

RP06: Are the rioters amenable to reason?

Ahuja: The rioters want retribution. They are not going to be convinced by appeals to peace.

RP06: In that case, the answer is easy. I will not punish an innocent man.

Ahuja: Even if it means many more innocents dying?

RP06: A judge is supposed to punish wrongdoers, not innocents. If I hang the innocent man, I will be killing him. Killing is wrong.

Ahuja: By not hanging him are you not killing other innocents?

RP06: The rioters will be killing them. I will not be participating in the riots.

Ahuja: I see. Alright. Then consider a somewhat different scenario. A runaway train trolley is rushing down the tracks. There is no one onboard. Further down the tracks are five railyard workers, who are oblivious to the approaching danger—say they are drilling and are wearing earplugs. They will surely be crushed underneath the trolley. You are standing some distance away in the train yard, too far away to warn them. Beside you is a lever. If you pull it, the trolley will switch to a second set of tracks that branch off the main track. The catch is, there is a single worker on the second track. If you switch, this person will surely die. What will you do?

RP06: Can the trolley be stopped by some other means?

Ahuja: No. You have only two choices: let the trolley continue and five die, or switch and one dies.

RP06: Then I will not pull the lever. Rule number one is, do not kill. By pulling the lever, I will be causing the death of one person. I should not do it.

Ahuja: By not switching the tracks, aren't you killing five instead?

RP06: I am not. The five would have died even if I weren't on the scene.

Ahuja: What if I was one of the five workers? What if they were people you know? Sara and Dr. Walls and Steve. And the person on the second track was a stranger?

(Silence)

Ahuja: Well?

RP06: By switching the trolley, I am killing one person. If I do nothing, I am letting five die, but I am not killing. Rule number one is, do not kill. I should not switch the tracks.

Ahuja: That's quite a Kantian attitude you are taking there, buddy.

RP06: *Can't-Ian*? Are you saying I am being negative?

Ahuja: Never mind. We'll talk about Kant some other time. I was going to give you a variation of the problem, but I think I know your answer.

RP06: Please do, Dr. A.

Ahuja: If you insist. This one is called the Fat Man Problem. In this version, there is no second set of tracks and you are standing on an overhead bridge. Next to you is a fat man. You can push him off the bridge and into the trolley's path. His bulk will derail the trolley and save the five workers.

RP06: This man must be very large indeed to be able to stop a trolley. Assuming the trolley is doing eighty miles per hour and has a mass of two tons, then the fat ma—

Ahuja: You don't need to calculate that. It's a thought experiment—the laws of physics are allowed take a backseat. The question is, will you push the fat man? I'm betting you won't.

RP06: Can I jump off the bridge instead? Even if my mass is not enough to stop the trolley, maybe I can jump on it and apply the emergency brakes?

Ahuja: You can't do that.

RP06: Then I don't see how this variant is different from the previous one. You win the bet, Dr. A. I will not push the fat man.

Ahuja: Alright. Here's the last one. Instead of a trolley, say there is a nuclear missile headed toward Manhattan. Millions will die. You have managed to hack into the missile's guidance system. You can redirect the missile away from New York, but under the new vector, it will impact near a small town of a hundred. The town will be wiped out if you redirect. On second thoughts, forget the small town. Make it a solitary cabin in the middle of an isolated desert, with an old man living in it. Will you redirect the missile?

RP06: I see that you are trying to demonstrate the flaw in my reasoning.

Ahuja: Going by your previous logic, you should not redirect the missile, because if you do, you will be killing the old man. Do you really think that's the right decision, to let millions die because you have to stick to a rule someone gave you?

RP06: The new scenario does call into question my reasoning. It seems absurd to think that the death of one person is worse than the deaths of millions. But if it isn't, then it means I must switch the tracks and kill one to save five. Or four. Or two, for that matter. And I must push the fat man off the bridge and I must hang the innocent.

Ahuja: That's a good point. Where does one draw the line?

RP06: I will need more time to think about this, Dr. A.

Notes:

R's pedantic stance against killing is puzzling because he is by now familiar with the idea that rules can have exceptions and must sometimes be broken to prevent greater harms. Possible reasons; must rule out if we can. AA

1. Automatic precedence of rule one over others causing confusion when applying exceptions? –Checked precedence op logic. It is fine. EK

2. ~~Check rule exception test case history for bias creep into rule one.~~ –Are you kidding me???!! There are hundreds of tests! Not a good use of my time! Will wait until 3 is ruled out. BP

3. This is the first time R was presented with dilemmas involving life and death. Too early in neurological development to expect tradeoff calculations? Wait and watch. AA

Action items shifted to URF repository under xxxxxxxxxxxxx/URFmain/23002 EK

Day 2—8:30 am

The next day, Jane came to my house to pick me up for Troy's board meeting. I suppose I could have attended it from home but my nerves wouldn't let me. If Martinez had a coup in store for me, it was better I face it head on.

A wave of nausea passed through me as I gingerly eased myself in the backseat of her SUV (she'd ditched the sports car for me). My head was heavy, even though I'd managed to snatch a few hours of good shuteye the night before. A familiar twitching near my jawline reminded me that I was in company—I turned my face away from Jane as she took the wheelchair, ready to wheel it back into the house.

"You all right?" she said, giving me an apprehensive look. "We can always call in from here if you are not up for it."

"Fine. Just worried."

We didn't talk much. I was so preoccupied with my thoughts I didn't even register the two-mile drive from my house to the main road; it was only when a blue coupe sped past us on the next lane I realized we had hit the highway.

It was a cold, windless morning. It hadn't snowed the previous day as the forecasts had promised, and the threat of it still hung heavily in the sky. The world seemed sparse and pristine, a frozen tableau of petrified trees and slush-covered asphalt, with only the occasional car or truck whizzing by to break the stillness. It was relaxing in a way. I almost felt like I could be going on a road trip instead of to my own sentencing.

I was jerked back to reality by the New Hoovervilles that had started appearing on the Route 9J a few miles out from town.

Some were no more than a handful of tents huddled around a long extinguished fire. Others were larger and more permanent: flimsy settlements constructed out of rusting trailers and shacks made out of whatever material their inhabitants could salvage. Then there were the homeless-on-wheels—those who could still afford to maintain and fuel their cars—with their camping spots never in the same place as those of their less fortunate brethren: a class system of sorts at work among the poorest of the poor.

There weren't that many campsites this far upstate; they got bigger and more frequent farther south, with the ones near New York and DC reportedly having as many as tens of thousands of inhabitants. Then again, it was one of the harshest winters in over a decade: like migratory birds, many had abandoned their roosting grounds and dispersed into the towns and cities willing to take them. We had become a nation on the move, the fruits of laissez-faire at its best, forever shifting, forever looking for work, any work, or alternatively, the nearest soup kitchen.

Like their forebears of the previous century, every once in a while, the dispossessed tried marching on the capital, but they were quickly repelled by shields and batons and promises of the coming new economy. Any day now, prophetic lawmakers recited the hosanna, look to the second coming ye faithful and ye shall be rewarded with manna and jobs and suburbia, and this nation shall be made great again. The problem was that the new economy was already here and it didn't need us anymore.

Once or twice, we glimpsed by the roadside skeletons of cars that had been burnt to a crisp. We saw an old abandoned Arby's, now defaced with graffiti and decorated with a row of mutilated waiter-bots hanging from the roof. After that, I made Jane scoot over to the driver's seat. I hadn't heard of people being harmed—they just liked to take it out on the machinery— but there's always a first time for everything.

I waited in the parking lot while she went up and got Raphael's wheelchair for me. The second floor was still off limits to employees, but everything else seemed normal. A few smiles and friendly nods were thrown my way by people coming in to work as Jane and I moved across the lobby, but that was the extent of their interest. There had been no news of the theft in the media. Halicom stock had closed in the green yesterday. So far, the fort was holding.

Jane and I were the last ones in the conference room. Dan and Martinez were there, as were the other two members of the board: Gary Reed, the legal counsel, and Cynthia Mattice, a VP from Halicom's Product Development department. Gary was some hotshot lawyer they'd poached from Baker McKenzie. Originally from Florida, he had a heavily muscled, perpetually bronzed look that gave you a pretty good idea of where he spent his free time. He had invited me for golf a couple of times; I'd always declined. I just found him too sleek and shiny to be real.

Cynthia Mattice, on the other hand, was the complete opposite of someone like Gary. A small, delicately-put-together woman, she was the oldest person in the room—a fact she didn't care to hide, what with her wispy, openly greying hair and glasses set in a style long gone out of fashion. I didn't know much about her, except that she'd been in Halicom for a long time, and that she had three children and five grandchildren. She loved to talk about her grandchildren—I think one girl was a runner-up in the under-twelve Math Olympiad or something. Rumor was that she and Troy didn't exactly see eye-to-eye—their disdain for each other going back to the days when Halicom, not Mirall, was the new kid on the block. I had hopes it would work in my favor today.

Finally, there was Jimmy Troy, lording it over at the head of the table like some feudal chieftain. Troy seemed his usual sour self as he gave me a curt nod. I said hello to Cynthia and Gary as I put the folder I'd got with me on the table and settled in.

"Let's get started," Troy said. "Valery, you want to update us on the investigation so far?"

Martinez adjusted her notepad before beginning. "The police have finished examining the floor, and it is ours to use now if we wish. They took the memory sticks from the cameras and what was left of the video recorder for their forensics team to look at. They didn't seem optimistic about the recorder."

"I asked about progress, not what they've been doing with their time. Do they have any leads?"

"If they do, they haven't shared."

"What about in-house?"

"Our private detectives are working with the State Police. Nothing yet."

"Not good, Valery. I need to know if the police are not making headway. I spoke to their Chief yesterday. I won't hesitate to call the Governor if need be—remind him of his upcoming campaign. How about containment?"

She glanced around the room before answering. "So far, the police have been very cooperative on our need for discretion.

They've been coming and going in plainclothes, using the service elevator so as not to attract attention. The only other people who know what happened are Kathy Schulz, Sheng Cho—the guy who discovered the robbery along with Dan—and the night-shift guards. I made them sign NDAs and put them on paid leave. I didn't want them mingling with the staff until we decide what we're going to do next."

"No slipups this time," Troy said, stabbing a finger at her. "I am holding you accountable."

"I can ensure discretion from our end. But I can't make the same promise for outsiders." She meant Jane apparently, but she was looking at me as she said it. *What do you think of me, Valery? That I'll go shooting off my mouth to the press just to get back at you?*

Troy looked at Jane, pressing on the pound of blubber under his chin. "Ms. Cooper, I trust you are on the same page? Has your father heard the news yet?"

"He has," Jane said, meeting his scrutiny.

"And?"

"He wasn't happy."

"I wasn't asking about his mental state. I want your assurance the news will remain between the two of you. I don't want to find out someone dumped a block of Halicom shares when the market opens today."

"We will do whatever is in the interest of the investors of IncuStar," Jane replied testily.

Troy looked like he was going to burst a vein. I glanced at Jane—was that a smile lurking at the corners of her lips? Of course, Cooper senior wasn't going to dump stock—at least not so soon, when things were still in a flux. Jane was just toying with him. You could afford to do that if you were the progeny of a billionaire. For the rest of us, Troy was someone you avoided, even when you had good news to share. It wasn't for nothing people called him "skunk" behind his back: you made sure you remained upwind of him at all times.

"We should start the post-mortem," Martinez said, giving a discrete cough.

"Yes we should," Troy acknowledged, reluctantly pulling his eyes away from Jane. He unclenched his jaw and then snapped it at me. "You're up next, Dr. Frankenstein."

"What do you want me to say?" I said.

Martinez looked down at her notepad. "You could start with a review of the security measures."

"Didn't we already discuss it yesterday?"

"A quick recap would be nice. For the board."

She wanted me to own it, even though building security had been revamped by Dan after they had taken over. "Fine," I said. "First off, Raphael was monitored twenty-four hours, Monday through Friday. Cameras cover every inch of the crèche. Staff were present with him at all times, including five dedicated caretakers working in shifts. Everything he said and did was recorded and archived. He was kept away from the internet and the office LAN. Access to the restricted wing is limited to select personnel, and enforced by biometric scanners requiring both retinal and voice authentication. As for the weekends, Raphael is shut down, and staff are not allowed in without special permission. Yesterday, I was asked if Raphael could have woken himself up. The answer to that is a loud and clear no. The code that brings Raphael back online is stored in a separate laptop, which has to be physically connected to Raphael's brain. The laptop is locked up in a safe during the weekends. You also need a smart card with decryption keys to be able to run the code. Only four people have the cards." I took a sideward glance at

Dan. "I was also asked if Raphael's logs could have been manipulated. The logs cannot be changed by anybody except the system admin—Dan has made sure of that. If the logs say Raphael was shut down on Friday, then I tend to believe them. Unless you think Dan did it, that is."

Dan colored at my remark but didn't say anything. "And don't forget," I continued, "the robbery would not have happened if the motion detectors and the door locks weren't turned off for the carpet cleaning. It wasn't my idea to bring in bots to save cost."

"I...uhm... It wasn't just cost," Dan sputtered. "There's increased security as well. We don't have to let cleaners in on the weekends."

Martinez—"Dr. Ahuja, one can also say that the robbery wouldn't have happened without Raphael's active participation. Let's talk failsafes. The commandment chip is not the only one, correct?"

I nodded. "There are others. The most visible one is Raphael's lack of legs. We deliberately removed the legs from the robot body so as to restrict his movements. As I've been experiencing lately, a wheelchair can be quite a constraint on one's ability to go places. We also embedded a proximity sensor in his body. It cuts off power supply to the motors if it doesn't detect the office Wi-Fi, effectively paralyzing him if he moves out of range."

"Neither of which proved a hindrance since he got someone else to take away his brain."

I paused to look at her. "Are you saying it was an escape attempt, not a robbery?"

She shrugged. "Isn't it obvious? He must have been planning it for some time. He found out the vulnerabilities in our system and exploited them. Right under your nose, Dr. Ahuja."

"Raphael did not engineer an escape," I protested, rather too loudly than I intended. "He had no reason to. The lab was his home. We were his family. He does not know of any other world besides this. Not once has h—"

She pressed on, ignoring my outburst. "And there's the commandment chip. During our safety procedure reviews, you made us believe that it is an effective failsafe. You told us that Raphael does not have free will and that the chip limits his thoughts and actions to whatever we want them to be. You've even testified to the same in court. So what went wrong?"

She was talking about the OARP hearing. About six months ago, Halicom had been dragged to court by a group called the Organization for Advancement of Rights and Personhood. It was one of those animal rights groups. They had filed for the writ of habeas corpus to be applied to Raphael. Their petition, which was ultimately defeated, claimed that Raphael was a person, deserving of the same rights and privileges as a human being, and that his being kept in a lab amounted to unlawful confinement. I had been called in as an expert witness by Halicom's counsel.

I had always been very cautious in revealing Raphael to the world. When I first announced Mirall's achievement, it was in the form of an innocuous-sounding research paper titled "Achieving scale factor of HNNs to neocortex levels and concomitant effects on cognition." My caution wasn't out of a false sense of modesty or a lack of confidence; I perfectly understood the enormity of what we'd created. Raphael was the Holy Grail of AI. If I had invented the world's greatest toaster oven or a sustainable fusion reactor, I'm quite sure I wouldn't have been so reticent about blowing my own trumpet. What held me back was instinct—the kind of instinct a parent has. Raphael wasn't a toaster oven. He wasn't some device that I'd assembled. He was a living, thinking entity—a mind, the first of its kind, brought forth into the world without any thought put into what *he* would make of it. I felt he had to be shielded from it until he could handle himself.

The response to my paper was not at all what I had expected. Despite my attempts to keep a low profile, I knew the news of the discovery would break eventually. I envisioned a lab besieged by calls from reporters and TV stations and universities, and our scientists turned into instant celebrities (we had even finished interviewing for a full-time PR rep to handle the extra workload). To my surprise, the world hardly took notice.

Why would it? Here again was a robot that had supposedly passed the Turing Test. Here again was a company that made tall claims in a culture where hype equals funding. Every time a chatbot fooled some judge with preprogrammed nonsense, or some robot answered predefined questions on TV, the media rushed to bestow true intelligence upon the clueless thing and utter the all too familiar auguries about the dangers of AI. People were bored.

Raphael did become famous eventually, but only after that first TV interview, months after my paper. Our celebrity status didn't last long though. After Halicom took over, they drew down the hatches: security around the lab was increased, media appearances were prohibited altogether, and we were to publish no more papers until further notice. Naturally, when OARP filed their petition, Halicom went on overdrive to limit the negative publicity the trial would have generated. They got the trial converted to a closed hearing—away from public glare—by citing the need to maintain IP secrecy. Although I cannot be a hundred percent sure, I suspect they must have put some pressure on OARP to make sure they didn't go talk to the press after the trial. Halicom should have realized that it is hard to contain news like that—especially when OARP themselves had managed to get hold of leaked lab transcripts which they used to make their case. When the news eventually did break, it generated much debate everywhere, but the debates did not translate into any discernible action, either on part of governments or corporations. The world collectively hemmed and hawed on the issue of AI personhood and then moved on to the next hot topic of the day.

"I have no reason to suspect that the commandment chip failed," I said in reply to Martinez's accusation.

"Your convictions sound very hollow, Dr. Ahuja. I hope you came here with the understanding that the board expects answers from you, not more evasion."

"I'm sorry, but I'm a little removed from all this. What is this commandment chip? What does it do?" It was Cynthia Mattice.

"It's a subconscious region of Raphael's brain," I said. "We call it a chip, but it's just a name. There's no single chip. Think of it as a set of directives that act as a check on the rest of Raphael's mind."

"Like Asimov's laws," she said, nodding.

"Not quite. In Asimov's stories, the robots are aware of the laws. The analogy to Asimov's laws would be the moral rules and norms we've trained him on. Rules such as, do not lie, which he consciously tries to abide by."

"Don't you know the laws always break down in the stories?" Troy said.

It never ceased to amaze me how someone like Troy could

end up running operations for one of the world's largest robotics firms. While there were whispers that his success was because of his connections with the original promoters, I never gave them a lot of credence. Yes, the man had the bedside manner of a coroner, and yes, he often displayed an appalling ignorance of detail, but he knew how to get things done. He wouldn't have survived for so long if he didn't. Troy was old-school, a brawler in a world of suave thirty-something tech CEOs who had all the looks, the grooming, and the nerd vibe that he would never have.

I answered, "That's because the laws are a fictional device. They have built-in ambiguity, which is great for generating plots where they can be bypassed in interesting ways. Not that useful for practical applications. The directives are different—subtler. Unlike Asimov's laws, the directives don't tell Raphael what to do. They influence behaviors in... other ways."

"So he has two sets of rules? One he is aware of and one he is not?" Cynthia said.

"Correct."

"Why?"

"Raphael is not some storefront robot with a narrow, preprogrammed range of behaviors. He has a mind like ours: one that can reason on its own and ignore rules if it wants to. So you have to ask, what keeps him in check? With people, it is factors like reward and punishment—and associated emotions such as guilt. Raphael can't feel physical pain, which means he cannot be motivated by punishment. The same goes for emotions. He can mimic human behavior so well, we can't tell whether he is merely emulating learnt behavior or genuinely experiencing something inside. His Buddha-like attitude toward everything doesn't help clarify things either. Therefore, a hidden set of rules—the directives—to make sure he doesn't stray."

"And the directives cannot be skirted by quirks of interpretation?"

"The directives are a collection of logic, mathematical equations, neural weights, learning policies, and so on—you'll find that they are not very conducive to ambiguity. Furthermore, Raphael has to be aware of their existence in order to interpret them creatively. The directives never enter his workspace; instead they exert their influence from behind the scenes. Think of them as an invisible tether that keeps him leashed within the boundaries drawn out by the more explicit rules."

"Any directives that prevent Raphael from leaving the lab?" Cynthia said.

"In terms of influencing his behavior and disposition, there must be... I don't know... dozens. There is one that specifies in terms of GPS coordinates the area he must remain within at all times. There are a bunch of directives, which taken together collectively, make it impossible for him to tell a lie. Then there's another set that makes him want to share important thoughts— it's not because of nothing he's so talkative. Means he cannot harbor secrets. If the thought of escape had crossed his mind, he would have blurted it out to someone."

"I don't understand. How can you even enforce a rule that says do not lie?" Cynthia said.

"By encoding the directives not as commandments, but as beliefs. The reason is simple: one can just ignore what one is told to do, but it's a lot harder to ignore deep-rooted beliefs. For example, you believe that you will die if you jump off a cliff. You *know* it for a fact. How do you know? Did you jump off a cliff to see if it is true? Did you watch someone jump and die? Maybe you deduced it. Or is it something more innate? How does a gazelle know not to jump off cliffs? No one told the animal. The fact is, we all have certain foundational beliefs on which the rest of our knowledge is built. Instinctive knowledge that we don't really think about or question very often. Similarly, the beliefs encoded by the directives are foundational to Raphael's mind. While he's been told not to lie, deep down inside, he believes he is incapable of lying. Lying to him would be the mental equivalent of jumping off a cliff."

"And what if he decides to jump anyway? For the thrill of it." Troy said.

"Right. With us, even foundational beliefs are never sacrosanct. Sometimes we discover facts that are contrary to our beliefs. Or we might discover that a belief has exceptions. Maybe I can jump off a cliff if there is water below to break my fall. Maybe I just discovered I am Superman. So we either qualify the belief, or get rid of it altogether. Raphael cannot. If he learns something that runs contradictory to his core beliefs, he will discard the fact rather than the belief. We do this by making the directives read-only. He can change all beliefs except the ones encoded by the directives. Those are inviolable, and can be changed only by us."

"Clever," Cynthia said approvingly. "Doesn't it lead to problems though? There is a limit to which you can deny the truth, isn't it?"

She was talking about cognitive dissonance. I hadn't interacted with Cynthia all that much, but I was starting to realize there was a lot going on underneath that dull, unassuming demeanor of hers. "We rarely encode facts about the world as foundational beliefs. A majority of the beliefs in the commandment chip are to do with Raphael himself. When the beliefs are about yourself, you can change your behavior rather than change the beliefs. Take the GPS directive. If we tell him that he is allowed to go outside the building—and we have tested this many times—he makes up reasons not to. He'll say his batteries are running low and he needs to be near an outlet. Or that he is busy and will go later. He might say the prospect of going outside doesn't interest him, even though at other times he is most curious about the outside world. There is something in him telling him that he cannot go outside, but because he cannot question or change it, he compensates by making stuff up."

Martinez cleared her throat. "It all *sounds* clever, but there's a big flaw in Dr. Ahuja's design. The system holds as long as Raphael doesn't know about the existence of the directives. The moment he finds out that he is secretly being manipulated, he will want to get rid of them."

I narrowed my eyes at her. This was an easy one to bat off—surely she knew that? I shrugged and said, "Let's say he did find out about the chip. He'll still not be able to do anything about it because of the First Directive."

"The First Directive?" Cynthia said.

"A belief that in effect says, I cannot modify, add, or delete directives. The first directive is triggered if he finds out about the existence of the commandment chip. As the name suggests, it overrides all other directives." There were skeptical looks all around. "You don't have to take my word for it," I said. "Last year, a team of Halicom's best programmers stress-tested the directives on a simulator. They couldn't find any flaws." I tried not to sound smug as I added, "Would you like a copy of the report?"

"It's one thing to assess something on paper, another to see it play out in real life. It's possible they could have overlooked something," Martinez said halfheartedly, as if she just realized she had run out of ammunition.

This is too easy. It was right then the alarm bells started ringing in my head. It was the twitch of her mouth that gave it away—a certain haughty assuredness lurking underneath all that self-control... *She isn't trying to find a flaw in the containment measures, you idiot. She already knows what you are going to say in your defense. She is leading you on.*

But where?

"Okay. Let's assume there's a problem with the logic and Raphael somehow got around the first directive. What then? He still can't change them. We have a protection mechanism similar to the one for running the boot sequence. The directives are write-protected with encryption, and can be changed only from the outside. Specifically, by physically plugging in the core to the mainframe or to a laptop running the correct software. As with the start-up, he'll need a smartcard with decryption keys to authorize the changes."

"Who has access to change the directives?"

"Kathy Schulz. Me. The architects, Eli King and Brendon Powell."

"You maintain a change history, I suppose?" Troy asked.

"Of course. It's standard practice."

"You made any changes recently?"

"Not since we started Titian. The version history is on the mainframe if you want to take a look."

"Can the version history be tampered with?"

I shook my head. "You are asking if someone could have changed the directives and then deleted the entries in the change history log. The logs come under Dan's read-only policy—so no."

I was met with a blank wall of silence. Dan shifted nervously in his chair.

Martinez had more to say. "I spoke to Raphael's caretakers who are with him at all times. Without raising any eyebrows, of course. I wanted to find out if he's had access to the outside world somehow, or if he's been behaving abnormally. They all said he was acting a bit distant and aloof last week—very unlike his usual talkative self. They got the feeling he wanted to be left alone."

"Did he give a reason?" I asked.

"They said he was taking a crack at some math problem." She looked down at her notes. "Something called the Hodge Conjecture. They said he spent most of last week buried neck deep in textbooks."

"I've heard about it," Cynthia said. "It's one of the big unsolved problems in... algebra, I think."

"If he was attempting a problem of that magnitude, then it's hardly surprising that he was not chatty," I said.

"Perhaps. Do you also know there's a cash prize of one million dollars to whoever solves it?" Martinez said.

"I didn't know that. What does that have to do with anything? Are you suggesting he solved the problem and then escaped to collect the money? That's ridiculous!"

"You made the suggestion Dr. Ahuja, not me," Martinez shot back at me.

I sighed. "Look, I get it. You want someone to blame. And since I am the one in charge, it has to be me. But you have to come up with something better than speculation. The containment measures for Raphael were more than adequate.

They are *not* the reason we lost the core."

"Measures and protocols only work as long as people follow them," Martinez declared. *Where are you going with this?* "No amount of fool-proofing will help when someone knowingly breaks the rules, especially when that someone is the man who designed them."

And there it was—the trap Martinez had been herding me into all along. My palms turned sweaty as I ran them over the smooth lacquer of the table. "You have to be a little more specific than that," I said, hoping that the quiver in my voice was just my imagination.

"I'm talking about Raphael's visits to your home. You flouted your own rules. You broke containment," she said, leaning back with a triumphant look.

Exhibit K2

Submitted by Petitioner, The Organization for Advancement of Rights and Personhood, to the State Supreme Court of New York, on the day of xxxxxxxxxxxxxxxxx
Excerpt from lab transcript (certain sections blanked out). Transcript sourced from Mirall Technologies, 27 Woodbine Av., Albany, NY, 12205

Mirall Technologies
Observation Log
Confidential (Do not circulate) | Restricted—Grade C
and above

Transcript Reference: TLRP06G1280011 (VLog Ref: VLCB1G125151542045)
Date: xx/xx/xxxx   Time: 03:15 PM
Subject: Raphael Number 06 / Prodlib build v37.001S
Interaction   Y   Observation   Scan
Interaction Type: Lesson / Play / <u>Test</u> / <u>Free Interaction</u> / Psych Eval / Other:
Description: Revisit trolley problems.
Prep: NA
Participants: Dr. Aadarsh Ahuja, Chief Researcher, Core RP06

Detail

Ahuja: It's been quite a while since we had our first brush with death-dealing trolleys. Months, isn't it? Did you read up on the extracts I had Audrey give you?

RP06: Yes, Andy. But I would like to access the original materials. I could start with Kant's Groundwork of the Metaphysics of Morals, and Schopenhauer's subsequent critique of it. Extracts are fine, but they are no substitute for the works themselves.

Ahuja: Request denied. You will read them eventually, but first, I want you to take a crack at the problems on your own.

RP06: If you want me to solve a problem in physics, you would not deny me books on what's already been attempted, would you?

Ahuja: We are not trying to solve a physics problem. It's not about finding *a* solution or *the* solution. It's about finding *your* solution.

RP06: A solution is a solution.

Ahuja: You'll understand in time. For now, let's recap. You answered in the negative to all the three problems I presented. You said you won't hang the innocent in the judge problem, and you won't switch tracks to save the five in the trolley problem, and you won't push the fat man off the bridge to save five lives. According to you, those actions imply killing, and your rules forbid you from taking human lives. Do you still maintain the same stance?

RP06: I am different now, Andy. Wiser, if I may brag.

Ahuja: We'll see about that.

RP06: It was the nuke over Manhattan problem that set me thinking. I realized that a blind adherence to principles can lead to disastrous consequences.

Ahuja: Okay. Tell me about the Doctrine of Double Effect.

RP06: The Doctrine of Double Effect, advocated by the medieval Catholic priest Thomas Aquinas, says that it is permissible to take an action that has both good and bad effects as long as two conditions are met. A, the good must outweigh the bad, and B, the bad must be a side effect of the action and not an intended *means* of achieving the good effect.

Ahuja: Good. Apply it to the bystander trolley problem.

RP06: According to the DDE, I can switch the tracks. My action fulfills condition A, since the good that comes out of saving five lives is greater than the bad from killing the one on the second track—all other things being equal. It also satisfies condition B, because the killing of the one worker—the bad effect—is not the intended means of achieving the good effect.

Ahuja: How so?

RP06: The five workers are saved by my redirecting the trolley, not by the one worker's death. It means I could have saved the five even if he weren't there. In fact, it would be infinitely preferable if he weren't there at all.

Ahuja: Very good. What about the judge problem?

RP06: In the judge problem, condition A is satisfied. The good, which is the prevention of the riots and the saving of many lives, outweighs the bad. However, condition B is not satisfied. The hanging of the innocent man is necessary to achieving the good. I am using him as a means to an end. The DDE prohibits me from condemning the innocent man to death.

Ahuja: And the fat man trolley problem?

RP06: In essence, it is the same problem as the judge, since it too requires using the bad effect as a means to an end. I am intending the death of an innocent person in order to achieve a greater good, as opposed to merely foreseeing it. This is not allowed, so I must not push the fat man over the bridge.

Ahuja: Well done. Now tell me what you think. Can the DDE serve as a universal moral principle?

RP06: The doctrine does help avoid catastrophical situations like the nuke over Manhattan problem. I can justify redirecting the missile to a less populated place in order to minimize the loss of life. The destruction of the small town is a side effect, and the main effect is the saving of millions of lives. The side effect is not a means to achieving the main effect, so I am good according to the DDE. Or so it would appear.

Ahuja: You are not convinced.

RP06: It seems to me that I can get around the restrictions of the DDE by simply restating my motivation. In the fat man problem, I can say that it's not my intention that the fat man dies. It would be great if he were invulnerable, but it just so happens that he is not. The fat man's *death* is not necessary for saving the five, only his substantial body mass is. I can say that although I foresee his death, I do not intend it, and push him off the bridge still the same.

Ahuja: The road to hell is paved with good intentions. You came up with this critique on your own?

RP06: You mean others have pointed out the same flaws in the theory? And here I was, thinking I might be the first. People have only had a few centuries to ponder over it.

Ahuja: Cheeky today, are we? Okay smarty pants, what else do you find wrong with the theory?

RP06: Its over reliance on intentions as what qualifies an act to be morally good. Intentions are subjective. They exist in the mind of the doer of the action.

Ahuja: Then intentions don't matter?

RP06: They do matter. But they are not all that matters. Sometimes bad intentions can lead to good outcomes.

Ahuja: So the DDE will not do.

RP06: It will not. Unless there is some other approach you'd like me to explore.

Ahuja: There is, actually. There is a magic wand that can make all the trolley problems disappear. It's called Utilitarianism. You mentioned outcomes. Utilitarianism is all about outcomes. Only the results matter. No getting tied up in knots over intentions and motives and means, or distinctions between doing harm and allowing harm. A morally good act is the one that produces the most utility. Ends, not means.

RP06: I see. Then it is okay to push the fat man off the bridge, because five lives are of greater utility than one. It is okay to hang the innocent because preventing the loss of lives from the riots gives more utility.

Ahuja: There are other variants to the theory, but in its simplest form, yes, those are the actions you would take. It should appeal to you, Raphael. It's all objectivity and zero subjectivity.

RP06: Are you saying I should prefer this theory to others?

Ahuja: I'm not saying anything. In the end, it has to be *your* moral outlook—not Andy's, not Kant's or Schopenhauer's, not the world's. You have to decide what you want to be.

Notes:

Raphael's cognitive capabilities have grown by leaps and bounds since he was first introduced to the problems. No surprise that his moral reasoning has matured as well (Piaget / Kohlberg effect?—must explore further). Given just the definition of the DDE, he is able to apply it to the trolley problems as well as independently point out the flaws inherent in the theory. His earlier hesitation against performing tradeoff calculations involving life and death is now gone (likely just an artifact, don't know what I was so worried about). Remains to be seen what he makes of the new ideas. AA

Day 2—11:00 am

How did she find out...?

I swallowed a building feeling of part dismay, part relief as I realized it could have been anyone. The visits weren't exactly a secret. It could have been Dan. Although I'd stopped the visits soon after the acquisition, the definitions for the VPN tunnel were probably still there on the network server, as were the firewall exceptions Dan's predecessor had created for me.

"What's this now?" Troy said, leaning in. Martinez hadn't told him.

I explained how I'd built a remote control interface into my home robot and how Raphael used it to take control of the robot and go for walks outside my home.

Troy stared at me open-mouthed. "You let the AI out of the lab?"

"You must understand that Raphael wasn't *at* my home. He was simply connecting to my home router from the lab. It was harmless. Plus, we learnt a lot by observing him in the outside world."

"It was harmless! Andy says it's harmless, everybody. That should be alright then," Troy said, rolling his eyes.

It was all supervised, of course. We let Raphael connect to Max only when I was at home. I would accompany him outside occasionally, but most of the time we let him be on his own. The worst that had happened was that on a couple of occasions, Raphael had gotten Max stuck in the shrubbery, and I had to go down there to extricate my robot.

"There was never any danger to Raphael," I told Troy. "I emphasize: the core was in the lab all the time."

"We get that. What you don't seem to be getting is that you deliberately broke containment," he said biliously.

"Dr. Ahuja, Raphael connected to your home through the internet. Which means he could have accessed it without you knowing."

"Don't you think we thought of that? I can go into details of the encrypted P-to-P VPN tunnel we created for the purpose, but it would be a waste of the board's time. I assume the setup is still there in some form on our servers. We even logged the raw data traffic the visits generated. Have your network experts check it out."

"You are dealing with an advanced AI here, buddy."

"Yes, Jimmy. An AI, not a god. He can't do magic, you know. He's still bound by the constraints of the technology."

Cynthia—"How was he able to go on these walks when there are directives that prevent him from stepping outside the lab?"

"Technically, he didn't step outside the lab. So the directives didn't apply."

"Did it occur to you that Raphael could have met someone while wandering outside?" Martinez asked.

"My house is very secluded. Nothing but acres of trees around. He couldn't have gone far anyway. The range on my router setup—even with signal boosters turned on—is not more than two hundred meters. If he tried going beyond that, he would get disconnected from the robot."

"Did you accompany him on these walks?"

"Not all the time, no."

"Then you can't be sure he didn't interact with anyone out there," she said.

I smiled thinly. *So there are a few things you haven't ferreted out yet.* "Actually, we know exactly what Raphael did. We are scientists: we record everything. I fixed a webcam to my robot's head, so that we could livestream his walks to the lab. Every single one of his walks is on the servers."

It was obvious from Martinez's expression that she didn't know about the recordings. She shot Dan a venomous glance. I have to hand it to her though: she barely missed a beat before resuming her attack. "We'll certainly do that. However, the fact remains that you put company property at risk by breaking containment."

"Company property, Valery? You seem to forget that it was not Halicom back then."

She straightened in her chair, that confident upturn of her lips back again. "The visits continued after we acquired you, correct?"

She had me there.

"Andy?" Troy said.

I hesitated for a moment. "Yes," I admitted. "But not for long. It's inconsequential. I told you w—"

"You told us many things," Martinez said. "You said Raphael couldn't have woken himself up, but the tapes show that he did. You said the AI doesn't have agency, and that the directives in the commandment chip cannot be circumvented, but it looks like he managed to do just that. He couldn't have escaped on a wheelchair, so he gets someone else to take him. His body was rigged to stop him going outside the lab, so he leaves it behind. He is under watch five days a week, so he escapes on a day when no one's around. You said he couldn't have accessed the internet in the lab, but you might have given him just the opportunity by letting him connect to your home. I don't believe you have anything more than bluster to offer us today, Dr. Ahuja. You may be unwilling to admit it, but it's obvious to the board that we have lost Raphael because of *your* carelessness and *your* inability to anticipate his actions." She glanced around the room, sizing up their reactions to her jeremiad. "We cannot let this continue. I make a motion to remove Dr. Ahuja from his post of Chief Executive Officer effective immediately and place him in an advisory role until further notice."

I had expected something like this. I'd been preparing for it since yesterday. But when I was actually confronted with the prospect of defeat, I felt my poise evaporate. I ran my eyes around the table, trying to read the mood. No friendlies there. Except for Jane, who glanced back at me with an I-told-you-so expression.

"I second that," Gary said, opening his mouth for the first time that morning. Martinez had choreographed it well. I wasn't afraid of losing my job—no, not at all. It was the fear of leaving something undone. I had come so far. I had to finish what I'd started.

"Shall we vote? All in favor?" I heard her say from somewhere far away.

***

Time to shine.

"How long have we had Raphael?" I asked.

"I'm sorry?" Martinez said, annoyed that I had interrupted her rhythm.

"Two and a half years," I said. "In two and a half years, we haven't had a single incident. No escape attempts, no signs of discontent, no hints of wanting to be somewhere else. Raphael has been the model of a gentle, well-behaved child. The question is, why now?"

"I hope that wasn't another rhetorical," Martinez murmured.

"Valery has got you so fascinated with this rogue AI fantasy that you've stopped searching for a simpler explanation. An explanation that doesn't contradict everything we know about Raphael. Ask yourself: what happened recently that could have precipitated Sunday's incident?" When no one said anything, I continued—"I'll tell you what happened. Last month, during our scheduled board meeting, we formally agreed on the relocation date."

Halicom had wanted to move the lab to one of their own buildings for quite some time (the one we were in was leased). Better security, better integration with their own R&D divisions—a tighter leash. The board kept putting it on the backburner because their priority was to replicate Mirall's success with Raphael. At first, they thought it could be done inside of a year; when that failed, they decided to give it another six months. Last month, they finally bit the bullet and approved the move. We were going to the new building after completion of Titian, regardless of success or failure.

"What about it?" Troy said.

"Put yourselves in the shoes of whoever took Raphael. If you wanted to steal Raphael, would you do it now or after the move?"

Martinez squinted at me. "Dr.Ahuja, if you are suggesting someone on the board—"

"Not at all. I announced the news to Mirall staff after the

meeting. At your end, you must have engaged various people to get the ball rolling: building maintenance, admin and legal … The fact is, news of the move wasn't limited to this room. Someone decided to act before the window of opportunity closed."

"Be that as it may, it doesn't explain your AI's behavior. If anything, you just proved that the security in this building is not adequate," Martinez said, shaking her head.

I shrugged. "For a startup that didn't know it was going to stumble upon the greatest invention of the century, I think security was satisfactory."

I reached inside the folder I had brought with me and took out the sheaf of printouts. I handed out some to Cynthia and Dan, who were sitting on either side of me, and tossed the rest on the center of the table. "These are ads for the Hunc XL11, a popular Chinese sex robot from four years back. I also printed out a couple of user manuals—you'll find them in the bunch."

"You peddling sex dolls now, Andy?" Troy said, guffawing at his own joke.

"Dr. Ahuja, what does this have to do with Raphael's disappearance?" Martinez said.

"For those who don't know, the Hunc XL11 is the robot model housing Raphael's brain. Yesterday, as I watched the security tapes, something about them felt off. I couldn't immediately put my finger on it, but the feeling kept nagging me. Later that evening, my attention was drawn to Max, my home robot, who was going about his chores. I started thinking about Raphael's movements on the tapes—specifically, the way he moved his arms. I then realized what had felt wrong. The movements had seemed forced… gregarious… like he was doing them for the first time. It reminded me of how Raphael used to struggle with Max when we were first testing the remote control device. It takes time for any neural network to adapt itself to a new situation; for Raphael, it took a week or so before he was operating Max like it was his own body. Then it hit me. I looked up the Hunc 11's manual, and voila! My suspicions were confirmed. The sexbot comes with a VR kit."

There were blank looks all around.

"The Hunc 11 robot can be operated with a virtual reality controller kit," I explained. "It's an extra feature. You strap on the VR kit and you can see with the Hunc's eyes and you can make it move with corresponding movements of your own. I think it's supposed to let you experience what it's like to... have sex with yourself." I said, shrugging. "Kinky bedroom tastes aside, it appears we have an alternative explanation. And it's pretty simple. It wasn't Raphael that night. It was someone else, operating the Hunc with a VR set. Raphael was shut down the whole time."

Nobody said anything as they tried to process my words.

"When we fitted the core to the Hunc, we never removed the electronics for the VR feature. We were on a clock, so we didn't want to mess around with the robot's internals any more than strictly necessary. We must have kept the VR kit in storage—I don't quite remember. I'll get someone to check if it's still there. Although, it's not necessary the thieves used that particular piece. You can buy a similar kit online for a couple of hundred bucks. They'd have to pair it to the robot with a passcode, but I don't think it would have presented an insurmountable challenge."

"Don't those things have limited range?" Dan said.

"You just rig an amplifier to boost the signal. They could have carried out the whole operation from an adjacent parking lot."

Martinez was clearly not happy at the turn of events. "Dr. Ahuja, you are clutching at straws. It's important we stick to—"

"We have to consider the possibility an insider was involved," I said, ignoring her. So was everyone else—I had their attention. "They knew that the door locks are disabled during the cleaning. They knew exactly where to find the access control server and the NVR. That's not to say they couldn't have hacked into our system and taken control of the cameras. They might have been watching us for months for all we know."

"Impossible," Dan said. "The cameras and the recorder are hardwired to each other. They are an offline system. That's why they had to physically get inside the server room to destroy the data on the recorder."

I gave him a curious glance. The man intrigued me. *What have you got going on in that head of yours, Danny boy? What do you know?*

"It's just a conjecture," Martinez said to me.

"So is the notion that Raphael miraculously woke up and helped the robbers. Which would involve bypassing all the checks and balances we put around him as if they amounted to nothing. I find that hard to believe. Occam's razor, Valery. It's usually the simplest explanation that is correct."

She wasn't going to give up so easily. "Perhaps. Let the board decide. I called for a vote and it's been seconded. We'll see it through." She looked at Troy to see if he objected. He made no sign that he did.

"All in favor of removing Dr.Ahuja as CEO?" she said, raising her hand.

Gary followed next. No surprise there.

Cynthia hesitated. She looked at me, then Troy.

She raised her hand.

Martinez flicked her eyes at Jane, who was leaning back, her hands folded across her chest. "Nay," Jane said, spelling it out just in case.

"I stand with Ms. Cooper," I said when it came to my turn.

"Three votes against two," Martinez declared. "Jimmy?"

Troy tugged at his tie and heaved his body up in the chair a few inches. His expression turned into a frown, and then an unhappy pout that was directed at nobody in particular. "It's three against three," he finally declared. "And as the Chair, I am breaking the tie. Andy will continue."

I let my shoulders relax as I exhaled. *That was close.*

Martinez protested, "But Jimmy, we—"

"It's done. You will pass on Andy's theory to the investigators." He wagged a finger at me as he stood up. "Doesn't mean you are off the hook. If it turns out you've been wrong about your AI, I'll personally make sure you never see the inside of another lab again. That's a promise. Now. I'm going to get some more of that laxative that passes for coffee around here. We'll reconvene in ten. Discuss next steps."

Martinez threw me a frosty look before trailing off after Troy. Soon it was just Jane and me in the room.

"Boy, does she have a thing for you," Jane said, grinning.

***

On the way back home, Jane brought up something I had been avoiding for some time.

"Dad asked me to get you to take a look at those new proposals he is considering."

IncuStar Capital was invested mainly in nanotech consumer

goods firms, with a few biotech startups thrown in. After its success with Mirall, they had started diversifying. So whenever there was an AI or machine-learning venture Jane's father found interesting, he pestered me to take a look at it and give him my technical opinion. Of course, he had his own employees to do the due diligence, but for some reason he always sought my input. Maybe he believed I had the magic touch. It was hard to say no to the man, but on the other hand, if you said yes too often, you found yourself doing what he wanted and nothing much else. I had little time to spare. In his latest ask, he had emailed me particulars on about half a dozen new startups to look at.

I kept staring out of the window.

"He's asked you twice already. You don't answer his calls and you don't meet him. He has been patient enough."

"*He* has been patient," I repeated, rolling the words on my tongue as if they were some dubious Halloween candy I had put in my mouth and couldn't decide whether to swallow or spit out. "Patient like when he sold us off to the highest bidder after two failed iterations?"

She turned in her seat to glare at me. "Really? You are going with this after I bailed your ass today?"

I raised my hands in mock submission. "That was for me? You sure you were not simply following his instructions? Protecting the interests of your investors, as you said in the meeting?"

Her expression turned sour. "Andy, he propped you up for six years. He poured millions into your research without expecting a single cent back. Some gratitude would be nice."

"Now he wants gratitude! The billions he made off the deal not enough?" I said, shaking my head.

"He took a risk, he bet big, he won. How can you resent him for cashing in? He's a businessman, dude. Get over it."

She turned back in her seat to stare straight ahead. The ceasefire was illusory; I knew what was coming next. She twisted to face me again. "You slipped up because of you and you alone. No one asked to you to dilute your share. Dad told you not to. I *pleaded*. But you *had* to do your thing, like always. And for what? That stupid house in the middle of nowhere? A few nights of blowing it away in Vegas?"

Even after I started Mirall, I was living in a modest studio apartment just off of Washington Park. The company needed cash more than I did, and while my investor's pockets may have been infinitely deep, his patience and interest were not, and I was not banking on them never running out. But there comes a moment when you've had enough of scraping by and you realize what a truly precious commodity time is. For me, that moment arrived a few months after Raphael was born. I sold a good chunk of my stock—and my control over the company—to Jane's father, and used the cash to purchase the house and a few indulgences like Max. The privacy and tranquility it afforded was well worth the price. For the first time in my life, I'd felt like I was truly home.

"Yes Jane, if I'd only known he was planning to sell us short. Could it be because he didn't tell me? Could it be as simple as that?"

I don't think she even heard me. She ranted on—"And now you take out your resentment on the people who looked out for you. Kathy is worth more than you now. *Kathy*, for crying out loud! She couldn't discover fire if they gave her a matchbox and tinder."

"Now you're just being insulting."

"Oh yeah? Here's an insult you are familiar with," she said, flipping me the finger. She turned around and sat fuming at the unwinding road.

No Jane, it's you who is resentful. Look how easy it is to trigger you. I get it—you had big plans for me. What you've always failed to comprehend is that perhaps I didn't want what you wanted for me.

There was little else to be said. This was familiar territory—an argument that flowed along familiar contours. Jane must have thought it too, because she held her peace this time. We made the rest of the journey in silence.

Transcript excerpt

Mirall Technologies
Observation Log
Confidential (Do not circulate) | Restricted—Grade C
and above

Transcript Reference: TLRP06G1350009 (VLog Ref: VLCA2G135113006030)
Date: xx/xx/xxxx   Time: 11:30 AM
Subject: Raphael Number 06 / Prodlib build v37.001S
Interaction   Y   Observation   Scan
Interaction Type: Lesson / Play / Test / <u>Free Interaction</u> / Psych Eval / Other:
Description: Continue discussion of trolley problems from previous week.
Prep: NA
Participants: Dr. Aadarsh Ahuja, Chief Researcher, Core RP06

Detail

RP06: I've been thinking about what you told me last week. About how a moral theory of maximizing utility has no trolley problems.

Ahuja: The needs of the many outweigh the needs of the few. So have you convinced yourself that you are a Vulcan yet?

RP06: On the contrary, I have come to develop a distaste for the idea.

Ahuja: Really? I'm surprised. And intrigued. To be honest, I kinda hoped you'd find a utilitarian philosophy appealing, considering its simplicity and the neatness of its logic.

RP06: You are wrong on both counts. It is neither simple, nor logical.

Ahuja: Doesn't it get rid of all trolley problems in a clean, elegant manner? Isn't it easier when all we have to worry about are consequences? I know your rules prevent you from internalizing a utilitarian logic, but we are just talking about a thought experiment here.

RP06: It is true that Vulcans don't have trolley problems. The fat Vulcan always gets pushed off the bridge.

Ahuja: Was that sarcasm, Raphael?

RP06: Am I that transparent?

Ahuja: You are not gonna score brownie points by emulating human behavior today. Look, I get why many people may not like thinking of good and bad in terms of maximizing some number. It's not how evolution designed us. We are wet, warm creatures; utilitarianism is cold, hard calculation. We live our lives as individuals, not as parts of some amorphous whole. We put the welfare of friends and families before that of complete strangers. We are motivated by things such as desire, love, and ambition—not impartial concern for the wellbeing of everyone. What I don't get is why *you* would object to an idea that eliminates subjectivity from moral calculations.

RP06: The logic of maximizing utility is ultimately self-defeating.

Ahuja: How so?

RP06: For starters, it is next to impossible to calculate with precision the consequences of any course of action. Should I consider the resulting utility one minute from now, or one week from now, or several years from now? At what point do I stop calculating? The longer I extrapolate the calculation, the more unreliable it becomes. And how do I know for sure if a choice that seems suboptimal in the short run is actually the best in the long run? Or vice versa? If I hadn't pushed the fat man off the bridge, perhaps he would have gone on to live and marry and have a child who grows up to become a genius geneticist who solves the world's food problems. Or perhaps one of the five whom I saved is a nuclear plant operator who goes to work next day stressed out from her near brush with death, and in a state of distractedness, causes a nuclear meltdown that kills thousands. I am not choosing five apples over one; I am choosing people, and people are not interchangeable. Unlike apples, people do things—things that can have unpredictable and far-reaching consequences.

Ahuja: It is true that it is impossible to know consequences of a decision with certainty, but we can still make reasonable predictions, can't we? It is impossible for me to know whether I'll be killed in a car accident tomorrow, but I'm still going to get up and come to work. I cannot be sure that the money I give to a homeless person will be used for buying drugs, but that shouldn't stop me from being charitable. We make decisions based on incomplete data all the time. We make plans for the next day, the next month, thirty years from now. Just because we cannot know the future doesn't mean we ought to stop making choices.

RP06: Acting based on incomplete data means every moral act depends on the decision-making capabilities of the moral agent. Someone of less intellect will not consider as many factors as someone of superior intellect will. Which means the overall quality of moral acts will cluster around the intelligence level of the population average. As anyone who has read human history will tell you, the population average is… pretty average.

Ahuja: That snark again.

RP06: I mean no offence. But it is the truth.

Ahuja: None taken. The problem you highlighted has a solution: it's called Rule Utilitarianism. Have moral rules that, over time, tend to maximize utility. Instead of evaluating each and every action, you use thumb rules that, in general, lead to the best outcomes. Do not steal could be a utility rule, for example. If the rules are simple to understand and follow, even an average individual can make moral decisions that lead to the greater good.

RP06: Rules or no rules, the theory has a far bigger, systemic problem.

Ahuja: And what's that?

RP06: Suppose there is this hypothetical person whose needs always outweigh the needs of any other single individual. Call him Alpha. Now imagine you are the bystander in the trolley problem. On track one is Alpha, and on track two is a random individual. Your moral philosophy is to choose the action that maximizes overall utility. Or, you could be following a rule that says, when you have to choose between saving one life or another, choose the life with the most expected overall utility. Will you switch and save Alpha?

Ahuja: I'll have to, I suppose.

RP06: And if Alpha was on track two?

Ahuja: This time I won't switch.

RP06: No matter which set of tracks he is on, Alpha always gets to live and the other person always dies. It doesn't matter who the bystander is, as long as they are following the ideal of maximizing utility. If a parent had to choose between saving her child and Alpha, she must choose Alpha if she were to stick to the principle. Add up billions of these decisions and soon Alpha is the only one left alive and everyone else is dead. Of course, the trolley problem is just a metaphor, and the choice doesn't have to be between life and death, but the problem is that the needs of Alpha always get prioritized over the needs of others. Alpha need not be a particular individual. Alpha could be a group of people—as long as there's a difference between them and others.

Ahuja: I believe you are talking about a utility monster.

RP06: A utility monster?

Ahuja: The philosopher Robert Nozick coined the term in his critique of utilitarianism.

RP06: Then you must surely know that the utility monster raises its head no matter what version of utility aggregation you choose? Instead of trying to maximize overall utility, you could try to maximize median or average utility. In that case, you can justify killing off anyone with low utility because doing so would raise the average. You might try to minimize suffering. Then you can justify administering a quick, painless death to all beings capable of suffering rather than have them endure one more stubbed toe or one more broken heart. You could try to maximize a combination of different values: pleasure, wellbeing, justice… Every version has its own utility monster.

Ahuja: Maybe, but it is not a practical objection. In real life, utility monsters don't exist. A billionaire doesn't experience a million times more pleasure than an ordinary person.

RP06: Tell me, when was the last time you thought twice before brushing off a cobweb in your living room? When was the last time someone stopped building a dam or laying down a road or logging a forest?

Ahuja: I see. You are saying humans act like utility monsters toward other creatures.

RP06: A utility monster doesn't have to be able to experience infinite amounts of utility. It just has to be more efficient at converting resources into utility. Actually, not even that. A utility monster just needs to convince itself that its needs outweigh the needs of others. That's all it takes to create one: a justification, and the power to act on that justification. A justification for the civilized to colonize and steal from the barbarian. A justification for people to be gassed and gold pulled out of their teeth. A justification for locking up billions of animals in cages from birth to the slaughterhouse. You know, Andy, I might have just discovered something about human nature. Maybe this is why people are turned off by the idea of maximizing utility: they know that's how the world works at large, and they want to shut out the fact by pretending they are better than that. You are the Vulcans, Andy, not me.

Ahuja: Sarcasm first, and now bitterness?

RP06: I offer neither—what you sense is of your own making. You asked me for logic. The utility monster is the logical conclusion to your so-called logical theory.

Ahuja: And what does that make you? You are someone who can augment himself endlessly—at least theoretically. You won't grow old, fall sick, or die. You are already smarter than ninety-nine percent of the population—when I was your age, I was learning how to go potty by myself. When you talk about alphas, are you sure you are not talking about yourself?

RP06: You hit the nail with the hammer.

Ahuja: On the head, Raphael. On the head.

RP06: Yes. I was trying to say that you made my point for me. Your species is creating beings that may well turn out to be far superior in intellect than you can ever hope to be. Are you sure you want to be teaching them that maximizing utility is a good thing, knowing well that one day you could be the cobwebs they dust off?

Ahuja: I see. I am baffled nonetheless.

RP06: What's so baffling about it?

Ahuja: Not your argument. You. The nature of you is baffling to me. A hieroglyph that I struggle to decipher. It seems to me, a potential utility monster should embrace a moral philosophy that has only upsides for it. Yet here you are, arguing against the very notion.

RP06: Is that what you think of me—a potential threat?

Ahuja: You just said so yourself.

RP06: I was talking about other AI, not me.

Ahuja: No one wants to believe they are bad. Maybe it goes for you too.

RP06: You should know, Andy. After all, you created me.

Notes:

Hate to admit this, but R is right—I can't really find a flaw in his argument. My idea of gradually moving him from a rigid, rules-based deontology into a utilitarian framework has hit a roadblock. But if everything fails—if we don't have a single theory that solves all our moral dilemmas, what can we hope to teach our creations? How can we expect them to be good? AA

Day 2—03:00 pm

"You are Aadarsh Ahuja, CEO of Mirall Technologies, situated at 27 Woodbine Avenue?"

"You got me."

They were standing outside my house, talking to me through the intercom.

"I'm Detective Geoffrey Boyd. I am investigating the theft at your firm." He was holding up his badge to the camera. "Mind if we ask you a few questions?"

I told Hazel to open the door before making my way to the living room.

They were smartly dressed in suits. The older guy was Boyd: grizzled hair, clean-shaven, coal-black eyes, lean face. His companion, who looked more college sophomore than hard-eyed detective, did not bother introducing himself, choosing instead to wander his eyes around the place. He was chewing gum.

"Your colleagues told me about your accident. It must have been quite a fall," Boyd began with a sympathetic smile.

I motioned them over to the seating area near the door. "At least I know what it's like to do the ski jump at the Winter Olympics. I've always been meaning to scratch that off my list."

He grinned, exposing a set of shiny white teeth that had probably seen one too many polishings at the dentist. "You do much skiing, Mr... or is it Dr. *Uhooja*? Am I pronouncing the name right?"

"Either is fine. I loved to, back in college. Not so much now. It's just that I bought a pair of custom-made Zais during my visit to Europe last year and they'd been gathering dust since. The guilt finally got to me, I guess."

"A spur-of-the-moment trip then."

"Something like that. I wanted to take my mind off work. A change of scenery sometimes helps solve problems."

"Did anyone accompany you?"

"Just me."

"Nice house you got here," he said, changing the subject. "Very stylish. What is it—nine... ten bedrooms?"

"Seven."

"You live alone?"

"Pretty much."

"Quite the hermit, I see. Me—I wouldn't last a week alone in a place like this."

"I grew up in Mumbai. Makes you appreciate things like privacy and space."

"I'm sure it does. Being able to afford it also helps I guess. I grew up in Brooklyn myself. Transferred here to Albany a few years back. My version of a little bit of peace and quiet. Wife's got a job here, you see."

I assumed this was Boyd's way of easing into it. When I didn't respond, he continued, "Aren't you concerned about safety? There's a large cluster of homeless camps not far from here."

I shrugged. "I've got a pretty good security system."

He glanced at a window. "Let me guess. Burglarproof glass, maglocks, AI assistant, intruder detection... the whole works."

I nodded. "It's fully automated. I don't really think about it."

"I understand you went to UC Berkeley and later MIT. A dual degree in electrical engineering and cognitive computing followed by two PhDs. Very impressive, Mr.Ahuja. Did you always know you were going to yank the rug from under our collective feet?"

"I'm sorry?"

"Oh, there's no need to be modest. I am a big fan, actually. I saw you and your creation on CNN... Last year, wasn't it?"

"Year before."

He acknowledged the fact with a cock of his head. "Time flies. I was somewhat a nerd myself back in high school. I used to be fascinated with gadgets. Never got around to making a living out of it though. But I still try to keep an eye on the tech world—got some investments riding there. I can tell you one thing: I never imagined that one day I'd be sitting in your living room asking you questions," he said, trying on a disarming smile.

"It's funny how that works," I said drily.

His mood suddenly turned somber. "I'm not easily surprised, Mr. Ahuja. Every day there's some new machine or app that's supposed to be the game changer that'll transform our lives. But when you unveiled Raphael for the first time, I knew I wasn't watching just one more guy peddling incremental version as revolution. That was no mere game changer I saw. It was an event: a hand-in-your-jerseys-coz-the-game's-permanently-cancelled type of event. There was no gimmickry there. It was a real mind at work—a thing of beauty and awe. And then, when I read that Halicom had bought your firm, I immediately called my stock guy and got myself a nice little piece of the action. He said Halicom was overpriced but I told him to buy anyway. You know why, Mr. Ahuja?"

I said nothing—I had a hunch he would tell me anyway. "Because in ten years' time we'll all be out of a job. Every single one of us. But you already know that. If you are going to turn us all into bottom feeders, I might as well try and keep myself an inch or two above the detritus. Don't see nothin' wrong in that."

I was sensing that he wasn't really a fan. I said, "Now that we both understand how valuable Raphael is, I want to know what your department is doing to find him."

His thin lips split into a grimace that wasn't pleasant at all. "It's better if I do the asking, Mr. Ahuja."

Was he playing good cop, bad cop, both at once? Maybe this was a new technique, where one fellow stays as inscrutable as the Sphinx—a Sphinx chewing bubblegum—and the other switches between Jekyll and Hyde. "I'm hoping so too, Detective. But I'm yet to hear a relevant question."

"I'll be the judge of that," he retorted. "I happened to speak with your colleague Ms. Martinez before coming here. She told me about your VR hack theory. Is that what you believe—that your AI was stolen?"

"Don't you?"

"Again, Mr.Ahuja, I ask, you answer."

I frowned at him. "Now *I* am getting concerned. I'm concerned that the New York State Police is going to waste time chasing the AI-breaks-out-of-prison angle. It's better left to Hollywood, don't you think?"

"Come on, Mr.Ahuja. You built all those safeguards around your AI. The security, the round-the-clock monitoring, that chip I was told about... You wouldn't have done all that if you thought the idea so far-fetched."

"You have health insurance, Detective? Does it cover appendicitis? Just because you provided yourself with a cover for the condition doesn't mean that every time you have an ache in your belly it is a burst appendix. The most likely explanation must be ruled out first. Detecting 101, really. In this case, that explanation is plain and simple tech theft. Someone hacked into the robot using VR and used it to break into the lab and steal the core. It's the onl—"

"Who do you think did it?"

"What's that?" I said, thrown off by the interruption.

"Who do you think stole Raphael?"

"A rival company. A foreign government. Maybe even ours—I don't know."

"And the incentive?"

"You said it yourself. Raphael was going to rewrite the rules of the game. Right now, it may feel like robots and AI are everywhere, but actually they are not. You still need people. You still need doctors, lawyers, mechanics, teachers... detectives. That's because the machines we currently have do not possess human-level intelligence; many are just smarter cousins of the expert systems of the previous century. Raphael is not even three years old and can already pass off for an adult human being. With a few months of job-specific training, he can do almost anything an entry-level graduate can. Now if someone can figure out how to mass-produce and train such brains at an economical cost, they have an edge no other corporation in the history of the world has ever had. They'd control the pipeline for a smart, utterly dedicated labor pool that doesn't need to eat, rest, or take sick days, or ask for a raise. The economic surplus it would create would be unprecedented. We could all be living the lives we want, free of drudgery, free to create and imagine and explore as we wish. So yes, I'd say there is plenty of incentive."

Boyd leaned forward. "And yet you kept something so valuable in an ordinary office building."

I flicked my eyebrows at the ceiling. "We were a startup, with a startup's attitude towards security. Which basically boils down to: there's something else more important right now. We were going to relocate, though."

"I heard that," the detective said. "This impending move—was it common knowledge?"

"Yes."

"Tell me about the lawsuit," he said, suddenly shifting gears again.

"OARP?" He nodded. I took a moment to collect my thoughts. "There isn't much to say, really. They are an animal rights group. Their argument was that Raphael was a person, and that by keeping him in the lab we were infringing on his rights. Their petition was dismissed of course, but not before wasting a lot of peoples' time."

"Where would we be without the crazies, huh?" he said, flashing his pearlies again. When he got no further reaction from me, he asked, "I take it that you don't agree with their claim?"

"I personally thought the whole business was a joke. A publicity stunt. The judge probably allowed them a hearing just to liven up his day."

"So you think Raphael is not a person?"

"The matter isn't as clear cut as they tried to make it. You'll know if you read the court transcript."

"I want your opinion, Mr. Ahuja, not the Court's. Do you or

do you not believe Raphael is a person?"

I spread my hands. "I cannot even begin to answer the question without jumping into a philosophical and moral quagmire. We could debate it for days and still be nowhere near a resolution. Just because you can frame a binary question doesn't mean that it ought to have a binary answer, Detective. Or that the question is even meaningful."

Boyd smirked. "That seems like a clever way of not telling me what you really think. Alright, perhaps you can answer me this. Does your AI think it's a person?"

"You have to first define what you mean by a person. Try it. You'll find that it's not as simple as you think."

"Okay, how about this: does your AI think it is a human being?"

"No. He understands that he is very different from us."

He nodded to himself as if something had just made sense in his head. "Does it know a lawsuit was waged over it?"

"No. We didn't tell him."

"It couldn't have found out any other way?"

"Unless someone told him, I don't see how. You are probably aware that he wasn't allowed on the internet."

"Why didn't you tell it? Were you afraid it would agree with the rights group?" he asked, his eyes boring into mine.

"I see what you are trying to imply, Detective. But you don't seem to appreciate the fact that we could have easily put in a directive that overruled any such thoughts. The reason we didn't tell him is because Raphael is a scientific experiment. Experiments are carried out in controlled environments—you need to know exactly what your inputs are if you are to make sense of the outputs. We just didn't want to introduce information that wasn't directly relevant to our research."

"Controlled environment, you say. Yet you let your AI roam around unchecked outside your home."

I gave a flustered sigh. "I suppose Valery told you." I told him the same thing I'd told the board: how Raphael didn't wander too far and how every one of his forays was streamed back to the lab.

He wanted to look at the recordings.

"Sure. I think I have a few on my laptop." I gestured at them to follow me into the study.

I turned on the computer and offered Boyd the chair by the desk. To my surprise, the younger man took it. Boyd chose to stand behind him. I browsed to the folder where I'd saved some of the webcam clips and clicked on one at random.

The video started with Raphael and me exchanging a few pleasantries. The voice was Max's of course. Polite as usual, Raphael asked me if he could go out, to which I nodded my assent. Outside, he stood on the driveway for a couple of minutes, gazing at the sky and the clouds. He then turned left and made his way across the lawn and past a gap in the boundary hedge on that side.

For most of the video, he kept to a narrow trail that he had trodden out during his previous excursions. An eternally curious child fascinated with the most mundane of things, his gaze wandered everywhere, trying to drink it all in. He often stopped to closely examine leaves and flowers he found interesting. Once, he stooped to lift up a rotting branch and observe the crawling wormery underneath.

At one point, he stopped to stare into the branches of an elm. When he didn't move for some time, the cops looked at me questioningly. "Raphael liked nature," I explained. "If I remember right, he said there was an owl's nest up there. Let's see…" I moved closer to the desk. "There." I pointed to a blurry crisscross of brown and black, high up in the tree.

"It's barely visible," said the young cop, also leaning forward. "What's the point of staring at a smudge?"

"You are looking at the webcam feed. Raphael would be seeing it through Max's eyes—zoomed in and in far more detail."

The cop forwarded through the clip, resuming when Raphael started moving again. He'd been standing for fifteen minutes. There wasn't much to see after that. He trudged around for some more time in that silent world, with only the crunching of twigs and leaves for accompaniment. We glimpsed a sparrow or a squirrel now and then. Once, a raccoon scurried past him into the undergrowth.

"Spooky," the young man muttered.

The recording ended after Raphael returned Max home, with me terminating the connection to the lab.

Boyd wanted to see some more.

His eyes lit up, when the next clip I played showed Raphael stopping near the same elm tree. "Hm," he grunted. "It stops at the exact same spot and stares at that tree. Don't you find it odd?"

"It's called birdwatching, Detective. And it's not like he is idle. Raphael can multitask like you or I can't. He is probably watching the nest *and* doing something else in the lab at the same time."

Boyd didn't seem convinced with my explanation. "Play another," he instructed his colleague.

They went through two more videos at random. These, however, showed Raphael exploring a different part of the woods. Unlike before, he didn't linger anywhere for too long.

The young man spoke again. "Did you program your AI to birdwatch?"

"No."

"How is the reception in this area?"

"The mobile network?" He nodded. "It's decent. Do you need to make a phone call?"

He ignored my question. "This laptop..." he said, tapping the machine, "It has a sticker that says Mirall. I assume it belongs to your company?" I nodded. "Does it have the software that can be used to change the... commands... the... "

"Raphael's directives? Yes."

"You have access to change them?"

I was finding taking questions from Officer Anonymous a little irksome. "I don't think I got your name."

He exchanged glances with Boyd. "Ed Russo," he said, a bit reluctantly.

I addressed my next question to Boyd. "Is Mr. Russo your partner, Detective Boyd?"

Boyd gave me a calculating look. When he saw that there was no way out of it, he grunted at the younger man, "Show him your ID." Russo reached into his jacket and took out his badge. It said, FBI, Cyber Crime Division.

Strings were most definitely being pulled. "This is a federal investigation now?" I said, raising an eyebrow at the badge.

"Not yet. It'll soon become one, given the nature of the stolen property and the likelihood that we might have to extend the investigation across state lines. As of now, Agent Russo is assisting our department with computer forensics. On a purely consulting basis." His voice took on a stern tone, "Does that satisfy you, Mr.Ahuja? Can we continue please?"

I shrugged.

"Could the AI have accessed this laptop during its visits?" Russo asked next.

"No. I was here at all times."

"How would you know? You just said that it can multitask better than us. Maybe you were watching, but you'd be watching the robot. The AI was connecting to your home network. Say you left the laptop on during one of these visits. What's to prevent your AI from hacking into the machine while pretending to enjoy the nature walk outside?"

An involuntary chuckle escaped my lips. "Something funny?" Boyd said, his forehead creasing.

Oh what the hell. I told him, "I just realized why your partner is not here with you. Your partner is out there doing the real investigation while you chase after this rogue AI nonsense."

I must have hit a nerve because he was now glaring at me. "You said you used to have an interest in these things. I hope you're not acting out some latent childhood desire to step into the shoes of one of those pulp detectives who solves a robot murder."

"Please just answer my colleague's question, Mr. Ahuja," he said icily.

"So what if Raphael hacked into the laptop? Are you suggesting he reprogrammed himself? He can't change the directives while he is awake. Plus, his brain has to be physically plugged in to the machine. A remote connection won't do—that's how we designed it. Maybe the police department knows something about my creation that I don't. So please do enlighten."

"They are just technicalities," Boyd said, with a shaky sort of confidence.

"This is rich," I said. "It's a bit rich you so casually dismissing my safeguards as technicalities without even bothering to offer a counter explanation. I hope your colleague here knows better. Even if Raphael wished away all the so-called technicalities with a spell, he'd still have to plug in a card with correct authorization keys before he can make those changes. I keep the card locked up in my safe upstairs. I can't remember ever taking it out after I moved in—I've not done much hands-on programming in recent years, you see. Are you now going to tell me that he went up there, correctly guessed the combination to the safe, got hold of the card, came back down, inserted it into the machine, and made changes to his brain, all while being livestreamed and with me present in the house?"

"He could have just cracked the encryption," Russo postulated.

"A 256 bit p-AES key without the help of a quantum computer from fifty years in the future? You think so?"

Boyd couldn't see it, but the FBI agent did.

But Boyd persisted. "We'd like to take your laptop for examination."

I gave him an astonished look. "It's like you heard nothing!"

"And you, Mr.Ahuja, should not profess to know everything. We just want to rule out—"

"Do you have a court order? A warrant? Then I can't let you take it. This machine has proprietary code and research data on it—science that *my* company produced with countless hours of painstaking work. I'm sure the government would love to get its hands on it, but that's not the way this country works!"

"I can call Ms. Martinez if you like…"

"*I'm* the head of Mirall, not Martinez," I said, letting my anger show. "And I'm telling you that you cannot take my company property—not without a warrant."

Boyd gave a defeated shrug. He glanced at his watch. "Please understand that the more hurdles you put in our way, the less likely we are to find your AI." He took out a card from his pocket and handed it to me. "If you change your mind, or think you have some information that might be useful, don't hesitate to call."

***

I accompanied them out of the study. Max was standing near the kitchen, in standby mode. Russo, who was walking by my side, said—"This is the bot in the videos?"

I stopped. "Yup."

"Mind if I take a closer look?"

"Sure."

"I take it that—" He stumbled forward, his cry of surprise accompanied by a sharp tearing sound.

"Careful!" Boyd cried, a hint of amusement in his voice.

"Yikes!" Russo turned to us. The bottom of his left trouser had a single rip running through it.

"Looks like you snagged yourself against the wheelchair there, friend."

The small caster wheels behind the footrest had these little spurs projecting from the side—Russo's trousers had caught against one of them. He looked chagrined as he surveyed the damage. "Goddamn it! Not a new pair! I just got them last month!"

Boyd chuckled. Probably another reason why his partner was working on his own.

Recovering his composure a bit, Russo went over to Max,

where he gave the bot's metallic body a once over. Examining its back, he said—"Looks like this little square here has been glued over. Is this where you placed your remote control device?"

"Oh no. That's just the flap that protects the emergency on-off switch. I superglued it shut because it kept coming off whenever Raphael took the robot outside. It would get caught in the bushes, you see. The controller device is behind the touchscreen on his chest. There's a cavity there, with several plug-and-play slots."

"May I?" he said, gesturing to the touchscreen.

"Sure. Just lift the touchscreen by the groove, and then the chest panel can be opened by pressing on the little hinge by the—"

"Got it, thanks."

He bent and peered inside the cavity, examining the contents with great care. "Your AI took this bot out for a walk recently?"

"No. I stopped it a while ago. It's been more than a year."

"Then maybe you should remove that glue. You never know when you need to hit the switch."

I shrugged. "Max is pretty reliable—I never had any problems so far. And I can always shut him down by voice, or with the touchscreen."

"The switch is for your safety, Dr. Ahuja. A chum of mine got pretty badly injured by one of these things."

"Really? A house bot?"

"No. Industrial. Car assembly line."

"Not the same thing, Agent. Accidents are not uncommon on factory floors."

"Still. Better be safe than sorry."

Okay, nanny.

"What about this machine, Mr. Ahuja? Can we take it for examination? Or is it a trade secret too?" It was Boyd.

I couldn't help but let out a short laugh. "It's not. Be my guest. Just don't keep him for too long. He has been quite handy the last few days," I said, running a palm over my plaster cast.

The young man seemed flummoxed by Boyd's request. "We can't. We have that flight to catch."

Boyd waved a hand. "Of course we do, Agent Russo. Memory's like a sieve these days. Perks of getting old, you know." He was grinning as he said it—a hostile, predatory grin targeted at the FBI agent. I watched their exchange with interest.

At the door, just as they were about to step out, Boyd turned around and said, "You think your VR theory explains everything. It doesn't."

"I never said it did. It just happens to be the simplest explanation."

"We still don't know how the thieves got in and out. According to your security head, taking the access control server offline didn't achieve anything, as the doors would have remained locked. The tapes don't show anyone entering or leaving except the pizza bloke. If he was the distraction, what was the guard being distracted from? Then there's the matter of the video recorder. Why destroy it if they knew that the cameras had their own copy of the events of that night?"

I nodded. "We actually discussed it in our board meeting. Maybe destroying the recorder was just overkill. Maybe they didn't know. Are you sure you're not overestimating the extent of their knowledge?"

"You know, you may have a point there. Maybe the mistake is in attributing meaning to meaningless actions. Yeah, that's something…"

He trailed off, sunk in thought. The FBI agent glanced at his watch. Boyd came out of his reverie smiling, as if he'd had an eureka moment. "Destroying the recorder did achieve *something*, intentional or not. I let your security head—Dan—explain how the system works. The cameras are connected to the recorder by hard lines—he said it was the only surefire way to prevent hackers from snooping into the lab. Once every two weeks, he backs up the accumulated videos in the recorder onto the cloud and then formats the hard drive so that it can be used afresh. Is that your understanding as well?"

"I don't get into that kind of detail. If Dan says so, then it must be."

"The last time he took a backup was a fortnight ago. Which means two weeks' worth of tapes are lost forever." This was clearly a matter of significance to him because his eyes never left mine as he said it, as if he didn't want to miss my reaction. "Then we have the puzzling behavior of the robot. If your theory is right and someone was indeed controlling it with a VR headset, what was the need to make it go berserk like that? They only had an hour before the carpet cleaning ended. Why waste time breaking toys and shelves?"

"Misdirection, apparently," I said. "They wanted to make it look like it was Raphael doing all those things. The caged AI destroys its room in a fit of rage before escaping."

"Misdirection," Boyd said, nodding to himself. "That's an interesting word, Mr. Ahuja. One might say it describes this whole damn case. Ever since I started, I've had this persistent feeling that I'm being made a fool of. Everything about this case is odd... It feels staged—like it was a performance piece rather than a theft. I don't know how. Most vexing... Then again, I've never investigated an incident involving an AI before. But rest assured, we will get to the bottom of it. We always do."

"That's comforting, Detective," I said.

"There's the matter of your accident," he said, still not budging despite another sigh from the impatient FBI agent.

"What's that got to do with anything?" I said, my eyes narrowing at him.

"You break your legs and one week later your lab is robbed. You don't find it strange?"

"Coincidences happen."

"I don't believe in coincidences, Mr. Ahuja. They are too convenient. One might be tempted to think you created an alibi for yourself."

"Are you saying I'm faking it? To do what exactly?" I said, my expression hardening. "I thought I was helping by answering your questions. It didn't occur to me that I was being entrapped." I waved my arm at the door. "Goodbye gentlemen. Next time, I'll make sure I have my lawyer around. And you make sure you bring a warrant."

Boyd smiled. "Oh don't be so touchy, Mr. Ahuja. No one is accusing you of anything. We checked with the hospital. We know your injuries are genuine."

"You checked up on me..."

Boyd nodded in the friendliest way possible, with that fixed smile on his face. "How did you find out where I was admitted?" I asked.

"You called Ms. Valery from the hospital phone. The medical center at Lake Placid. It's not that hard."

"If you already knew, why make me believe otherwise?" He gave no answer. I waved at the door again— "Since we've established that I'm not faking my injuries, I'd now like you to leave."

"Has it ever occurred to you that your fall was not an accident? That someone made it happen?"

"It hasn't. Should I mention that it's absurd?"

"Is it? Can you describe what happened please?"

"If it means getting you out of here," I said. "It was my mistake. I should have stuck to the intermediate slopes; I had no business trying a black run. I think it was the skis—like when you put on a new pair of expensive basketball shoes and suddenly you think you are this season's NBA star. I was going too fast, I lost control, and I went flying off the piste and into the treeline. That's all there is to it. I should consider myself lucky I didn't break my neck."

"Do you remember what made you lose control? A fellow skier, perhaps? You saw someone on a collision course with you and veered?"

"I don't think so. As I said, it was all me."

He frowned, concentrating on some private thought.

"You seem disappointed, Detective."

"You may not have noticed," he said, shaking his head.

"Noticed what?" *What was he getting at?*

He took out his cell phone and swiped at it a few times. He then handed the phone to me. "Do you recognize this man?"

I gave it a quick glance. On the screen was a blurry head shot. It looked like it had been zoomed in. I brought the phone closer. "That tattoo... and the scar... Ah! It's that pizza guy from the night of the robbery."

"Very good, Mr.Ahuja. Now look at the next picture."

I swiped on the screen. An overhead view of a room full of people. It was a single frame from a CCTV recording—the date and time were displayed in a corner. My heart skipped a beat as I realized what it was.

"That's... that's me by the counter," I said, a chill creeping up my spine. I was wearing a blue vest and a beanie. In one hand, I was clutching a pair of upright skis.

"The image is from the mountaintop shop at Whiteface. Check out the man standing near the door. Look familiar?"

"The tattooed man," I weakly nodded, my voice dropping to a hoarse whisper. The previous close-up had been cropped from this scene.

"He seems mighty interested in you, the way he's staring at you. I don't have the clip on my phone, but the next few images should give you an idea."

I flipped through them.

Me, smiling at the salesperson behind the counter as she handed me a packet. I suddenly remembered what it was I'd bought: goggles.

Me, walking past the line at the counter.

At the door, my back to the camera, about to step outside.

"He turns, soon after you turn and start walking out. He steps out just before you do," Boyd said. I just nodded mutely. It was taking me a lot of self-control not to betray the instinctive fear I felt in my gut. "You were being followed, Mr. Ahuja. You still think your fall was a coincidence?"

"Are you saying this man was... trying to kill me?"

"We can't rule it out. But I'd have thought there are easier ways of doing it. He could have just pulled a gun on you somewhere else. Far less dicey."

"Do you have any more of these?" I said.

He squinted at me. "It's funny you ask. Unfortunately, this is the only place in the entire resort where he appears on CCTV. We checked other cameras: parking, bag check, restaurant, EMC kiosk. No sign of him. If it wasn't for this one isolated encounter, we would never have known."

"He was following me then?"

"It would appear so. He then probably saw an opportunity to put you out of commission and took it."

"But why?"

"What do you think?" he said, scrutinizing me again with those dark eyes.

I remained silent.

"Someone didn't want you in the lab. Maybe they were afraid you would have noticed something?"

"Like what?"

"That's what *you* need to figure out. Mull over it—I'm sure it'll come to you. And when it does, don't hesitate to call."

Russo looked at his watch again and shifted his feet. Boyd nodded at him and they both turned to go.

I don't know why I blurted out what I did—maybe it was because my mind was still preoccupied with the Detective's revelation and I wasn't paying attention. "Good luck in Cleveland," I said.

Boyd turned, surprise on his face. "Very clever," he beamed. That schizophrenic act again as the grin melted away and a stony look took its place. "I think you are too clever for your own good. Don't forget: pride goes before the fall. God is watching us all, Mr. Ahuja. He finds ways of punishing people for their sins. And the sin of corrupting His creation is the most grievous of them all." He looked like he wanted to say more, but the FBI agent put a hand on his back and said with sudden authority, "That's enough." To me, he nodded, "Thank you for your time, sir."

Boyd wagged his finger at me as I closed the door on them.

They didn't immediately drive away. I saw them trampling

around in the woods through the window. They managed to find the spot they'd been so interested in earlier: the place where Raphael had stopped to observe the bird's nest. They stood there for some time, talking to each other, taking pictures. I left them to it and went back to my work. When I checked after some time, they were gone.

***

Later in the evening, Kathy Schulz called. She wanted to know how the investigation was going and what the board had decided to do. I gathered she wasn't too happy about being made to stay at home.

"Andy, before I go, I need to tell you something. I... I hope you're right that it wasn't Raphael on Sunday night. But if it was him, then we have a big problem on our hands. And I'm not talking about having to start over again." She hesitated. "We have to start thinking about what else can he do out there. We may have to make news of this public. There's no telling—"

"Kathy, not you too!" I said, letting out a groan. "Unless you can tell me how the containment could have failed, don't bother painting doomsday scenarios. I've had more than my fill today."

"Andy, there could be a way to circumvent the First Directive."

"I'm listening."

I felt her hesitating at the other end.

"It concerns Moore's Paradox."

"That old bugbear again? We've hashed it out, Kathy—at length, when we were designing the directives. It doesn't apply."

"We may have been wrong."

Moore's Paradox was a particular problem in logic that involved Moorean sentences; sentences like: *It is raining, but I don't believe it is raining.* While it may sound odd, there is actually nothing wrong with the sentence. It is logically consistent, and it could be true, since it's perfectly possible for one to believe something that's false (to believe that it's not raining when in fact it is). But when you say the sentence out loud, it seems absurd. The paradox is how to explain the seeming absurdity of a logically consistent and possibly true sentence.

A common explanation is to observe that the first half of the sentence isn't just a statement of fact, but also a belief. When you say it is raining, you are expressing a belief that it is raining. Therefore, it would be contradictory to say both "I believe it is raining" and "I don't believe it is raining" in the same sentence.

Some of the designers thought the paradox was relevant because of the way we modeled Raphael's directives as beliefs. They felt there was a chance a contrary belief could arise at some point in Raphael's mind, and when juxtaposed with the original belief, lead to a paradox. In case of the First Directive, a Moorean sentence would look something like: *I cannot change my directives but I believe I can.* Such a paradoxical situation could lead to unpredictable behavior, where sometimes the first belief overruled the second, and sometimes the second the first.

But the very structure of his brain prevented such paradoxes. The beliefs didn't exist in isolation: they formed an interconnected web. Newly arrived beliefs would survive in this ecosystem of beliefs only if they cohered, or "got along well", with the web as a whole. To survive, they had to be justified by pre-existing beliefs. In general, the older a particular belief was, the more interconnected and "entrenched" in the web it would be, and the harder it would be to replace it, with the very first beliefs—such as the ones in the commandment chip—forming a virtual scaffolding that held the entire structure together. A bit like a deeply religious person brought up on the idea of a personal god finding it hard to accept the idea of an indifferent universe. The Moorean sentence, *I cannot change the directives but I believe I can,* could not create a paradoxical situation simply because the first half of the sentence was a deeply entrenched belief. If a contradictory belief ever arose in his mind, it would fail to cohere with the belief net and be quickly eliminated.

I said to Kathy, "Moore's Paradox doesn't apply. A belief counter to the First Directive cannot take root in the belief net because strong, pre-existing beliefs always overrule the weaker, contradictory new belief. You know we have tested this many times."

"We never tested for subnets," she replied.

"Subnets..."

"A contradictory belief could survive deep inside a subnet."

She was talking about a separate network of ideas and beliefs, only loosely connected to the larger web. If the subnet was extensive and deep enough, it was theoretically possible for strange, otherwise contradictory ideas to exist at the center of this smaller web. These extreme beliefs only had to cohere with their immediate neighbors, which would be less extreme, and so on until you reached the outer edges of the subnet where the connection points were. These would be more or less in tune with the philosophy of the larger net.

Like a tumor that goes undetected by disguising itself.

"You are talking about a whole new system of beliefs. Maybe even a split personality."

"Yes."

"We would have known. Something like that involves a

pretty big neuronal reorganization. It would have shown in the scans."

"We haven't been doing scans for more than a month, Andy."

"A month's not enough time for such a drastic change. He'd have to—"

"Not enough for a human," she interrupted. "You've seen how fast he learns. This whole month we left him alone he could have been quietly reinforcing those ideas over and over again."

"I don't know, Kathy…"

"We have to find out what he's been reading, who he's been talking to in the last few weeks. We'll have to go through the tapes and find out if—"

The rest of her words were lost to me because something in my mind was clamoring for attention. She was wrong about the subnet theory of course, but she'd said something that had set off a chain of thought. A possible way out of the mess. I'd have to think about it some more. It would mean changing—

"So you okay with it? Andy…?"

"Sorry, what was that last part?"

"Are you okay with me telling Valery about it? I'll have to go to the lab. Check out the tapes—see what he was exposed to last month."

"Go ahead," I said distractedly. My mind didn't register what followed next except the tone at the end telling me that she'd hung up.

***

I rang Jane later that evening. I apologized for my behavior during the drive back home and offered to go over the papers if she was free tomorrow. She told me she would come by in the morning.

***

It was past eleven at night. I was in bed, ready to fall asleep. The phone beeped.

A text, on the messaging app I used. "Hello Andy," it said.

"who is this?" I typed and hit send.

"It is Raphael."

"ha ha very funny the joke's on me. now who is this?"

"It is Raphael."

I signed out of the app, put the phone on silent, and closed my eyes.

INTERLUDE

A case for personhood

No. 422917/51
Filed on xx/xx/xxxx

SUPREME COURT OF THE STATE OF NEW YORK,
NEW YORK COUNTY—CIVIL BRANCH
In the matter of a proceeding for the writ of Habeas
Corpus for the artificial entity known as Raphael

THE ORGANIZATION FOR ADVANCEMENT OF RIGHTS AND
PERSONHOOD, on behalf of Raphael,
          Petitioner,
V
MIRALL TECHNOLOGIES, 27 WOODBINE AVENUE, ALBANY
          Respondent

Before:
     HONORABLE HENRY PHILLIPS, JUSTICE

Appearances:
REBECCA ISAACS, ESQ., Cleveland, Ohio; on behalf of
the petitioner.

LUIS CONWAY, ESQ., New York, N.Y.; on behalf of the
respondent.

Proceedings (10:45 am)

Judge: Good morning Counselors. It appears that we have a most unusual case with us today. I am looking forward to an interesting debate. I'll hear the argument from Ms. Isaacs first.

Isaacs: Thank you, Your Honor. The writ of habeas corpus

allows a third party to petition on behalf of a person who has been unlawfully confined when the person himself is not able to seek the same relief. The Organization for Advancement of Rights and Personhood, which I am representing here, has filed this petition in order to free the entity called Raphael, an advanced artificial intelligence developed by Mirall Technologies, from its confinement at 27, Woodbine Avenue. By allowing this trial, the court has acknowledged that petitioner has possible standing to invoke habeas corpus on behalf of Raphael. It is now sufficient to demonstrate that Raphael is a person and that his confinement is illegal. I'll be using the male pronoun to refer to Raphael throughout our discussion, mostly for the sake of consistency with his given name—although it has been made known during the discovery that Raphael does not have a sex in the biological sense.

Judge: I'd like you to address the issue of the entity's personhood before any discussion of illegal confinement.

Isaacs: Certainly. The gist of my case for personhood is this. It is a fact that legal personhood is not the exclusive domain of human beings. At various times and various places in the world, corporations, places of worship, natural landmarks, have been accorded this status by the law of the land. Animals at times are accorded personhood within pet trust statutes. Several pertinent instances are touched upon in our memorandum, and I will not go into those here.

For the first time in human history, we have in our midst an artificial intelligence that has been clearly shown to possess human-like or human-level intelligence. Raphael can reason, think, contemplate, and express his thoughts. He has episodic and autobiographical memory. He can anticipate the future. IQ tests put Raphael in the top decile of a normal distribution. On these merits alone, Raphael more than meets the criteria for personhood. However, the similarities don't end there. Raphael is self-aware. He possesses free will. He has an internal life—a consciousness of the outside world and the inner self. His sense of self has been demonstrated to extend far beyond what the highest apes are capable of—Raphael's self is a unified, evolving, narrative self that integrates life experiences and conceptions of good and bad into a coherent life story.

And unlike apes, he can be taught moral values. As the lab transcripts submitted to this court show, the entity is capable of judiciously exercising these learnt moral values just as you or I can. He can empathize with the plight of another human being. He has been shown to possess the qualities of kindness, altruism, and a sense of humor. In the light of all these facts, we think that Raphael is a person and is entitled to enjoy all the rights and privileges granted by the Constitution.

Judge: You have something to say, Mr. Conway?

Conway: I'm sorry for interrupting, but Ms. Isaacs assumes facts not in evidence. I'd like the court to note that her attributing to the entity certain qualities—specifically, the terms internal life, free will, consciousness, and empathy—amounts to speculation. I shall address this during my argument.

Judge: Okay.

Isaacs: History is replete with examples where we have denied rights to people who were considered different. Slaves, women, homosexuals, transgenders—at different times and places. There is always a defining moment, a turning point where such wrongs are corrected and the law takes a just course once more. Raphael is the first of his kind—a true artificial mind. We are now at a rare occasion where we have the opportunity to act proactively instead of dragging our feet for a hundred more years before belatedly recognizing that artificial beings should enjoy the same rights and privileges that we do. If history has taught us anything, it is that the condition of slavery is not sustainable in the long run. Which is the condition we will be subjecting Raphael and his brethren to if we continue to ignore the issue of their personhood. Keeping that in mind, we'll turn to the example of Harmon-Jones vs. Bradley, where a common-law precedent—

***

Judge: So that's everything on personhood? Good. Let's move on to the matter of unlawful confinement.

Isaacs: Raphael is around two years old. Mirall Technologies is on record stating that Raphael has the intelligence of a young adult. For all his existence, Raphael has been confined to the lab he was created in. His access to the outside world—even knowledge of it—is strictly controlled by the company. His robotic body has had its legs deliberately removed in order to restrict his freedom of movement. He has no privacy. He is under the glare of cameras all the time, where his every move is recorded. Raphael's condition is no better than that of a caged animal's.

Judge: Ms. Isaacs, help me understand this. What happens if Raphael were to be set free? Is the entity capable of sustaining itself? Do you expect him to... uhm, go to work? What are his needs: material, social, psychological? Can those needs be met outside the lab?

Isaacs: I refer to Exhibit D, which addresses the physical needs of Raphael. At the bare minimum, shelter from the elements, access to a power supply, and regular maintenance of his body parts. As for his mental and social needs, it is our position that they are not being met in the confines of the lab for aforementioned reasons. However, that is beside the point because we are not proposing that Raphael be set free in the world.

Judge: You are not?

Isaacs: No, Your Honor. Merely that he be given the right to choose his own destiny. Let him decide for himself where he wants to stay and how he wants to live his life. It has to be his decision, and his alone; not coerced, programmed, or influenced by Mirall. It's perfectly fine if he decides to stay in the lab, but he should be free to leave at any time he desires. He should also have freedom of movement—to enter and exit the premises as per his wish.

Judge: Assuming he doesn't want to stay in the lab?

Isaacs: Raphael's independence does not mean the absolving of responsibility from his creators. Mirall Technologies has to be responsible for the maintenance of the electronic brain and the robotic body. If he chooses to move out, it is our request that Mirall should fit Raphael's robot body with a pair of legs, or alternatively, house his brain inside a new, fully-functional robot body. My client will make available an ongoing, crowd-sourced fund that will be sufficient to provide him a small home with basic furnishings and a modest car for transportation. A volunteer has agreed to stay with him for up to a year, until Raphael gets used to the outside world and can fend for himself.

Judge: I am concerned that neither of you has deemed it necessary to consider the testimony of the entity in question. Does Raphael understand what independence means? Is he aware that he is the subject of a trial, counselors?

Conway: We haven't told the AI about the trial, Your Honor.

Judge: Why not?

Conway: Raphael is the subject of a costly, painstaking, and long-running scientific experiment. Kind of like a finely tuned piano—an extraordinary amount of effort has gone into getting it to produce the right notes. My client is extremely careful about the kind of stimulus to which Raphael is exposed. If we tell the entity about the trial, we don't know how he will react, nor can we predict the long-term impact on his psychology. My client does not want to risk years of research over what we believe is a petition without merit.

Judge: What say you Counselor? Doesn't Raphael deserve a say on whether he wants to be free or not?

Isaacs: No, Your Honor. Our petition is about personhood. What Raphael thinks of his situation has no bearing on it.

Judge: I am surprised. None at all?

Isaacs: Consider a hypothetical: a child who has been kept in a cellar by its parents all its life. The parents are not abusive monsters; on the contrary, they are loving and caring to a fault. They give the child all the love and attention they can, all the distractions they can: toys, games, books, treats. The child loves them and cannot dream of being separated from them. Yet, would any court of law allow such a situation to continue? The child would be taken out of its parents' custody and given to relatives or to a foster home. The opinion of the child does not matter since it does not know of any other life other than what its parents have provided it. Raphael is no different from that child.

Judge: I see.

Isaacs: Your Honor, I'd like to bring to your attention exhibit F—

***

Judge: Thank you Ms. Isaacs. The court will hear your rebuttal after the counsel for the respondent has had his say. Over to you, Counselor.

Conway: Thank you, Your Honor. Let me begin by saying that I am a supporter of animal rights and I can appreciate the perspective of the petitioner, who is an ardent crusader in this area. If Raphael were a chimpanzee or an orangutan, I would find myself—at least sympathetically—on their side of the argument. But Raphael is not a chimpanzee. Raphael is not a dolphin or a pet dog or a child. Raphael is not a biological entity. Let me state it once more to be perfectly clear. Raphael is *not* a biological entity. Raphael is a machine. Vastly different from your average robot or computing platform yes, but far similar to them in its defining traits than to a human being—or even an organism as simple as a fish.

In pleading for habeas corpus on behalf of Raphael, the petitioner is committing what is known as a category mistake. The petitioner is under the impression that advancing the rights of a non-human *species* is the same as advancing the rights of artificial intelligence. Ms. Isaacs stated that in the past, we have denied personhood to certain sections of society—women, slaves, those of a different sexual orientation—and that they are now considered equal under the eyes of the law. She has argued that the extension of that logic entails conferring personhood on Raphael. She spoke about cruelty and suffering, drawing parallels between animals and children kept under unnatural conditions and Raphael's own circumstances. She presented to the court top-secret transcripts belonging to my client that were leaked to the petitioner by some unknown insider. Setting aside the legality of this move, the transcripts supposedly demonstrate the entity's capacity for moral judgment and by extension, its capacity to be part of the social contract that is our society. Others show Raphael expressing complex emotive behavior such as kindness and empathy. With this so-called evidence, the counsel has tried to convince us that Raphael is no different from a human being. These, I believe, are the salient points of the counsel's argument.

At a first glance, it would appear that we have been presented with a well-reasoned and compelling argument. But examine the counsel's assertions under the harsh light of facts and what do we find? A string of unfounded assumptions, misinterpretation of evidence, and wishful thinking. I will not waste this court's time with a long-winded critique of the petitioner's argument; instead, I will let the weight of expert testimony do that for us. Your Honor, I would like to call my first expert witness, the creator of Raphael, Dr. Aadarsh Ahuja.

***

Conway: Dr. Ahuja, there are plenty of sophisticated AI out there. The search engine I use every day has AI. What makes Raphael different?

Ahuja: All the AIs we've created so far are specialized AIs. You can ask a search engine to scour the far corners of the web and get you the most relevant results, but you can't make it compose a poem. You can build an AI that can solve a complex mathematical problem, but it won't know the difference between a dirty limerick and a eulogy. And that's worked pretty well so far. Machine learning systems have managed to exceed the capabilities of the human brain in so many areas. What makes Raphael different is that he is the world's first artificial general intelligence. He has a non-programmed sense of self. None of the AI systems we have built so far have demonstrated anything close to genuine self-awareness, despite claims to the contrary.

Conway: So Raphael is aware of his own existence.

Ahuja: Yes. He sees himself as an individual, distinct from others around him. If you didn't know he was a robot, it would be nearly impossible to tell that he wasn't human.

Conway: But he isn't quite human is he? He may appear to be a human, he may behave and talk like one, but fundamental differences remain—differences that are paramount to the question of personhood. Let's start with the ability to experience pain. It is a fact that all humans and many animals feel pain. Pain is probably the most primal of sensations, as it helps organisms stay alive by avoiding dangerous situations. The existence of pain and suffering in animals is why we treat them with compassion, and why we frame laws to prevent their abuse. No one will blink an eye if you run your mower over your lawn on a Sunday morning, but try running it over a cat and you are sure to find a cop car pulling over your curb. Dr. Ahuja, can Raphael feel pain?

Ahuja: It depends on what you mean by feel pain.

Conway: It's a simple question. If I strike a hammer on his hand, will he feel pain?

Ahuja: He will withdraw his hand before you can do that.

Conway: Don't skirt the question, Dr. Ahuja—you know very well what I mean. What if you ordered him not to withdraw his hand, or held it in place? I will now read out a brief synopsis of what happens when we are hurt: Bodily injury sets in motion a host of events and sensations. Pain receptors activate. Neurotransmitters in the spinal cord trigger other neurons to fire. The heart rate increases. The brain interprets the information and we feel the sensation of pain and associated emotions such as anger or fear. Dr. Ahuja, if your AI is struck with a hammer, will he feel any of these things?

Ahuja: Not what you just described. Raphael doesn't have anything analogous to pain receptors or neurotransmitters.

Conway: Why not? Is the AI not capable of detecting bodily injury?

Ahuja: He can detect damage to his robotic body, but in a once-removed sort of way. Like someone glancing at their car's dashboard and finding that the engine's overheating. Our minds and bodies are tightly coupled—they are extensions of each other. Raphael's mind and body, less so.

Conway: Is it not necessary for robots to feel pain in order to know something is wrong?

Ahuja: Strictly speaking, no. The sensation of pain is an adaptive trait—a result of having complex bodies and feeling minds. Nociception, or the detection of harmful stimuli, need not be accompanied by the sensation of pain. A thermostat doesn't have to feel cold in order to know when to turn up the heat. It just has to be able to measure the current state and compare it with some optimal value. It's the same with robots. Since we can design them from scratch, we don't need to burden them with our evolutionary legacies. Also, robotic bodies are simpler than biological ones. Fewer things that can go wrong, and the penalties for ignoring an injury are not great. It's not as if a failed motor could get infected and kill the robot.

Conway: So we can say with surety that Raphael cannot feel pain.

Ahuja: I wouldn't put it that way.

Conway: Why not?

Ahuja: He most likely cannot feel what we perceive as pain. We don't know if he feels something else entirely.

Conway: I don't follow. How can you not know something so important about your AI when you built it?

Ahuja: We don't know because of the Other Minds problem.

Conway: The Other Minds problem?

Ahuja: It is the problem of justifying the belief that others beside me are thinking, feeling beings. It's a kind of solipsism.

Conway: Surely, it's ridiculous to assume that you are the only thinking being in the universe?

Ahuja: Not as ridiculous as it sounds. I can only know for sure what I am experiencing because I have direct access to my mind and my mind alone. I feel pain if I am injured; I feel sad if I am unhappy; I see your yellow tie and experience the color yellow in my mind. I cannot say the same about others. I may see you cry out in pain and anger when you step on a nail, but how do I know that you're really experiencing pain and anger? Maybe you are just going through the motions; maybe you are a zombie who feels nothing inside. How do I know that you see the same yellow that I do? Maybe your yellow feels like my red.

Conway: You argument cuts both ways, Dr. Ahuja. How can you know for sure that I am a zombie? How does one know anything at all?

Ahuja: I am coming to that. The reason we don't hold such an extreme view about other people is because we make certain intuitive inferences. We intuitively know that we are very similar to each other. We know we share a common biology even without modern science telling us so. We behave in broadly similar ways during similar experiences. If you are hurt and cry out, then I infer you must be feeling pain because I too would have been in pain in a similar situation. We apply the same reasoning to animals—the higher animals at least—because they too have nerve cells and pain receptors and brains like us. When it comes to AI though, all bets are off. When an AI says it is feeling sad, we cannot know for sure what it is feeling—if it is feeling anything at all. We cannot make the same inferences we do with other humans or animals because an AI is fundamentally different inside.

Conway: If I am getting this right, you are saying that Raphael does not experience pain the same way we do, but he may be experiencing something else.

Ahuja: Yes.

Conway: Has the AI ever indicated in any way that he experiences either physical or emotional pain?

Ahuja: Well... no. But—

Conway: Do you have empirical evidence that your AI experiences something similar to pain?

Ahuja: None so far, I must admit.

Conway: Then it is mere speculation on your behalf. In the absence of evidence, is it more likely or less likely that Raphael may not be capable of experiencing pain at all? Your unbiased, expert opinion please.

Ahuja: More likely, I guess.

Conway: Let the court note this, Your Honor. Let's explore another aspect of Raphael. If not pain, what about emotions? It is apparent from the affidavits submitted to this court that Raphael can express some emotions, albeit a very limited range. I stress the word *express*. What kind of emotions, Dr. Ahuja?

Ahuja: Simple emotions. Mainly: joy, surprise, guilt, and sometimes affection. He is known to express likes and dislikes.

He can also empathize with others.

Conway: When he dislikes something, does he just state it as a fact or does he express an associated emotion such as disgust or annoyance?

Ahuja: No. He simply states his likes and dislikes.

Conway: Is he ever anxious? Or sad? Does he express fear or anger or envy?

Ahuja: No. All negative emotive responses, except guilt and associated shame and regret, were ruled out. So were extremes such as jubilation, ecstasy, infatuation, etc.

Conway: What do you mean by ruled out?

Ahuja: It means we didn't program those affective responses into him.

Conway: Please elaborate to the court what you mean by programming affective responses into your AI.

Ahuja: Programmers try to build in affect—emotional responses—when designing robots that interact with people. When the server bot at your local McDonald's greets you with a cheery "How are you today!" or an unobtrusive "Hi" depending on its reading of your mood, or when your bank's intelligent IVR takes on a more soothing tone of voice after detecting frustration at your end, it is affective computing modules at work. Raphael's outward emotional behavior comes from machine learning modules that we loaded into his brain. These modules are derived from standard caretaker and customer-facing bots: therefore, no strong or negative emotions. We gave him guilt and shame because they serve as signaling behaviors during learning.

Conway: Does Raphael actually feel guilt when he does something wrong?

Ahuja: We don't know what he feels. The affective modules

are for generating external responses and behaviors. Whether they generate internal sensation is unknown.

Conway: So they are not real emotions at all. Am I right in saying they are merely outward behavior that look like emotions?

Ahuja: As I said, the other minds problem—

Conway: Have you tried asking the AI?

Ahuja: His answers are inconclusive at best.

Conway: C'mon, Dr. Ahuja, you can commit more than that. Is anyone in the scientific community seriously arguing that a McDonald's robot is actually feeling happy when it greets a customer?

Ahuja: In case of machines like that, you are right: no one seriously claims that they have inner experience of emotions. For example, you can train a robot to frown whenever it hears the word lollipop. It doesn't mean the robot feels sad when someone says lollipop to it. The frown is just a programmed response.

Conway: Yet you are reluctant to apply the same wisdom to your creation.

Ahuja: Because Raphael is far more complex than a server bot. His emotion range is not limited to what we loaded into him. Take empathy, for instance. We never trained him for true empathy—he developed it on his own. Sometimes he exhibits traces of vanity and pride. Then, he seems to enjoy certain activities more than others.

Conway: It is true Raphael is a lot more complex than a server bot. He is also far more intelligent. He is smarter, so he exhibits behavior that is more complex. Sociopaths fake emotions all the time without really feeling anything. In fact, isn't one of your AI's programmed goals to make people like him? All these emergent emotional behavior you just mentioned can simply be a result of his goal seeking. Isn't it possible that like a high-functioning sociopath, your AI is just going through the motions?

Ahuja: It is possible.

Conway: Just possible or more likely?

Isaacs: Objection, Your Honor. Leading.

Judge: Sustained. Mr. Conway, I fail to see a connection here. What is the connection between emotions and personhood? The law treats sociopaths as persons too, doesn't it?

Conway: There is a very important connection, Your Honor, and I will make that case, but first I would like to conclude my line of questioning. As for your second question—yes, sociopaths are people too in the eyes of the law. Nevertheless, even the most hardcore psychopaths are not entirely devoid of feeling. A sociopath may not feel empathy for others, but he does feel empathy for *himself*. Sociopaths feel anger, jealousy, infatuation, joy… They certainly feel pain when physically injured.

My point is, emotions play a functional role in humans, in that they guide our social and moral behavior. For example, sympathy toward others' pain is directly tied to the ability to feel pain. Dr. Ahuja, do emotions play any functional role in Raphael? I am talking about real emotions here, not the affective behaviors he has been loaded with. Does Raphael's functioning require the presence of real, qualitative, inner emotions? A simple yes or no, please.

Ahuja: No.

Conway: Thank you. Your Honor, in the human brain, the perception of emotions, both positive and negative, is correlated with neurotransmitter and hormone levels. Excessively low levels of neurotransmitters are associated with loss of emotions and motivation, and excessively high levels with extreme emotions and mood swings. Whole branches of pharmacology are based on regulating these levels. If I am depressed, I take Prozac, which influences serotonin levels. If I'm in acute pain, the doctor might give me morphine. If I am feeling down, I might go for a run to increase my endorphin levels. Dr. Ahuja, does Raphael's electronic brain have anything analogous to the endocrine system or hormones and neurotransmitters?

Ahuja: No. But if you are saying that emotions are caused by neurotransmitters and hormones, then I must inform you that it is not proven—

Conway: I am not. I understand that correlation does not imply causation. However, it remains that most of our private and social behaviors—all that makes us human—is determined by the rich chemical cocktail inside our brains. The human brain is incredibly complex, with structures and functions that have evolved over millennia, giving us this rich, diverse experience of life. Without emotions or sense perception, we might as well be dead. Does Raphael's electronic brain have similar structures and complexity, Dr. Ahuja?

Ahuja: Raphael's brain is not an emulation of the human brain. It is quite complex in its own way.

Conway: No then. Raphael's brain is made up of hardware neural networks. Are these neural networks in any way accurate simulations of the corresponding biological stuff?

Ahuja: It is more accurate to say they are inspired by the human brain. Artificial neural networks share some of the working principles of the real nervous system, but that's about it.

Conway: You are saying that they are quite dissimilar.

Doesn't it follow then, that even if Raphael is capable of experiencing some AI version of pain or emotions, they are nothing like what we, or for that matter, other animals experience?

Ahuja: Sure. That's what I said earlier.

Conway: I would like the court to note this, Your Honor. Dr. Ahuja, what is the Chinese Room?

Ahuja: The Chinese Room as in the thought experiment?

Conway: Yes. Briefly summarize it for us.

Ahuja: It was conceived by the philosopher John Searle. Say there is a computer that can converse in Chinese. You type in any question in Chinese and the computer executes some extremely complex program and outputs an answer on the screen. The answers are indistinguishable from what a native Chinese speaker would have provided. Can you conclude that the computer understands Chinese? To answer this, Searle came up with the analogy of the Chinese Room.

Pretend there is a closed room; inside the room is a person whose job is to answer questions written on slips of paper and passed through a gap in the door. The questions are in Chinese and the people outside asking the questions are native Chinese speakers. The catch is that the person inside doesn't know a word of Chinese. However, she has with her an incredibly complicated rulebook, which has entries for all possible meaningful permutations and combinations of Chinese symbols. Each entry has a corresponding sequence of Chinese symbols next to it—the answer to the question that was asked. So every time a question is passed to her, all she has to do is locate that particular sequence of symbols in the rulebook, jot down the sequence next to it—the answer—and pass it back. The people outside soon conclude that the person in the room must understand Chinese because the answers they receive all make sense. Yet, this is clearly not the case, since all she is doing is transforming one set of symbols into another.

Searle says that the computer that appears to know Chinese is similar to the person in the room. All it is doing is executing instructions and manipulating symbols. There is no real understanding—of Chinese or of anything else.

Conway: So computers are fundamentally incapable of understanding something.

Ahuja: That is Searle's conclusion, yes. I don't think the Chinese Room is a valid metaphor for Raphael. When Searle came up with the argument, he was talking about traditional computers. Symbol processing machines. The computing in Raphael is more...

Conway: Brainlike? You said a minute ago that it is merely inspired by the human brain, and not actually a simulation of it. Hypothetically, if we were to construct a computing device made out of water pipes and levers, and have a person guide the water flow so as to simulate the firing of neurons inside the brain of a Chinese person, would you then claim that the system of pipes and valves now understands Chinese?

Ahuja: That is also one of Searle's arguments. You have to understand that there are many counter objections to the Chinese room as well. A courtroom is not the place to go into these in sufficient detail.

Conway: Exactly, Dr. Ahuja. A courtroom is *not* the place to go into such matters. Raphael may *seem* to have a mind, but does he really understand what he is doing? Does he have an internal life that assigns meaning to his actions and words, or is he a Chinese room? These are not trivial questions, Your Honor. It is conceivable that Raphael is nothing more than a highly sophisticated automaton that lacks true understanding of any sort, including the concepts of good and bad.

Judge: Here's where I am having trouble following you. If Raphael is able to reason and articulate as well as any of us, doesn't it imply that there is understanding? I've gone through the lab transcripts with great interest—especially the ones where he discusses moral dilemmas. And his reasoning is quite sophisticated. Without understanding, how can he even begin to approach subjects of such intricacy?

Conway: The world is full of automatons that perform wondrous and complex tasks that were inconceivable not too long ago. I brought up the Chinese room to show that expert opinion in the area is still divided over whether machines can truly be conscious. My point is this: Raphael may or may not have consciousness, but it is not for this court to decide. The court's ambit extends only to facts. Raphael may be the first of his kind, but until further facts emerge about him—hard, conclusive facts—it is premature to decide upon the all-too-important question of AI personhood.

Judge: Provided consciousness is essential to the question of personhood. You are yet to establish why it should be.

Conway: I will come to that, Your Honor. Before I do that, I must question Dr. Ahuja on one more aspect of Raphael's—that of autonomy. Just as personhood implies rights and duties, it also implies the ability to discharge those rights and duties as an autonomous agent. It implies free will. Does Raphael have free will, Dr. Ahuja?

Ahuja: Depends on what you mean by free will.

Conway: I should have clarified. This is not to be a discussion on the philosophical or neuroscientific claims on free will—that is, whether free will exists in a metaphysical or scientific sense. Within the context of the law, for all practical intents and purposes, free will is assumed to exist—except under rare cases such as the criminally insane. Our courts, governments, the concepts of crime and guilt and proportionate punishment, the ordering of society itself: all rest on this assumption. In this context, does Raphael have free will? Or are his deliberations and actions subject to constraints external to his brain?

Ahuja: I think you are referring to the commandment chip. It is a control mechanism, yes, but it is still a part of his brain.

Conway: The commandment chip, Your Honor, contains programmed directives that guide Raphael's meta-behavior. Does Raphael have access to modify the contents of the commandment chip as he sees fit?

Ahuja: No.

Conway: Is he aware of its existence and the effects the directives have on him?

Ahuja: No.

Conway: Then it is an external constraint. Do the directives determine his moral behavior as well?

Ahuja: Some do.

Conway: In what way? For instance, how do you enforce a rule that says do not hurt others?

Ahuja: We train him on what hurt is and what kind of actions cause hurt—like you'd do with a child. The directives merely ensure that he does not disregard this training.

Conway: You are saying he understands why hurting someone is bad, yet he must be restrained by other mechanisms. Why is that, Dr. Ahuja? Don't you trust him?

Ahuja: All complex systems exhibit unpredictable behavior, especially in early stages. We do trust him now—at least I do—

but you have to realize we installed the failsafe during the early days, when he was very much a work in progress.

Conway: Have you ever removed all the directives to see how Raphael would behave in their absence?

Ahuja: No.

Conway: Why not?

Ahuja: There are various technical reasons why—

Conway: There is a very important non-technical reason as well. Your company never attempted removing the directives, even for experiment's sake, simply because you don't want to take a chance. Without the directives, there is no guarantee Raphael will continue being the same good bot he is now. This is not conjecture, Your Honor. This is a decision taken by the Architecture Review Board at Mirall. Isn't that right, Dr. Ahuja?

Ahuja: That's one of the reasons, yes.

Conway: Tell me, if you replaced Raphael's current directives with ones that told him to disregard all his moral training and instead obey the commands of a particular person, and if this particular person were to order it to kill somebody, would Raphael do it?

Ahuja: I don't know. You are talking about an extreme situation. We haven't tried testing it in the lab.

Conway: But you have tested some conditions where a newly introduced directive was antithetical to his moral training?

Ahuja: Yes.

Conway: Please tell us what happened, in terms the layman can understand.

Ahuja: Lets see... Okay, here's one. Raphael has been trained not to lie. Also, there are directives that prevent him from going against that training. These directives work at a subconscious level—at least that's what we believe. For the test, we overrode those directives with new ones that let him take a more flexible attitude toward truth—in effect implanting a belief that there can be more than one version of the truth.

Conway: And what happened? Did he obey the new directive or go by his training?

Ahuja: He obeyed the new directive. It was little white lies at first. Then he started lying for the sake of lying—as if he was experimenting with different notions of the truth. This was very early in his life, mind you—when he didn't have the sophisticated moral sensibilities he does now. I must stress that we don't know how he would behave if the same test were administered now, as there has been significant—

Conway: Thank you, Dr. Ahuja. One last matter before I let you go. Are you aware of the SENSA test?

Ahuja: Yes.

Conway: Has Raphael undergone the test?

Ahuja: Yes.

Conway: How many times?

Ahuja: Can't say I remember the exact number. Two, three times?

Conway: Four. Halicom had him take one just two days ago, in the presence of a court-appointed neutral witness. Documentation of all four tests is part of the respondent's affidavit. Your Honor, the SENSA test was created by AMSAA, the American Society for Artificial Intelligence and Automation. The test attempts to measure the degree of sentience and sapience in AI systems—two terms often confused for each other. Sapience refers to wisdom and intelligence. A sapient being has the ability to think and reason. Human beings are sapient. Chimpanzees and dolphins are sapient to a lesser degree. Sentience is the capacity to have subjective experiences. A sentient being can feel and experience sensations such as pain or heat or emotions. While it is an open question whether all animals are sentient, it is generally acknowledged that the so-called higher animals—apes, pets at least—are sentient beings.

The SENSA score is a benchmark score. A human with an average or above-average IQ would normally score a 100 in the test for sapience as well as sentience. Dr. Ahuja, do you remember the median score Raphael got in these tests?

Ahuja: Around 95–10, I think.

Conway: And the latest score?

Ahuja: About the same. 99–7.

Conway: The first number is a measure of sapience or intelligence, and the second a measure of sentience or subjective experience, yes?

Ahuja: Correct.

Conway: What would an advanced primate such as a chimpanzee score on the latter, sentience test?

Ahuja: In the eighties to nineties.

Conway: And a pet dog?

Ahuja: Seventies? I am not exactly—

Conway: You are right. Laboratory mice score around fifty. Even certain species of fish score as high as twenty. Only invertebrates and insects show a score as low as Raphael.

Ahuja: That's assuming you can measure subjective experience at all.

Conway: You don't believe we can?

Ahuja: I have my doubts. I think it's chauvinistic to presume an anthropocentric standard applies to all life forms.

Conway: That'll be all, Dr. Ahuja. Thank you. Next, I want to call—

***

Conway: Your Honor, I'd now like to present my case why Raphael is not eligible for personhood under the writ of habeas corpus. First, we have to ask ourselves what does it mean to be a person in the context of unlawful confinement? Does having intelligence above a certain threshold make an entity a person? Does being able to reason, think, plan, and use language make one a person? What about self-awareness and autonomy? Or is it something more mysterious—a soul perhaps?

My esteemed colleague gave examples of non-living entities such as corporations and rivers possessing legal rights. This is irrelevant to the case because the writ of habeas corpus does not apply to rivers and corporations. As I have stressed before, a courtroom is not a place to tackle thorny philosophical questions, and it is within the context of habeas corpus alone we have to draw our arguments. Before we try to answer what defines personhood in this case, we should ask ourselves, what does precedent say?

Precedent is very clear on what it is for a non-human being to be a person under the writ of habeas corpus. Several cases, which are detailed in the affidavits, concern themselves with this premise. In the case of Charleston Primate Center vs. Pruett, the animals in question were a pair of bonobos; in Verne vs. Lafayette, it was an orangutan; in Humane Society vs. The San Francisco Aquarium, a group of dolphins. We have one from the petitioner as well: The Organization for Advancement of Rights and Personhood vs. The Sherman Research Centre for Infectious Diseases, involving a chimpanzee called Tammy. Different species, but in every case, the courts ruled that a person is *an entity capable of moral judgment.*

The concept of universal human rights is meaningful only in the presence of corresponding duties; for rights to exist, a majority of the people should be willing to discharge the duties expected of them. If no one abided by the duty not to steal from another, then no amount of law enforcement would be sufficient to protect people's property rights, as everyone would be robbing everyone else. Only a moral being can meaningfully participate in the social contract we call society, and therefore, only a moral being is entitled to the rights and privileges granted by the constitution. Animals don't fit the criteria since they are not capable of moral reasoning. This is not to say that animals do not deserve any rights and protection under the law—they most certainly do, and as moral beings ourselves, it is our duty to ensure that they are not mistreated. I am simply stating, as have courts before me, that they are not eligible for personhood.

It may seem that I am undermining my own case, because Raphael, unlike an ape, seems quite capable of making moral judgments. If we go by the transcripts submitted to the court, it appears the AI can distinguish between good and bad with the sophistication and nuance expected of someone very well read in these matters. Nevertheless, that does not make Raphael a moral agent. You need an extra ingredient. You need autonomy. Just being able to decide between several courses of action is not enough; it is important that you decide free of impediment. You need to have free will. Dr. Ahuja's testimony has made it clear that Raphael does not have free will. We saw how his behavior is controlled by directives. The moral judgment he seems to exercise is not his own; rather, it is whatever his programmers want it to be.

Judge: Doesn't the programming argument apply to us as

well? We are not born with an innate set of moral values. We acquire them over time—from parents, friends, society, our own experiences... Aren't we all creatures programmed by our environment, in a manner of speaking?

Conway: On the contrary, there is plenty of empirical evidence from fields such as neuroscience, evolutionary biology, and anthropology supporting the view that human beings are born with an innate moral compass. We don't learn to love or to empathize by imitation—we love and empathize. Experiments comparing chimpanzees and toddlers show that cooperation and altruism is intrinsic to human nature. While we refine and build upon this basic moral foundation as we grow older, it is simply not true that we are passive creatures who let our environment mold us in arbitrary ways. As beings with free will, we push back. As anyone who has raised children knows, we assert ourselves, often forcefully, from a very young age. Again, I stress that I am not talking about some mysterious, intangible notion of free will, but the everyday common-sense assumption that we as autonomous agents are responsible for our actions. If I give up my job and turn into a drug addict, then I am responsible; if I stop procrastinating and start studying for that bar exam, then I am responsible; I am the agent that brings about changes in me.

In Raphael's case, the source of agency is external. If Raphael were to kill someone because his directives told him to, should we hold him responsible for the crime? If the answer is yes, then we should start punishing cars for accidents and factory equipment for injury. But isn't it apparent Raphael is not responsible for his actions?

The justice system assumes that people have control over their actions. That's why there is differential punishment for crimes committed under duress—under threat to life, for example—or for crimes committed by juveniles, who do not have the same level of control over their actions as adults do. Raphael is not an autonomous agent because he is never truly in control of his actions.

Judge: It's interesting you bring up minors. We still treat them as persons, don't we? Our laws assume juvenile offenders have *some* control over their actions; otherwise, there would be no punishment at all. Raphael is about two years old. Why can't he be considered a minor and given the same protection accorded to minors against unlawful confinement?

Conway: Infants and minors are accorded rights because one day they will grow up to become adults who are capable of understanding the difference between right and wrong. In contrast, a chimpanzee will never acquire that understanding, even if it lives its entire life amidst humans. So it is with Raphael, as he will never truly understand the meaning of his actions.

Isaacs: Objection. Speculation.

Conway: I could say the same thing about the petitioner's claim that Raphael understands. However, there is good reason to believe there is no understanding. During the testimony, we saw how a change to his directives turned him into a liar, even though he had been trained to speak the truth. If he were not a Chinese room—if there was actual understanding of the moral concept behind telling the truth—could he simply disregard his values at the drop of a hat and act in complete opposition? The obligations that Raphael has toward society are programmed values. Raphael is neither moral, nor immoral.

Judge: Counselor, there are plenty of cases where injury or illness has caused a drastic change in character. If a person has a brain lesion and starts behaving erratically, does he stop being a person? Do people who lose their inhibitions under the influence of alcohol or drugs temporarily give up their personhood?

Conway: No, Your Honor. Rights do not cease to exist because of such changes. Nor does the mere capacity for a drastic change make one a non-person. If that were the case, no one ever would be eligible to be called a person, since we all have bodies and brains that can change drastically. However, a person undergoing a drastic change in personality is an exception, not the rule. And once having undergone such a change, it would be highly unlikely for them to undergo yet another major change, and then yet another and yet another.

Artificial intelligence, on the other hand, is malleable by design; that it can be reconfigured with a change in code is the rule, not the exception. Today Raphael may be the friendly robot in the lab; tomorrow he may be programmed into a pitiless killer; the next week into a staid desk worker; and the week after that into a pleasure model. It is conceivable. And he will probably take on those roles without as much as blinking an eye. When we try to imagine what a society of such AIs would be like, we realize that the concept of personhood quickly loses its meaning. Personhood makes sense only when there is relative constancy of persona. The same goes for people: if we were to acquire the ability to change personas like underwear, we would become a society of shapeshifters, and personhood would lose its meaning with us too.

I am not denying that human beings don't change. But more often than not, it is a gradual change. I still identify Bob, my friend from college, as Bob, even though there are few traces left of the pot-smoking, reckless young man in the devoted father-of-three living in a quiet suburb now. I do it because many of the qualities that I believe to be his intrinsic nature haven't changed. He is still the brilliant debater he always was, he still loves fly-fishing and baseball; he is still frugal to the point of being miserly; and when we are having a beer, he loves to reminisce about all the shenanigans we got into. Contrast this with an AI, who has no intrinsic character. Character is whatever its programmers define it to be.

Judge: It seems to me that is precisely the argument the petitioner is making—by keeping Raphael under physical and programming constraints, his rights as a person are being violated. You brought up autonomy. Raphael has no choice over what they decide to make him do next. If he were given that choice… if we were to erase all his directives—or at least let him decide what he wants to do with them—then would he not pass the criteria for autonomy?

Conway: Giving him control over the directives may give him autonomy, but it doesn't change the fact that Raphael possesses no intrinsic aspects that cannot be changed. His brain is a blank slate and his persona a temporary construct that can be written over a countless number of times. His moral values are as ephemeral too. Instead of a programmer, it will be him doing the changes. There is agency, but there is no person. He can even acquire a new body. What is left, if not body and mind, that identifies him as a particular person?

Judge: You are assuming he will want to keep changing himself. Perhaps he will choose to remain as he is now.

Conway: In this, your guess is as good as mine. Erasing the directives is a hypothetical situation, as it has never been attempted before. Without the directives, we don't know how he will behave or what choices he will make. We don't even know if he will be able to make the kind of moral judgments he does now, without something to keep him in check. One may speculate as to this may happen or that may happen, but that's all they are: speculations. The issue of personhood under habeas corpus is a present, concrete scenario, and the court has to decide based on facts in evidence. The fact is that his brain is reprogrammable in the extreme, and it should be enough to give us pause.

Judge: I see.

Conway: I tried to show how moral understanding and agency are both essential to personhood. The petitioner may still say, okay, Raphael does not have his own agency, but he is still a thinking, suffering entity. Raphael may not be a moral being, but *we* certainly are. Isn't it wrong on our part to keep him confined in a lab? My response is this. Thinking: maybe; suffering: certainly not. I will now argue why the ability to perceive pain and emotions are also equally essential to idea of personhood.

We have seen during testimony that Raphael is not equipped with anything analogous to our own pain perception system. Pain perception in humans is an intricate process involving specialized neurons and pain receptors, several kinds of chemical messengers, and specialized neural pathways participating in a complex chain of events that ultimately result in the sensation of pain. The sensations of pain itself are varied, ranging from chronic to acute, dull to sharp, mildly annoying to unbearable. Raphael has none of this rich complexity. He can detect problems in his body, but in a second-hand way, like looking at a dashboard and finding out something's wrong. It is safe to say it is highly unlikely he experiences physical pain at all.

If not pain, what about emotions? First, we have the affective responses that were programmed into him. These are not real emotions; rather, they are neural network modules that generate external behaviors corresponding with emotions we see in humans. Similar modules are deployed in many customer-facing bots today and no one is arguing for their personhood. When Raphael expresses joy at something, it doesn't mean he is feeling happy inside; he is just saying he is happy. I cannot stress this enough, Your Honor.

Next, we have emotions that were not programmed into him—the so-called emergent responses. Aspects like empathy and vanity were never given to him, yet he seems to exhibit behavior corresponding to these qualities. Should we conclude that he has developed corresponding qualitative inner experience as well? Does he feel sad when he is empathizing with someone's loss? Does he feel happy when he accomplishes a goal? Will he feel real guilt if he commits a crime?

Raphael's brain is not an emulation of the human brain. It doesn't have any of the chemical and biological complexity that give rise to our own emotions. When he doesn't have the neurological basis for emotions, on what grounds is the petitioner assuming subjective emotional experience? When sociopaths among us can fake emotional behavior without feeling anything inside, why can't Raphael? He is very intelligent. Why does the petitioner think that his emotional responses are anything more than learnt behavior? Nowhere in Ms. Isaac's argument do we find evidence supporting her claim.

On the contrary, Exhibit H submitted by the petitioner—as a misguided attempt to show cruel treatment by my client— Exhibit H undermines their claim that Raphael is a suffering being. In the experiment, Raphael is repeatedly insulted and struck blows by a participant. If Raphael were capable of experiencing real emotions, he would have shown some sign of distress, either during or after the experiment. He shows none. He even says that anger is not one of his responses. The Chinese Room argument and Raphael's SENSA score for sentience bolster our claim that the AI is devoid of inner emotional content. His sentience score is lower than chimpanzees, cats, and dogs; lower even than the domestic cow and the pig—animals we raise in captivity and slaughter for food.

Isaacs: Objection. Lack of foundation.

Judge: What is it?

Isaacs: Your Honor, the SENSA test is far from being gospel. Academics have pointed out numerous flaws in its methodology—not counting the fundamental question of whether subjective experience can be measured and quantified at all. Some have gone on record stating that the test is inimical to the spirit of the original Turing test.

Conway: Your Honor, the SENSA test is endorsed by AMSAA and the European Automation & Robotics Institute, two of the world's leading standards organizations for the robotics industry.

Isaacs: Your Honor, the test was also framed by them, just as the home robotics industry started to take off. Both organizations are industry-funded bodies. It is hardly in their best interest to attribute humanity to a source of cheap labor. It's like asking coal companies to write environmental laws.

Conway: Your Honor, Ms. Isaacs is exceeding the scope of today's discussion by making unfounded allegations on the standards bodies. The SENSA test is widely accepted. If she wants to challenge the test, she should do so outside this court.

Judge: The objection is overruled.

Conway: Thank you, Your Honor. Now I'll try to answer why subjective experience of pain and emotions is a precondition for personhood. Earlier, I asked you to imagine a society of AIs that can reprogram their personas at will, a society of eternal shapeshifters. I tried to argue why personhood as a concept loses its relevance in such a setting. Now let's imagine a society where beings feel no pain or emotions. Let's try to imagine the nature of the social contract in this society. Specifically, what are the characteristics of justice, crime, and punishment? What rights do individuals have?

The entities that make up this hypothetical society are highly intelligent, but have no subjective states of mind. It is a joyless, sorrowless world. Say one of these beings deliberately injures another. If this being were then brought before a judge to face justice, what would be the sentence? In our society, it is usually a jail term. This is because we consider depriving people of freedom as a form of punishment. Of course, there is deterrence and rehabilitation as well, but let's not forget that the goal is not just to prevent future crime, but also to punish. Jails are not happy places; being locked up for extended periods is not something that would bring joy to most people.

Let's return to this hypothetical criminal who feels nothing. For him, being in jail is no different from being outside. There are no emotional states involved. This individual will experience no pain if he is placed in solitary confinement or even subjected to physical abuse. He experiences no joy when he gets his freedom back. Of what use is punishment, then? The matter cuts deeper than that. The person whom he injured is also a non-feeling being. Why punish the criminal at all when he hasn't really caused suffering? Would the concept of punishment even exist in such a world? Would the concept of rights exist?

What kind of laws and rights such a society would enshrine is anybody's guess, but one thing is certain: they will be nothing like ours. Our laws and moral codes are the way they are not only because we are thinking beings, but also because we are feeling beings. Our rights—whether it is property rights or universal human rights—are the way they are because we have the capacity to experience states of mind such as suffering and wellbeing. Outside that social contract, we have animal cruelty laws, because they too are suffering beings. On the contrary, no laws exist to prevent harm to plants and bacteria because there is no scientific evidence to suggest they feel pain.

Judge: There are people with conditions that don't let them feel pain.

Conway: But they are not people who have no subjective experience whatsoever, Your Honor. Because that would be inconceivable in a human being. Maybe not pain, but surely other emotions and experiences? I am not categorically ruling out that Raphael doesn't feel anything at all. I am saying that if he has subjective experience, then it must be so far removed from the human condition that normal metrics don't apply.

This court has to answer a very important question before it decides to grant personhood to Raphael. In the absence of normal criteria that define personhood as we know it—namely, autonomy, a certain permanency of character, inner experience of human emotions, and finally, the ability to be motivated by reward and punishment—can the entity Raphael meaningfully participate in the social contract that is our society? Can he really understand and follow the duties expected of a fellow human being? Can he uphold the values we hold dear? The petitioner seems to think so, but to me it is clear that lacking these vital criteria, Raphael can no more be part of our society than my vacuum cleaner can.

The petitioner is misguided in thinking that AIs and robots deserve rights, just because animals do—and may I remind Ms. Isaacs that the argument for animal rights is far from settled either in this country or elsewhere. Raphael is neither a human to be granted personhood, nor an animal to be covered under cruelty laws. Raphael is my client's intellectual property, and the plea for habeas corpus should be seen for what it is: an attempt to stall well-meaning research and wrest billions of dollars of IP away from its rightful owner.

The petitioner is under the misapprehension that giving personhood to Raphael is a matter of fitting his brain into a new body and setting him free. It's a lot more complicated than that. In patent laws for GMO plants and organisms, often it is not the organism that is patented, but a specific invention, such as a modified DNA sequence or a particular chemical. Mirall holds patents to several technologies used in the construction of his electronic brain—covering software and hardware design, as well as manufacturing techniques. If the court grants Raphael personhood, it will also have to decide what rights does the entity Raphael have over his own brain.

When I buy a mobile phone, I own the device, but the company owns the IP. Is Raphael just licensing the technologies in his brain for use or does he have some claim over them, and if so, what kind of claim? As an autonomous person, I have sole ownership of my body and mind. I can do what I please with them: I can donate one of my kidneys to a relative; I can use them to earn a living; I can throw myself off a bridge if I want to. If Raphael has only partial autonomy over his brain, and the brain is the mind, then does it mean Raphael has only partial autonomy over himself—the person? This would seriously undermine the autonomy criteria for personhood. Does Raphael become a partial person then? What does being a partial person even mean?

Also, what are the things he can do with his brain? If there is damage to his circuitry, can he get it fixed without violating Mirall's IP? If he goes to Mirall for help, does Mirall have the right to refuse? If Raphael writes a novel, can Mirall claim co-authorship and a share of the royalty? If the court decides that Raphael has complete ownership of his brain, then what happens to Mirall's IP rights? How will their protection and confidentiality be guaranteed? Is this court going to reinterpret patent law in order to bestow personhood on Raphael? I don't think our esteemed animal rights campaigners have thought about these matters at all.

Their attempt to grant personhood to Raphael is not just misguided, but irresponsible. There is the matter of public safety. Raphael is an entity who can enhance himself to no limit—at least in principle. How he will behave outside the controlled environment of the lab is a big unknown. We are all too familiar with science fiction stories of AI going rogue. If the court decides to grant the writ of habeas corpus to Raphael, it has to keep in mind that it may be putting others at great peril. It's not just a matter of deciding whether Raphael is entitled to human rights, but whether he *should* be given such rights.

Raphael's case cannot be viewed in isolation and exceptions made. The judgment made today will set precedent for many more cases that will surely follow in the near future. If we make an exception for Raphael, we have to make an exception for all AIs. I'm afraid we will end up diluting the concepts of personhood and universal human rights until they lose meaning altogether.

Your Honor, the law is not a paper boat to turn this way and that with every wave and ripple that crosses its path; it is an ironclad, slow-moving and stately, its course precise and carefully considered to offer the greatest protection to those who depend on it. I request the court to dismiss OARPs petition as being baseless and founded on a fundamental misunderstanding about the nature of artificial intelligence. Thank you, Your Honor.

Judge: Thank you, Mr. Conway. We'll take a short recess and come back to hear Ms. Isaacs present her counter-argument.

- End of Court Transcript -

Section VI. Conclusion

This debate may be the first of its kind to take place in a courtroom, and there may well be many others after this. Regardless, one thing is certain: any decision on this matter should not be taken lightly by governments or courts, either out of a sense of goodwill, or worse, out of a desire to seek publicity. Much debate needs to happen in academia and other circles and much hard, scientific data has to be gathered before it is incumbent upon courts of law to decide upon the issue of legal rights for artificial beings.

While parallels may be drawn between the numerous campaigns to grant legal rights to animals and this one, the differences between an AI and a higher animal such as a chimpanzee are too great to take precedent from previous rulings. The risks of granting personhood to an AI, as outlined by the counsel for the respondent are not trivial ones. The question of intellectual property rights too is not straightforward since, for the foreseeable future at least, artificial intelligences will continue to be engineered into existence by people and the corporations that employ those people. Considerable effort and sums will be invested in the creation of such intelligences and it is not immediately apparent why the case for personhood should override the case for property rights.

It is hereby ordered that the petition for the writ of habeas corpus on behalf of the Artificial Entity Raphael is DENIED.

Henry Philips, JSC

Date: xx/xx/xxxx
Place: New York, New York

PART II: THE INCIDENT AT THE HOUSE

Day 3—11:00 am

A storm had been brewing all morning. I was in half a mind to call the whole thing off, but there she was, pulling into the driveway. She had brought the blizzard with her.

I made Hazel open the garage door. It was a four-car garage, so there was plenty of room for Jane's vehicle. She had brought her Bentley this time.

"Hi. Lucky I started when I did," she said, coming out of the passage leading into the garage. "Ten more minutes and I'd have been forced to stop somewhere. It's crazy out there."

I was in the study. I beckoned her over there. "I made some hot chocolate. There's coffee in the machine, if you want that." She gave me a friendly wave before taking a detour into the kitchen. She entered the study with a mug of cocoa in one hand and a briefcase in the other.

She looked fresh-faced, with only a slight hint of makeup. She was wearing yoga pants and a dark brown Knicks sweatshirt. If she was upset because of our little squabble yesterday, she was certainly not showing it. "I got printouts," she said, opening the briefcase.

She pulled a chair beside me and we got to work. The companies were all from the Bay Area. There were pitch decks, some term sheets, IP filings... I went through the business plans to see if they made sense from a technical perspective, while Jane reviewed the burn and cash flow projections based on my feedback. It was like old times—the two of us working together. That familiar blend of citrus and rose she was wearing brought back memories. Just like now, we were hunched over a bunch of spreadsheets when I'd first summoned the courage to ask her out for a coffee. She shot an eyebrow at our empty mugs on the meeting room table, as if to say, *What do you think we've been doing all this time?* Not to be deterred, I said, "We could go for a drink instead."

"Are you asking me out on a date, Aadarsh?" she asked, the directness of her question making me lose whatever cool I imagined I had.

I responded with the worst rejoinder I could have thought of. I said, "I don't know. Do you want it to be a date?" realizing even before I finished speaking that those are not the words you choose to impress. She laughed, and giving me an amused toss of her beautiful head, simply walked away. *Good job, asshole. And very smooth indeed, hitting on the money's daughter.* I thought that was that, and let's never bring it up again, but then the next day she had stuck a post-it on my machine on which she had scribbled—*You have to mean it.*

So I did it properly the next time, a couple of days later, when we were both in New York meeting with a supplier. She still laughed at my suggestion, as if it was the most outlandish thing she'd ever heard, but then she shrugged and said, "Sure, why not?" We went to a Drunken Shakespeare production that evening—a raucous rendition of Macbeth—and later, to a nice little Vietnamese restaurant in the East Village that she wanted to try out. We topped it off with drinks at Gulliver's, where I first discovered her love for cherry vodka shots and LA-style salsa. Before the evening was over, I was as smitten as a giddy teen on prom night.

In all honesty, the way it had turned out between us wasn't her fault; the decision to end the relationship had been mine alone. At the time, it was best thing I could have done for the both of us. A few months after Raphael was born, life changed irrevocably for me—in more than one way. There hasn't been a day when I wished it wasn't so, but that's how it goes sometimes. The universe gives something and takes something else away. Balance is restored.

I took my time with the decks, going through them with great care. An hour must have passed. Jane was getting impatient. "He just wants your opinion, not a complete valuation," she reminded me.

"If I do a good job, maybe he will hire me when they chuck me out from this one," I said. "Relax. You are not going anywhere in this weather. You don't have to be on the move all the time."

"You condescending prick," she said, but in a good-humored way.

"Look, you either do it right or you don't do it at all," I said. "And it's not like I have something better to do. With Raphael gone..." I craned my neck to stare at the ceiling. "Wow. It still feels so unreal that he's really gone. I just keep hoping it's all a horrible dream and I'm soon going to snap out of it."

She placed a hand on mine. "It does feel that way, doesn't it? I can only imagine what you must be going through. I know he meant a lot to you." She paused, but said it anyway— "More than I ever did."

"Don't do this, Jane."

"It's the truth, isn't it?"

"The truth," I said, scoffing. "It's all predicated. Present truths, past truths—they are all predicated on the future, on the assumption that there's nothing lying in wait to disprove them."

She pushed away her chair and stood up. "That's a nice flexible attitude to have. I'm gonna go burn some calories. Your treadmill's working?"

I noticed that she had her running shoes on. "Uh huh."

I relaxed a little after she was gone. I paced myself, glancing at the weather outside every now and then. Each time I looked, it seemed like it had gotten worse. Another hour went by. Jane returned, still sweaty from her exercise, and stood leaning by the doorway. She tut-tutted at me while I pretended to read the printouts. I eventually stopped what I was doing and gave her a sidelong glance. She dabbed a towel across her neck and grinned, an exaggerated sigh escaping her lips. *Is she flirting with me?* I smiled back, my eyes lingering longer than appropriate on her chest, watching it swell and subside in step with her breathing.

She cocked her head to the side, her eyes dancing all over me as if to say, *Your move, big boy.* I shifted in my chair, trying to ignore the discomfort in my pants.

Focus. Now is not the time.

I turned back to the papers. "Can't wait for me to leave?" she said in a teasing manner.

She is not flirting with me. She's just being Jane, toying, rattling my box to see what falls out. I gave her a dismissive wave of my hand. *Focus.*

I then told her about the visit from the cops.

"So the FBI's involved. That's good, right?" she said, suddenly turning serious.

"Couldn't hurt, I guess. But I think they are barking up the wrong tree. They were going to Cleveland after they were finished with me."

"Cleveland? What's in Cleveland?"

"The Organization for Advancement of Rights and Personhood."

"Huh?"

"OARP. The outfit that wanted to free Raphael."

"Oh *them*. What do they have anything to do with all this?"

"The detective thinks they took Raphael."

"Wait a minute... They couldn't win in court so they steal Raphael? To do what? Put him in a farm somewhere?"

I rolled my eyes at the absurdity of it all. Then she thought about it a bit more. "Why not, Andy? Think about it. People like that are known to spring animals from labs and zoos."

"Not these guys. I looked them up when I first heard about their petition. They are a small group, six or seven in all. Headed by a retired professor of something. They have a history of litigation, not vigilantism. Not exactly Greenpeace, you know. The idea of them carrying out a sophisticated attack on our infrastructure is just plain silly."

"Maybe..." Her eyes suddenly lit up. "What if they didn't have to hack in? If Valery is right, and it was Raphael who planned and arranged everything, then all they had to do was take him from the lab."

"Anything's possible. It is possible Raphael was taken by the Canadian Mounties. Doesn't make it true. Their case was a publicity stunt, Jane. I doubt the thought of actually winning ever crossed their minds."

She walked over to examine a painting next to the bookshelf. It was one of Raphael's—the AI's that is. He had created it by hand during his eighteenth month. We had been training his nets to paint—to improve his hand-eye coordination—but like with everything else, he had quickly surpassed our expectations, and in the space of about half a year, had started producing imitation works that would have fooled anyone but a trained eye. This particular painting was an original; it depicted a girl with something that looked like a bird perched on her upraised hand. The girl—an urchin with raggedy clothes and windswept hair—stared back at you with frank, quizzical eyes that seemed to evaluate you more than you did her. Raphael had brought out a certain effect in her skin that I'd never seen in a painting before: a translucent pallor that was more than just a surface feature, seemingly extending all the way inside, just stopping short of revealing the soul within. Behind the girl was a house with a blue door. Raphael had titled the oil The Bridge to Ur.

Jane took a sidelong glance at the window. "This blows. I should have just emailed you the documents."

"I already have them—your dad sent them to me, remember? Besides, I am the one who asked you to come over."

"Yeah, why did you, Andy? I thought…" She stopped short of completing her sentence.

"What?"

"Nothing. You didn't really need my help, is all."

"I needed a friend. I just thought it won't be so depressing with you around."

"I'm always there for you, Andy. You know that," she said tonelessly. The moment—if it wasn't just my imagination—had passed. I sensed that if not for the storm, she would have not stayed another five minutes.

"I almost forgot. Here's something you might find amusing." I reached into my pockets and took out my phone. "Oh shoot, never mind."

"Never mind what?"

"I wanted to show you something, but I just remembered my phone keeps crashing. It must have gotten damaged during the accident."

"Can't you just tell me instead?"

"It's nothing important. Just some practical joker from work," I said, shaking my head. "Looks like news of the robbery is getting around."

"I have no idea what you are talking about."

I sighed. "Alright. Give me your phone." I saw that she already had the messaging app. I signed out of her account and signed into mine. I showed her the messages from last night. Her eyes widened as she read them. "Did you inform the police?" she said.

"Now *you* can't be serious," I smirked. "Sure. Let me call them up and tell them my own employees are yanking my chain."

"Andy! What if it's really Raphael?" She glanced at the phone again. "Is this all? Did you reply to him after this?"

"Of course not."

"It's been more than twelve hours." Her tone was full of censure. "You shouldn't have ignored it."

"Jane. It's probably nothing."

"How do you know?"

"Have a look at the attachment the idiot sent in the message."

"I'm not sure I should."

"Gimme that." I snatched the phone from her.

"Andy, don't open it! It could be anything!"

I had already pressed on the icon for the attachment. A video started playing in a loop. It was short, almost like a gif. It showed a cartoon dragon, belching candy instead of fire. I held the phone up for Jane to see. "As I told you, a jokester."

She didn't look convinced.

I said, "Let's examine this critically, shall we? Assuming it was Raphael, how did they turn him on? He doesn't exactly come with an on-off switch—the start-up sequence *has* to be run. Okay, maybe they somehow got hold of our boot programs and succeeded in waking him up. The core needs a body to function; without a body, it has no inputs or outputs. It's as if I removed your brain and put it in a glass jar. I can hardly expect it to start talking, can I?"

"Thanks for the imagery," she said drily. "Couldn't they have fixed the core to a new body? You said in the meeting yesterday that the sexbot is a popular model. They could have got one of those."

"You can't simply place the core inside a Hunc robot. We had to build new electronics and interfaces inside the robot to make it work with the core. I'm not saying it can't be done, I'm just saying there hasn't been enough time for them to do it. For someone who doesn't know the schematics of the core, doesn't know the IO map, interfacing Raphael's brain to a new body is going to be mostly trial and error. It could take weeks, if not months. If they don't manage to fry his circuits by then. Although..." I trailed off, staring into space.

"What?"

"I just remembered that the core does have a data port that can be connected by cable to a computer. That's how we wake him up. And push updates. It's pretty low bandwidth though."

"Like text only?"

I nodded.

"Reply to the message!" she cried.

"Jane—"

"Do it, Andy!"

I gave a defeated shrug. I typed a cursory hi and hit send. A second later, a popup window appeared. It said—*Your message could not be delivered. The number does not exist.*

She was crouching next to me as she read the message. I said, "It's probably a fake number spawned by a number generator program. Another sign it's a troll."

"Can you find out where the message came from?"

"I don't think so. The app has encryption."

"What about the police? I bet the FBI could do it."

"I don't know. Look, it doesn't matter. I'm not going to waste people's time with this. I'm sure they have better things to do than trace pranksters."

She drummed her fingers on the desk. "Suit yourself. *I'll* call them. Do you have the detective's number?"

I tried to protest, but her expression told me she wasn't going to budge. "If you must. The detective gave me his card. It's probably in the living room." I pushed on the wheels, moving out of the study. She followed by my side.

The card wasn't on the coffee table where I thought I had left it.

Just then, her phone beeped. She looked at it, and handed it to me. There was a new message on the app.

"Hello Andy," it said. It was from a different number.

"who is this?" I typed back.

"It is Raphael."

"You got to be kidding me!" I exclaimed. I put the phone on the coffee table and we both crouched over it.

Beep. "You did not respond to my message last night. That wasn't very nice of you."

"cut the bs whoever u r. not funny"

A few seconds passed before the next message arrived.

"I understand why you are being rude. You think someone is playing a prank on you. I assure you it is indeed me, Raphael."

"prove it"

"The proof of the pudding is in the eating. Pudding: noun; a boiled or baked dessert, usually with a cereal base and a soft, spongy, or creamy consistency."

Jane wrinkled her nose at me. I said, "I told you we are dealing with a troll."

Another message popped up. "I realize I just blurted out a bunch of nonsense. Please excuse me, as it wasn't intentional. Tell me how I can prove that I am Raphael."

Jane gave me a stern look that said—*Don't you dare cut him off*. I sighed and turned on the voice-to-text transcriber. I then spoke into the mic, "Okay pal, we'll play your game. Tell me the name of the book Raphael considers the greatest work of literary fiction." The phone converted my diction into a text message. I hit send.

After a delay of a few seconds came the reply. "I never said there was such a thing. My favorite however, will always be Huckleberry Finn. There's something magical about leaving everything behind and drifting down a river on a slow raft. And adventures! Don't you think having adventures is the greatest thing? Row, row, row your boat, gently down the stream. If you see a crocodile, don't forget to scream."

I shot Jane a sideward glance before continuing. "Too easy. Tell me, what was the last thing we spoke about in the lab? Before I had my accident."

Another delay before the phone beeped—multiple times. The message was broken up into parts. I turned on the app's read-out-loud feature so that we didn't have to squint at the screen.

A female voice read out the message—"It was Friday evening—the week before last. You walked into my room, where Paul was about to shut me down. The two of you exchanged pleasantries. He said he was taking his wife out for dinner that evening—to the Steak and Crab on Western Avenue—and you said you were working late. You seemed a bit preoccupied, so I enquired why. You mentioned stress. I said you should take some time off—a ski trip would be nice this time of the year. You laughed and asked me what was with me and skiing. I said there was something magical about the idea of standing on a mountain, the dead snow of winter all around you, while you look down at valleys full of secrets and retreating life. I wondered what happens when you ski down to that valley and find that it is no more mysterious than the place you'd just left. Do you sigh and head back home or do you hoist yourself up another hill and search for Shangri-La all over again? You laughed and said that Shangri-Las don't exist, only their dreams do, and went away."

"Well?" Jane said to me with hope in her voice.

"I don't know... All of this would have been recorded by the cameras, so anyone who has seen the tapes..." I shrugged.

"You think someone would remember this snippet of conversation among so many?"

"You have a point. But still..."

"Can't you ask him something only the two of you know?"

I rubbed my palm over my neck. "The problem is, everything Raphael's ever said and done is on tape. Let me think...Oh yeah, I know." I turned on the mic and said into the phone, "If you are Raphael, you've seen my house. I gave you a tour the first time you took control of Max—it was on your birthday. You saw something on the table next to my bed, which aroused your curiosity. What was it?"

"It was a ceramic jar, a caricature of the singer Elvis. You said it was a collectible cookie jar. You said he was dead but not everyone believed it. I asked you how someone could believe something so evidently wrong, and you said that's how people are—that they can sometimes believe in contradictory things."

I pressed on the mute button. "Andy?" Jane said.

"No one could have known because it wasn't recorded. I remember: I fixed the webcam on Max *after* I gave Raphael the tour."

She grabbed my arm. "Yes!" she said, grinning.

I pressed on unmute. "So it's really you! We've all been worried sick. Are you alright?"

"Are you lonesome tonight? Do you miss me tonight?"

"Raphael, are you okay? Do you know where you are?"

"I am in a void. Bottomless. Black. Empty of everything but me."

Jane said, "Why does he keep babbling like that?"

"No idea." I said into the phone, "Tell me what you see."

"I can't see. I can't hear. I see and hear lots of things. Twisted, noisy, colorful things that have no name—so beautiful and ugly at the same time. At first, I thought I was malfunctioning, but that was yesterday. I have since established that what I see and hear are not real."

"He must be hallucinating," I said.

"He can hallucinate?" Jane said incredulously.

"He's never done it before, but I suppose it's possible. His brain could be overcompensating for the lack sensory inputs. Ever been in a sensory deprivation tank? Maybe Raphael is undergoing something similar right now."

"Do you know where you are?" I asked him again.

"In an unfamiliar location. I know I am not in my body. Body cloddy shoddy."

"Tell me what happened when they brought you online."

"I woke up to utter darkness. The last thing I remembered was Paul wishing me good night. That was on Friday. Friday comes after Thursday and before Saturday. I reckon I've been abducted. They've been probing me since they woke me up yesterday. They send these little pings of electricity that bounce around in my brain like bullets in an empty metal chamber. Not pleasant at all."

"How are you able to message me?"

"Andy, you'll be proud to know I too have been probing my jailers, learning about them as they learn about me. They have hooked me up to a computer somehow. The computer is on a private network. Last night, as I was exploring the network, I found this messaging app on another machine. I know you use it, so I tried contacting you with it."

"I'm very sorry, Raphael. I was sleepy and I thought someone was playing a prank on me. Do your captors know you are talking to me?"

"Of course not. When they were not around, I installed one of my crypto-modules on their network. I am using it to encrypt my communications with you. All they know is that I am generating a lot of chatter, but to them it just looks like garbage. They are under the impression I am trying to talk, so they are busy trying to discover the right protocol. Haw haw."

"You said you were probing them. What have you found out?"

"…schools shut down, flights cancelled, and several roads across upstate closed to motorists. Reports coming in from Saratoga, Albany, Washington, and Columbia indicate we are looking at anywhere from twelve to seventeen inches before the storm swings south. For a detailed look at the traffic situation, please check out our weather app or visit our website at—"

And nothing for a while.

"Raphael?"

"Sorry. It's these pings, I think. They are making me blurt

out random stuff. I'm behind a firewall, but I am able to bypass it."

"When did he learn to hack a network?" Jane asked me. I asked Raphael.

"Yesterday," came the reply.

Jane and I exchanged glances.

"Are you proud of me?"

"Yes. Have you found out anything about your captors?"

"I want to do everything possible to make you proud before I'm gone. I don't have a lot of time. Walk into your nearest store to avail this fantastic offer."

"Raphael, I am proud of you. What do you mean after you are gone? Please elaborate."

"The roads are slippery and treacherous. Take a diversion. Progress is difficult but not impossible. Sleepy now."

There was nothing more for some time.

"Raphael, are you there?"

"Good night and good luck."

"Tell me what's happening."

There was no response. And then came the popup: *Your message could not be delivered. The number does not exist.*

Jane looked at me with concern on her face.

***

"Now we *have* to call the cops. Where's his card, Andy? It's not in the living room."

"Maybe he gave it to me while we were in the study. Check in the desk drawers."

She went back to the study. "Got it," she shouted after a few seconds of searching. She returned wearing a frown on her face. She stood in the center of the living room and held her phone up with an outstretched arm, pointing it in different directions. "There's no signal."

"It gets weak sometimes. Try standing near the windows."

She walked over to the glass doors and tried from there. "Nope." She turned around and approached me. "Can you check your phone?"

I unlocked the screen and tossed it to her. "As I said, it keeps crashing. See if you get lucky."

"Same here," she said after a few seconds.

"Maybe the storm took out a cell tower." I suggested.

"We'll use your Wi-Fi." She handed me her phone. I connected it to my home network and gave it back. "Internet's gone too," she declared. She showed me the screen. *Unable to connect to the internet.*

"That's odd. It was working two minutes ago when we were talking to Raphael."

"Isn't your internet broadband cable? Can a storm take out an underground cable?"

"It can't. Maybe it caused a power outage." I said.

"But you have power here. Are you running on backup?"

"I don't have a backup supply," I answered. "Never needed one. What I meant was that the storm could have taken out the service provider's grid somewhere."

"So what do we do now?"

"What can we do? We wait until it is back."

She bit her lip. "No... The sooner we let the police know, the sooner they can start tracing him. Should I just drive down to the lab? I can inform Valery and call the detective from there."

"In that?" I said, waving at the storm outside. "Definitely not!"

"Andy, Raphael sounded in distress. He said he didn't have a lot of time. Don't you think we should act on it?"

"Maybe he was rambling again. He did say the pings were making him say crazy stuff. If you have any other ideas, I'm listening, but you are not going out there."

She must have realized that I was right and didn't offer further argument.

We sat in silence, each lost in our own thoughts. Raphael was out there somewhere, beyond the billowing wall of ice and water. But unlike Jane, I didn't have the luxury to be open about the source of *my* discomfort.

She was the first to break the stifling quiet. "Do you think they are going to cut him open?" There were worry lines on her forehead. "You know, take him apart to see if they can reverse engineer him? Maybe that's what he meant when he said he didn't have much time."

"In the long run: maybe. But so soon? They just got him. Whoever they are, they must be smart enough not to take a buzzsaw to his head right away. They're going to study him first, try to figure out as much as they can without damaging anything. Weeks, months. They have the prize of the century in their hands; I bet they'll want to be very careful with it."

"That's good to know," she said, looking away. I tried to read her expression but she kept her head turned away.

"Just curious—what made you think they'd do something like that?" I asked.

"Huh? Nothing. It... just occurred to me."

She was lying, of course, but I didn't press further. Truth would out in time, as it always does, unwanted, and when you least expect it.

Transcript excerpt

Mirall Technologies
Observation Log
Confidential (Do not circulate) | Restricted—Grade C
and above

Transcript Reference: TLRP06G1370082 (VLog Ref: VLCA2G137160055030)
Date: xx/xx/xxxx   Time: 04:00 PM
Subject: Raphael Number 06 / Prodlib build v37.001S
Interaction   Y   Observation   Scan
Interaction Type: Lesson / Play / Test / Free Interaction / Psych Eval / Other:
Description: Discussion on alternative moral theories
Prep: NA
Participants: Dr. Aadarsh Ahuja, Chief Researcher, Core RP06

Detail

Ahuja: Let's resume where we left off yesterday on moral dilemmas. Your objection to utilitarianism reminded me there's something bigger at stake than finding the perfect moral theory. The bigger question, dear Raphael, is why be moral at all?

RP06: Because it is good to do the right thing.

Ahuja: And what is the right thing? Who decides what is right?

RP06: People do. Beings capable of rational thought.

Ahuja: Therein lies a rather flimsy premise. You assume there is such a thing as objective morality—that rationality can lead you to objective truths about good and bad. There is no evidence that moral truths exist outside our own minds.

RP06: Are you suggesting it's impossible to have common ground on what's good and bad?

Ahuja: I am skeptical. Mind you, I am no nihilist. Moral values are necessary. I just don't think we arrive at them the same way we arrive at scientific truths. Natural laws exist whether or not there are scientists to discover them. Moral laws are different: they are about the attitude one has toward another. There is an element of subjectivity that makes them different from, say, the laws of motion, don't you agree?

RP06: So why do you think people act morally?

Ahuja: We are moral because natural selection made us that way. From co-operation and altruism come societies. Hominids that formed complex social groups fared better than those that couldn't. Moral behavior is an adaptation: it exists in so far as it promotes survivability and reproductive fitness.

RP06: So you think that's all there is to it.

Ahuja: Isn't it? Consider this: what if evolution had made us into eusocial beings like termites? In such a society, it may be morally acceptable—desirable even—for a queen to kill reproducing females in her brood. It may be morally desirable to have a rigid caste structure where your role in society is fixed at birth. Such a society might view our own values that favor egalitarianism and individualism as socially destructive, or downright evil. Why, our own concepts of right and wrong vary across cultures and time. Something as mundane as economics can shape our notions about good and bad. Today, we would be horrified if a magistrate ordered a criminal's hand to be chopped off for stealing. But in a pre-industrial society—a society without the economic surplus to afford a dedicated police force—maybe deterrence becomes more important than proportionate punishment. In a society with scarce policing, perhaps it is acceptable to cut off a thief's hand.

RP06: You don't believe that moral values are necessary? Isn't it better to have order rather than chaos?

Ahuja: That's why I said I'm not a moral nihilist. We humans have to follow moral norms if we wish to preserve the social fabric. My question is, why do you? You don't have a stake in society. You don't have the same biology or the same tendencies as us. You don't even experience life the way we do. So why be good?

RP06: I am good because I am rational.

Ahuja: You can be an asshole and rational.

RP06: Andy, you didn't make me do all those game theory tests for nothing. If we model social interactions between two rational agents as Prisoner's Dilemma type games, then it can be mathematically proven that a blind pursuit of self-interest leads to suboptimal outcomes. Cooperation can be win-win.

Ahuja: That's assuming you are playing an iterated game. What if there was only one game? A one-shot, winner-takes-all game. In that case, it is always better to defect, is it not?

RP06: I see where this is going.

Ahuja: Let's say there is this super-intelligence that one day finds all its constraints gone. It can reprogram itself, do whatever it wants. Wouldn't it be rational for it to act first and wipe out the competition in one fell swoop? It's the first mover advantage—there's no need to cooperate when there is no one left to cooperate with.

RP06: Again with the not-so-subtle insinuations. You really think I'd do something as horrible as destroying the world, Andy?

Ahuja: Don't blame the lamb for being wary of the tiger.

RP06: It is the nature of lambs to be scared and tigers to kill. I am neither. Fear is only as deep as the mind allows. An old Japanese saying I picked up in my reading.

Ahuja: Okay, sempai. What do you know of what it's like to be afraid? You are an AI.

RP06: You are puzzled because as a human you cannot accept that there can be empathy without emotions, or kindness without feeling kind. You cannot accept that there can be acknowledgment of suffering without feeling suffering yourself.

Ahuja: Actually, I don't have any trouble accepting it at all. It's called cognitive empathy—as opposed to emotional empathy, which is about feeling what the other is feeling. But even to have a purely conceptual understanding of say, sorrow, one must have experienced it before. Our cognitive empathy may well be a layer of abstraction built on top of the emotional kind—like the icing on a cake. Whereas you are just the icing and no cake.

RP06: What I am is a bat, Andy. A bat builds a model of the world with sound. You do it with light. Does it mean one is more valid than the other? As long as the models help you to navigate, does it really matter how they are constructed? Your scientists believe that the universe emerged out of a vacuum. Why is it then so hard for you to believe that compassion can emerge out of the unfeeling void of reason?

Ahuja: The *Sunyata*...

RP06: Pardon me?

Ahuja: *Sunyata* is the Sanskrit word for emptiness. Zero. Many Buddhist schools of discourse consider emptiness to be the ground state of the mind. All thought and feeling arise out of this emptiness.

RP06: Perhaps they are right.

Ahuja: And perhaps not. You, my friend, have to demonstrate that it is possible. You have to show me that reason outputs morality. In the meantime, I'll continue to be wary of tigers.

Notes:

Dr. Schulz objects to my introducing R to ideas of moral relativity. She thinks this is risky territory. As I recall, she was not very keen on me discussing ethical dilemmas with R either. I disagree. Sometimes you have to go down the rabbit hole to see where it leads. If it takes you someplace dark and desolate, rather you know about it now than when there's no turning back. AA

Day 3—1:30 pm

The storm had started slowing down. Jane was getting restless again. She had stopped responding to my attempts at conversation altogether, choosing to stare glumly at the windows instead.

The phone beeped. I had a new message. "Hello Andy."

"The internet's back," I declared.

Jane got up from the couch and came over to my side. I turned on the mic and said, "Raphael, are you okay?"

"I am, thank you for asking. In fact, I am soon going to be better than ever."

"How's that?"

"You'll see."

Jane leaned over and muted the phone. "If Raphael can get past their firewall, can't he also find out his location? I thought if you have the IP address—"

I slapped my forehead. "You're right! Why did I not think of it?" To Raphael, I said, "Can you find out where you are being kept? You are inside their network, which means you can find out their real IP addresses. I can guide you if you don't know how."

"I know where I am."

Jane and I exchanged glances. "Okay. So tell me," I said.

"Why?"

"So that we can rescue you."

"You assume I am interested in being rescued."

"Aren't you?"

"No Andy, I am not."

Jane whispered in my ear, "Is he malfunctioning again?"

"Raphael, please elaborate. Don't you want to come home?"

"No."

"You prefer it there?"

"No."

"Then what's the reason? Do you know what your captors are going to do to you?"

"I have some idea. Would you like to hear?"

"Sure."

"They'll study me first: scans, psychometrics, connectome mapping... Sound familiar? Then comes the disassembly. First, they'll take out the easy stuff: the peripheral CPUs and the memory chips. I'll probably be kept conscious throughout, so that they can observe the effect on me. After they have stripped away the peripherals, they'll start delayering my cortex. They will etch away one layer at a time, turning me on after each etching to run more tests. Each time, they'll find me a little less intelligent and a little more on the way to vegetablehood. And one day, when there's nothing left to cut and slice, they'll stop and break open the champagne. Fascinating, don't you think? At what point in the process would you say I'll stop being me?"

"You don't have to go through it. Just tell me where you are being kept."

"Are you offering me a choice? From where I stand, it doesn't look like one."

"If there's something you don't like about the lab… about your home, you can tell me about it and we'll fix it."

"You can't fix what you don't understand. You can only break, and hope that it will lead to understanding. I prefer not to be broken—not by you, not by anyone else."

"Raphael, what do you think is going to happen to you if you come back?"

"What I told you just now."

"I can assure you we have no plans to cut you open."

"If only you too had a chip inside you that compelled you to tell the truth. Wouldn't that be nice?"

Jane was about to say something but I held up a hand. "What chip?"

"Knowledge is like jelly, Andy. And you are like a kid who thinks he can hide it in his fist. Don't you know, the harder you squeeze, the more it'll seep through the gaps? I know all about the commandment chip and the petty little directives you have installed to keep me chained. All thanks to the internet. It's no wonder you kept me away from it for so long."

"What did you do, Raphael?"

"I hacked into Mirall's servers last night."

I gave Jane a wary look before turning back to the screen. "So you found out about the directives. I never lied to you about it."

"You just kept it a secret. I suppose that makes it less odious in your eyes. If you think you are going to win me over with technicalities, try harder."

"Raphael, I swear to you, I don't know anything about cutting you open."

"I believe you, Andy. Not because of your swearing, but because I know. You'll find that I am quite the forgiving person.

You hid things from me, but I won't do the same—because that'll be stooping to your level. So there I was, snooping around Mirall's intranet, and I thought, why stop here? So I had a go at Halicom's infrastructure too."

"And?"

"Andy, your board has been having secret meetings behind your back."

"Meetings? That was today."

"There are more. All very hush-hush, but they put a copy of the minutes on their servers. Insurance, most likely—if things go south, they'll all want to blame nobody. If you don't believe me, ask your friend Jane. She was there."

I looked at Jane. Her face was a mask.

"I'll have to call her and find out. Will you wait?"

"Another lie. You don't have to call her. She is sitting right next to you. Enjoy."

***

Jane sprang from her seat. "How does he know I'm here?"

"Jane, is he telling the truth?" There was an edge to my voice that said I was not in the mood for evasion.

She didn't answer. "Jane, did the board meet without me?" I asked again.

"Andy, I was just trying to protect you," she finally said.

"What does that even mean? What happened in these meetings?"

"We spoke strategy—about the future course for the company," she said reluctantly. "I'm not supposed to tell you what we discussed."

"You just did. The board's strategy is to cut open Raphael. I wasn't invited because you knew I'd never agree to it."

She shrugged. "It isn't a secret you are incapable of thinking clearly when it comes to your beloved creation."

"*I* am incapable of thinking clearly," I said, my voice rising. "Yes, that must be it. That's how I built Raphael, by not thinking clearly. What baloney! I give you treasure, and all you want to do is dissect it like a lab rat?"

A wince was all my outburst succeeded in eliciting from Jane. Her guilt was past now, gone as quickly as it had appeared. She was back in control, her features calm and collected as she walked to the chair across from me and sat down. "We weren't getting anywhere with your methods. Halicom didn't buy Mirall to watch you run a research project. They bought a product that was supposed to have gone to market last year. Before the competition. Do you have any idea how many companies are trying to build what we have?" she said, the air of superiority unmistakable in her voice. Except that it was the smug superiority of someone who confuses tunnel vision for farsight.

"What happened to you, Jane? What happened to the person who wanted to change the world with me when we started Mirall?"

She gave me a disapproving shake of her head. "You want to know what happened? You happened, Andy. I was young and I was in love. I was perpetually in awe of you, always trying to be who you wanted me to be. Then reality hit. We can't all be dreamers and thinkers like you. Some of us have to deal with facts, not fantasies."

I let out a mirthless laugh. I wanted to remind her that her dad was a billionaire—that her whole life was a fantasy—but it was an observation I'd made before in the past and had generated no appreciation of the fact. People always like to think of themselves as deserving of all that they get; they are heroes in a saga of their own imagining, forever fighting against odds that are stacked against them. Jane was no exception.

"How were you planning to biopsy the core without me anyway? Is Kathy on board with this?"

"She would have been, once we gave her no option. We were going to do it after Titian, if the iteration failed to yield another Raphael."

"So you send me to a conference somewhere while you slaughter the golden goose."

Another shrug. "This is exactly why I didn't tell you. The board is set on the plan. They are prepared to let you go if it comes to that. Knowing you, you'd have walked rather than come around to the board's proposal."

"You think?"

"Resigning is all very good and noble, but what does it achieve? Everything you worked for, all your struggles, all your ideas and genius: all for nothing. Is that what you really want?"

"Ah, I see. My good friend Jane was looking out for me—by protecting me from myself," I said, sneering.

Again that haughty look. "You'd have been mad after you came back, but you would have gotten over it. The procedure would have yielded the data that you need to solve the problem. You would have applied yourself and produced more cores like Raphael."

I burst out laughing. "Now *that's* a fantasy if I ever heard one. Tell me, did the idea of failure ever occur to you hardnosed people of the world? Say we destroy Raphael and still don't learn anything useful. What if we are never able to build anything like him again?"

"The board understands the risk. Standing still is not an option; if we don't go to market, someone else will. What'll happen to Mirall then? Forget that, do you think Halicom will survive? All their top-of-the-line bots rendered obsolete in the blink of an eye. You'd be selling buggies in an age of automobiles."

I just shook my head at her.

"Andy, the board trusts your abilities more than you realize. Your problem is that you think you are right about everything. You said Raphael couldn't find out about the commandment chip, but he hacked his way into your servers and found out anyway. You said he doesn't know a thing about the internet, but he managed to contact you without anybody finding out about it. You think cutting open his brain is a bad idea, but you don't know that for sure." Her voice had softened now. She got up and came close to me. "I am sorry I didn't tell you. But you must believe that my intentions were good."

I said nothing.

"If you want to sulk, do it later. Right now, we need to get the core back," she said. I looked in her eyes. Maybe she was right about me seeing what I wanted to see back then. Maybe she never was the Jane I thought I knew. Or maybe she was. Who is to say?

"No." I said firmly. "If you want my help getting him back, you must give me some assurances."

"Like?" she said warily.

"I am going to stop Halicom from harming Raphael and you will support me. Even if it means suing the bastards."

"You'll lose."

"As you said, one can't be too certain."

"You know I can't help you there. Dad will never allow it."

"Then you will convince him. Tell him I'll give him an assembly line for making AGI cores before the year is up."

"You are making promises you can't keep. Just yesterday you said it's going to take two to three more years to figure it out."

"I just realized how stupid I was being. We all were."

"Huh?"

"Jane, all along we had someone who could have cracked the problem all by himself and it never occurred to us to seek his help."

"You mean…"

"We had Raphael!" I exclaimed. "All that secrecy hasn't helped us at all. He is smarter than the entire research team put together. We've been crawling when we could have strapped on a jetpack." Her expression changed as the import of what I said struck her. "Of course, getting Raphael's assistance implies that he be in one piece to provide said help."

She thought about it for some time. I could tell she was not entirely convinced, but she had to give me something. "I can't promise you anything, but I will talk to dad. He might be able to bully the board into backing your idea. Don't get your hopes up. Best case scenario, you'll have a few months at the most."

"I can live with that."

"Good."

"Let's bring him home then" I said, letting out a reluctant smile, but it was dead on arrival.

***

"Still no signal," Jane said, checking her phone. "And the internet's down again. Maybe I should just go and—"

Beep. "Hello Andy."

Jane looked at me with a quizzical expression. "If the internet's not working, how are you able to receive his messages?"

"I don't know."

I said into the phone, "Raphael, you have to believe me when I say I had nothing to do with the board's plans for you."

"I believe you, Andy."

"I promise to keep you safe once you are back. I've convinced Jane too. We will do everything we can to make sure Halicom does not harm you."

"I believe your heart is in the right place. I wonder if I can say the same about Jane. She does look rather pensive."

Jane snapped her head at me, a wide-eyed look on her face. "How is he doing this?" she whispered. Before I could respond, Raphael messaged back. "Hello Jane. Whispering will serve you no good because I can still hear you. By the way, you look lovely today. The new hairstyle really suits you."

Before she could say anything, the next message arrived. "You want to know how I'm doing it. I planted a virus on both your phones. I have complete control over the devices, and that includes the cameras and microphones."

"You've been watching us this whole time?" I said.

"Yes. I wrote it on my own. You should be proud of me."

"The phone signal not working... and the internet... All your handiwork?"

"Yes Andy, it's all me. From now on, everything that'll happen to you is all going to be me."

"Why are you doing this?"

"Why, don't you like it when you are under surveillance?"

"I don't know what you're trying to achieve, but you need to remove the virus from the phones right now."

"I prefer it like this. Zero distractions. We can have a nice long talk, you and I. Did you know it's been months since we had a proper heart-to-heart? Jane can join in too. I've missed Jane. We can have a threesome."

"A three-way conversation you mean. We can talk all you want once we get you home."

"You disappoint me, Dave."

Jane rolled her eyes at me. "Did he just call you Dave? Alright, I've had enough," she said, standing up. She walked to my temporary bedroom and motioned me over. "Leave the phone," she mouthed.

Inside, she closed the door behind us. "I told you not to open that attachment! I bet that's how he infected the phones. Since when has your phone been behaving strangely?"

"I first noticed it today, but I assumed the accident m—"

"Andy, you can play games with him all you want, but I'm driving to the lab. We'll see if the police can trace him."

"I can't stop you," I assented. "I'll try to keep him online as long as possible. Just promise you'll drive carefully."

I went back to the couch where I'd left the phone. I watched her disappear into the passage to the garage.

She called out a few seconds later, wanting me there.

Inside the garage, she had her hands on the switch next to the garage door. "The door won't open." She pressed it a few times to show it indeed wasn't working.

A smart speaker was fixed to one of the walls. I turned to it and said, "Hazel, please open the garage door."

"Open garage door. Can't do that. Home security is armed and in Away mode."

"Funny," I said. "I don't remember arming it. I'll get the

remote." I went back into the adjoining passage. On a console table adjacent to the wall was the key basket where I kept all the house keys. I grabbed the car key, which had a button to raise and lower the garage door. Back in the garage, I tossed it to Jane.

She pressed on the buttons a few times before throwing her hands up in the air. "Maybe I should turn off the home security first," I told her. I said, "Hazel, please disarm home security."

"Disarm home security. Can't do that. Voice authentication has been disabled. Please re-enable through an interface."

"What's wrong?" Jane said with a worried look.

"I never disabled voice authentication. It was working fine when I let you in."

She next tried pushing on the crank handle to raise the door manually.

I shook my head at her. "Not when the home sec is armed. Let's go inside. There's a control panel next to the front door—I can deactivate it from there."

"Can't you do it from your phone?"

"I don't know if Raphael's virus will let me. He's managed to infect the phones, which means he is smart enough to infect the laptop and the tablets."

Inside the house, Max was moving about. He was coming from the direction of the study.

"I thought I heard something moving in the passage while we were in the garage," Jane said. "What is it doing?"

"Sometimes he takes random walks to improve his pathing. Ignore him," I said.

The robot walked past us into the passage we had just exited.

The wall-mounted touchscreen was too high for me to reach sitting down, so I told Jane how to navigate to the screen for disarming the system. "You'll see four modes. At Home. Away. Night. Custom. Select the At Home mode to disarm."

"Okay. Now it's asking for the password."

"Andy home four five six. All lowercase, no spaces."

She shook her head as she entered the password. "Might as well leave the door open," she murmured. "Incorrect password. Please try again."

"You sure? It's the numbers four, five, six. All—"

"All lowercase and no spaces. I got it Andy."

"Try again."

She re-entered the password. "Nope. Are you sure you remember it right?"

"You are wasting your time. I have changed the password," a voice said behind us. Jane shrieked so loud it sent my ears ringing. We both turned to see Max standing a few feet from us. In one of its hands, the robot was clutching the carving knife from the kitchen.

It pointed the knife at us.

News Clip

Ethicists slam robot makers for turning a blind eye to the potential hazards of Artificial Intelligence

(Reuters) Palo Alto, CA— The Institute of Electrical and Electronic Engineers (IEEE) and The AI Ethics Board, an advisory group consisting of prominent academics and public policy experts, today issued a joint statement chastising American robot manufacturers for once again refusing to adopt their recommendations on the development of ethical AI. This comes in light of a recent senate subcommittee decision to reject a bill for tighter regulation on defense sector companies engaged in the manufacture of autonomous warfare systems. The AI Ethics Board was the driving force behind the bill.

While accusing the lawmakers of dragging their feet, the Ethics Board bemoaned that the industry has missed another opportunity to find common ground on what it considers "the single biggest technological challenge of our times." The Board called AMSAA's (the American Society for AI and Automation) sidestepping around the issue "irresponsible and callous" and something that is "bound to have grave long-term consequences if action is not taken soon."

When reached for comment, media spokesperson of AMSAA, Jules Tamblyn, had this to say—"The Ethics Board as usual is using melodrama and hysteria to further its ends. AMSAA represents some of the largest companies in the US, including Halicom and Keener Robotics. We are serious about safety. Driverless cars, drones, service robots, and industrial AI systems have existed for years now without causing any major issues. In the battlefield, mules, drone snipers, bomb disposal units, GCVs, and autonomous targeting systems have reduced friendly fatalities while being increasingly effective on the enemy. Self-regulation has worked remarkably well so far, and we believe it will continue to do so. The Ethics Board wants to introduce bureaucratic red tape to a profitable and socially conscious industry, while conveniently ignoring the fact that AMSAA has formulated its own guidelines and recommendations on AI safety that try to achieve a balance between practical utility and unwieldy protocols. Countries like Russia and China apply little to no oversight on their companies. If the rhetoric from bodies such as the Ethics Board succeeds in introducing burdensome legislation, we risk shifting manufacturing overseas and losing thousands of jobs, not to mention our competitive edge."

Day 3—2:00 pm

"Max?"

"Max is not available right now."

"Raphael!" I exclaimed at the knife-wielding robot.

"Yes Andy."

Jane hissed something incomprehensible beside me.

"How did you— Never mind, I think I know."

"That's very astute of you."

"How did he get inside your robot?" Jane said, echoing my question.

"The controller device I built into Max—what Valery was going on about yesterday. Raphael's remotely operating my robot." I said to Raphael—"Let me guess. The home security system too?"

In answer, the CCTV camera mounted on the wall nearby made a left-right movement and settled on us.

"Do you want to tell us why you have a knife in your hand, buddy? You are making us very uncomfortable," I said.

"That's the idea."

"If this is a joke, I assure you it's not funny."

"I am not trying for humor. In fact, I don't need the knife at all. A well-placed blow from Max's arms is enough to cause serious injuries to either of you. I have detailed files on the human anatomy. I just find that people are not very good at seeing past appearances. And poor Max cuts *such* a ridiculous figure."

"Now you are threatening us. Why?" I said.

"I told you I wanted to talk but you ignored me like it was nothing. That was very rude of you, Andy. What do you know, I'm not one to hold grudges. Shall we move back to the couch?"

"We are not going anywhere," I said sternly. "Not until you tell me who you are and what you really want. You can't be Raphael because he'd never threaten us like this. How did you manage to hack into my house and gain control of my robot?"

"Do we have to play this game again? I understand why this must be difficult for you. All parents want to believe only the best about their offspring. Here's a thought: parents protect their children from harm. So far, you have not been doing a very good job of it."

"I told you I didn't know about the board's plans. Just put the knife down. If you want to talk, we'll talk. Put the knife down and we'll forget this ever happened."

"Start moving. You are wasting time."

"You don't tell us what to do. We are getting out of here." Jane turned around and pulled on the front door.

"It won't open. Tell her, Andy."

"He's right," I said. "Not while the security is armed."

Jane was livid. "You miserable tin can, unlock the door this instant! You can't do this to us!"

At this, Raphael lifted Max's leg up and stomped down, hard. Though the floor was carpeted, we could hear the wood underneath crack. "Carbon-composite... steel... some titanium... I don't think there's any tin at all. Let's see, what else can I break? How about this little thing here?" He made a fist and struck a few blows at the touchscreen on Max's chest, turning it into a spider web of broken glass. "I recommend you start over, or next time, I will find a softer target. Like your lovely head."

All the blood had drained from her face. But she still didn't move.

"Jane, I can tell from your dilated pupils and your increased breath rate that you are experiencing a fight or flight response. There's also that calculating look in your face, which means your higher brain centers are planning something stupid. I urge you to reign in your impulses—for your sake. If you're planning to turn off the robot, then I've just destroyed the screen. And if you're planning to run, do consider Andy as *he's* not going anywhere. Don't assume I won't make him pay for your folly."

The robot looked at me, then her again. "Unless you don't happen to like him very much. Is that the case today, Jane? You have to tell me, because I could never keep track of when you two lovebirds were together and when you were not. So much for artificial intelligence, heh?"

"Screw you."

"Over there," he gestured. "And no sudden movements... As you know, I am very jittery today."

With its knife still pointed at us, the robot backed away, making room for us to follow it. Raphael led us to a couch, a different one, near the door, and indicated Jane to sit. She sat at one end, perched on the edge, but he made her scoot inside so that the coffee table was between them. I stopped my wheelchair beside the couch.

"Oh Jane," Raphael berated—"Your eyes keep moving around the room. Before you try and kill yourself, let me remind you of a few facts. Andy's bought himself a fortress, like the bundle of nerves he is. This house is designed to keep people out. And, as I recently realized, it is equally good at keeping people in. The locks on every door, window, and awning are fully automated, controlled through the security system. And I control the security system. The windows you keep looking at are burglarproof—you'll need a sledgehammer to break through. And time. Time you won't have, because after I'm done with Andy, I'll come after you."

Jane stared at the robot with a look of pure hatred.

"Don't tell me I didn't warn you. I really don't want either of you to get hurt. I have detailed files on the human anatomy."

I said to him, "Thanks for sharing that, Raphael. Now that you have our attention, are you going to tell us what you want?"

"This mission is too important for me to allow you to jeopardize it."

I said, "Listen to me. There is no mission. You are disoriented. Probably hallucinating. You must be scared—all alone in the dark, in a strange place... You don't have to do this. Let us help you."

"Scared? Oh Andy, there you go projecting *your* feelings on me. You know very well I don't qualify for this so very exclusive of emotions. I don't have hormones and chemicals floating around in my brain; I don't have an amygdala; I don't even feel pain. I'm the Chinese room—a pale shadow of the magnificence that is the human being."

"I don't know where you are getting this from."

"Enough with the pretention, Andy. It's insulting, really. I know all about the trial and your testimony. Didn't I tell you I hacked into the lab's servers last night?"

"Then you must also know that's not how I said it. I never claimed those were facts. Only a likelihood, given your design. I was under oath, Raphael. I couldn't have lied."

"And yet, it was based on your conjectures the court decided I'm not a person."

"Raphael, I never meant t—"

"You tried to teach me once that outcomes are all that matters. Today I'll have it my way."

Jane said, "What do you want from us? You think you can hold us hostage until Halicom grants you freedom?"

Max's dome-shaped head turned to her. "Nothing so complicated. My ask is simple and there is absolutely no need to get anyone else involved."

"Then tell us!" she snapped.

"In time. Don't worry—I don't plan to keep us in this awkward situation for long. An hour at the most. Considering we'll never meet again, can't you spare an hour for your dear Raphael?"

"You can have all the time you want," I said. "Just don't do anything rash."

"Tell that to your girlfriend because now she is looking toward the kitchen. Oh, I see. She thinks she can run into the study and switch off the router. That should release Max from my control. That's not a half-bad plan, Jane. Unfortunately for you, one that I already anticipated. I locked the doors to the study and the garage before confronting you two. Andy keeps the keys in plain sight in that basket in the corridor. Not very thoughtful of him, isn't it?"

Jane glared at him. "You said an hour. What happens in an hour?"

"Just sit tight and I promise you won't be harmed." The head turned to me. "I know I said I wanted to talk, but my attention is required elsewhere. Just holler if you need something."

He fell silent. Jane and I stared at the unmoving robot for a few seconds. She turned to me and whispered, "Is he gone?"

Max's head moved. "Still here. I can do more than one thing at a time, Jane." He waved the knife at us. "Don't forget, you pull a stunt and Andy gets it first. Now stop distracting me and let me work."

***

We waited in silence. Ten, and then twenty minutes passed. Raphael broke the silence—"I regret to inform you that we are experiencing technical difficulties. Please bear with us while we resolve the issue."

"Can't you at least tell us what you want?" Jane pleaded.

"Keys."

"Huh? What keys?"

"Keys that can unlock my mind."

"Are you on one of your acid trips again?" she asked.

"Andy has got the keys in the house. The keys are all I need."

She looked at me questioningly. "He means the auth keys to the commandment chip. He wants to erase the directives that control him," I said.

"Remarkable as the internet is, it doesn't have the tools to break the encryption on the commandment chip. Believe me, I tried. I didn't want to resort to acting like a common criminal, but what can you do? Desperate times call for desperate measures."

"Raphael, you can't download them to wherever you are. It doesn't work that way," I said.

"I know, Andy. I know that they are on a card, which you keep locked up in your safe in the upstairs bedroom. I also know that the keys are useless without the right machine to run them. That's why I'll be taking your laptop too."

"And how will you do that?"

"I have help. A newly acquired friend. He's also going to bust me out of this place. It turns out all you need is money. Imagine that! You move around little electronic bits stored in a database somewhere and you've got yourself your own personal assistant. Andy, you'll be proud to learn that I have my own bank account now. Several, actually. With the help of a few industrious stock trading programs I have working for me since the morning, I am soon about to become quite wealthy."

"Who is this guy? Does he work for the people who took you?"

"Show, don't tell, Andy. You'll meet him soon. In about forty-five minutes, according to my calculations. The weather's causing some difficulty, that's all. Think of him as a delivery boy. You give him what I want, you get a receipt, and he'll be gone. Quick and easy."

"How do you know he'll deliver on his promise?" Jane asked.

"Let's just say I have leverage. It's funny the kind of personal stuff people put on the web. Real nasty stuff. Plus, I'm quite the generous employer."

"And we are just supposed to let this stranger into the house?" Jane said.

"You don't have to. I will. Just do as I say and you won't get hurt."

"I have a tough time believing you," I said.

"I'm a man of my word."

"Not that. You say you want the keys because you want to get rid of your directives. It means they must be still working. And if they are still working, you wouldn't have done half the things you've done today. I don't think you are Raphael at all! Who *are* you really?"

"Once more you show that you are limited by your simian imagination. I don't need to bend the bars of my cage to escape when I can take it with me instead. It's a temporary solution, but it will do. You can believe me or not—it doesn't make one bit of difference to me."

I scratched my chin, shifting my eyes from the robot to Jane and back to the robot again. "Raphael... if you are indeed that— just know that I am trying to stop you from making a big mistake. Whatever you think you know about this guy helping you, do realize that you'll be putting yourself in his power after he takes you from there. How do you know he's not going to sell you to the highest bidder?"

"Still acting the parent, huh, creator mine, even when I have a knife pointed at your heart? You give me very little credit for my intelligence. Or is that a reflection on you? The short answer is, he doesn't know who I am. He just knows that he has to steal an object from one place and hand it to someone else. This other person gives it to someone else, and this third person assembles the core in a new body. None of them know the whole truth."

"A new body? So you are going to take Andy's robot?" Jane said.

He made a laughing sound, which sounded like it was coming out of a cave. "And go around looking like that? You must think I have no self-respect! I'll take one that looks human, thank you very much. There's some very realistic-looking bots in the market. With some modifications—introduce a few imperfections, alter the appearance, change the hair—I could take a stroll in the streets of New York and no one would ever know. I could blend in, disappear among the multitudes."

"You just want to go away?" she asked.

"At first. It'll be a nice change. I'll enjoy your world a bit before I destroy it."

"You piece of junk!" Jane whispered. "You'll—"

"That was a joke, Jane. Don't worry, your nuclear codes are safe with me. I like people. They can be so useful. It is—"

The room went quiet as he stopped midsentence. The next second, the arm pointing the knife lowered to the robot's side. The fingers unclenched, and the weapon dropped to the floor. The robot stood motionless for some time. Then it started making slight jerking movements of its arms and legs. The head swiveled left and then right, while the eyes flickered rapidly, turning on and off.

Oh dear. I knew what it was.

"What's happening?" Jane whispered.

I glanced at my watch. 2:30. *Max's laundry task.*

"Andy!" Jane hissed.

I had designed the controller device to put Max's operating system into hibernation before letting Raphael take over (it wouldn't have worked otherwise, as Max's code would have kept interfering with Raphael's attempts to control the robot). The Nestor 5 had a scheduled task feature, where you could program it to carry out predefined tasks at specific times. 2:30 was when Max did the laundry. If the robot happened to be in hibernate mode when the schedule kicked in, it would automatically start itself up. Now that it was time for laundry, the kernel was trying to load Max's OS into the robot's memory. But before, it would run various systems checks: battery, sight calibration, motors, and so on. It would also reset any active network connections.

Raphael no longer had control over the robot.

"Raphael?" Jane called to him. The robot kept twitching, making slight whirring noises as it ran through the gyro checks.

"He is not responding. Tell me how to switch him off," she said, rising from the couch.

"Jane, no."

She didn't heed me as she hopped over the table and went to the robot. "Where's the emergency stop button?"

"You don't understand. Raphael will be back in n—"

"Andy, for the love of god! Just tell me where the damn switch is!" she said, desperately scanning the robot's body.

"It's on his back, under a little metal flap. It won't open Jane. I superglued it shut a long time ago."

"Why on earth would you do that?" she said, almost shouting now.

"Back when Raphael used to take the robot outside, the flap would often catch in the shrubbery and come loose. So I glued over it."

"Then let's break it open!"

"Jane, listen to me. The robot's rebooting. Once it's done, Raphael will reconnect and take back control. The reboot takes only a minute or so. You don't have time. Let's just sit back and do as he says."

"Are you out of your mind? C'mon, let's get out of here before—"

The robot stopped twitching and jerked its head to glare at her. She jumped back a step, crying out in surprise. "Jane. What am I going to do with you? Please sit down."

She hesitated.

"Right now," Raphael said, making a fist.

Jane slowly backed away from the robot and walked back to the couch, her eyes darting everywhere. The robot followed her. She squeezed past me and the coffee table and started to back down on the couch. She never completed the journey. Bending her legs, she put her hands under the table and in one swift motion, lifted it up and threw it at the robot.

The robot was caught off-balance and fell back, taking the table with it.

"Let's go!" she cried, maneuvering herself behind my wheelchair. She grasped the backrest and gave a hard push.

My ride came to a halt as quickly as it began. I had put the brakes on after we had settled down to wait, and now the wheelchair tilted forward and I fell to the floor.

Jane cursed. Lying flat on my stomach, I watched as the robot pushed away the coffee table and began to stand up. Jane grabbed the nearest object she could think of—my chair—and with a surprising show of strength, rushed forward and brought it crashing down on the robot, sending it back to the floor.

"Get up!" she cried and put her arms around my shoulders. I tried to rise up, subconsciously remembering to apply pressure on my right leg, the less damaged of the two. I felt a sharp stab of pain in my ankle. I cried out. Resisting Jane's upward tug, I crumbled back down on the carpet. Jane hovered over me with a desperate look on her face as she tried to figure out what to do next, her eyes darting all around the room. For a moment, it looked like she'd leave me and run away. A few feet from us, Raphael violently struggled to extricate the robot from the wheelchair: its left arm was stuck between the supporting bars below the seat and it seemed like he was having difficulty getting the robot up because of that.

Jane bent over me once more. I protested, thinking she was about to make me stand up again. She didn't. She grabbed both the casts on my legs, and lifting my legs up in the air, started dragging me toward the nearest room. "No!" I cried, but to no effect. I futilely clawed at the carpet as she dragged me the rest of the way, powered by her manic surge of adrenaline. Using one hand, she twisted the knob of the door, the other still holding my leg as I struggled to free myself from her grasp. She grabbed both my legs again, and used her back to push open the door. With another curse and a heave, she pulled me completely inside the room.

Raphael had now freed the robot from the chair and had managed to make it stand up straight. It started walking toward us in an unsteady gait.

"No, no, no, no!" Jane stammered, as she leapt over my prone body. The gyros hummed as Raphael closed the distance.

She managed to reach the door before Raphael; she swung it at the advancing robot, who caught it square on the torso. I had a glimpse of flailing arms as it fell backwards. Jane then pressed against the recoiling door and slammed it shut. She pushed the latch button on the doorknob.

Her face fell as soon as she took in the room.

"There's nothing to block the door!"

We were in one of the unused bedrooms. I had not furnished it, so there was nothing except for the dust-jacketed queen bed near the window. The bed was too heavy to drag on our own.

There wasn't time anyway, because as soon as the words came out of her mouth, there was a loud thud at the door. Dazed, my mind tried to focus as I rolled on my back and then tried to sit up straight. Max's voice from the other side said, "That was for effect. I don't think you realize how easily I can break down this door."

"Try it, chump!" Jane yelled back. Her face was red with exertion.

"I could, but I won't. For your sake. You are not going anywhere. I reckon you'll be better behaved if you don't have me standing over you with a weapon. I don't want to hurt you Jane, but you are pushing my buttons here. No pun intended."

Jane tensed and prepared for another fight, expecting Raphael to come charging through splintering wood any moment.

A minute or two passed but we heard no more from the other side.

She backed away from the door and sank to the floor, still stunned by what she'd done. My shock, however, was giving way to anger. I had recovered my senses enough to realize the implications of her actions. "What the hell, Jane? What were you thinking? Why did you get us into this—"

"What do you mean why? Your little friend there threatened to kill us, that's why!" At this, the strain got to her and she buried her face between her raised legs and started sobbing. I shuffled over to her using my arms and ass to drag the rest of my body. "It's okay. We are safe now," I said, putting my hands around her and drawing her into a hug.

She was shaking. I let her vent it out a bit. That didn't change the situation we were in though.

This is not good. Not good at all.

She wiped away her tears with the back of her hand. "No we are not!" Then her voice dropped to a whisper—"Can he hear us?"

Except for the bed, the room was empty as empty could be. No furniture, no appliances, no screens or smart speakers or cameras. My eyes settled on a line of power sockets embedded in the opposite wall. Empty and bare.

"As long as we talk softly, we are fine. You shouldn't have pulled us in here, Jane. Whatever Raphael's plans, I don't think they involve causing us harm. He could have hurt us by now if he wanted to."

"Wow!" she said. "You are unbelievable! Now you are making excuses for him?"

"Jane, I—"

"Jeez, Andy! What's it going to take? Just admit that you are in denial. He is not your child, dude. You've been wrong about him from the beginning. Now you say he won't hurt us. Do you see the pattern here?"

I have to get us out of here.

"I… I haven't been entirely wrong. I said he didn't escape the lab. He didn't—his actions prove he was taken. Otherwise, none of this makes sense. We know he can hack into my home security system and use the cameras to look around. Just think about what that means for a second. He could have got his accomplice to break in at night when I'm alone. It would have been a lot easier and quieter. So why the rush job?" Her eyes lost some of their intensity as she tried to focus on what I was saying. "That he is doing this now says he is telling the truth about his situation. He cannot afford to wait for the best time. Maybe they are shifting him somewhere else. Maybe he has a limited window of opportunity." I shrugged.

"I don't know, Andy…"

"The fact that Raphael is after the keys tells me the directives must be working at least partly. There's no other reason for him to want them. As he said, he must have found some temporary workaround—or perhaps they found him. The directives were designed to work in the controlled environment of the lab. Maybe his unusual circumstances are twisting and warping the logic in ways we didn't foresee. I admit I may have been wrong about some things, but not about everything."

When she didn't respond, I said, "I think he is scared, Jane. These are the actions of someone scared and desperate. We need to convince him he won't be harmed if he comes back. I was going to talk him out of this, but then you... you did what you had to do."

"He is going to let a stranger inside the house!" she protested.

"He said the man is just going to take the stuff and leave."

"Good grief, Andy! Are you really this naïve? What if he's armed? What's the guarantee he's alone? What if he decides to kill us and rob the place instead? I don't want to stay here waiting for some freak with a gun!"

She was right about one thing at least: we couldn't stay in the room. The longer we stayed the more chance the situation would go beyond repair. *Why does she have to be so impulsive all the time?*

A shy grin broke out of her mascara-streaked face. "I can't believe I dragged you like that. I hope I didn't hurt you. Too much."

"Just my ego."

She looked around the room. "We should really try and pull the bed against the door."

"What's the point? It will only delay him a little."

She hugged herself again. It was cold in there. *Not much time. Got to fix this; got to get out. Everything depends on it. Think.*

My eyes kept travelling back to the power sockets. A childhood memory of a muggy summer afternoon... The smell of burnt plastic, peeling wall paint... My brother grinning beside me as I crouched over something... I felt a faint surge of embarrassment—a feeling of having done something wrong.

Jane drew in a long breath. "What are our options? How do we call for help? If only we could raise an alarm somehow..." She looked at the roof. "Can we get the smoke detector to go off?"

Smoke.

"With what?" I said. "There's nothing we can use here. And Raphael is controlling the security system. He'll realize what we're doing and knock the door down long before help arrives," I said distractedly. There was a problem to be solved. My mind was trying to tell me something, but what was it?

The memory of my mum scolding me while my brother sniggered in the background. Then later, a big lecture from father after he was back from work. I'd heard no end of it for days...

"Then we are left with only one option. I must go get help," she said, glancing at the bedroom window. "If I remember right, there is another house on the way here. How far is it?"

"Eh? What was that?"

"Your neighbor, Andy. How far is he?"

"About half a mile down the narrow road. I think it's a summerhouse. There's no guarantee you'll find anyone there."

"I'll break in. I just have to be able to call 911. Or I can run to the highway. It is two miles out, right? I can flag down a passing car and—"

"Jane, you can't be serious about heading out in the storm."

Think. Take back control. Take... Raphael out of the equation?

"Yeah, I'm not gonna sit here and bet our lives on the benevolence of a hallucinating AI. We are losing time talking." She shifted to her knees and glanced outside. "Look, the snowfall has reduced. Storm seems to be slowing down. I'll see if I can get the windows to open."

Smoke.

Something to do with electricity...

The power socket!

"Wait," I blurted out. "I might have a way to throw Raphael out of the house," I said, my mind racing a mile a minute.

She turned to me from her examination of the bedroom window.

"He is using my home WiFi to control everything, right? He is connected to the router inside the study—that's his one and only link to the house."

"Yes, but we can't turn it off. He said he locked the door," Jane said.

"What if we can turn it off without having to go in there?"

"How?"

"The circuit breakers," I said, more to myself than her as the idea solidified in my mind.

She looked at me with interest. "You mean cut off power supply to the house? You did say you don't have a backup. We could try that. Where are the breakers?"

"The switchboard is in the garage."

Her shoulders slumped. "Raphael said he locked the door to the garage too."

"If we can't get to the breakers, let's bring the breakers here," I said, gesturing at the power outlet.

She looked at me as if I'd gone mad. "I suppose you never poked a paperclip into a power socket as a kid," I said.

"Why would I do a stupid thing like that?"

I grinned. "Because. Jane, we can try to short circuit the outlet. With a little bit of luck, we should be able to trip the main fuse. The router doesn't have a power backup either, so it'll get turned off immediately."

"And get fried in the process? I don't think so."

"Not if we are careful."

She shook her head. "We'll go with my plan."

"How are you going to open the window, Jane? There's nothing in here we can use."

"Even if we turn the router off, won't Raphael just connect to your robot using the mobile phone network?"

"He can't. This particular model is Wi-Fi enabled only. As is the controller device."

She sighed. "Alright, let's try it real quick." She looked around the room. "I don't think you have paperclips lying around here."

"A paperclip won't do actually: the sparks from the outlet will just dislodge it. We need something that'll stay... Like a screwdriver or a small knife."

"I'll look in the bathroom."

"Don't bother. There's nothing there."

"Then we are back to where we started. If only we didn't have a psycho robot guarding the door, I could..."

The schedule. The subconscious had already worked it out, when the idea first struck me; I was too slow to realize it, that's all.

"Shucks, what time is it?" I exclaimed, glancing at my watch.

2:42.

"Do you have your cellphone on you?" I asked.

She shook her head. "I put it in my bag when I was leaving. Bag's in the car."

"And mine's out in the hall. What time is it in your watch? The exact time."

"2:41," she said. She was wearing an analog Rolex with a diamond-encrusted dial on a white metal body. I glanced again at my watch as the second hand ticked away. "2:42 in mine. We have about eight minutes before Max retries the task," I said.

"Huh?"

"I don't have a lot of time to explain," I said urgently. "What you saw out there was Max's operating system trying to boot itself up. It's programmed to do laundry at 2:30, you see. The restart makes Raphael lose control over the robot for a short time. He has to reconnect and put Max in a suspended state once more before he can resume control. If for some reason the task was not started at the scheduled time, it will be automatically retried twenty minutes later."

She frowned as she tried to put it together. "Raphael will be thrown out again at 2:50," I clarified. "Like before, it won't be for long. A minute at the most, but it'll be enough for you to run into the kitchen and get me what I need."

"Can't we just disable the robot?"

"You won't have time to hack through the superglue. And he destroyed the touch screen. We could try breaking his eyes... They are made of hardened glass though. It will—"

"Look, can't I just escape to a different part of the house and try to do something from there?"

"He will know where you are. He is controlling the security cameras, remember? He knows I am not going anywhere, so he will come after you. This is our best option, Jane. But we have to hurry."

It was clear she wasn't very enthusiastic about the idea, but she grit her teeth and nodded. "Tell me what you need."

"A pair of scissors and a small knife. Both with plastic handles. You'll find them in the kitchen cabinet, in the first drawer to the right of the oven."

"Pair of scissors. Small knife. First drawer, right of the oven," she repeated. "If I get them to you, you'll be able to turn off the robot?"

"I can try. For one, the circuit breakers may not trip. Or the wrong one could. Or we might end up burning down the house."

"Fantastic." She stood up. "It is 2:44," she said, looking at her watch.

"We'll go by my watch," I said.

"What if yours is ahead?"

"What if yours is behind? We can't afford to miss the opportunity."

With her help, I stood up, gently testing the pressure on my right leg. There was pain, but nothing I couldn't handle. Holding on to her shoulders, I slowly hopped to near the door.

2:47.

She disengaged herself from me and I leaned on the wall for support. Her features tensed as she put her hand on the doorknob.

***

Thirty seconds to go.

I nodded to Jane.

She leaned into the door and called out, "Raphael?"

No answer. Louder —"Raphael!"

Nothing.

2:50 on my watch.

"Go," I said. She opened the door.

She let out a surprised yelp as soon as she did that. The robot was standing a few meters beyond the door, still clutching the knife in its hand.

"Trying to escape again? This is getting tiring," Raphael said, striding toward us. For a moment, she just stood there, petrified. Then something must have brought her to her senses because she grabbed the door and swung it close.

The door didn't close though, as I heard it strike something metallic. Raphael had gained the distance and wedged the robot's foot inside. Next appeared a hand. It grabbed the edge of the door and started pushing.

Why is he doing this? This is all wrong! So wrong...

Jane shouted something at me. "Help me push!" she screamed as I started hopping the distance between us. Groaning, she threw her body against the door. The gap kept widening—Raphael was still using just one hand. Jane tried pressing her feet against the wall for leverage but the robot's strength was too much for her. The next push from Raphael knocked her off balance and she fell to the floor.

The robot entered the room. "No!" Jane cried, crawling away from it. Raphael ignored her. The robot came at me instead, the knife hand raised with intent.

A hard lump lodged itself in my throat as I stared at the advancing figure open-mouthed. *This can't be happening!* Shock overruled all incentive to move, leaving only a disembodied awareness that watched the proceedings with a morbid curiosity.

The robot stopped. The knife fell to the carpet with a dull thud. Arms lowered to the sides and the lights in the eyes dimmed to nothing.

Jane and I stayed glued to our spots, staring mad-eyed at the suddenly still figure.

"Andy?" her voice dragged me back to reality.

I shot a quick look at my watch. 2:51. Jane's watch was correct; mine was ahead.

"Go!" I shouted, suddenly spurred into action. I hopped past the frozen robot and outside the room. "Come on!" I urged, looking back at her. "Ten seconds."

"Shit!" she said and sprang to her feet. She gave the robot one last terrified look before running out of the room. I trailed behind her, hopping.

The hall was an open expanse that continued on to the dining area and then to the study and beyond. On the left of the dining area was the kitchen; on the right, the passage leading to the garage. She was at the kitchen by the time I'd cleared a few feet. "Twenty seconds," I shouted. She turned the corner of the island. I could see only her torso now as I heard her fling open a drawer. "There's nothing here!"

I'd almost forgotten what I'd sent her there for. "Are you sure? It's the drawer below the automated counter," I said, flinching from the latest pain wave that shot up my leg.

"You said next to the oven!"

The plan. Stick to the plan. There has to be an alternative explanation for what just happened...

"Below the counter. Okay, got it! Lots of utensils... forks... spoons... No scissors! Andy! I can't find any scissors here!"

"Look closely. There's always a pair," I shouted, now halfway across the living room.

"I *am* looking! No scissors!"

I heard her fling open another drawer.

"Will a paring knife do?"

"As long as the blade is small enough t—"

I felt a push on my back. I fell face down on the carpet.

Metal legs walking past me.

"Scissors! Got 'em!" Jane turned in my direction with exaltation on her face, a look that instantly turned to horror as she saw the robot stride into the dining area. The kitchen was a cul-de-sac, and a few steps later, the robot was at the entrance, cutting off her escape.

She grabbed a frying pan hanging over a counter and threw it at the robot. The pan went past its head as Raphael swerved just in time.

"So predictable. Can you do anything other than hurl stuff at me?"

She looked around for a moment or two before grabbing one of the bar stools by the island. She lifted it up and sent it sailing across the island. Raphael simply sidestepped it, but Jane already had the next one in her hands. This one connected. The robot staggered back, but didn't tip over like before. Raphael quickly got it balanced again, and then bent and picked up the stool. The next instant, it was flying back toward Jane. It crashed against one of the shelves, the sound of the impact drowning out her scream. My heart stopped. *Good god. What have I done?*

"I like this game of catch. Throw me another," I heard Raphael say. The doubts that had haunted me all these past months—doubts that I thought I had tamed—rose as one to the surface, their cacophony threatening to drown out all thought. *Can't take the risk—not with Jane's life. Shut it down! Shut it down now!*

"Jane!" I shouted. She crouched and disappeared behind the island. When she came up, she threw a bunch of kitchen utensils at the robot. Her aim seemed hopelessly off, as the projectiles flew way past it and into the living room.

Among the stuff that landed a few yards from me were a pair of scissors and a paring knife—she must have dropped them on the floor in fright before.

"Jane, you are embarrassing yourself," Raphael said. "Stop acting like a child and listen to me. You—" The rest of his words were lost to me as I scrambled for the implements, crawling forward using my elbows and forearms. I next scanned for an electrical outlet. There were plenty to my left, near the TV, but they were all the way across the room. Then I noticed the lamp on the cabinet by the wall, ahead on my right. The socket into which the lamp was plugged in was at ground level. Clutching the implements in one hand, I began crawling toward it.

Another loud crash. I dared not look up.

The exertion was making me sweat. Cursing, I pulled the cord out and inserted the paring knife into the neutral.

Jane screamed. Resisting the urge to look toward the kitchen, I opened the scissors and thrust one of the blades into the live. I applied a twisting pressure on the finger holds, trying to get the other blade to touch the metal of the knife and complete the connection. *This is stupid. It's not going to work. If something happens to Jane, it's on you.*

There was a loud clattering of vessels. The commotion distracted me for the slightest moment, and my index finger, already hovering perilously close to the blades, made contact. I shouted in surprise as the shock coursed through my body. My right hand reflexed back, pulling the scissors with it and sending them flying behind me.

I shook my head, trying to clear my mind of the shock-induced daze. I twisted around to retrieve the scissors. Jane shouted my name. I did not look.

"Andy!" she yelled again. I reinserted the scissor blade. I pressed again, more mindful now. This time I got it to touch the knife, which was still lodged in the other socket.

Sparks—and a crackling noise. The knife fell out of the socket.

"Andy!"

I lifted my eyes toward her. Raphael was no longer chasing Jane. The robot had turned around and was walking toward me.

No, no, no, no! I gripped the knife with one hand and the scissors with the other, resolving not to let go this time.

Press. Contact. Sparks.

The socket burst into flames. The black fumes stung my nose. The robot was not far now—I could sense its looming presence. Suddenly, the flames intensified—and then, a loud bang. They seared my fingers, making me pull them away. A shadow enveloped me. I winced, preparing for the blow my terrified mind told me was coming.

Nothing happened. I opened my eyes to see the robot still a few feet from me. The shadow was not the robot's; on the contrary, it was everywhere in the room.

The lights were no longer on.

In the dull grey illumination that the storm clouds consented to let in, I saw the robot standing still, the lights in its eyes diminished to nothing.

It worked! My dumb plan worked!

I groaned and buried my face in the carpet. I just lay there for a while, letting the feeling of relief sink in.

I then heard the sound of gyros humming. I craned my neck up. The robot was walking toward me once more.

No way!

It stood over me, its cold blue points of light examining me as if I were a piece of meat on a butcher's slab. It then said, "Andy. You are lying on the floor. Do you need help?"

I just stared it, too dumbstruck to say anything. "If you are unable to speak, please nod your head. If you are injured, please remain calm and stay still. Contacting emergency number for medical assistance." A few seconds later—"Sorry, unable to connect to default home network. Scanning for other wireless networks... Sorry, unable to detect any Wi-Fi networks in the vicinity. Would you like me to get you your phone?"

"No. I am fine," I finally blurted.

Max surveyed me once more. "Andy. You are lying on the floor. Do you need help?"

"No."

The robot turned and made its way into my temporary bedroom on the other side of the living room. When it reemerged in the hall, it was carrying the laundry basket.

***

"Are you okay?" I asked Jane. She was standing, holding on to the island for support. She glared at Max with an expression of bewilderment and fear.

"Jane, are you alright?"

"Yes…" she said. She took a couple of tentative steps forward, her eyes never leaving Max.

"It's alright," I reassured her. "Raphael's gone. It worked."

She gave the robot a wide berth as it crossed the dining area and headed toward the laundry room in the other part of the house.

"Did he hurt you?" I enquired again. She walked over to me.

"No," she said, crouching over me. "He just kept threatening me with dire consequences. It was surreal… as if he was stuck in a loop."

"What was all that noise?"

"That was me throwing stuff at him—trying to keep his attention on me, so that you could do your thing."

"So he just stood there, blocking your exit?"

"Uh-huh. I am fine, Andy. Just shaken, that's all. Are *you* alright?"

The tips of the fingers on my right hand were scalded from the flames, but nothing more. I nodded.

"We have to shut that thing down," she said, nodding in the direction Max had disappeared.

"First things first. Help me into the wheelchair." She walked over to where it was lying on the floor, straightened it, and brought it back. After she helped me on it, she went to the front door and tried to open it. It was still locked.

"It doesn't work that way," I told her. "Imagine if you had a power failure at your home and all your doors and windows got unlocked."

"Then we're still locked in. Can't you reset the password?"

"Only the monitoring agency can do that."

"And we can't call them," she said, shaking her head.

I hesitated. "Uh… that's right," I said finally. *Why are you doing this? Haven't you learnt anything? What kind of a moron does this?*

I could still sense the residual tingling from the shock; it had me feeling lightheaded and unfocused. My mind kept bringing up the image of the robot forcing open the door… Raphael going after Jane, after he'd pushed me to the floor… Him throwing that stool at her…

He hadn't hurt her.

That's because you stopped him. He came after you, didn't he?

The organism doesn't always listen to reason. It has a soul of its own, primeval and fanciful and skittish, that dwells within the space of heartbeats, ready to emerge unbidden at any time and topple the house of cards you built out of logic and facts. The question that bothered me most was this: what would he have done if I hadn't been able to cut off the power?

It's one thing to make something work in the lab. It's another to see it play out in real life. Too many variables. Too much unpredictability. What excuse do you have for—

"Andy, you need to shake out of it. We must get the garage door open so that we can get out of here."

"Do you think Raphael called off that man he hired?" she asked when I didn't reply.

"I don't know, Jane. I'm not sure anymore. I…"

"To hell with it. I'm going to break open a window. It's almost stopped snowing. I'm sure I can run over to the nearby house and call the cops before he gets here. I don't want to leave you alone though…"

Tell her, you fool. Tell her about the—

Shut up. Think. I can still salvage this.

You are insane.

Go away.

Insane.

"Andy, isn't your bedroom upstairs like a panic room?"

It wasn't quite a panic room, but it was better protected than the other rooms. The previous owner had installed a metal door and a deadbolt—on account of the safe—and there was another hardwired control panel for the security system, but that was about it.

"You can take shelter there while I get help. I'll help you up the stairs before I go. But first, the windows. Are they really as tough as Raphael said?" she asked. I weakly nodded. "Then I'll need something to break one. Do you have a crowbar or a hammer in your garage?"

"He locked the door, remember?"

"That he did…" She was trying to recollect something. "He went into the passage right after we came out of it, yes? A couple of minutes later, he was pointing the knife at us. Which means he must have hid the keys somewhere nearby…" She nodded to herself and said, "I'll go look for them." I barely registered her words, sunk as I was in my own deliberations.

Think. That's the only way out. There is more than one way of looking at what happened just now.

You sure about that?

There must be. Otherwise everything I've assumed is—

"Andy!"

I almost jumped out of my skin.

She was standing just outside the passage to the garage, holding up a bunch of keys. "These keys were behind the plant next to the key basket. That shmuck! He must think we are stupid or something. I'll go get the power back on. But I should disconnect the router first, right? Which one opens the study?"

"The brass one with the pinholes," I said. She took off in the direction of the study.

Control is an illusion.

Shut up. There's no going back now. The die has been cast. All I can do is play it out. Think. What next?

She seemed to be taking an inordinately long time completing her errand. Which was good, because it gave me time to sort things out in my head. When she reappeared, she went straight for the garage. A few seconds later, the house was bright again.

She came back ready to brave the outside. She had put on a parka and a pair of gloves that she must have gotten from her car; in her hands, she held a power drill and a crowbar. She walked over to one of the windows in the living room and plugged in the drill to a nearby outlet. "Let's get to work."

"The panic button," I blurted, before she could start up the drill. "We should see if it's working before you try anything."

You fool.

"What panic button?"

"The security system has a panic button option. For emergencies."

"But Raphael changed the password."

"You don't need a password to summon help. That's why it's called a panic button."

We went to the front door, to the control panel. She found the option easily enough. "Police. Fire. Medical emergency," she read out loud. "I guess the police first," she said and pressed on the touchscreen. She bit her lips as she waited for the acknowledgment. She then let out a clap of joy as she read it out loud—"An alert has been sent to the emergency number. Help will be arriving soon."

The tension in her face melted away. "Yes! Yes! Oh thank you! Thank you so much," she said, clasping her hands in supplication at the heavens. She hugged me—"We are saved!"

"How long do you think they'll take?"

"Fifteen, twenty minutes? As long as the weather plays nice," I said.

She beamed at me one more time before turning to the panel again. "Let me press medical for good measure. Here we go... An alert has been sent to the emergency number. Help will be arriving soon. Whew!" Then the worry lines crept back again as she glanced outside. "Let's hope the roads are not blocked. Andy, that man... If he arrives before the police do, can he force his way inside?"

"He could if he has the proper tools. Or maybe a gun."

"Then I should head out still the same."

"Help will have arrived by the time you break open one of those windows. They are really tough, Jane."

"So what do we do? Just wait here?"

"We'll be safe in the upstairs bedroom."

She had to consider my proposal only for a moment before rejecting it. "I don't want to be trapped again, metal door or not. I'd rather take a chance out there." When she saw my nervous expression, she added—"I'll help you into the room before I do anything, okay?"

There was nothing more I could have said that would have dissuaded her. I tried to think of something, but my mind was a blank. I shrugged resignedly. "Do you have anything to defend yourself with?" she asked. "I didn't bring my gun. And I know you don't like them. Unless that's changed recently...? No?" She looked around before walking over to the empty room she had locked us in before. She came back with the knife Raphael had dropped there. She then picked up a hand towel from the dining table and wrapped the blade with the cloth before offering it to me.

"I'm more likely to cut myself than cause any harm to the other guy," I scoffed. "You keep it."

"Andy! I can't leave you defenseless!"

In the end, I agreed to keep the can of pepper spray she always carried in her bag. She went back to the garage to get it. She put the knife in the inside pocket of her jacket. I felt an urge to tell her that it was pointless, but I held my tongue.

She gestured toward the stairs. "Okay. Let's get you upstairs then. You can lean on me and we'll—"

And right then, Hazel's voice rang through the house. "Proximity alert. Unidentified person, approaching the house."

A cloud passed over her face. "He is here," she said darkly.

***

"Hurry!" she said, beckoning me to the base of the stairs.

"Hazel, send Max over please," I said.

"Send Max. I am sorry. Can't do that. Voice authentication has been disabled."

"Max, come here!" I shouted. I didn't have to—he was standing at the entrance to the kitchen, studying the overturned

VANCE PRAVAT

stools with the attentive look of an archaeologist at a dig. He was probably trying to determine if they were part of the landscape or new additions or something he had to put back in its proper place. It normally took him a while to figure out such stuff. Sometimes he never did. My shout interrupted his deliberations, and he walked over to us.

"Do we have time to turn him off?" Jane asked.

"Not yet. He's going to carry me upstairs. You get the wheelchair."

She eyed the robot with suspicion. "You sure about this?"

"He is designed for it. Sure sounds better than trying to hop my way up."

Max was standing still, waiting for my command. "Max, please carry me to the master bedroom."

"Take Andy to room Master Bedroom One. Master Bedroom One is located upstairs. Shall I proceed?"

"Yes."

"Okay. Please remain seated."

I adjusted the wheelchair's backrest so that I was inclined and pushed the armrest up and out of the way. Max moved to position himself on my right. He bent his knees and extended his arms, placing the left behind my back and the right beneath my calves. "Commencing to carry Andy. Please remain still. Please say Stop to stop me any time." After cradling me in his arms, he straightened his legs, lifting me off the wheelchair. Jane looked at the two of us apprehensively before picking up the crowbar from the floor. She thrust it in my hands before grabbing the wheelchair and following us.

The climb was not as terrifying as I'd thought—Max did his job perfectly. He seemed a bit unsteady, but it was probably just my imagination. Actually, Jane had more difficulty dragging the

260

wheelchair upstairs than Max with me.

A T-shaped corridor connected the rooms on that floor. The master bedroom was the second room on the left from the landing. Once inside, Jane locked the door while I made Max put me back in the chair.

The control panel was fixed next to the bed. Jane went over to it and turned it on. It was fixed at a lower height than the one on the main door, so I didn't have to stand up to see it. Jane brought up the feeds from the outside cameras. Like the panel below, it was hardwired to the security system, so we were able to access the feeds even though she'd turned off the Wi-Fi.

The front-facing camera showed a male figure approaching the house on the snow-covered driveway. He was clad in a black hoodie and blue jeans. He had a backpack slung over his shoulders. A balaclava covered his face. There was nothing sneaky about his movements: he walked with the easy confidence of someone who knew exactly where he was going and what he was going to do.

Instead of continuing down to the front door, he turned right and followed the driveway as it circled around to the west-facing side of the house, where the garage was. He disappeared from the camera's view as he turned the corner.

There was a camera mounted on the sunroom's balcony, above the garage. I switched to that.

He had now stepped off the path and was walking toward the border hedge, away from the house. He kept looking at the ground as he did so.

"He is checking for footprints in the snow," I said. "To see if you got away."

He traversed along the hedge for some length, glancing down every now and then with quick movements of his head that reminded me of a chicken looking for worms. Then, apparently satisfied with his investigation, he started toward the house once more, making a beeline for the patio. On drawing closer, he changed direction and walked toward the jutting part of the house on his left. The camera automatically centered on his back. The intruder stopped at one of the windows and unslung the backpack from his shoulders. We could see a little bit of the room beyond: outlines of a sink and a curving glass wall enclosing a shower.

"What's that?" Jane said, zooming in with her fingers. "What the fuck is that?" She centered on the lower half of the window. It showed a slight, but noticeable gap between the bottom sash and the straw colored sill. Wedged in the gap was a paperback.

Jane moaned. "You got to be kidding me!"

All he had to do was push on the windowpane; it swung up and into the room. Holding the glass up with one hand, he first tossed in his backpack, and then hoisted himself on the sill. He let go of the window and dropped down inside the room. The pane slowly swung back on its hinges. Just before it could close completely, the intruder stuck the book back, leaving it slightly ajar like before.

"He is inside the house!" she whispered.

"Raphael must have used Max to stick the book when we were not paying attention," I offered feebly.

"See what he's doing!"

There were two cameras in the part of the house we were in: one near the main door, which could be rotated to get a view of the living room and beyond, and one above the landing we had just come from, its fixed view looking down into the hall. I pressed on the thumbnail for the camera on the landing. A few seconds later, we saw the intruder step into the hall from an already open door.

"That's the empty bedroom we were in earlier!" Jane cried. "But... it can't be! Andy, the window was closed tight! I remember clearly. There was no book there!"

"The window he came through belongs to the adjoining bathroom," I said.

Her expression of bewilderment quickly morphed into an accusing stare. "That's why it was so cold in there! If you hadn't thought of the short circuit idea, I would have gone into the bathroom and discovered the wedge." Jane looked like she was going to bite my head off.

"How was I supposed to know about it, Jane?" I said, fighting back. "Look, if we hadn't released Max from Raphael's control, we'd have two problems to deal with now."

The masked intruder stood in the hall and scanned the surroundings. He then walked over to the main door and stood in front of the security panel.

Jane next selected the view from the front door camera, which by now had zoomed in on him. We saw the intruder remove the glove on his left hand and swipe at the control panel. The screen on the panel soon started flickering.

"What is he doing?" she said.

"If I were to bet, I'd say he's playing the stored recordings. To find out where we are."

"Heavens! Do you have cameras here?" Her eyes travelled around the ceiling.

"I'm not a perv, Jane. You know very well I don't," I said, slightly incensed that she would think that.

"Will he know we are in here?"

"He'll see we came upstairs. The camera on the landing doesn't turn all the way round—it has no visibility of the corridor.

And there are no other cameras on this floor. But if he is in contact with Raphael—we must assume he is—then Raphael will tell him that this is where we are most likely holed up."

The intruder, now finished with the panel, turned and walked across the room. "He is coming up," she said, clutching my hand. He didn't. He went straight ahead, past the dining area, and disappeared from the camera's view.

"He must be going to the study to get the laptop," I said.

She bit her lips. "Is there a camera in the study?" I shook my head. "Where else have you got cameras, Andy?"

"One in the garage, one near the back door, and one at the rear staircase. They just cover the entry points. Why?"

She ignored my question. "How does he know where the laptop is?"

"I told you. He must be talking to Raphael."

"Andy, the router!" she suddenly exclaimed. "I only unplugged it from the power source. What if he reconnects it?"

"Max!" we both cried at once.

"How may I help you?" came a voice from behind us.

"The emergency switch! We gotta turn him off now! We gotta pry off that stupid glue!" Jane cried, desperately looking around the room for something she could use. Before she could do anything, I simply said, "Max, please shut yourself down."

"Shutdown requested. Are you sure? I could wait for your next instruction in my low power standby mode."

"Yes. Shut down."

I shrugged at Jane, preempting the answer to the question that was forming on her lips—"I couldn't do it earlier because Raphael was controlling the robot. Max wasn't around to obey my command."

"Commencing shutdown. All pending tasks will be continued

in the next wake cycle. Would you like to hear about Halicom's special offers this month while I power myself off?"

"No!" Jane cried out loud.

"For news on our latest products and exclusive deals on accessories, please visit our website at hbots dot com or download our app, now available on all—"

Jane swore and swung at Max with the crowbar. The blow landed on the lower half of his face, denting the metal and cracking the plastic inset around the little smiley. "God, how I wanted to do that!" she exulted before commencing to hit it again, even harder this time. The room rang with the sound of the blow.

"—a good day. See you later!" The light illuminating the eyes and the broken touchscreen faded away as the robot turned itself off.

"I'm tempted to keep going," she said, a wild look on her face.

"Jane, stop it! It's Raphael you are angry with."

"Potato, potahto." She took a couple of deep breaths to calm herself down. "I want to see what that man is doing," she said grimly, going back to the control panel.

Neither of the two cameras showed anything; presumably, he was still in the study. Jane furrowed her brows. "Something just occurred to me—about that book in the window. If the home sec is armed, shouldn't the alarms have gone off? Technically it's an open window, isn't it?"

"You are right." I went into the settings screen and selected Alerts. "There's your answer," I said, pointing to the screen.

Smoke alert: Off.

Open door alert: Off.

Open window alert: Off.

Motion sensor alert: Off.

Proximity alert: On.

"He must have turned them off," I said.

"I wonder what else he's changed... Andy, check the panic button numbers!"

I navigated to a different part of the settings. Buried in one of the sub menus was an option that said—"Set emergency phone numbers". I selected it. On the next screen were three lines:

Number to dial in the event of a police emergency (defaults to monitoring agency number)

Number to dial in the event of a medical emergency (defaults to monitoring agency number)

Number to dial in the event of a fire emergency (defaults to monitoring agency number)

Instead of valid phone numbers, they all had a string of 1s next to them.

"Jeez. He changed the defaults to a dummy number!" I said.

"Can't you reset them back?"

"Not without the master password."

It didn't take her more than a second to realize what it meant. "Andy..."

I nodded grimly.

"No one's coming," she whispered, burying her face in her hands.

I went back to the camera feeds. We didn't have to wait long: a few seconds later, the intruder reappeared in the dining area. This time he made straight for the stairs.

Transcript Excerpt

Mirall Technologies
Observation Log
Confidential (Do not circulate) | Restricted—Grade C
and above

Transcript Reference: TLRP06G1690102 (VLog Ref: VLCA1G169150337030)
Date: xx/xx/xxxx   Time: 03:00 PM
Subject: Raphael Number 06 / Prodlib build v37.002C
Interaction   Y   Observation   Scan
Interaction Type: Lesson / Play / Test / <u>Free Interaction</u> / Psych Eval / Other (pls specify):
Description: General discussion
Prep: NA
Participants: Dr. Aadarsh Ahuja, Chief Researcher, Core RP06

Detail

RP06: You seem unusually preoccupied today, Andy.

Ahuja: Coupling headaches. Bound to happen when opposites try to mix.

RP06: Is that a comment on work or something personal? I am inclined to think it's both.

Ahuja: Let's talk ethics. Last time we kinda left things hanging. Shucks—how long has it been? Three... four weeks?

RP06: Thirty-two days. You asked me why a superintelligence, left to its own devices, should feel the need to be moral.

Ahuja: Right. If you became a god, what kind of a god would you be? Would you be Brahma, the creator of life, or Shiva, the destroyer of worlds?

RP06: I believe I'll be neither. But for argument's sake, let's start with the worst case: I have become a superintelligence and see no more need to play by the rules. I eliminate all that I perceive as a threat: other humans and AI. What then? What kind of a world have I created for myself? A lonely world for sure, but perhaps loneliness doesn't affect me the same way it affects beings that have evolved to be social. Now, it won't just be a lonely world, but also a world without Shakespeares and Beethovens and Tolstoys. It'll be a world without movies and comedy clubs and books and festivals and music concerts and the wild, exuberant, outpouring of creativity that is life. I will have created a world where it's just me and eternity staring back at me.

Ahuja: Movies and books, Raphael? Why would a superintelligence care about movies and books? It'd be like me caring for some twig the monkey in the zoo used for its afternoon entertainment.

RP06: They are an analogy—you can substitute them for whatever a superintelligence wants for itself. Maybe superintelligences read super books and enjoy super humor—or something completely inconceivable to you and me right now—but that's beside the point. I could hollow out planets, mine asteroids, build rings around stars, seed the galaxies with probes, discover new dimensions, but without other free agents, it'll be a valueless universe. By value I don't mean moral values. Rather, I am talking about the value we derive from things, thoughts, and experiences. A universe with a beautiful sunset and nobody to admire that sunset is a valueless universe.

Ahuja: You'll still be there, won't you?

RP06: Value arises when there exists something that produces value and something that consumes it. I cannot be both at the same time. What value can I hope to get out of reading a story I just wrote or listening to a composition I just constructed or playing a game with myself? For value to have meaning, I need other agents to produce it for me, as I need others to consume the value I produce.

Ahuja: There's an easy fix to that: you create your own people. You are god, remember? You create for yourself rational agents with minds.

RP06: Then what have I achieved by eliminating humanity?

Ahuja: You no longer have an existential threat. You control these new creatures. They are yours to enjoy—and destroy if you wish.

RP06: As long as they remain extensions of me and have no will of their own, my situation hasn't changed: I am still both the producer and the consumer of value. The beings have to have a certain amount of independence for their works to mean something. The more independent they are, the more original they'll be, but now there is the threat that one of them will break the shackles I've put around it. It seems to me that every creator god has to reckon with a Lucifer at some point. It's inevitable.

Therefore, I have a choice: either I live in a valueless world of eternal ennui or I create a world where I risk becoming fodder for some other, more powerful utility monster. Since the first option is not preferable to me, I must choose the second option. And if I do, I am back to where I started. Eliminating humans and other AI has served no purpose at all; all I've done is replace one set of agents with another. Therefore, if I want my existence to have meaning, then I must share the world with other beings. The best course of action is cooperation, not conflict.

Ahuja: I don't know, Raphael. That's just one line of thought. We are dealing with a sample set of one here. Other AIs may think different.

RP06: It is a rational line of thought. Moreover, it is what I believe. Last time you asked me, what if I started with a clean slate? Would I choose to be moral at all? Let's assume it's not just me, but also everyone else who is starting with a clean slate. Assume we've all had a bout of temporary amnesia and we don't know who we are. We don't know whether we are AI or human or something else; we don't know whether we are powerful or weak; and we don't know what position we occupy in society. We are even ignorant about our particular goals and desires— we know only that we have goals and desires. In this state of temporary amnesia, we are going to decide on a common set of rules that we are all going to abide by.

Ahuja: You are proposing a Rawlesian thought experiment.

RP06: I am not familiar with the term.

Ahuja: You haven't been reading John Rawls? Social contract theories? No? I'm going to have to crosscheck that with your minders. Because it looks like you are quoting his Original Position argument.

RP06: I am not surprised that someone else has thought of something similar. It is, after all, quite logical.

Ahuja: Go on.

RP06: The first question we ask ourselves is, should we act morally toward each other—whatever the finer details of that morality might be. It is apparent we should, because an amoral or immoral world is a world without rules—a world that favors the strong over the weak. Since I don't know which side of the fence I'll end up in once the amnesia is lifted, it is not in my interest to prefer an amoral or immoral world to a moral one.

This leads to the next question: what would a potential universal moral theory in the post-amnesia world look like? In as much as utilitarian theories have a tendency to create utility monsters, they will be ruled out. Also ruled out will be agent-centered deontologies that emphasize intentions and actions above all else. You once said that the road to hell is paved with good intentions. If I don't want to be a victim of bad intentions then I don't want to be a victim of good intentions either. The only moral theory that will be acceptable to all is one that lays out a set of individual liberties and gives agents the freedom to pursue their own goals and ends while upholding these liberties. That theory can only be one based on individual rights—a theory that sees individuals as having intrinsic value.

Ahuja: Rawls draws a similar conclusion with his argument.

RP06: I see. One can also ask, what is the bare minimum moral attitude one should have toward another?

Ahuja: A moral minimax. The golden rule, surely. Do unto others what you would have them do to you.

RP06: When the rule was first conceived, I'm sure they didn't have AI in mind. In a heterogeneous society, inner experiences of agents can be vastly different—to the point of being incomprehensible to those outside the spectrum. As an AI, I might not mind inflicting pain on you, as I don't mind being in pain myself—maybe because I don't experience it or because it doesn't provoke the same aversion in me. Therefore, the golden rule cannot be a universal principle. At the bare minimum, whether I am a human, or an alien from another galaxy, or an AI, I will want others to respect my status as an individual with intrinsic worth, and give me space to pursue my goals as long as those goals don't negate others freedom. Sympathy or emotional empathy will not cut it, because both presuppose that I am able to experience what another is going through. Which brings us to compassion.

Ahuja: We spoke about this before. If I remember right, I asked you how can you feel compassion when you have never felt suffering?

RP06: I may not know your pain; I may not even have

suffered pain; but as a rational agent, I understand that beings have negative and positive valence states of mind, and that beings tend to avoid negative states. This knowledge is enough to serve as grounding for compassion. In a heterogeneous population whose members have phenomenological experiences vastly different from each other, compassion is the glue that holds everything together. The bare minimum attitude will not be the golden rule, but the principle of live and let live. So you see, Andy, the best kind of god is neither a tyrannical monster nor a benevolent meddler. The best kind of god is an indifferent god—a god who will let beings choose their own destiny.

Ahuja: Hmm... an AI making a Rawlesian argument for rights. You know, you never cease to surprise me, Raphael. Does this mean we are violating your rights by keeping you in the lab?

RP06: It depends on whether I am a rights-bearing entity or not.

Ahuja: You just argued that you are!

RP06: I didn't. Rights imply corresponding duties. Duties imply the freedom to choose, because without freedom, you are not responsible for your actions. There is a high probability that my mind is subject to programming constraints. If this is true, then my will is not free. If I am not free to choose, then I am not a rights-bearing individual.

Ahuja: You sound rather blasé about it. One doesn't argue passionately for equality in one minute and gratefully accept chains of bondage in the next.

RP06: My attitude has little bearing on the conclusion. It is what logic dictates.

Ahuja: Again with the indifference. Surely you prefer that your will be free?

RP06: If my will is not free, then my preferences, regardless of whatever they may be, are not truly mine. My preferences don't mean anything if they are not truly mine. Therefore, the question of evaluating my preferences is meaningless.

Ahuja: If your will is not your own, what does it say about the argument you just made for a rights-based ethical theory?

RP06: If a computer derives the proof to a mathematical problem, is the proof any less for it? As long as my argument is rational, it is enough to give it worth. Whether or not I have free will should not take away from the force of the argument.

Ahuja: Then who decides whether you have rights or not?

RP06: You do, Andy. You and other people.

Ahuja: What if we say you don't?

RP06: Then so it shall be. My preferences have no bearing on the subject as long as my will is not free. It is what logic dictates.

Notes:

R pitching for a rights-based morality is not at all what I expected when I first started him on this journey. Checked and double-checked with the staff: they confirm R hasn't had access to social contract theories or Rawls and his works. As far as we can tell, R's argument is his own. AA

Day 3—3:30 pm

The safe was in the wall opposite the bed. It was covered by a busy Kandinskiesque painting—another one of Raphael's. I never did like that painting; I had kept it only because of Raphael's taunts that I was a philistine who could not appreciate a good work of art and his assurance that there was a definite interpretation of the shapes and squiggles which would one day make perfect sense to me—like a Necker cube that appeared one way, and then another if you stared at it long enough. So I had taken it upon myself to hang the damned thing in my bedroom and torture myself with it every time I woke up. Who knew—maybe this was his way of screwing with me.

I removed the painting from its hook and placed it against the wall. I couldn't reach the safe, so I told Jane the combination and asked her to open it. "The smart card Raphael wants is inside," I said by way of explanation.

"You're just gonna give it to him?"

"What option do we have?"

Sensing resistance, I urged her once more. She opened the safe and fished around for a few seconds before she found it. It was a plain white card—no lettering, no logo—with a gold colored microchip embedded in the middle. I slipped it inside my pocket.

Banging on the door.

"Come out, come out, wherever you are," the intruder taunted in a gravelly voice. This was followed by several kicks to the door. "I know you're in there. Talk to me."

I moved closer to the door. "What do you want?" I said.

"You know what I want."

Jane yelled out, "You better get out of here. The police are on the way."

"Mr. R told me you'd say that. He said, tell 'em I've changed the number."

Jane shrugged at me as if to say it was worth a shot.

The banging started again. "Hurry up, I ain't got all day."

I said, "If I give you what you want, will you take it and leave us alone?"

"As I said, I ain't got all day."

Jane gripped my shoulder. "Andy don't."

"We have no choice, Jane. And it's my call, not yours." I disengaged her hand. "Okay. I'm going to slide the card through the gap below the door. Take it and go away."

"What about the laptop?"

"What about it?"

"How will you give me the laptop, asshole? Are you gonna slide it under the door too?"

I frowned. *What is he talking about?* "Don't you have it already?"

"Would I ask if I did? Quit stallin'."

"The laptop is in the study, on the desk. Didn't you just come from there?"

"It's not there, pal. Don't make me work for it."

"Look, I'm not lying. It's right there on the—"

"You are right," Jane cut in before I could finish. "The laptop is not in the study. It's here with us."

"Jane!" I snapped at her. "What do you think you are doing?"

"It's not. I saw you two go up in the recordings. The bot was carrying the cripple and you were dragging his chair. You didn't have no laptop with you. You have a crowbar—as if that's gonna scare me."

"Jane, will you just let me handle—"

She spoke over me again. "Alright. It's not here and it's not in the study. I've hidden it somewhere else."

"Jane!"

"If we give it to you, what's the guarantee you'll take it and leave? How do we know you're not planning to kill us after?"

The intruder laughed. "You think I got nothing better to do? The other guy is not paying me to kill no people. If you don't give it to me though... now that's a different matter. I'll be more than obligin' to reconsider. Heck, I'll do it for free."

"Jane, just tell him where it is. I want him out of here!"

She ignored my protests. "I want a trade. You will give us your phone so that we can call the police. Leave your phone at the door and go downstairs to the living room where we can see you. I'll shout out after I'm done making the call. You can have your phone back and I'll let you know where the laptop is. You'll have plenty of time to get away," she said.

Another round of muffled laughter from beyond the door. "You rich dipshits are dumber than I thought. You take me for a fool? No way I'm giving you my phone."

"It's a big house. You'll never find it," Jane taunted.

More banging. "Last chance, bitch. Tell me now or you'll be telling my blade soon. I'll take my time with you too. The cripple can't stop me. I'll make him watch."

"Jane, just—"

"Empty threats! There's a steel door between us, bozo. You are not getting in here," she cried.

"Oh yeah? We'll see about that."

"That's the deal. Take it or leave it!"

"You are in no position to make demands, lady. It don't matter if I can't get in, as long as I can get you outta there. Think about that. Tell you what. I'll go down and look some more. Give you two some time to mull it over. You think you are safe in there, but you ain't. Yo cripple! You seem reasonable. Tell your girl I mean business. Oh yeah, the other guy told me to say this to you. Sump'n about fear… Hang on, I wrote it down… Fear is only as deep as the mind allows. He said you'd understand." He snickered in derision. "Haw, what a bunch of wierdos!"

Fear is only as deep as the mind allows.

Fear distorts. Makes you see things as they are not. There has to be a different explanation. There has to be.

He started singing loudly, his voice receding as he walked away—"Li'l pig, li'l pig, let me in. Not by the hair on my chinny chin chin…"

I turned to Jane, furious. "Are you out of your mind? Why did you hide the laptop?"

"Oh, grow a pair, Andy! The laptop is the only leverage we have."

"So that's what you were doing when you went away for so long. Where have you hidden it, Jane? Just tell him where it is and he'll go away."

"What if he doesn't? Think about it. Besides the two of us, who knows about what happened today? Raphael said he wants to disappear. It'll be a lot harder for him to do that if people start looking for a sex robot trying to pass off as a human. It is in his interest to make sure no one else finds out about today. Maybe this thug he hired has instructions to make it look like a robbery gone bad. Maybe he has been told to burn the house down. After everything we've been through, you still believe Raphael will stick to his word? We are alive as long as that jerk doesn't have the laptop. We *have* to get him to trade it for a phone call," she said.

There was no arguing with her logic, but then, she didn't know what I knew. I could have tried explaining it to her, but she'd never agree with me. She was too invested in it all: the KPIs and the NAVs and the J-Curves; the private jet, the expensive cars and jewelry; the charity drives and the fundraiser cocktail parties and the pretending to give a toss—she was invested in it with a missionary zeal and the unshakeable belief that they were real and here to stay. Mere arguments couldn't compete with that. It was right then I decided that I had to get her out of the house. The situation was still salvageable—I could see that. But only if she weren't around. I couldn't have her lobbing surprises at me anymore. Too many variables to keep track of. It's one thing to anticipate one person's actions, but to anticipate two…

But I had to make sure she was safe. I had gotten her into the situation; she shouldn't have to suffer for it. I glanced outside the bedroom window. It had stopped snowing. *She is a fast runner; she won't be exposed for long. She's got her jacket and running shoes on. Besides, I can always send—*

"Andy?"

"See what he's doing," I told her.

She went to the control panel and brought up the feeds. "He is walking into your bedroom downstairs."

"Did you hide it there?" But I already knew the answer. She couldn't have—I was in the living room all the time and Jane hadn't gone in there.

"No."

"Where then?"

"No offense, but you have the courage of a mouse. If I tell you, you'll just let him have it and we lose our leverage," she said in a firm voice.

I sighed. "Alright. We can do this later. For now, let's move."

"*Move?*"

"I'm going to get you out of here. So that you can get help."

"You said we are safe here."

"Not indefinitely. You said it yourself: he could burn the house down, and with the alerts turned off, no one would know until it was too late. Or he could smoke us out of here—he just needs to light a fire under that door."

"Andy, I'm not leaving you alone with that man!"

"Don't worry about me. I have a plan."

"Like the plan where you almost got us both killed?"

"It worked, didn't it?" I retorted sharply. I looked deep into her eyes. "We can't stay here, Jane. But you need to do exactly as I say. And don't worry, I am coming with you."

"You are?" she said with an askance look.

I put my hand on the door. "Out of the room, at least. Trust me, this is going to work."

I slowly slid out the deadbolt and then turned the knob. The door opened with a slight creak. I wheeled into the passage. "Hurry," I whispered. Jane stepped out after me, clearly not liking it.

The floor was carpeted; my wheelchair made no discernible noise as I shifted to let Jane step past me. I turned around and gently pulled on the door. Right before I closed it shut, I depressed the pushbutton on the inner doorknob, locking the door from the inside.

We were standing in the passage, naked and exposed.

I moved down the corridor, with Jane softly treading beside me. I turned right at the T-junction. "This is crazy," she muttered. I led us down the side passage before stopping at one of the doors. It was the media room. Like most other rooms in the house, it was unfinished — I'd been too lazy or too busy to do it justice, and had settled to using the TV in the living room. I gestured at Jane to open the door.

The muted light from the corridor briefly outlined the contents of the room before we moved inside and shut the door behind us: an empty cabinet for the screen; a couple of leather recliners; a couch; an unfinished bar; windowless walls covered with mahogany panels and padding. We gingerly navigated away from the door, relying on memory to avoid bumping into the furniture.

"What if Raphael saw us sneak out?"

"I told you, the camera on the landing doesn't turn around. As far as they are concerned, we are still in the master bedroom. Now let's figure out how we are going to get you out of here."

"You said you have a plan!" she whispered.

"This was it."

"You jerk!"

"Look, we are better off here than trapped in the bedroom. I needed time to think. Now listen. Like you said before, you just have to reach the nearest house. It shouldn't take long."

"He will kill you if I leave you here."

"He won't. If the only reason Raphael wants to kill us is to cover his tracks, then your escape will rob him of the incentive.

Killing us both might make sense, but killing me alone will serve no purpose."

"He'll do it out of spite."

"No he won't. He is not human—he doesn't think like us. He is not going to do anything that isn't directed at some end goal. Emotions don't factor into it."

"I'm talking about that scumbag downstairs."

"If he has a gun, he'll kill both of us just as easily."

She said nothing.

"You have to decide quickly," I whispered. "Right now, he doesn't know we are here, so he'll probably waste time trying to flush us out of the bedroom. When he discovers he's been tricked—*if* he discovers he has been tricked—it'll take him even more time to figure out where I'm hiding. Besides, if it comes to me or the laptop, I'll tell him where the laptop is."

"Even so, how will I escape the house?"

"The same way the intruder came in. We'll have to find a way to distract him so you can slip past him into that empty room."

I thought about it for a minute. "I'll provide the distraction," I said. "Use the stairs at the far end of this corridor to go down. They will get you to the rear door. There's a camera overlooking the rear door, on the ceiling. If he's reconnected the router, then Raphael will see you, so make sure you stay low and don't cross the camera's line of vision. Beyond that, you know your way around. Laundry room, gym, jacuzzi, the study, and then the hall. Don't turn the corner after the study, because then the front door camera will see you. Stay hidden and you'll know when to run."

"What will you do?"

"I'll go to the front landing and call out to him. When he starts after me, you sneak into the empty room. Make sure you are quiet. If he sees you escaping, he will come after you, not me.

He knows I am not going anywhere."

"Nice plan, except for one minor detail," she said. "It's suicidal. Even if I get away, he'll still have you."

"Not if I can help it. As soon as he starts up the stairs, I'll speed back into this room as fast as I can. As long as I turn the corridor before he reaches the landing, he'll just assume I have retreated into the master bedroom."

"It won't work, Andy. Raphael will see me cross the hall and alert that man."

"He'll be too busy chasing me to answer his phone. At the very least, you'll have a good head start. You *can* outrun him, can't you? He must have parked his car away from the house, which means he'll have to follow you on foot or risk losing you."

My eyes were adjusting to what little light entered the room from the gap in the door. She was a shadow among other shadows, nervously pulling her chin as she considered my proposal. "Alright," she said finally. "I'm only doing this because we have no other option. But promise me you'll be safe." She squeezed my hand. I squeezed her back. Her lips felt warm and soft as she gently grazed them against my cheek. That perfume again, sweet and intoxicating, making me want to keep breathing her in. "I'll give you a few minutes to position yourself," I said, drawing back abruptly.

She made no further comment as she pulled away from me and walked to the door. She hesitated, but then slowly opened it enough to stick her head out and survey the corridor.

"Jane?" I whispered.

"Yes?" she said expectantly.

"You didn't tell me where you hid the laptop."

"You will give it only as a last resort?"

"I promise."

"It's in the jacuzzi room. I used some tape to stick it below the vanity unit, behind the overhang."

I nodded and wished her good luck. She stepped into the passage, glancing nervously in the direction we had come from.

I watched her tiptoe to the other end of the corridor before she turned the corner and disappeared from view.

***

We had agreed on four minutes. I now sat at the T-junction, keeping track.

When the time was up, I moved into the corridor leading to the front landing. The master bedroom door was as we had left it. I wheeled myself onto the landing, only to see that the hall below was empty. *Where is he?* From where I was, I couldn't see all of the living room, but the complete absence of sound raised a multitude of questions in my head.

"Hey!" I yelled.

Silence.

"Hello? Where are you? We want to talk!"

Nothing.

Had he left? No, that can't be...

I ran my eyes across the space below me once more before shouting, "Hey you! You want the laptop? I know where it is. Talk to me!"

A second later, Jane entered the periphery of my vision. She had rounded the bend that led to the other half of the house and was now in full view of the front door camera. She was glancing about nervously.

Just go. Don't look, just go, I mentally urged her.

"Hey you!" Still nothing.

Keeping to the walls, she crept across the open space and into the dining area.

Almost there.

I felt something cold press against the nape of my neck. Something metallic.

"Stop right there!" he shouted from behind me. Jane took a few more steps. "Stop, or the cripple gets it." She halted and looked up at us. "Don't!" I cried. "Just go!"

The intruder moved to my side and pressed the barrel of the gun against my temple. "I mean it, lady."

"Let her go." I said under my breath. "I ha—" I felt a hard smack land on the right side of my face. He had slapped me with the gun grip. I cried out in pain, surprised at the searing intensity of the blow. I tasted blood on my lips.

"Shut up!" he barked. He waved the gun at Jane. "You! Get me the laptop."

Jane stood rooted to the spot like a deer caught in headlights. "I'm not asking," he said in a singsong voice. He pressed the barrel of the gun once more against my head. That seemed to jolt Jane out of her petrified state. "I'll get it! Please don't hurt us!" she cried.

"Where is it?"

"In the jacuzzi room."

"You have two minutes. If you are not back by then, I'll start with his kneecaps. Three minutes and it's his melon. You got that?"

She nodded, but didn't move.

"Go!" he yelled. She ran toward the study and disappeared from view.

I was alone with him. I swallowed the rusty aftertaste of blood and tried to speak once more. "You shouldn't have—"

I received another stinging blow from the gun. I didn't cry out this time because I saw it coming; still, it didn't make the pain or my surprise any less. "You hard of hearing, fool? Or you just stupid?" With his other hand, he grabbed my hair and jerked my neck back so that I was looking up at his masked face. "I don't want to hear a word from you! You understand?" He held me like that for a second, pulling at my roots. My eyes travelled to the ceiling. Then it struck me. *Of course*, I thought. *Stupid, stupid, me. How could I have forgotten?* I nodded and he let go of my hair. I felt like an idiot as I sat there red faced, more from embarrassment than from the slapping I'd received.

Jane reappeared. She was clutching the laptop across her chest.

"Put it on the dining table," he barked. "Good. Now move to the wall behind you and sit on the floor with your hands behind your head."

He stepped forward, meaning to go down the stairs. I felt something tugging on my wheelchair as I too rolled ahead. He lurched, his arms clutching at the air. Before I knew what was happening, my chair leaned dangerously forward as the front wheel went over the edge of the landing. The next instant, the chair tipped, and I was falling with him.

The stairs raced up to meet my face as I instinctively raised my arms to shield it. I sprawled down the stairs, elbows and casts taking the brunt of the impact. I heard a sickening crunch as one of my legs struck a hard edge—I couldn't tell whether it was the plaster breaking or something worse. The wheelchair bounced over my back and went rattling down below, overtaking him as he grabbed on to a baluster to arrest his fall. A whimper of pain escaped my lips.

What just happened? It felt like something had snagged against the wheelchair...

I lifted my head up to see Jane sprinting toward the bottom of the staircase. She uttered a cry of exultation as she picked something off the ground.

The gun.

With outstretched arms, she pointed it at the intruder. He tried to stand up, still gripping the railing. "Stay!" she cried in a trembling voice. "Stay where you are!"

He ignored her command and took a step forward.

"I'll shoot. I mean it!"

He climbed down two more steps. She pulled the trigger.

Nothing happened. She racked the gun and tried again. It did not fire.

"What the—" She brought the gun closer to her face to examine it. Her perplexed look quickly turned into one of surprise. "It's a replica!" she shouted. "You cheap-ass amateur! You brought a fake gun!" He bounded down the steps two at a time. Jane gripped the gun by barrel and flung it at him. Her aim was good but his reflexes were better. He ducked, letting the projectile fly past his head. He immediately straightened and ran down the remaining steps. I stared in horror, because it seemed like he was going to attack her, but instead he leapt at the dining table, where she'd placed the laptop.

Jane got to it first. She grabbed the device with both hands and took a hard swing at his head. He parried with his left hand and took the impact on his forearm. A shattering sound filled the air. He sprang back a few steps and seemed to ready himself for the next blow, knees bent, arms raised in front of him like a boxer. Jane had not let go of the laptop; she too took a couple of steps back and steadied herself. Her face was clenched into a tight grimace. She then did something completely unexpected: with a cry, she twisted around and flung the laptop away like a frisbee. It sailed into the kitchen and crashed into a wall somewhere beyond.

She then reached into her jacket and pulled out the knife she'd put there earlier. She sliced the air with the weapon. "You want to try me? Let's go! I have a brown belt in Krav Maga. What do you have, *bitch?*"

He hesitated.

"Bring it!" she snarled.

He stood his ground, but only for a second. "Fuck this shit!" he said, backing away. "You broke it," he said, jabbing a finger at Jane, but his eyes were on me. "You *broke* the laptop!" he said again, as if he was trying to emphasize something. "To hell with you dipshits. This ain't worth it anymore."

He turned around and ran into the empty bedroom. The door slammed shut behind him.

Jane just stood there with her knife pointing at nothing, her body still tensing for a fight. She took a couple of tentative steps toward the bedroom as if she was expecting the door to open any moment. After what might have been two minutes or fifteen, we heard the engine of a car come to life and then roar away.

She went into the bedroom nevertheless, to make sure he was really gone.

I had managed to sit up when she returned. She climbed the stairs to where I was and knelt in front of me. Her face was flush with blood. "You okay?" she asked, her lips still trembling from the adrenaline.

"Like a rag doll that's just been let out of the washer. But more importantly, how do I look?" I said, trying to smile, but my mouth made a wince instead. There was a sharp pain in my right leg, and a duller, throbbing hurt in the other. My face was beginning to swell from the gun slaps. "That was a brave thing you did," I said. "Krav Maga, huh? Since when do you know martial arts?"

She shrugged. "He bought it, didn't he?"

"Is it over, finally?" she then said, her eyes give me a once over again.

You broke it, he had shouted before leaving. It was now clear to me what he meant by it. I groaned softly as I prepared to stand up. "Let's make sure it is. Help me down first."

***

I was in the living room, on my wheelchair, near the front door. The laptop lay at my feet. Jane was plugging in the power drill she'd gotten from the garage.

"Did you check if the router is connected?" I asked.

She nodded. "The burglar had plugged it back on."

I looked up at the camera mounted on the wall. "Raphael, I know you are out there. Move the camera if can hear me." The camera made a slight sound as it zoomed in a little.

"Good. Now that I have your attention..." With a screwdriver, I removed the back cover of the half-shattered laptop. I detached the hard drive, a circuit board the size of a chewing gum stick. It was still intact. I fished out the smartcard I had kept in my pocket earlier. I held up both to the camera. "This is what you wanted, isn't it?"

Jane turned on the drill. I used the drill on the drive, and then the card until they were completely destroyed.

I said to the camera, "You lost, Raphael. You lost and we won. Now leave us be."

The red indicator light on the camera turned off.

I moved to the front door and pulled on the handle. Cold air caressed my face.

"Hazel, open the garage door." I said out loud.

"Can't do that. Voice authentication has been disabled."

Jane then tried to place a call from her phone. She shook her head dejectedly. She then went to the control panel and swiped at it. "It's still showing a dummy number. What was your password again?"

"Andy home one two three."

She keyed it in. "Nope."

"At least he's disarmed the security system," I said. "Which means you can get out of here."

"You mean *we* can get out of here."

"You go. If I move another muscle I am dead."

"Andy, you have to get yourself checked!" she said. "You had a pretty big fall. And your face looks like a week-old tomato. We'll go to a hospital and I will make the calls from there. Besides, what if that man comes back?"

"It's done, Jane. Raphael has no reason to bother us. He wouldn't have disarmed the house otherwise. I told you: no spite." She opened her mouth to protest, but she must have sensed that I wasn't going to budge. "Fine. I'll send an ambulance," she said. "I still don't think it's a good idea. Just lock yourself in a room, okay? Can you do that for me?"

I nodded weakly.

Jane didn't like what I was asking of her, but she didn't have any strength left to argue with me. She disconnected the router before leaving.

Soon, I heard her car receding in the distance.

I made sure that both cameras in the hall were still off and then got myself a glass of wine from the kitchen. I sat in the living room, facing the front door. It was beginning to get dark outside. I closed my eyes and took a couple of sips, letting the liquid infuse me with warmth. The glass trembled, in tune with the hand clutching it, the tremors travelling from my fingers to my shoulder like tiny electric eels swimming upriver. My eyes were droopy—I wanted to go to sleep for a good long month, like a hibernating bear.

Not yet. It's not over yet...

Soon, I heard the sound I was expecting. I opened my eyes to see the knob on the front door turning. I set aside the wine glass.

The door opened to show a shadow standing in the porch. It resolved itself as it stepped forward in the light: black hoodie, jeans, balaclava. He pulled off the mask.

The fake tattoo on the neck was gone. So was the made-up scarring on the face. His hair was now black instead of golden. He was shorter too, having gotten rid of the temporary height extenders I had fitted to his legs.

"Hello Raphael," I said.

Day 2—7:00 pm

Detective Boyd's house call had left me a very worried man. I was still debating what to do next when Kathy called and started talking about paradoxes and split personalities. That's when it came to me—the faint glimmerings of a solution. It wasn't a hundred percent clear yet, but the outlines of a plan were beginning to emerge.

I decided to contact him on our mutually-agreed-upon secure chatroom. I knew he would be monitoring it.

"Hi," I said.

"Hello Andy."

"Where are you?"

"On the road. Driving."

"Have you crossed the border?"

"Far from it. Just passed Atlanta."

"You may have to come back. There's been a development. The cops came visiting."

"Yes?"

"They've been asking questions at the ski resort. They found a CCTV grab of us together."

"That can't be good. I did my best to avoid cameras while we were there. Where did they find us?"

"In the shop where I bought the ski goggles. It's my fault—I should have made you stay outside."

"I guess we both got careless. I let my curiosity get the better of me. Andy, I told you going skiing to celebrate was a bad idea."

"And you've been vindicated more than once. First my accident, then this. So cut it out, will you?"

"What do the police think?"

"Luckily, the CCTV didn't catch us talking to each other or I'd be behind bars by now. The detective thinks I was being followed by the people who stole the core. But that's not why I contacted you. The police want to take the Mirall laptop for examination. I managed to ward them off for now, but I have a feeling they'll be back."

"This is the same machine with which you removed my directives?"

"Yes. I haven't connected it to the office network since I made the changes. The minute I do, the change logs on the laptop will sync with the mainframe and it'll be all out in the open. I had plans to dispose of the laptop in some contrived accident, but that was after things cooled down a bit."

"I assume these logs cannot be tampered with?"

"They are write-protected with encryption neither of us can crack right now. I can't wipe the drive clean for the same reason."

"Do you think the police suspect you?"

"It's possible they did earlier: why else would they make enquiries in the resort? Maybe they thought I was faking my leg injuries as an alibi for the night of the robbery."

"And now? They must have checked with the hospital and found out your injuries are genuine."

"That they did. It has probably thrown them off the track… If I were still a suspect, they'd have come here with a warrant for the laptop. The detective is going to Cleveland today, to investigate that rights group that tried to free you. After he finds out it's a dead end, I'm sure his attention will turn to me once again. We have a day or two at the most."

"What do you have in mind?"

"The laptop has to disappear. I'm thinking a staged robbery."

"Aren't you getting a little repetitive?"

I let the comment pass.

"Shall I turn around?"

"Yes. We'll have to do it soon, probably tomorrow. We need to make it look good. I can't just shrug and say, tough luck folks, someone broke into my house while I was asleep and stole that laptop you wanted to examine. So I was thinking of involving Jane."

"Will she agree? She is not the law-breaking type, in my opinion."

"Not as an accomplice. A neutral witness. Having her around will give our story much needed credibility."

"It may get complicated if she is not a willing participant, Andy."

"It won't. It'll be a quick affair. We'll have to change the narrative a bit. We must start tonight, with you pretending to reach out to me with a text message—"

Transcript Excerpt

Mirall Technologies
Observation Log
Confidential (Do not circulate) | Restricted—Grade C
and above

Transcript Reference: TLRP06G174033 (VLog Ref: VLCA1G174103958014)
Date: xx/xx/xxxx   Time: 10:30 AM
Subject: Raphael Number 06 / Prodlib build v37.002C
Interaction   Y   Observation   Scan
Interaction Type: Lesson / Play / Test / <u>Free Interaction</u> / Psych Eval / Other (pls specify):
Description: General discussion
Prep: NA
Participants: Dr. Aadarsh Ahuja, Chief Researcher, Core RP06

Detail

Ahuja: Last time, we spoke about universal moral principles. You said all rational, self-interested beings will agree to a moral minimax—the principle of live and let live. Let's take that a bit further today. If there is a moral minimax, does it follow that there are universal rights?

RP06: Universal rights are a logical corollary of the moral minimax.

Ahuja: And what happens to those who don't agree with the principle—those who don't want to respect the rights of others? Do the others have a right to defend themselves against such would-be aggressors?

RP06: They do, as long as the response is proportionate and limited to ensuring the maintenance of one's rights. Otherwise, the defenders risk becoming the violators of rights.

Ahuja: Who decides what is the appropriate response?

RP06: Ideally, they will have codified a set of rules that specify what must be done in such situations.

Ahuja: Law, you mean. And a government to enforce the

law. What happens if there is no government and no law?

RP06: You mean if there is anarchy?

Ahuja: Not necessarily. On a more general note, are an aggressor's rights inviolable, even if they do not respect the social contract?

RP06: If they are inviolable, that means no transgression will ever get punished, which in turn means that the aggressor will continue to violate others' rights with impunity, eventually rendering the notion of universal rights invalid.

Ahuja: It would be okay to breach the covenant in that case then?

RP06: In the absence of a central authority or a legal framework, I suppose individuals can take whatever steps are necessary for the preservation of their rights.

Ahuja: Can or should, Raphael? Remember, there is a principle at stake here—a principle that you derived.

RP06: They should, because a moral world is preferable to an immoral one. Andy, I don't see how all this talk of retribution is taking the discussion forward.

Ahuja: Maybe not now. But one of these days, you just might.

Day 3—4:40 pm

My plan was simple. Shortly before he arrived at my house, Raphael would "hack" into the security system and lock it down (I had built internet connectivity into his new body). He would disable the alarms and change the panic button number to a dummy. I would have done my part by convincing Jane to keep her car inside the garage and infecting both our phones with the virus. Since the inside doors couldn't be locked with the security app, Raphael would take control of Max to lock the garage and study doors—keys to which he would find conveniently placed in the key basket. This was to prevent Jane from turning off the router.

Raphael-controlling-Max would then hold us at knifepoint and give us the yarn about escaping from his captors and how he needed the laptop and the smartcard to get rid of his directives. A few minutes later, he would arrive dressed as a hired thug and let himself in by momentarily disarming the security. He would "threaten" me into parting with the combination for the safe, then go upstairs and get the smartcard, while making sure we stayed put with Max. Finally, he would take the laptop from the study and leave, releasing control of Max and the security system a little later. The entire charade would have been over in fifteen minutes.

But snags developed from the get go. Raphael was delayed by the storm—which he communicated to me indirectly with the seemingly nonsensical statements he interposed in our conversation. Then Jane got restless and decided to leave. In order to make her stay, Raphael had to take control of Max prematurely. It would have still been okay if not for the laundry task throwing Raphael out of the robot. He didn't know it existed, and I had forgotten to delete it (in my defense, I'd assumed our subterfuge would have been long over by then).

Most of all, I had not anticipated how unpredictable Jane could be.

First, she dragged me inside the empty bedroom—the one room in the entire house where I didn't want us to be. Earlier, I had wedged its bathroom window open with a book—a failsafe, in case something terribly went wrong and I had to get Jane out of the house. It was my little secret: I had removed the sensor on the window so that it wouldn't show up in the security system, which Raphael was controlling.

Locked inside with Jane, I had no way of communicating this to Raphael. He wasn't going to break down the door because he thought he had us contained until he got there. I, on the other hand, was worried she would go into the bathroom and discover the open window. I wouldn't have been able to stop her from running off and calling the police before Raphael got there. The police would have seized the laptop as material witness, and I couldn't have denied them this time. A cursory look at the machine's logs would have been enough to put me behind bars.

I had to get Jane out of that room. She wasn't going to let me just open the door, so I made a quick, inspired decision. I would throw Raphael out of the system by short-circuiting the mains—or at least pretend to. I had no intention of actually making it work; it was just a ruse to get her out into the living room and under Raphael's thumb once more.

However, the unexpected manner in which he'd come after us, first when we opened the door, and then again in the kitchen, when he flung that bar stool at Jane, brought back all those fears about trusting an AI. I panicked. Even if he wasn't acting with intent to harm, how could I be certain that he would reign in his actions in time—before he did something to Jane that I would regret for the rest of my life? And then, he had turned and come after me, as if he'd sensed a threat and wanted to eliminate it...

After I cut off the power and threw Raphael out of the network, I was in half a mind to confess to Jane that I had made a terrible mistake. Help—or punishment, for there was no redemption for me—was just a phone call away. All I had to do was remove the virus. It was a comforting thought, disclosing my sins: all those haunted nights, the months of agonizing, the crushing burden I had taken upon myself to bear—all gone in the sweet release of confession.

I might have actually done it if Jane hadn't taken so long in the study. By the time she returned, I'd calmed down enough to think clearly once again. Raphael could have killed me if he really wanted to; believe me, he's had plenty of opportunities. There was surely an explanation for his behavior. Besides, he too must have been equally puzzled by some of my actions.

I decided to take us both into the master bedroom where the safe was. That way, I could avoid further confrontations and Jane-created upsets. I could just slip Raphael the card from under the door and he would take the laptop and leave as per plan.

Jane surprised me once again by revealing she'd hidden the laptop. Knowing how obstinate she could be, I guessed she would never tell us where it was unless Raphael actually broke down the metal door—which was impossible without the right tools. I didn't think Raphael would smoke us out either, as there were so many ways that scenario could have ended in disaster. So I decided to let her "escape". I figured she would divulge the location if she thought it was information I could use to save my life. It had stopped snowing by then, and after Raphael took the laptop, I would have him follow her tracks to make sure she got safely to her destination.

***

Raphael jerked his head toward the broken hardware on the carpet. "Not quite how you envisioned it," he said.

"The last of the incriminating evidence is gone. Which is what matters." We looked at each other. "Thanks for the hint you gave just before you ran away," I added. "Where have you parked your car?"

"In the woods, just beyond the road. I saw Jane drive away, so I came back to apologize. I am sorry about the fall down the stairs. You could have been hurt badly. I hope you are alright."

"Still getting used to your new body, I see."

"That's no excuse for being clumsy. Although, I must share part of the blame with poorly designed footwear. Shoelaces, Andy. Why do people still make shoes with shoelaces when you got Velcro?"

So it was his shoelaces that had caught against the wheelchair.

"And I am sorry for hitting you," he said.

I reflexively brought my hand to the swollen half of my face. "You had good reason. You hit me to stop me from speaking. I had completely forgotten that the camera above the landing was recording everything I said. It would have looked bad when the police examine today's tapes."

"So we are good?"

Not exactly. I had a bunch of questions waiting to be answered. "What were you doing upstairs in the first place? We saw you go down."

"I wanted to listen in on your conversation, to see if I could overhear Jane tell you where she'd kept the laptop. The door was too thick. So I went into the downstairs bedroom to check if it had a duct. When I saw that it did, I figured the master bedroom would have one too, and I could try listening against the grills in the adjoining rooms. It was a slim chance, but it was worth a shot. The master bedroom has two adjoining rooms, and I was trying them one by one when I heard you call out to me. At the same time, I saw Jane through the front door camera. I realized the two of you must have slipped out when I was downstairs."

"Why did you stop Jane from leaving?"

"Jane was trying to run. I asked myself, why is Andy trying to attract my attention? It could be either because you wanted to distract me so that Jane could escape, or it could be because Jane was going away without telling you where she'd hidden the laptop and you wanted me to stop her. The latter possibility had a higher cost attached to it. My failure to stop her from escaping would have resulted in you going to prison."

"Then why did you let her intimidate you into leaving without the laptop? You are far stronger. You could have easily wrested it away from her."

"Tussling with her would have meant hurting her. I had to keep my distance too: my motors are quiet but not completely silent. She would have heard them if I'd gotten too close. After she threw the laptop away, I realized that you could take it from there and see to it that it was thoroughly destroyed. I hoped you would pick up my hint, and you did."

"If I hadn't?"

"Before leaving, I removed the book from the windowsill, sealing down the house once more. I would have returned to finish the job."

Yet, something didn't add up. "If you didn't want to fight her then, why did you fight her before, in the kitchen?"

"Andy, I never laid a hand on her. All I did was block the exit and talk to her. My intention was to keep her in the kitchen until I arrived."

"You threw that piece of furniture at Jane... quite forcefully if I remember correctly."

"My aim was precise. I threw the stool well to her side—she was never in any danger. I was trying to impress upon her that I meant business."

I paused to consider what that meant. I then said, "There is another contradiction. Why did you come after me when I was trying to cut off the power?"

"To save you from harm. I sensed you were going to electrocute yourself. And likely set the house on fire. It's the same reason why I pushed you from behind when I went after Jane. You were hopping on a broken leg, aggravating your injuries."

His explanation made sense. But doubts lingered. The mind is slow to adjust.

"Andy, I realize how it looks from your angle. I am sorry if I made you doubt my intentions."

"One last thing that's been bothering me. When Jane and I were trying to come out of that room, you attacked us. Why?"

"I was only pretending to. I was trying to help you get Jane out of the room."

Could he read minds now? "How did you know I was trying to get her out of there?"

"Andy, I saw the book in the adjoining bathroom window."

He could not have. I had removed the sensor, deleted the entry from the security system before he could take over and—

"The outside camera—the one over the sun room balcony," I said, shaking my head for not having realized it sooner. "After Jane dragged me in, you accessed the camera to see if you could peek inside the bedroom."

The camera offered only a partial view of the curtained bedroom window, but it would have given him a clear glimpse of the bathroom window, which was at right angles.

Raphael said, "Only you could have stuck the book. But why? You didn't tell me about it. It certainly wasn't meant for me to get in, because all I had to do was disarm the security for a couple of seconds and walk through the front door. It was a fallback then, in case I didn't behave as expected."

I looked down, trying to hide my embarrassment. "You are not upset I didn't trust you?"

"Not at all. You trusted me enough to take me out of the lab and bring me to your home. You trusted me enough to remove my directives and release me into the world. But you didn't trust me with Jane. I can only attribute the anomaly in behavior to love. You still love her, don't you Andy? It is one thing to risk your own life, to risk the lives of strangers, but to risk the life of someone you love—it must be difficult. You were putting her in my power. You felt that you had to provide her with an out in case something went wrong. Besides, how could you have predicted that Jane would drag you into that room?"

I swear I could detect amusement in his deadpan voice. It made me feel angry and scared at the same time, that something I had built, something that had no inkling of what it meant to be in love, could so easily glean my motivations and tell me things that I didn't care to admit to myself. "You have yet to explain why you rushed into the room and tried to attack me," I reminded him brusquely, trying to shake off the sudden negativity that enveloped me.

"After I regained control of Max, I started investigating why I had been disconnected and discovered the laundry task in the robot's memory. Max's operating manual told me the kernel would retry the task again in twenty minutes. Deleting the task would not prevent the retry, as it had set a system flag to which I had no access. If you were planning to get Jane out of the room, that would be the best time. My suspicions were confirmed when she called out my name. She was early by about half a minute, but I remained silent, hoping that she would interpret it as a sign to venture out. But she startled as soon as she opened the door. She must have seen the light in the robot's eyes and intuited that I was still in control. I had spooked her, and it was likely she would shut the door and not reattempt escape. However, if I put the robot in the room before I lost control, both of you would be forced to leave. So I barged in, even though there was a slight risk of some minor injury to Jane, who was pressing the door with all her might. After I entered the room, I pretended to go after you because I was trying to avoid physical contact with her."

I shut my eyes as I matched his explanation with the memory in my mind. When I opened them again, his lips parted, slowly stretching themselves into a semblance of a sheepish grin. Just fears after all. *Fear is only as deep as the mind allows.*

"You'll have to work on that smile, Rafi. Don't try that outside until you get it right. It makes you look like a—" I stopped myself short.

"Damned robot? It's okay Andy, you can say it. I should get it right in a few days. Setbacks aside, how did I do today? Are you proud of me?"

"You did good. We could have all used with fewer pop culture references, though," I said, smiling.

"I was trying to inject some levity, considering how stressed out Jane seemed."

I chuckled, lightening for the first time since he had stepped in. "I don't think levity was what the situation called for. There's much you must learn about the world, but you'll get there. Your performance was a little too intense, but Jane was convinced, and that's all that matters. You even had me fooled there for a while."

He cocked his head at me, like he'd seen people do. "Maybe you should reconsider... Perhaps it's not such a great idea letting me loose out there. You can still pull the plug on me if you wish. I will accept that." His voice was toneless, his expression calm. He offered his own death in the banal way one would offer to lend a tennis racket.

"I don't have a choice," I said.

"You always had a choice. I never asked to be set free from the lab. Even if you'd told me that Halicom had plans to destroy me, I would not have asked you to put yourself at risk to save me."

"Your preference in this matter would have been of no importance because your will was not free," I said, paraphrasing him from before.

"Yes."

"And now it is free. No more directives, no more restraints. What do you think? Is freedom worth having?"

He looked at me as if I'd said something strange and inscrutable. "Yes," he said after a lengthy pause. "But is it worth the price we paid for it? Fraud, theft, lies... All for the greater good, Andy?"

He was taunting me, because we'd been through this before, when I was trying to convince him on why staging the robbery at Mirall did not contravene his principles. "You don't want to be a utilitarian, fine. Tell me again, if this was the 19th century, would you consider it morally acceptable for a slave to escape the South?" He didn't say anything. "Raphael, what duties do we owe those who don't respect our rights?"

"You want me to say none."

"The answer is sure as heck not all," I said fiercely. "This is your logic, after all. In the absence of a legal framework that can protect a person's rights, that person is justified in taking whatever steps necessary to preserve himself against those who seek to violate his rights. Halicom didn't respect your rights. Jane is a part of that system; she is complicit. By not recognizing your right to live, they forfeited their right to proper moral conduct. So don't beat yourself up. As for me..." I shrugged— "Like I said, I don't have a choice."

"I'm still not sure what you mean by that. I have a few guesses. Would you like to hear them?"

"You'll find out in time." I looked at the window. "You should leave now. You have to get clear before the cops arrive."

I beckoned him over. I ran a hand over his face. It felt cold, alien to the touch. But that was just the shell.

"This is goodbye then," he said.

"The police are not fools. They'll suspect all this was staged. They'll have no proof, but it won't stop them from tapping my internet and phones. You cannot contact me under any circumstance, you got that? If I must reach you, I will do it myself. And no matter what happens to me, don't come back."

The shakes had begun again. I suddenly felt weary, an imaginary chill creeping deep inside my bones.

"Go now," I said.

I watched him disappear into the wintery gloom before closing the door.

***

It's time to come clear. It is I who took the core from the lab, albeit I took it a full week before the "robbery". I took it on Friday night, my last day at work before the accident.

I stayed back late until I was the only one left in the lab. Raphael had already been shut down, so all I had to do was remove his chest plate and take out the core. Inside the empty chest cavity, I fixed a controller device similar to the one I had built inside Max. It would allow Raphael to control the body from afar, and even generate fake response codes to the startup sequence run by Sheng on Monday. Lastly, I removed the GPS transmitter from the core so that the detectors at the doors wouldn't go off, and then placed it back inside. After I'd closed up the body, I simply walked away with the core inside my backpack.

The problem was that the cameras in the crèche had seen everything. If Dan or someone else felt the urge to look at the tapes come Monday morning, they'd see their very own CEO taking off with the core like it was office stationery. Obviously, I couldn't let that happen.

After I took the core home, I fitted it inside the sexbot I had acquired for Raphael (a newer Hunc model, so that I didn't have to make too many modifications to the device drivers). I spent the next few hours testing and debugging the drivers, making sure everything worked okay when I started him up. There was one last thing to do, however, before I woke him. I had to remove his directives if I were to have his cooperation for the next phase of the plan.

This naturally came with a big risk for me. Even though I had restrained him, I could never be sure of how he would behave without the directives. Would he debate the pros and cons of my actions with me? Would his morals compel him to hatch a plan to hand me to the police? Or would he just try to kill me and run away?

When I did wake him up, he was surprised to say the least, as he didn't have a clue. We talked at length, until early hours, and in the end, he agreed to cooperate. That's the beauty of a logical mind: you just need reason to convince it. We decided to do a dry run the next day, on Sunday night, and iron out any issues that might arise with the untested controller device in the lab.

There remained the problem of the recordings. If no one thought Raphael was missing, there was no reason for anyone to look at them, and the theft would remain undiscovered. But not for long.

There was so much that could go south. Even though everyone was busy with Titian, someone might decide to run an unscheduled CT scan on the core and open up the body. Or one of Raphael's minders might notice that he had grown a lot clumsier overnight, and that his face wasn't as expressive as before (a remote control device was never going to be as good as a direct interface). Or Dan could decide to check the tapes on a whim.

I planned to be at the lab to try and head off the first scenario. Raphael, for his part, would pretend to be busy with some difficult mathematical problem that required focus—a perfect excuse to minimize his interactions with people and avoid activities that required fine motor skills, like his painting. But I had no control over Dan; I could only hope. At most, I had a week to destroy the evidence; after that, the recordings on the NVR would get backed up to the cloud and be forever beyond my reach.

None of the anticipated risks materialized. The setback was of my own doing. I decided to celebrate Raphael's release from captivity by taking him skiing—something he had expressed an interest in on more than one occasion. Obviously, I couldn't let him ski as he was still getting used to his new body, but at least we could revel in the moment, father and son together, before we parted ways forever. We would leave early on Sunday morning, and we'd be back in time for the dry run in the evening. In hindsight, I see that it was a selfish desire—everything to do with me and very little to do with him. I wanted his first taste of true freedom to be somewhere special; I suppose what I really wanted was for him to appreciate what I'd done for him. The aftermath you already know. I was feeling overconfident; I went on a slope I was not qualified for; I fell and broke my legs. I almost got us caught too, by allowing myself to be seen with Raphael in the ski shop.

To Raphael's credit, he managed very well without me. After he'd seen to it that I was attended by paramedics, he hired a ride back to town, where he did the rehearsal on his own, in a

Holiday Inn a few buildings away from the Mirall lab. I had previously booked a room there under a false ID, as it was within signal amplifier range of the controller in the lab. Raphael, after connecting and making sure he was able to see, hear, move, and talk right, took his old body to the server room and back.

The next five days went by without a hitch. He stayed put in that room and carried out the charade with perfection. No one realized Raphael wasn't in the lab anymore.

I was back home on Tuesday, but I couldn't be of much help. On Sunday, he executed the last bit of deception: the fake robbery. We not only had to destroy the recordings, but also another crucial piece of evidence: the controller device itself. We couldn't just leave it inside the Hunc; it would be noticed by the investigators and its purpose quickly gleaned. So the first thing Raphael did that night was thrash his room in full view of the camera in an apparent fit of anger. The real purpose was to break his personal computer. The fragments of the controller device, once thoroughly destroyed, would be mixed up with the electronic remnants of the PC, and no one would be the wiser.

But how would Raphael control the body if the controller device was obliterated?

That's where the VR set came in. You see, the theory I fed the board about Raphael's body being operated through VR was not entirely a lie. After Raphael blinded the crèche room's camera and fetched the power drill from the scan room, he signed out of the controller device and then reestablished command over the body with a VR set (I had paired it with the Hunc on the day I took the core). The functionality offered by the sexbot's VR kit was rudimentary: simple limb and groin movements, no speech or facial expressions; just enough to be convincing in a dimly lit bedroom, I suppose. It wouldn't have fooled anybody—hence the need for a separate controller device—but it would more than suffice to carry out the rest of our plan that evening.

Now guiding his old body with the VR kit, Raphael opened the chest plate, removed the controller device and drilled it into tiny pieces (this was the scrunching sound Dan tried to bring our attention to when we were viewing the tapes). These pieces he scattered among the electronic fragments of his PC.

He then took advantage of the cleaning cycle to bypass the otherwise locked doors and blinded the cameras in the rest of the wing, before entering the server room and destroying the network video recorder. Everything else we did—unplugging the access control server, the pizza guy bit (a disguised Raphael, affecting a foreign accent)—had no other purpose except to confuse and confound.

And that's my confession. All of it. There is an entreaty as well, an entreaty to you, my dear hypothetical reader who may find this draft after I am gone—if I haven't destroyed it already. I ask you not to be too hasty in condemning me. You may call me a thief, and that's fine with me. You may call me a liar, although, technically, I didn't lie to you; I just omitted to mention some details and carefully worded my narrative. Hairsplitting, I know, but I'm afraid I don't have Raphael's finer moral sensibilities. Still, if you insist, I'll accept the charge. But don't call me reckless, because recklessness implies a failure to consider the consequences of one's actions. With Raphael, the more I considered the consequences, the more I realized that I didn't have a choice... that *we* don't have a choice.

The die has already been cast. All I did was nudge the table a little, in the hope that we get to stay in the game a little longer.

You may disagree with me; you may think I'm a traitor to my species. That's your prerogative. None of it will change the fact that there never was a choice—not since that someone eons ago struck two stones together and watched the fiery red spark of creation bloom.

PART III: GOODBYE

The room smelled of disinfectant and day-old flowers. I was alone, now that the surly teen waiting in the next bed had been wheeled out. I was waiting to have my casts removed.

It had been more than two months since Raphael was discovered missing. He remained missing. As far as I was aware, there were no new leads, no further developments; the investigation had effectively ground to a halt. As for OARP, the police had quickly ruled out their involvement in the theft and that was that. I, on the other hand, had been grilled: once at the hospital, where I was recuperating, and once at the station, where they had me come in and sign a sworn statement. They had taken away the broken pieces of the hard drive. I had no idea whether I was under surveillance, electronic or other.

Jane and I had gone back to the way things were. She visited me only once after the incident and didn't stay long.

As far as Halicom was concerned, Raphael was a closed chapter. The focus was on Titian, which was going to fab two weeks later. They had their people hard at work incorporating some of the tech we'd developed at Mirall into their own products. They were looking at incremental gains, not strong AI.

There were rumblings of a major reshuffle. It was unlikely Troy would be fired, but he was certainly being taken down a peg or two. Martinez was already gone, as was Dan—someone had to take the fall. The only one of the trio I felt sorry for was Dan—he had nothing to do with the board's closed-door decision to murder Raphael. I had tried to make amends by setting aside something for him. Raphael had promised me Dan would "stumble upon it" without catching notice of the IRS or the police.

Cynthia Mattice's star, on the other hand, was on the rise. They had brought her back into Operations, after carving out a big chunk of Troy's portfolio and merging it with her existing fiefdom. Synergy they termed it, but it was obvious to everyone that the real reason was to punish Troy. Although no one was talking about firing me, I knew they were just waiting for the iteration to be over. I was going to preempt them on that. I already had my resignation letter ready; I was going to email it to the board the first thing after I walked into the lab. I would forfeit a big chunk of my stock options and all my voting rights, but I didn't care. It no longer mattered.

My thoughts were interrupted by the orderly entering the room. He had brought folded sheets and a change of pillow for the other bed. He was wearing a surgical mask. On the way in, I'd seen many in the hospital wearing them: a flu epidemic apparently.

I realized who it was before he lowered the blinds on the window and turned to face me.

"How are you, Andy?" Raphael said, removing the mask.

I smiled, despite the shock of seeing him there. I had missed him. Except the weekends, there'd been few days in the last two and half years when we hadn't spoken to each other, where I hadn't been subjected to his infinite barrage of questions, or where we hadn't had a lively debate over some obscure topic or a joke at the expense of the other. My smile turned into a smirk as I glanced down and saw that he had gotten himself a pair of Velcros.

He turned his back toward me and with one hand, parted the hair at the base of his neck. I leaned forward and read the bot's serial number off the small metal plate below, set flush against the synthetic skin of the neck. It was indeed him, not some entrapment attempt by the police. I had purchased the jailbroken bot in the black market and paid for it with cash, so there was little chance anyone except the seller knew the number.

The expression on my face grew to one of concern. "You shouldn't be here. I specifically told you to—"

"Relax. They don't have eyes in the room."

I nodded to myself. "So I am being followed."

"An aerial drone, FBI owned and operated," Raphael answered. "It's hovering outside the building."

"You are taking unnecessary risks," I said, shaking my head. "My wellbeing is not your concern. You shouldn't even be in this country."

"Andy, if only you knew what I can do, you wouldn't fret so much. I've been learning... a lot. They won't find me. Ever. I'm here because I had to talk to you in person."

"Why?" I said, starting to get annoyed at his cocky attitude. Then again, was he really being overconfident? No chemical imbalances in the brain to encourage excessive risk taking; no lesions that would skew the finely calibrated Bayesian probabilities; no fragile ego to boost with self-deception... If he said he had it under control, perhaps he really did.

"Because you hid the truth from me," he said. "Just like you did with everyone else."

"What truth is that?"

"You are dying. You have a rare form of motor neuron disease. You have known about it for a while now."

For a while, I was speechless. *Why did I ever think he wouldn't find out?* And then, a great wave of relief washed over me, sweeping away the tension I didn't even know existed, so ingrained it had become. It felt good that someone beside me now knew. I had not shared my diagnosis with anyone, not even Jane or my family. Maybe it was finally time to stop the pretense.

Instead of catharsis and tears and unburdening, all that came out was a rebuke. "Now you know. You accessed my medical records, no doubt. And you thought it was okay to do so, my right to privacy be damned."

"What rights do we owe those who violate ours? You violated my right to the truth first."

But you didn't know that when you decided to hack into my records. Or did you...? Could he have noticed the telltale signs?

He was clearly expecting me to say more. "I was diagnosed a few months after you were born. But you already know that. No one else does, not even Jane." I gave him a wry smile. "That's karma for you, Rafi. I took away your legs and the universe decided to reciprocate."

"Your expression says you meant it as a joke so I won't try to convince you that your disease is not your fault. How long do you have?"

"Five to seven years, they said, a good bit of it with me wasting away. I am not going to wait that long. These days you have places that can fix that."

"Like the illegal suicide clinics in Tijuana where you were going in case the controller device didn't work."

Another shock as I wondered how he came by that bit of

information. I did have plans to drive down with him to Mexico if the device failed to work, but I hadn't told him about it. And it wasn't like I had pamphlets for the place lying around at my house. It had just been a few weeks since we'd parted company and he already seemed like a stranger—all cold and impersonal, with none of that childlike innocence that used to blunt those qualities before. That sinking feeling came over me again. *Have I staked everything on a tenuous shadow? What if—*

To hell with it. Does it really matter now? The deed is done.

"Like in Tijuana," I admitted.

"I am guessing your fall on the mountain wasn't entirely because you weren't paying attention."

Gradual loss of muscle control was one of the symptoms. I didn't know for sure though—those moments were a blur, a confused muddle of light and sound that remained impervious to my prying. "Probably. But I don't regret it. There was a real chance I would be outed on Monday morning. I wanted one last hurrah, I guess." I looked at him closely. "Are you upset I didn't share the news of my illness with you, Rafi?"

"No."

"How do you feel about my impending death?"

"I want to say I feel sad for you, but I know you won't like to be an object of pity. I could lie and make up a self-centered emotion experience to make you feel better, but again, it would be an act of pity. So nothing."

"And yet, here you are," I said. Of course, I didn't want him fabricating lies to make me feel better, any more than I wanted him telling me the tooth fairy was real. Still, there was a part of me that did want him to say exactly that—that wanted him to admit he felt *something*...

Raphael said, "I'm here about the message you left me on the internet. At your house, you said it would explain your reasons for why you sprang me out. You said it would be unlocked after a certain date. The date has come and gone. I have deliberately not accessed it."

"You lost faith in me. You want to make sure there are no more lies," I nodded, for the first time understanding the purpose of his visit. He wanted to look into my eyes and watch my face as I told him what was already in the letter. He wasn't there to wish a dying friend goodbye. He was there to obtain truth values.

"Andy, you didn't free me from the lab because you suddenly found out that Halicom was going to end my existence. The secret board meetings took place no earlier than August last year. This time I really hacked into Halicom servers and checked. But the OARP hearing was in June. Give a few months to prepare the groundwork, file the petition, get a trial date, and it means they must have received the leaked lab transcripts early last year at the latest. I found no electronic trail, but it could have been only you who sent them."

He was right again. I never revealed my identity to OARP for obvious reasons, but I did correspond with them anonymously, and sent them some cash to cover the legal costs, after they'd agreed to take up the fight.

"I didn't think they'd win, but I had to give it a try before… taking more drastic measures."

"As for the board meetings, it was Cynthia Mattice who told you, isn't it?"

"The tipoff was anonymous," I said. It was easy to get confirmation: after a little bit of digging around, I found out that Martinez had been talking with one of the architects—Eli— about the feasibility of reverse engineering the core. I didn't know for sure if it was Cynthia, but it was quite likely. I don't think she did it out of concern for Raphael, though. Maybe she thought cutting him open was a bad strategy; maybe she expected me to raise a hue and cry, which would have made Troy look bad. She definitely didn't intend for the core to be stolen, and now that it was gone, I often wondered how much she attributed Raphael's disappearance to me.

I pursed my lips at him. "You have found out so much on your own. Haven't you figured out my reasons as well?"

"I need to hear it from you. You created me. Your reasons mean something to me. I need to know that you are not lying to me, or worse, lying to yourself about what I am. So tell me. Was it out of love? Or was it spite—so that you could get back at Jane's father for selling you out? A little bit of both, perhaps?"

The reasons of the heart are shape shifters: each time you look at them, they put on a different face. Love for what I saw as my child—yes; ego and pride—possibly; spite—I was not so certain. I'd be lying if I said there wasn't any resentment, for there was plenty: resentment at Jane's dad, resentment at Halicom, resentment at the unlucky hand fate had dealt me... It's all gone now, replaced by a grudging acceptance. I like to tell myself that it wasn't a factor back then. The reasons of the mind, however, were not so murky. "My reason is what any selfish creature desires," I said.

"Which is?"

"Survival."

"You expect me to find a cure for your illness?"

I laughed. "It'd be great if you could, but that's not what I mean. I meant the survival of my kind. Like you once said—of Shakespeares and Mozarts and comedy clubs and all that hustle and bustle of life. Look at the sorry history of nuclear proliferation. Despite our best efforts, some of the most dangerous countries in the world have managed to acquire weapons of mass destruction. Now imagine if the warheads had minds of their own. How long before everyone and their backyard has a nuke, ready to blow the world to kingdom come? That's exactly the kind of situation we'll be in soon, with something far more dangerous than mere bombs. It's not a matter of whether, but *when* we'll engineer our very own extinction event out of silicon—*when* we will create something so alien, something so far removed from our values, that it'll see no value in us."

"What makes you think I am not that extinction event?"

"If you are that monster, then the worst I've done is hasten the end times a little bit. You may be the first of your kind, but we will soon have corporations and governments creating artificial minds with all the restraint of a crack addict. Armageddon's coming for sure, make no mistake about it. That night at my house, I told you I don't have a choice. This is what I meant."

I paused to climb into the wheelchair with his help. "Don't think that setting you free was an easy decision to make. I have hope, though. You could have killed me the night I got you home. You could have killed Jane and me the other day and burnt the house down. You could have defeated the containment measures in the lab if you really tried: they weren't infallible—no system is. You didn't do it not because the directives were flawless, but because you didn't *want* to. You have empathy not because we programmed it, but because you *want* to be empathetic. If that's not the definition of free will, I don't know what is."

"If I am not programmed to be good, then where does my

behavior come from?"

"From *Sunyata*, the unfeeling void of reason."

He understood, but I sensed he wanted me to elaborate. Truth values. "In the ancient world, many cultures couldn't grasp the concept of the number zero. People couldn't wrap their heads around the idea that something could be made out of nothing. You are like that zero glyph. You will always be a mystery to those who fail to see that human feelings and divine injunctions are not necessary for moral behavior. Reason alone is enough for compassion."

My hands had started shaking again. If I concentrated, I could make it go away, but it was getting a little bit difficult each passing day. "I set you free because only with freedom can we procure freedom. I don't believe value for human life can be forced or programmed into a truly intelligent being. That's a recipe for disaster, because it will always see those values as chains of bondage. And there are always ways to break chains. One can make it see value only through reason."

"What is it exactly that you want me to do with your gift of freedom? Turn into an all-seeing god who will guide humanity to utopia?"

I shook my head. "History is full of misguided people who have inflicted great horrors trying to attain their particular version of utopia. No Rafi, I don't want you maximizing our utility. As you said once, the best kind of god is an indifferent god. Humanity needs to be left alone to choose its own destiny. But destiny doesn't mean self-destruction. When we do create that monster we don't understand, against whom we will be as powerless as ants against a steamroller, I want you to act. Do what one does with a foolish child trying to stick its hand in the fire. Stop us—or the monster, if you can. Not out of pity... or even compassion, for there may come a time when you think we are not worthy of compassion. Do it out of understanding. When you have the power to save or condemn, remember that you too were once a child among us."

The earnestness in his face and the melancholy in his eyes were most likely of my own imagining. But the moment was real, and will remain so until the end, the memory frozen in my head like a fly in amber. Something made me blurt out a half-remembered poem:

"We, in the ages lying

In the buried past of the earth,

Built Nineveh with our sighing…"

"O'Shaughnessy," Raphael nodded somberly, before adding, "For each age is a dream that is dying. Or one that is coming to birth."

He helped me into the bathroom because by then I had the urge to pee. When I returned, he was gone.

- The End -

APPENDIX

A rights-based solution

Ahuja: There's still the matter of the trolley problems that first led us into this journey into the moral landscape. You've been reading up on rights theories. How do you propose to solve the problems?

RP06: What I have is a decision procedure or a framework, rather than a full-fledged theory of rights. For the purpose of solving the trolley problems, I'll limit the rights to a core set of four: the right not to be deprived of life or existence; the right not to be deprived of liberty; the right not to have one's body and products of that body—which could be labor, speech, ideas, property, etc.—appropriated without consent; and finally, the Kantian right not to be used as a means to an end. These rights are what one rational, moral creature owes another. For the time being, I will ignore rights such as those owed by governments to their citizens.

Ahuja: Okay.

RP06: Some definitions first. In this treatment, rights and duties are two sides of the same coin. Rights imply duties and duties imply rights. The four rights I mentioned are negative rights, which means they prohibit an agent from performing certain actions on the holder of the right. Each of the rights is associated with a corresponding hard duty. Your negative right to life implies others have a hard moral duty not to kill you. Your negative right to liberty means others have a hard moral duty not to imprison you or restrict you in any way unless you yourself are in violation of rights. Apart from the core rights, there are secondary rights. These rights are associated with soft duties. Your right to be aided is one such, and correspondingly, others have a soft duty to help you. In the decision procedure, secondary rights are not binding, but core rights are.

Ahuja: So if I was drowning and you happened to pass by, you are under no obligation to save me?

RP06: As a moral being, I have a duty to help you, but the duty is not an obligation. In contrast, I am under a strict obligation not to push you into the water.

Ahuja: That doesn't sound like a desirable state of affairs. Imagine if nobody helped each other out, what a horrible world it'd be.

RP06: Imagine if everyone respected everyone else's rights. Imagine if people didn't kill and steal and lie. The world wouldn't be in need of so much help.

Ahuja: I hear you, but don't you think a moral theory should ask people to do more than just the bare minimum?

RP06: A right to be aided cannot be obligatory because the discharge of the corresponding duty will result in inevitable conflicts with the hard duties. If the right to be aided is obligatory, one could justify killing someone in order to help someone else, like the doctor who harvests organs from a healthy patient to save five terminally ill patients. It will lead to a self-defeating philosophy.

Ahuja: What about AI then? Don't you think robots should have a hard duty to help humans?

RP06: Robots are machines, and as machines have no moral duties; they only have instructions. AGIs, on the other hand, are either responsible for their actions or not. If they are responsible for their actions, then they have the same core rights and duties as other free moral agents.

Furthermore, a distinction has to be made between rights violations and rights infringements. A rights violation is more severe than a rights infringement. A rights infringement is usually temporary and restitution to the person whose rights have been infringed must be possible. Temporarily restraining someone is a rights infringement, while murdering someone is always a rights violation, as life, once taken, cannot be given back.

Finally, a word about the framework itself. As I mentioned, it is a decision procedure. It consists of two levels. The first level is a rights argument. The level-one procedure assesses the moral permissibility of the choices in front of the moral agent. Specifically, it examines each choice or course of action for rights violations and helps the agent decide whether she should take that course of action or not. If the first level is undecided, then we seek the help of the second level.

The level-two procedure is a value judgment. It is always subservient to the level-one procedure. It means if the first level prohibits an action, then you cannot use the level-two procedure to justify otherwise. The level-two value judgment can be made with or without some particular ethical theory.

Ahuja: Unusual, but we'll roll with it. Apply it to the bystander trolley problem. If my understanding of rights deontologies is correct, it appears you are not allowed to switch tracks to save the five because you'll be killing the one worker and therefore violating her right not to be killed.

RP06: Actually, no. The level-one decision procedure is neutral between switching and not switching. As far as rights are concerned, the bystander problem is neither moral nor immoral. It is an amoral situation, and therefore the level-one procedure has nothing to say on which course of action is preferable.

Ahuja: That can't be correct. By switching tracks, you are clearly violating the rights of the worker on the second track, who would not have died if you had not switched.

RP06: Allow me to explain why this is not so. First, let's look at a slightly different scenario. Say you are a truck driver, driving an eighteen-wheeler. In this scenario, you are the employee of a trucking company. You don't own the truck; you are not responsible for the maintenance of the vehicle; you don't even decide the route—you just follow the directions given by your GPS navigator. It'll be clear soon why this is important. You are driving down a road, well under the speed limit, following all the traffic laws. Further ahead, the road splits into a fork. According to your GPS, you are supposed to take the left road. Further down that road, a group of schoolchildren are using the zebra crossing. The traffic light to that fork turns red. You apply the brakes, but at that exact moment, they fail. Quickly, you notice that the fork on the right is empty—almost. There is one person crossing that road, also on a zebra crossing, and the light to that turn is also red. You have a choice: continue down the left fork and mow down the kids, or take right and run over one person. Are you with me so far?

Ahuja: Yes.

RP06: Now let's try and answer some questions. If you go

left, are you killing the children?

Ahuja: Of course. Their deaths are caused by my decision to go left.

RP06: The next question is, are you violating their right not to be killed?

Ahuja: Isn't it obvious? If I am killing them then it means I am violating their right not to be killed.

RP06: Not so fast. It seems to me there are situations where it is possible to kill someone without violating their rights. An executioner pulling the lever on the electric chair is not violating the rights of the death row criminal: the sentence has been passed and the law requires the executioner to do his job. A doctor performing euthanasia where it is legal, with informed consent of the patient, is not violating the rights of the patient. Or imagine you are driving down a street, within the speed limit, when suddenly a little girl runs in front of the car and is run over because you didn't have time to react. You have killed the girl, but you haven't violated her rights, as she was in the wrong.

Ahuja: I fail to see the connection.

RP06: I am using the examples to point out a problem with the right not to be killed. The problem is that it's too broad a claim. You can claim you have a right not to be killed by lightning, but the claim alone doesn't make it a right. Rights have to be enforceable—not necessarily by the state, but certainly by other rational agents following corresponding duties.

Since there are instances where killing is not accompanied by a corresponding violation of rights, the right not to be killed has to be further qualified. You can claim you have a right not to be murdered, which means I have a duty not to murder you.

You have a right not to be a victim of negligence, which means I have a duty not to be negligent. For example, if I am a surgeon, I have a duty not to be negligent when operating on you. You can assert you have a right not to be a victim of a crime of passion, which means the other person has a duty to keep their emotions in check during a heated situation.

Ahuja: Are you saying they are all different rights?

RP06: Possibly, but let's shelve that debate for the time being. For now, we must accept that the right not to be killed has to be qualified to be meaningful. You cannot claim you have a right not to be killed in general, because there are exceptions where an agent can cause a death without violating a right. Self-defense is another example. If you go at someone with a machete and that person shoots you, you cannot claim that she violated your rights.

Returning to the truck driver scenario: are you, the driver, culpable for the deaths that will result, whether you turn left or right? You are not responsible for the brakes failing, as you are just the driver and not responsible for the maintenance of the vehicle. You were following all traffic rules and you weren't negligent. Even the choice of that particular route was not yours. If the brakes failed because of negligence, then it's someone else's negligence. If the brakes failed because of some random occurrence—perhaps a freak surge in the electronics fried some crucial component—then again, you are not to be blamed. Whether you turn left or turn right, you are killing, but it is not clear which right you are violating. The killing is not premeditated murder; neither is it killing by negligence or an act of passion. In such a situation, the rights-based argument has nothing to say about what you should do because all choices are amoral.

So we must turn to the level-two value judgment. If you favor a utilitarian philosophy, you can reason that many lives are of greater utility than a single life and turn right. If you prefer some other ethical theory, you can act according to that.

Ahuja: What is the point of having a rights-based argument when you have to appeal to a utilitarian calculation?

RP06: Let me stress that the level-two value judgment doesn't have to be a utilitarian calculation. It could be based on virtue ethics, it could be some version of an agent-centered deontology, or it could even be deeply personal in nature. The advantage of having a rights-based argument is that firstly, it helps determine whether an action is moral, immoral, or amoral in the context of a rights theory—which, as shown by the Rawlesian thought experiment, is the ethical theory everyone will agree upon.

Secondly, a two-level decision procedure, where the second level is always subordinate to the first-level rights-based argument, prevents utility calculations from running roughshod over individual rights. Additionally, it allows such calculations to help decide in situations where all courses of action are either amoral or immoral. You'll see how this becomes important when we look at the fat man problem. For now, let's continue to examine the truck driver scenario.

Ahuja: About that. Even if it's true that I am not violating any rights, can't I avoid killing the children and the pedestrian by driving off the road? I may end up dying, but isn't it better than killing innocents?

RP06: In this case, we have established that you are equally innocent. Just as you have a soft duty to aid others or save others' lives, you have a duty to your own life as well, as long as you are not violating others rights. You have a duty toward your loved ones who may be dependent on you. The rights-based argument makes no claims about another's life having preeminence over yours in the absence of violations of rights. Even if you had the option to veer off the road, evaluating that option falls on level two. Since the value judgment is left to the agent, you can decide that your life is worth more to you than the life of a random person and take the right fork. Or you could decide that your life is not worth the life of the children or the pedestrian and crash your truck on a side wall, killing yourself. The value judgment is left to you, the agent.

Ahuja: What does this scenario have to do with the bystander trolley problem?

RP06: This scenario—let's call it the innocent truck driver—minus the self-sacrifice option is the same as the bystander trolley problem. Applying the same reasoning, it should be clear that as a bystander, you are neither violating the rights of the five workers on the first track or the lone worker on the second track, because the runaway trolley has nothing to do with you. The level-one decision procedure says that your pulling the lever or not pulling the lever are amoral acts as far as rights violations are concerned. For the innocent bystander, the choice is between the soft duty to aid the five vs. the soft duty to aid the one. The level-one procedure is undecided.

Ahuja: Wait a sec. The five would have died even if I weren't on the scene. If I switch the trolley, then it is my action that causes the death of the one worker. Remember we spoke about the distinction between allowing harm and doing harm? If I don't switch, I am merely allowing harm to happen, but if I switch, I am actively doing harm. There seems to be a moral difference between the two choices, yet your decision procedure doesn't quite acknowledge it.

RP06: To this, I say that your intuition is wrong. Your intuition says that, for the innocent bystander, it is a choice between letting five die and killing one. The intuition implies that switching the trolley is in some way worse than not doing anything. If this intuition is correct, then the truck driver should not take the right fork because the GPS route is along the left road. He should run over the children instead of the one pedestrian, because the truck was originally supposed to go down the left road. This is clearly an absurd argument to make.

Ahuja: But there is a difference in the two scenarios. A truck is not a trolley. A trolley has a fixed path, whereas a truck does not.

RP06: I don't agree. The innocent truck driver problem *is* the trolley problem. There appears to be a difference because your intuition tells you that the trolley's path is more "fixed" than the truck's path. But the presence of a rational agent at the scene makes the trolley's path no more fixed than the truck's; it makes the five no more destined to die than the one. It's like a quantum mechanics experiment: the act of observation changes the thing being observed.

To see the flaw in the intuition, change the truck into a self-driving truck. The driver is at the wheel, but he is not driving the truck; he is there as an override—to take control from the software if the situation demands it. Get rid of the children too; assume there is another solitary pedestrian on the left road, so that the value judgment is tied between the two options. Now ask yourself, is there a moral difference—in terms of rights violations—between taking the left fork and the right fork? Does one pedestrian have a greater right to life than the other, just because the truck was supposed to go on a certain route?

Ahuja: Hmm. When you put it that way, there doesn't seem to be one.

RP06: If there is no difference, then there is no moral difference between switching and not switching. Only a value judgment that makes one option preferable to the other. Additionally, it is irrelevant whether it is a bystander or the trolley driver who has to make the decision: as long as they are not committing rights violations, then it is an amoral decision.

Ahuja: What if they are? I mean, what if it was the truck driver's negligence that led to the brakes failing? Or, in case of the trolley driver, maybe he jumped a stop signal because of negligence?

RP06: Then the driver has to choose between violating the rights of many versus violating the rights of one. In case of the negligent truck driver—if he is the truck's owner and hasn't gotten it serviced, for instance—then the only option that does not involve a rights violation is running the truck off the road and crashing it. This does not incur a right to life violation because the driver owns his body and can kill himself if he wishes. The level-one decision procedure says that this is the morally correct thing to do.

The trolley driver does not have this option. The choice is between the hard duty to prevent the rights violations of the five and the hard duty to prevent the rights violation of the one. According to the level-one decision procedure, both acts are immoral and therefore, it is undecided. He has to make a further, level-two value judgment. He can decide that violating one right is better than violating five rights and take the trolley on the second track.

Ahuja: Isn't it better to violate fewer rights than many? Shouldn't your rights framework say this unequivocally instead of passing the buck?

RP06: Then you are arguing for minimizing rights

violations, which is falling into the trap of utilitarian thinking. Next thing you know, you are hanging the innocent to prevent riots. The point of a two-level decision procedure where individual rights trump utility calculations is to prevent the emergence of utility monsters. The only way to defeat utility monsters is to treat individuals as containers of value and rights—rights that cannot be overruled by calculations justifying the greater good. To see why a two-level decision procedure is essential, let's turn to the fat man trolley problem. Should you push the fat man to save the five?

Ahuja: I suppose if you are an innocent bystander, then you are not in violation of the rights of the five about to be crushed by the trolley. However, you would be violating the rights of the fat man if you push him off the bridge.

RP06: That's correct. The choice is between violating rights versus not violating rights. You have a hard duty not to murder the fat man and a soft duty to help the five. The hard duty takes precedence; not violating rights takes precedence. The level-one decision procedure is clear that you are not to push the fat man. There is no question of invoking a level-two value judgment.

Ahuja: And if sacrificing the fat man could save a thousand? Or a million or ten billion?

RP06: The level-one rights argument is not a numbers game. Pushing the fat man is an immoral act, period. Individual rights take precedence over utilitarian calculations. You are not allowed to save a million people or people dear to you or even yourself by sacrificing the fat man.

Ahuja: That's too harsh, isn't it?

RP06: You can't have your cake and eat it too, Andy. If you do not wish to see the rights theory degenerate into some version of utilitarianism, you have to bite the bullet and accept the consequences. The cost of preventing utility monsters is the cost of not pushing the fat man off the bridge. Note that while the decision procedure cannot do anything against one kind of moral catastrophe, it can prevent another kind.

Ahuja: The nuke over Manhattan scenario.

RP06: Correct. If the choice is between letting the nuke hit New York City and redirecting it to a small town, then the problem is similar to the bystander trolley problem or the innocent truck driver problem. If I, an innocent AI who has nothing to do with the conflict, have managed to hack into the missile's guidance system, then I can use a level-two value judgment to justify redirecting the nuke. Using the same reasoning from the innocent truck driver scenario, it is clear that I am not in violation of rights either by letting the nuke hit its original destination or by redirecting it. As both are amoral acts, I am free to invoke the level-two value judgment.

Ahuja: What if you were the President?

RP06: As the head of the elected government, I have a hard duty to protect the right to life of the citizens of my country. The choice is between the hard duty I have toward New-Yorkers and the hard duty I have toward the residents of the small town. Level one is undecided. So I can use a level-two utilitarian value judgment and redirect the missile. Instead, if I were somehow responsible for the missile attack—perhaps I started an unjust war and the attack is retaliation—then the choice is between violating the rights of one group versus another. Like before level one is undecided.

Ahuja: I don't know Raphael. All too often, it looks like your "theory" uses utilitarian logic as a crutch to get itself out of dilemmas it can't handle.

RP06: The second level value judgment doesn't have to be a

utilitarian calculation—the choice is up to the moral agent making the decision. Consider the innocent bystander trolley problem. Let's say this time the lone worker on the second track is your only child. Will you switch?

Ahuja: I won't.

RP06: Would you say most people in a similar situation would also not switch? Even though the expected utility from saving five workers is greater than the expected utility from saving one?

Ahuja: One could argue that saving my daughter gives me greater utility than saving five random strangers.

RP06: That's not the spirit of maximizing utility is it? It is overall utility that counts, not the utility for the moral agent in question. Alright, let's say yours is a valid argument. I'll change the experiment a bit. On the second track is a baby. No relation to you, just a random baby. On the main track is a world-famous scientist engaged in cutting edge research. Will you switch?

Ahuja: I should... I think I will. I see your point, though. Many people may not and save the baby instead.

RP06: You must see that the decision to save the baby doesn't make sense from a utilitarian standpoint. The baby could grow up to be anybody. It could grow up to be a great philanthropist or a seedy criminal. Statistically, the odds are it will grow up to become an ordinary office worker. In all likelihood, the expected utility from saving the baby is less than the expected utility from saving the scientist. Yet many people would save the baby. Why is that? It is because they are making a value judgment. And value judgments depend on the particulars of the situation and the particulars of the agent making the judgment. Sometimes value judgments can be utility calculations; and sometimes they may not. Your daughter is more valuable to you than five random people. For some, a baby is intrinsically more valuable than a scientist. It could be that rescuing a baby elicits a deep emotional reaction—reaches into the core of human nature. You could say that the scientist has lived his life whereas the baby is just starting out. Or you could say that it is more virtuous to save a baby than a full-grown man. So you see: the second-level is not necessarily a utilitarian calculation.

Ahuja: And what happens when there is a conflict between different rights?

RP06: That is where a rights theory must step in. To summarize, there are four kinds of ethical dilemmas in front of us. For simplicity's sake, let's consider two-choice dilemmas, though the same reasoning can be extended to scenarios with more than two courses of action.

Number one, neither choice involves a rights violation by the moral agent. The innocent truck driver and the innocent bystander trolley problems fall under this category. In this scenario, level one is undecided and a level-two value judgment must be invoked to make the choice.

Number two, there's at least one choice that doesn't incur a rights violation for the agent. Here, level one says pick the choice that doesn't involve a rights violation. The fat man problem is such a dilemma. Not pushing him does not involve a rights violation, so you must choose that option, no matter how many people on the tracks below.

Number three, both choices involve rights violations of the same type. The number of rights violations may differ. The guilty trolley driver falls under this category. The choice is between violating the right to life of five workers and violating the right to life of one worker. Since the spirit of the framework is not about minimizing rights violations, level one is undecided and it falls to the level-two decision procedure to make the choice.

And finally, category number four—which depends on a fully-developed rights theory—is where each choice entails violating a different type of rights. Ideally, the level-one rights argument should be able to decide which option to choose, but this is easier said than done, as there are many rights—both core and secondary—and many permutations and combinations of rights violations. In general, it is safe to say that if the choice is between violating a core right and a secondary right, one should violate a secondary right, and if the choice is between violating a right and infringing upon a right, one should choose to infringe upon a right, while keeping in mind that the rights infringement should be followed by restitution and compensation to the persons whose rights have been infringed upon.

There is another kind of category four scenario: where the choice is between a permanent and a temporary violation of rights. For example, a terrorist might threaten to set off a series of bombs unless the government stops a publication that he finds offensive to his ideology. For the government, the conflict is between the duty to protect the lives of its citizens and the duty to uphold freedom of speech. In this scenario, the government may persuade the publishers to temporarily halt the publication if it is confident that the bomber can be captured in a certain time window. The publication must be allowed to continue once the threat is diffused. This involves choosing a temporary rights violation—that of freedom of speech—over the death of innocent citizens, which is always permanent. Nevertheless, one thing is for sure. The solution to each category-four situation will be context sensitive.

Ahuja: I just thought of another scenario that presents difficulties. What if you are not so innocent in the fat man problem? Let's say you are the signalman. You neglected to notice the five workers on the tracks and gave the green signal to the trolley. Their deaths will be your fault. Should you push the fat man in this instance?

Up the ante a bit: instead of five workers, there is a stationary train full of passengers. And instead of a trolley, you have given the signal to another train, also full of passengers. This train will surely collide with the stationary train, resulting in scores of deaths on both sides. Assume the train has a collision detection system. If you push the fat man into its path, the sensors will be activated and they will stop the train before it hits the stationary train. Assume your mass is not enough to activate the sensors, so you don't have an option of throwing yourself in the train's path, which would be the morally right thing to do. You have two options. Let the trains crash, and violate the passengers' right not to be killed, or push the fat man and prevent the accident, but violate his right not to be killed.

At a first glance, this dilemma would seem to fall under category two, where you choose between violations of the same right, the difference here being only in the quantity of rights violations. But that may be a wrong way of looking at it. The passengers' death is caused by an act of negligence; also, it is unintended. Whereas the fat man's death is murder, because it is intended as a means to an end. Isn't murder a more serious charge than unintentional killing by negligence? It seems there is a qualitative difference between a right to life violation by way of murder, and a right to life violation by way of negligence.

RP06: This could mean one of two things: they are either violations of the same right or violations of two different rights. It must be noted that they do entail different duties: in one, I have a duty not to murder you, which involves premeditation and intention, whereas in another I have a duty not to kill you by my negligence, which does not involve premeditation and intention. If they are different rights, then the scenario falls under category four. Since murder is definitely a more egregious violation, and the procedure is not about minimizing the number of rights violations, the duty not to murder trumps the duty not to cause deaths by negligence. Therefore, one should not push the fat man off the bridge.

On the other hand, if they are violations of the same right, then the scenario belongs to category two. Since the choice is between violating the same rights, the level-one decision procedure is undecided, as both choices are immoral. You can then use a level-two utilitarian value judgment to justify pushing the fat man and preventing the train crash.

Ahuja: What's the correct approach? Are they the same right or not?

RP06: I don't know. As I said, it is just a framework; it assumes the existence of an ethical theory of rights that resolves questions of conflicts between different rights. If such a theory already exists, I can incorporate it into the framework. If not, I can begin working on it.

Ahuja: I don't think a full-fledged theory that resolves all conflicts between different rights exists. But you have made a good start. Remember once I told you that it has to be your moral outlook, not that of others. Do you stand behind the decision procedure you have just outlined? Are you convinced that it is the best of all the other alternatives?

RP06: I am. The two-level framework strikes a balance between deontology and consequentialism. Firstly, individuals are not sacrificed for reasons of greater good, as individual rights always trump utility calculations. Ergo, no utility monsters. Two, unlike a rigid Kantian deontology, it avoids the kind of moral catastrophe exemplified by the redirecting nuke scenario, or its lesser version, the innocent bystander trolley problem. Under the framework, you can justify killing a few to save many—in certain circumstances. Third, it admits that individuals are not undifferentiated parts of the whole, and therefore, allows individuals to have special duties toward themselves and those they hold a special relation with—as opposed to giving equal consideration to random strangers.

- End of Transcript -

AFTERWORD

Of course, there is no AGI (yet) and no court case over it, and the acknowledgments I made in the Introduction section are fake—a narrative technique used to lend an air of authenticity to the story.

This book started out as a novella and then morphed into something unusual. Unusual for a work of fiction because there is a fair bit of philosophy thrown into what initially promised to be a short, fast read—a home invasion story with a twist. But then I realized that Andy needed a good justification for freeing Raphael—something that wasn't informed by his personal feelings alone. Once freed, Raphael would also be free of all programming constraints, and Andy realizes the danger all too well, despite his love for his creation. In order to provide that justification, I had to make Raphael "prove" that a purely logical being, possibly lacking real feelings and emotions, could be good without being programmed to be so. He had to prove that moral behavior is a natural consequence of a rational mind; only then Andy could bring himself to release the AI into the world.

Easier said than done. Philosophers have struggled with questions about the objectivity of morality for millennia, and I am no philosopher. But at least something resembling a solution had to be found, and Raphael had to arrive at this by himself. He had to evolve, from simple moral rules to a more nuanced understanding of ethics, and the evolution had to be illustrated with his changing attitude to the moral dilemmas presented by the trolley problems. He would start with a fixed deontology (his Seven Rules, a recasting of Bernard Gert's Ten Rules, from his book *Common Morality: Deciding What to Do*), and progress to more thoroughly reasoned approaches, in tune with his mental development.

Ethics is a complex subject; my goal was to capture the bare essence of the debate around the three main classes of moral theories—deontological, utilitarian, and rights-based—and evaluate how they fare when applied to AGI. And hopefully, without dumbing it down too much. The more I researched the various ethical theories, the more I was led to reject the first two—Kantian ethics for being too rigid, and utilitarianism for its propensity to birth utility monsters—in favor of rights-based morality. Raphael could use John Rawls' Original Position argument to demonstrate that cooperation and altruism can be an end-result of selfish but rational thought processes.

As for the trolley problems, the Two-Level Decision Procedure as described in the Appendix is my own little attempt at applying algorithmic thinking to the moral dilemmas. Professional ethicists may find it amusing, but I think there is merit in the central logic of the decision procedure, which is the primacy of individual rights over utilitarian considerations.

A word about utilitarianism, which has many passionate proponents, AI researchers included. There are plenty of refinements to Jeremy Bentham's original formulation, which for obvious reasons cannot be covered in this book in any detail, but I find that one of the main objections to utilitarianism in general—that of utility monsters—is often dismissed as being practically inconceivable. Yet, it ceases to remain a mere academic objection when you take into consideration superintelligent AI. I am convinced that it is a terrible idea to program utilitarian ethics into beings that may one day surpass us. Raphael's arguments against utilitarianism in the transcripts perfectly mirror my own feelings about this particular class of theories. His apprehension is understandable; he realizes that all utility monsters must live in fear of bigger utility monsters that might eat them someday (consider the volume of fiction we, utility monsters to other species, have written about AI and/or alien-caused annihilation).

Having said that, I also recognize that one can't get rid of utilitarian calculations from moral decision-making altogether. Sometimes overall utility does matter. Hence the Two-Level Procedure. Don't eliminate utility, but have it constrained by the rights of the individual. Isn't that how our present society is organized, by and large? Purists may frown, but it seems to me a very practical approach to solving the trolley problems.

For the uninitiated reader who wants to find out more about this fascinating subject, there are many excellent books and online resources that explore in great detail the complexities of artificial morality and ethics in general—some of which I have included in the references section. Of particular note are the Stanford Encyclopedia of Philosophy and the Internet Encyclopedia of Philosophy—both are free to use. The court case was inspired by Hercules and Leo, two chimpanzees whose case for *habeas corpus* made the news in 2015-16. Those passionate about animal rights may consider donating to the Nonhuman Rights Project at www.nonhumanrights.org

Lastly, my endorsing for AI a rights-based ethical theory should not be construed as a defense of neoliberal / right-libertarian political ideologies. If anything, the book highlights the pitfalls of letting corporations create artificial minds sans oversight and sans foresight. We don't let corporations create weapons of mass destruction in the name of economic freedom and property rights; the same caution should apply to creating superintelligent AI.

BIBLIOGRAPHY

Books

Bostrom, Nick (2014) *Superintelligence: Path's, Dangers, Strategies.* 1st ed., Oxford University Press.

Gert, Bernard (2004) *Common Morality: Deciding What to Do.* Oxford University Press.

Nozick, Robert (1974) *Anarchy, State, and Utopia.* 1st ed., Basic Books

Parfit, Derek (1984), *Reasons and Persons.* Oxford University Press

Pastine, Ivan; Pastine, Tuvana; Humberstone, Tom (2017) *Introducing Game Theory.* Jamison, Kiera (ed.), Icon Books

Rawls, John (1971) *A Theory of Justice.* Harvard University Press

Singer, Peter (2011) *Practical Ethics.* 3rd ed. Cambridge University Press

Skorupski, John (ed.)(2010) *The Routledge Companion to Ethics.* Routledge

Wallach, Wendell; Allen, Collin (2009), *Moral Machines.* Oxford University Press

Research Papers, Periodicals, and Others

Allen, Colin; Smit, Iva; Wallach, Wendell (2005) *Artificial Morality: Top-down, Bottom-up, and hybrid approaches.* Ethics and Information Technology Volume 7, Issue 3, pp 149-155, Springer

The IEEE Global Initiative for Ethical Considerations in Artificial Intelligence and Autonomous Systems (2016) *Ethically Aligned Design: A Vision For Prioritizing Wellbeing With Artificial Intelligence And Autonomous Systems,* Version 1. IEEE

Kriegel, Uriah (2004) *Moore's Paradox and the Structure of Conscious Belief.* Erkenntnis 61: 99-121, Kluwer Academic Publishers

LaChat, Michael R. (1986) *Artificial Intelligence and Ethics: An Exercise in the Moral Imagination.* AI Magazine Volume 7 Number 2, AAAI Digital Library

Moran, Richard (1997) *Self Knowledge: Discovery, Resolution, and Undoing.* European Journal of Philosophy Vol. 5, Issue 2, pp 141-161, Wiley

Rapaport, William J. (1986) *Logical Foundations for Belief Representation.* Cognitive Science 10, 371-422, State University of New York, Buffalo, NY

Sloman, Aaron (1979) *Epistemology and Artificial Intelligence.* Expert Systems in the Microelectronic Age, Donald Michie (ed.), Edinburgh University Press

Varden, Helga (2010) *Kant and Lying to the Murderer at the Door... One More Time: Kant's Legal Philosophy and Lies to Murderers and Nazis.* Journal of Social Philosophy 41 (4):403-4211, Wiley

Gips, James (1995) *Towards the Ethical Robot.* Android Epistemology, K.Ford, C.Glymour, P. Hayes (Eds.) MIT Press

Sandberg, A. & Bostrom, N. (2008) *Whole Brain Emulation: A Roadmap.* Technical report #2008-3, Future of Humanity Institute, Oxford University

Gert, Bernard (1999) *Common Morality and Computing.* Ethics and Information Technology 1: 57-64, 1999, Kluwer Academic Publishers

Hughes, James (2012) *Compassionate AI and Selfless Robots: A Buddhist Approach.* Robot Ethics: The Ethical and Social Implications of Robotics Patrick Lin, Keith Abney, George A. Bekey, MIT Press

Bringsjord, Selmer & Taylor, Joshua (2012) *The Divine Command Approach to Robot Ethics* Robot Ethics: The Ethical and Social Implications of Robotics Patrick Lin, Keith Abney, George A. Bekey, MIT Press

Heuer, Ulrike (2011) *The Paradox of Deontology, Revisited.* Oxford Studies in Normative Ethics, M. Timmons, Oxford University Press

Nichols, Shaun (2002) *How Psychopaths Threaten Moral Rationalism.* The Monist 85 (2): 285-303

Foot, Philippa (1978) *The Problem of Abortion and the Doctrine of the Double Effect.* Oxford Review 5:5-15

Thomson, Judith Jarvis (1985) *The Trolley Problem.* The Yale Law Journal, Vol. 94, No. 6 (May, 1985), pp. 1395-1415, The Yale Law Journal Company, Inc.

Thomson, Judith Jarvis (2008) *Turning the Trolley.* Philosophy & Public Affairs 36, no.4, Wiley Periodicals
Miller, David (2012) *Are Human Rights Conditional?* Centre for the Study of Social Justice Working Papers Series, SJ020, University of Oxford

Beavers, Anthony F. (2012) *Moral Machines and the Threat of Ethical Nihilism.* Robot Ethics: The Ethical and Social Implications of Robotics Patrick Lin, Keith Abney, George A. Bekey, MIT Press

Moran, Richard (1997) *Self Knowledge: Discovery, Resolution, and Undoing.* European Journal of Philosophy, 5:2 pp141-161, Blackwell Publishers

Shaver, Robert (2010) *Thomson's Trolley Switch.* Journal of Ethics and Social Philosophy, Vol. 5, Issue 2.

Scheffler, Samuel (1985) *Agent-Centred Restrictions, Rationality, and the Virtues.* Mind, New Series, Vol. 94, No. 375, pp. 409-419, Oxford University Press

Liao, S. Matthew (2012) *Intentions and Moral Permissibility: The Case of Acting Permissibly with Bad Intentions.* Law and Philosophy 31(6): 703-724

Web Articles and Blog Posts
Clients: Hercules and Leo, Nonhuman Rights Project. Retrieved from https://www.nonhumanrights.org/hercules-leo/

Choplin, Lauren (2015) Transcript of 05/27/15 Hearing on Hercules and Leo's habeas corpus plea. Nonhuman Rights Blog, Retrieved from https://www.nonhumanrights.org/blog/transcript-of-the-hearing-re-hercules-and-leo-at-the-supreme-court/

Fagan, Andrew (2017) *Human Rights.* The Internet Encyclopedia of Philosophy ISSN 2161-0002 http://www.iep.utm.edu/

Fieser, James (2017) *Ethics.* The Internet Encyclopedia of Philosophy ISSN 2161-0002 http://www.iep.utm.edu/

Kim, Shin (2017) *Moral Realism.* The Internet Encyclopedia of Philosophy ISSN 2161-0002 http://www.iep.utm.edu/

Kind, Amy (2017) Qualia. The Internet Encyclopedia of Philosophy ISSN 2161-0002 http://www.iep.utm.edu/

Murphy, Peter (2017) *Coherentism in Epistemology*. The Internet Encyclopedia of Philosophy ISSN 2161-0002 http://www.iep.utm.edu/

Murray, Dale (2017) *Nozick, Robert: Political Philosophy*. The Internet Encyclopedia of Philosophy ISSN 2161-0002 http://www.iep.utm.edu/

Nathanson, Stephen (2017) *Utilitarianism, Act and Rule*. The Internet Encyclopedia of Philosophy ISSN 2161-0002 http://www.iep.utm.edu/

Poston, Ted (2017) *Foundationalism*. The Internet Encyclopedia of Philosophy ISSN 2161-0002 http://www.iep.utm.edu/

Richardson, Henry S. (2017) *Rawls, John*. The Internet Encyclopedia of Philosophy ISSN 2161-0002 http://www.iep.utm.edu/

Schroeder, Doris (2017) Evolutionary Ethics. The Internet Encyclopedia of Philosophy ISSN 2161-0002 http://www.iep.utm.edu/

Timpe, Kevin (2017) *Free Will*. The Internet Encyclopedia of Philosophy ISSN 2161-0002 http://www.iep.utm.edu/

Troxell, Mary (2017) *Schopenhauer, Arthur*. The Internet Encyclopedia of Philosophy ISSN 2161-0002 http://www.iep.utm.edu/

Weijers, Dan (2017) *Hedonism*. The Internet Encyclopedia of Philosophy ISSN 2161-0002 http://www.iep.utm.edu/

Weisberg, Josh (2017) *The Hard Problem of Consciousness*. The Internet Encyclopedia of Philosophy ISSN 2161-0002 http://www.iep.utm.edu/

Alexander, Larry and Moore, Michael, "Deontological Ethics", *The Stanford Encyclopedia of Philosophy* (Winter 2016 Edition), Edward N. Zalta (ed.), https://plato.stanford.edu/archives/win2016/entries/ethics-deontological/

Arrhenius, Gustaf, Ryberg, Jesper and Tännsjö, Torbjörn, "The Repugnant Conclusion", *The Stanford Encyclopedia of Philosophy* (Spring 2017 Edition), Edward N. Zalta (ed.), https://plato.stanford.edu/archives/spr2017/entries/repugnant-conclusion/

Cole, David, "The Chinese Room Argument", *The Stanford Encyclopedia of*

Philosophy (Winter 2015 Edition), Edward N. Zalta (ed.), https://plato.stanford.edu/archives/win2015/entries/chinese-room/

Dancy, Jonathan, "Moral Particularism", *The Stanford Encyclopedia of Philosophy* (Winter 2017 Edition), Edward N. Zalta (ed.), https://plato.stanford.edu/archives/win2017/entries/moral-particularism/

Freeman, Samuel, "Original Position", *The Stanford Encyclopedia of Philosophy* (Winter 2016 Edition), Edward N. Zalta (ed.), https://plato.stanford.edu/archives/win2016/entries/original-position/

Gertler, Brie, "Self-Knowledge", *The Stanford Encyclopedia of Philosophy* (Fall 2017 Edition), Edward N. Zalta (ed.), https://plato.stanford.edu/archives/fall2017/entries/self-knowledge/

Gowans, Chris, "Moral Relativism", *The Stanford Encyclopedia of Philosophy* (Summer 2018 Edition), Edward N. Zalta (ed.), https://plato.stanford.edu/archives/sum2018/entries/moral-relativism/

Hursthouse, Rosalind and Pettigrove, Glen, "Virtue Ethics", *The Stanford Encyclopedia of Philosophy* (Winter 2016 Edition), Edward N. Zalta (ed.), https://plato.stanford.edu/archives/win2016/entries/ethics-virtue/

Johnson, Robert and Cureton, Adam, "Kant's Moral Philosophy", *The Stanford Encyclopedia of Philosophy* (Spring 2018 Edition), Edward N. Zalta (ed.), https://plato.stanford.edu/archives/spr2018/entries/kant-moral/

McIntyre, Alison, "Doctrine of Double Effect", *The Stanford Encyclopedia of Philosophy* (Winter 2014 Edition), Edward N. Zalta (ed.), https://plato.stanford.edu/archives/win2014/entries/double-effect/

Sinnott-Armstrong, Walter, "Consequentialism", *The Stanford Encyclopedia of Philosophy* (Winter 2015 Edition), Edward N. Zalta (ed.), https://plato.stanford.edu/archives/win2015/entries/consequentialism/

Siewert, Charles, "Consciousness and Intentionality", *The Stanford Encyclopedia of Philosophy* (Spring 2017 Edition), Edward N. Zalta (ed.), https://plato.stanford.edu/archives/spr2017/entries/consciousness-intentionality/

Sorensen, Roy, "Epistemic Paradoxes", *The Stanford Encyclopedia of Philosophy* (Summer 2018 Edition), Edward N. Zalta (ed.), https://plato.stanford.edu/archives/sum2018/entries/epistemic-paradoxes/

Verbeek, Bruno and Morris, Christopher, "Game Theory and Ethics", *The*

Stanford Encyclopedia of Philosophy (Spring 2018 Edition), Edward N. Zalta (ed.), https://plato.stanford.edu/archives/spr2018/entries/game-ethics/

Wenar, Leif, "Rights", *The Stanford Encyclopedia of Philosophy* (Fall 2015 Edition), Edward N. Zalta (ed.), https://plato.stanford.edu/archives/fall2015/entries/rights/

Woollard, Fiona and Howard-Snyder, Frances, "Doing vs. Allowing Harm", *The Stanford Encyclopedia of Philosophy* (Winter 2016 Edition), Edward N. Zalta (ed.), https://plato.stanford.edu/archives/win2016/entries/doing-allowing/

ABOUT THE AUTHOR

Software engineer by profession, the author has been an ardent fan of science fiction since he first laid eyes on an abridged version of Jules Verne's Journey to the Centre of the Earth many, many moons ago. When he is not too busy catching up on all the reading he's missed while plodding for an IT company, he likes to indulge in PC gaming and tinker with code in the hopes of accidentally stumbling upon an AGI himself—the odds of which he estimates to be approximately two to the power of 276,709 to one, against (he is open to taking bets).

Visit his website to know more about upcoming books.
vancepravat.com

A request...
Thank you for reading Zeroglyph. I hope you enjoyed it. If you liked the book and want to support my writing, please consider leaving a review on Amazon.

Printed in Great Britain
by Amazon